Rota

Jessica Adams ... int 'ED ON OR BEF... THE L...
OM WHICH ' *Vog* BORROW
Cosmopolitan astrologer. She was also a team editor
on the *Girls' Night In* series in aid of the children's
charities War Child and No Strings. Her novels
include *Single White E-Mail*, *Tom Dick and Debbie
Harry*, *I'm a Believer* and *Cool For Cats*.

For more information about Jessica Adams, visit
her website at www.jessicaadams.com

Acclaim for Jessica Adams

'An original and entertaining tale about life and death'
The Times

'A heart-warming, funny book with a serious core'
Glamour

'A brave and witty novel . . . Fantastic stuff'
New Woman

'Very human, very moving and frequently very
amusing . . . original and well-written'
Wendy Holden, *Sunday Express*

'Warm, witty and wise'
Cosmopolitan (Australia)

'A comical and compulsive read'
B Magazine

SHOULD I STAY OR SHOULD I GO?

Jessica Adams

BLACK SWAN

TRANSWORLD PUBLISHERS
61–63 Uxbridge Road, London W5 5SA
A Random House Group Company
www.rbooks.co.uk

SHOULD I STAY OR SHOULD I GO?
A BLACK SWAN BOOK: 9780552999441

First publication in Great Britain
Black Swan edition published 2009

A CIP catalogue record for this book
is available from the British Library.

Addresses for Random House Group Ltd companies outside the UK
can be found at: www.randomhouse.co.uk
The Random House Group Ltd Reg. No. 954009

The Random House Group Limited supports The Forest Stewardship
Council (FSC), the leading international forest certification organisation.
All our titles that are printed on Greenpeace approved FSC certified
paper carry the FSC logo. Our paper procurement policy can be found
at www.rbooks.co.uk/environment

Typeset in 11/14½pt Giovanni Book by
Kestrel Data, Exeter, Devon.
Printed in the UK by
CPI Cox & Wyman, Reading, RG1 8EX.

2 4 6 8 10 9 7 5 3 1

For Francis Clayton,
also known as Sage

Acknowledgements

Thanks to all at Curtis Brown and William Morris
and Emma Buckley, Lynsey Dalladay, Katie Espiner,
Fiona Inglis and Louise Thurtell.
Very special thanks to Peter Clarke and
Imogen Edwards-Jones.

Chapter One

I am moving to Australia because I want to see some wildlife that isn't a pigeon. This is not the kind of thing I can admit to Australian immigration officials, but it's the way I feel this afternoon. The next time I see a bird in the wild, I'd quite like it to be something that doesn't strut around like James Brown singing 'Sex Machine'.

Male pigeons are like 1970s medallion men: if they could wear cheap aftershave and leave their shirts undone, they would. I can see one of them in front of me now, stalking a female. Soon she will be lured back to his loft, and after copulating with him, she'll be left to bring up the chicks on her own.

There is a dirty teaspoon on the next table and the temptation to throw it at James Brown is very strong. He is now trying to eat a cigarette butt. He also has the pigeon equivalent of man boobs. If my chest looked like that, I wouldn't puff it out.

When Nash and I finally land in Australia there will be emus, not pigeons. There is one decorating the national coat of arms, on Form 80. I bet emus don't try to eat cigarette butts.

I am studying Form 80 like a woman possessed at the moment, because today Nash and I have our final meeting with Nice Heidi from Australia's Department of Immigration and Citizenship.

Should Heidi throw me any trick questions about recent war crimes, terrorist activity or freedom fighting I am ready for her. The answer will be no, no and no. Unless you count the woman I shoved out of the way outside the tube just now in order to get a free shampoo sample.

Nash and I are using shampoo from the pound shop at the moment. It may not be shampoo at all. It could be mayonnaise. The label is printed entirely in Arabic.

When I had a proper job, I also had proper hair. It was short and blonde, streaked and conditioned, blow-dried and moussed. These days, I have one-quid hair.

I read through all the letters from Nice Heidi. She has been in charge of our application for months, steering us gently towards a sympathetic doctor when Nash and I had to take our health exams, and coaching us with our Character Requirements form.

Heidi even got us over the awkward bits about our relationship. Not the awkward bits *within* the relationship, of course, because that would have made her a counsellor – or possibly a modern miracle worker. Rather, Nice Heidi's role was to find out if Nash and I constituted a bona fide couple in the eyes of the Australian government.

Heidi needed to test all this, because Nash is the sponsored employee going to Sydney and I am merely the secondary applicant. In other words, I'm a WAG, but without the handbag. If all goes well, Nash will be the next Head of Music at St Joseph's Boys' School, North Sydney, and I will be – according to Form 80 – his interdependent partner.

Nice Heidi has been very kind throughout, waving away my embarrassing employment history, and even overlooking the fact that Nash and I share neither a bank account, mortgage or bills to prove we've been together for longer than six months.

After two years together we still don't split the bills. Instead, Nash pays for everything, and I clean all the rooms on the top floor of the Swiss Cottage International Travellers' Hostel, where we're currently living rent free.

That's why I've got rubber-glove hands. I sniff them now to check, and sure enough my hands smell like the inside of an old hot water bottle.

Nash and I have never even discussed a joint bank account. I think both he and the bank manager would be too frightened. Even as a child, my piggy bank had a crack down the centre.

There is a mad hope in my heart at the moment, and it all hinges on Australia. It's the kind of deranged optimism that defeats everything. Being broke, being stuck in the pouring rain in this café, and even being surrounded by over-sexed pigeons.

I have never been to Sydney (Nash has) and I have

never been married (Nash has), but in my dreams, I see us on Bondi Beach a year or two from now, standing on the sand in our wedding clothes while he puts a ring on my finger.

By then, Vintage Alice will be a shop, not just an imaginary fashion design label. All the ideas I have about recycling old clothes to make new ones will finally become a reality. All the plans I have to single-handedly wipe out size zero skinny jeans and the tyranny of the smock top will have succeeded.

If I keep picturing these dreams perhaps they will become real. Isn't that the theory? In my heart, there is no credit crunch.

There are practical reasons why Australia might turn things around, too. When we move to Sydney, Nash and I might lose all the problems we have here – namely, not having any money and being forced to live in two rooms on the top floor of the Swiss Cottage International Travellers' Hostel.

All the good bits I love about Nash – the sexy, soulful, sensitive musician bits – are bound to come back once he stops working so hard and worrying so much. And he can get a motorbike again and ride it on those long Australian highways that go on for ever.

I just want to design clothes for Vintage Alice, make women feel wonderful, grow my hair and go barefoot.

The last time I went barefoot in London, I skidded on a tomato sauce sachet and fell on someone's old nappy. That just about sums this place up.

Form 80 is terrifying. Nice Heidi says she is very happy with my employment history, but . . . what if some all-powerful Australian official suddenly scans the form at the last minute and realizes that my last proper job was Woman With Key In Back – that I spent last summer painted silver, standing on a crate outside Covent Garden station while small children threw crisps at me?

Worse still, what if the Australians find out that I'm not a fashion designer after all, as I printed in such beautiful letters on the form, but a wannabe fashion designer who only made three dresses last year, and who spends her whole life doing McJobs? The sad thing about Form 80 is there just aren't enough boxes to fit all the casual and part-time work in my life.

Nash says that's the price you pay for spending your entire university life being terrified of exams, watching daytime television and eating instant noodles. Not to mention your entire fashion college life hiding in the library reading all the *Vogue*s.

When Nash was at university, of course, he was in the Chamber Orchestra and the University Funk Group. Yes! The University Funk Group! He was also in the Italian debating society, which is where he learned to speak proper Italian, which is how he seduced me – not in Italy, though, in The Slug and Lettuce in Clapham when we were both somewhat drunk.

We wandered home via Clapham Common, where he kissed me for the first time before nobly helping me onto the back of his motorbike, then driving me home.

I still like kissing him. And I still occasionally have day-dreams about all the things we've done on the back of that bike. It just doesn't happen very often, that's all.

Perhaps it's the fact that we have sex on a proper bed now. Or maybe it's the fact that it's a bed from the Swiss Cottage International Travellers' Hostel.

The bed has the kind of mattress you flip over to cover up the stains, then realize the stains are worse on the other side.

Nash is fifteen minutes late now and we're due at Australia House at 4 p.m. I can't text him because my phone is out of credit, and he probably can't call me because he's stuck on the train.

There are even more pigeons outside now. Someone has stopped their car and chucked the contents of their ashtray onto the pavement, so that dozens of orange cigarette butts are being tossed around in a gigantic pigeon football game.

I think about my conversation with Nash this morning, when we tried to come up with a practical way of breaking the news about Australia to everybody.

If you include relatives, friends and all the teachers at Nash's school, we have about a hundred people to tell – not easy.

Nash suggested that we send everyone a bulk email, but I told him that if we did that, nobody would ever speak to us again.

'Spam is for Viagra, Nash.'

Anyway, half our relatives aren't even online. Or, as one of my uncles so quaintly puts it, 'In the internet'.

My best idea about breaking the news was a Christmas party, though preferably at someone else's house, rather than our rooms. If we tried to have a going-away party in the hostel, people would only bang into the trouser press and stun themselves on the fold-up ironing board.

I don't know what we'll do about a farewell event. I expect we'll probably just go to the pub, as usual. My God. It's quarter to four already. Where is Nash?

When he finally arrives at the café, he has damp hair, flat curls, a drip running down his neck and a soaked leather jacket. Despite this, of course, women turn their heads to look at him. Nash could be covered in sewage and he'd still be unfairly good looking.

He sweeps the rubbish off one of the adjacent tables and picks up part of an old newspaper.

'Bloody England,' Nash shakes his head as he puts the paper down. 'It's all floods and David Beckham's feet. And Woolworths and Wedgwood. Bloody credit crunch.'

I pull the paper away. 'You only read it so you can moan. Anyway, you're so late we're going to have to run.'

'Can you please just stop lecturing me?' He yawns.

'Can you please just stop moaning?'

Nash looks through his G'day Australia pack, deliberately making me wait because I've just told him off. Nice Heidi at Australia House gave us these packs on our last visit. There is a giant wall map inside, which Nash finds irresistible.

'Woy Woy,' Nash picks out a town with a teaspoon, playing for time to annoy me. 'Woy Woy and Wagga Wagga. Does everything have two names in Australia? Imagine if they did that here. People would be forced to live in Stoke-on-Trent Stoke-on-Trent. Think about it Alice. If you'd grown up in Woy Woy, instead of England, your favourite band as a child might have been Duran Duran Duran Duran.'

'Hmm.'

According to this library book I've been reading, if I could only share jokes like these with Nash – in other words, laugh at them – it would be a good sign. It would mean that after being on separate journeys, we would have ended up on a small bridge.

We've already got the big bridge. That's the Sydney Harbour Bridge. However, according to my library book, we need lots of little bridges if we're ever going to get married. Not just the big obvious ones.

I do want to get married. Despite the fact that right now I could strangle Nash with my own black opaque tights, asphyxiating him with the gusset.

We set off for Australia House, me dragging him along in the rain, when Nash suddenly pulls me under his umbrella.

'Put yours away,' he says, grabbing my silly tartan umbrella that never keeps the rain off. Then he pulls me inside his coat and I put my hand in his pocket.

It's like this between us all the time at the moment. The day begins with an argument and ends with a kiss. Or the day starts with a kiss and ends with an argument.

He tastes of chewing gum and instant coffee from the machine at his school. But I love the smell of him. No matter how annoyed I get with him, it's that warm, familiar Nash scent that always pulls me back.

Because there is a crowd of people pushing against us from the other end of the Strand, Nash and I hop into the gutter and half walk, half run, along the double yellow lines. It seems to take for ever. Australia House is always further away than you think, rather like Australia, I suppose.

'Why are you so short?' he complains as he pulls me along.

'Why are you so tall?'

'Why are you so blonde?'

'Why are you so curly?'

We've been saying this kind of thing to each other for so long that we hardly notice we're doing it.

When we arrive at Australia House, we wipe our feet on the front doormat – on the national coat of arms as it turns out – so that the people watching the CCTV cameras can see how clean and responsible we are, then we take the lift to Nice Heidi's office.

The receptionist tells us Heidi won't be a moment in an accent which means it comes out this way: 'Hardy warnt be a marment.'

I read some weird Australian women's magazine with the accusatory headline RUSSELL CROWE – YO-YO DIETER? while Nash looks at his map and quietly laughs at more silly place names.

Still no sign of Nice Heidi. I inspect Robyn's keys and letter instead.

Robyn is my cousin. The last time we saw each other we were six years old. She stuffed a Mars bar up my recorder and I put a dead hamster to sleep in her Barbie bunk bed. Apart from that we got on brilliantly.

My impression of Australia so far is down to Nice Heidi and Cousin Robyn, both of whom are helping me feel braver about moving. If they're all like Heidi and Robyn in Sydney, I think I can cope.

Robyn's letter reads:

Dear Alice and Nash, please use the spare
bedroom as long as you need to. Call me if you
need anything before you get here. See you
when I get back from Bali – can't wait!
Love Robyn xxxx

'She's a four-kiss person,' Nash says, reading over my shoulder. 'I didn't see that before. She has four kisses on her letter.'

He continues reading out silly place names from the map of Australia. 'How about this one, Alice? Delicate Nobby. Imagine living in Delicate Nobby!'

'You're just making that up.'

I think about my new library book. It's called *Should I Stay or Should I Go?* Nash took one look at it and banned it, saying it was a calculated misuse of a perfectly good Clash song.

The book is full of little tests to help you decide if you

18

should stay with your partner or run away screaming. I borrowed it hoping to pass all the tests that suggested you should stay. So far I'm cheating slightly, but so far it seems the answer to the question, 'Should I stay or should I go?' is 'Yes, all right then, stay.'

'Goodness me, Alice, what a relief!' Nash said when I told him. 'Otherwise I would have cancelled our flights to Australia.'

I read the book again this morning, after he had gone to work. One of the questions in the test asks if my memories of the best-ever times with Nash still make me feel good. I think about this now as he reels off Australian place names.

The answer to the best-ever-times question is easy, because Nash and I were so in love two years ago. The phone calls went on for hours. I used to wear his leather jacket when he wasn't there, just to feel closer to him. I even used to draw his nose over and over again. It's a noble nose. Quite Roman and dignified.

Once I found out his real name was Sebastian I doodled it all over the place, so that even today I find old notebooks or bills with his name on them. And drawings of his noble nose, of course.

Because he'd been married before, when I first met Nash he seemed sexier, somehow. Older, wiser and altogether more experienced. You know that film *The Horse Whisperer*? He was like a woman whisperer.

My love life before had been Jon (workaholic mountaineer) three Pauls (they all seem to run into each other now) and after that, years of nothing.

I was forever single in London – possibly the cruellest city in the world for a woman on her own . . . or a pigeon.

When Suzanne dragged me along to the pub after work and said that an interesting man would be there, it was hard to feel inspired.

Nevertheless, Nash was more than interesting. And to say it was good with Nash at the beginning is an understatement. It was bloody incredible.

But now it just feels like hard work pretty much all the time. I wonder how long do you have to slog away before you know it's time to give up?

Hopefully we won't have to find out. That's what Australia is for.

I wonder if we'll swim with our arms around each other, when we get there? That's one of the daydreams that keeps me going at the moment. In my fantasy, Nash and I are swimming with our arms around each other at Bondi Beach (not sure how we'll stay afloat, but anyway) and frolicking like young dolphins.

Once we get to Bondi Beach we'll rediscover each other, recycle the relationship and make sure we never have another conversation about the Swiss Cottage International Travellers' Hostel again.

I dream that Australia will be like a born-again baptism for us. New country, new life, new beginning. We can wash the last year in London off our backs – not to mention all the tomato sauce off our shoes – and start all over again.

Dr Ray Stein, the author of *Should I Stay or Should*

I Go?, wants to know what we once did together that made us feel close. That one's easy. I worshipped Nash. He wanted to be idolized and I did it. I actually sat at his feet when he strummed his guitar, like some 1960s babe in a beret.

The fact that Nash could say long sentences like 'I love your earlobes' in Italian was part of it. So was his funniness. I wonder if he's still as funny as he was then and decide he probably is. The problem is more likely to be me. At the moment I'm not finding this map-reading thing very funny at all.

Heidi comes out of her office and calls us in.

Nash gives me a look and puts his G'day Australia pack away.

I try to work out how Nash is feeling and realize I don't really know. He's as cool as ever, despite the fact that this is one of the more life-changing moments in his world. Very little ever shows on Nash's face, though. He's laidback, chilled, born in an ice bucket, cooler than the fish fingers at Asda.

Perhaps that's why it remains my challenge in life to make Nash happy, or at least make him passionate about me again, just so I can get the satisfaction of watching him crack.

We follow Heidi into her office and see all the documents on her desk.

My God. This is it. We're actually going.

Nash gives the smallest sigh of relief. He *must* be feeling it now.

My own heart is thudding and the whole thing feels

slightly unreal, as if I'm watching myself watching myself.

'Hi Alice,' Heidi shakes my hand, 'Hi Nash. Is it still raining outside?'

Poor Heidi always asks us about the weather, basically because she never knows what's going on outside in the real world. Australia House is like a hermetically sealed tomb.

'Can't wait to get to Bondi Beach.' Nash smiles and she smiles back, going a bit fluttery.

'Not long now then,' Heidi reassures him, and Nash and I exchange looks. 'Everything's ready to go for you here, guys, I just need a couple more signatures and then we're done.'

She always calls us guys. Nash says it makes him feel as if he's in a Western.

When Heidi thinks we're not watching, she checks her watch, and I realize she's probably dying to go home. She lives in Wimbledon. At this time of day that's like travelling to Serbia.

She excuses herself to go and find an extra bit of paper that I appear to be missing.

'We should celebrate after this!' I squeal at Nash. 'Let's go and get some champagne!'

'OK,' Nash says calmly and hands me some coins. 'That's our budget. I believe that's enough to buy one can of lemonade. Let's go crazy.'

What is it about Nash today? I can normally cope with his ice-man approach to life, but this is practically polar bear.

'This is the most important day in our relationship since we moved in together,' I tell him, 'and you want to go home and sit in the horrible hostel and eat baked beans.'

'We are eating baked beans because you don't have a job,' he says.

'Shut up. I do have a job. I'm trying to create my own label.'

'Maybe. Wait until you get to Australia and earn some money, then we'll have champagne.'

'When are you ever going to understand the fashion industry? It doesn't happen overnight.'

'I know, I know. We've been through this.' Nash affects a bored look.

Heidi strides in with the missing bit of paper and we both clam up like naughty children.

'All right guys?' she enquires.

Despite my worries about Form 80 it seems we are in the clear.

'Well, I hope you'll be very happy in Australia,' Nice Heidi says, remembering her script as she hands us our visas and documents. Then she weakens and adds, 'Say hello to Bondi for me.'

'My God,' Nash says later as we go down in the lift. 'I think Heidi actually had a tear in her eye when she told us to say hello to Bondi.'

'She must miss it. I would.'

Nash laughs at me. 'You've never even been there.'

'Yes, but I sort of know. I know that I'd miss it if I was from there and I was stuck here.'

We walk back along the Strand in the rain, sharing Nash's umbrella again, and I ask him one more time if we can have champagne to celebrate. If nothing else it will numb the slight shock I feel. After all this time I can't believe we're finally ready to go.

'Alice! We're broke!' Nash protests.

'Well maybe not champagne. Just a glass of wine then. We can share it in front of a fire somewhere.'

No reply from Nash.

Then . . . 'I'm not going home with you!' I hear myself shouting. 'I'm going to Trafalgar Square!' Then I storm off across the street without looking back.

I doubt that Nash will come after me, but just in case, I use the back streets so he can't find me. Then I stand under my umbrella in the rain, taking a last look at the lights, the lions and the fountains.

It may be one of several last looks at London – we still have two months left – but what if we're too busy with other things? This could be the last time I see Trafalgar Square for two years. Maybe even longer if we stay in Australia.

If it all goes well.

I stand in the rain and try not to cry. When I was a kid, Dad used to bring me to Trafalgar Square all the time. I suppose millions of people must stand here and remember their childhoods.

I am feeling guilty that I haven't rung my mother. I should have done it as soon as I knew we had this final interview with Nice Heidi, but I couldn't face it. Nash hasn't told his parents either. We agreed that we would wait until the visas were in our hands, to make absolutely sure it was happening, but we both know we're just being cowards.

Neither of us really knows how to tell our parents we're leaving them. How can I tell my mother I'm moving to the other side of the world when she no longer has anyone left except me? How can I tell my mother, that great lover of all things English, that I've simply had enough?

The rain is falling in front of the floodlights around the square, making the kind of dash-dash-dash pattern you see in cartoons. Robyn says the rain in Sydney is quite different. It's torrential, as a rule, and often warm.

Oh, England. It's all very well to talk about a lovely new life in a lovely new place, with a lovely fresh start – but the reality is we're dumping this country and everyone in it. It feels exactly like dumping a boyfriend. The churning fear and horrible guilt are about the same.

I've tried my hardest to live here and be happy all my life, but it just hasn't worked. *Dear England, I'm sorry, but it's not me, it's you.*

In one of the quizzes in *Should I Stay or Should I Go?*, you're supposed to find out if the problem with your relationship is in your environment or in you.

Amazingly, I got Nash to fill that bit in. I've still got the piece of paper in my handbag.

I look at it now in the floodlights.

Alice fed up with England due to cost of living – cannot pay for leg waxing. Embarrassed about constantly being filmed on thousands of CCTV cameras across London with hairy legs.

London so expensive, had to sell motorbike. Now have to catch bus and train to work – Dante's bloody Inferno. *Nine concentric circles of hell etc.*

Backpackers at hostel complain about guitar coming through walls. Forced to live in cheap, non-soundproofed hostel because of extortionate London rents. Cannot afford to move because promotion chances tied to London school.

What Nash and I need is sunshine, sea, music, flowers and enough money to buy a glass of white wine at the end of the day. It's not much to ask, is it?

I look around Trafalgar Square at the hoodies. Honestly, it's like living among a bunch of novice monks.

Mum has always wanted us to move to Sussex, to be near her, but I don't think the answer lies there. Nash and I need to go somewhere so big it will make our problems seem small, and so far away that our differences will fade into the distance. We need a really, *really* big leap.

I take one last look at Trafalgar Square, in case it is my last look, and cross the road to St Martin-in-the-Fields.

A service is in progress, so I go inside to absorb all the Englishness and get a better idea of what I am about to lose.

The church smells of mould and candles, just as it always has. It's also full of non-believers, like me, who are only there to get out of the rain. We all sit at the back, partly because we're too embarrassed to sit at the front, and partly because it's the best place for a quick exit if it all becomes too . . . religious.

The Bishop of London begins his sermon. He lets us know that a real donkey will be in church for their Christmas service. I give him ten minutes before I escape. I was sent to an Anglican school, but none of it really stuck. And I know I've been looking for England here, rather than God, but the Japanese tourists with their Burberry brollies have made it impossible to find.

Maybe I should just give up on this forced farewell to London and catch the tube after all. Nash must be halfway home by now.

Suddenly a man on a penny farthing bicycle honks his horn at me, and wobbles from one side of the road to the other while various drivers honk him back. He is wearing a tweed suit, bicycle clips and a deerstalker hat. He is also about 250 years old.

A group of girls on a hen night yell at him from across the pavement. They are drunk, screaming and dressed like red devils. The bride is wearing a Viking helmet and a giant pair of fluffy monster feet.

Maybe this is God's joke. I went looking for England in a church, and it has decided to find me instead.

People get it wrong when they say the English are eccentric; we're just escape artists.

It's only now that I'm leaving it all behind for ever that I notice the madness. That group of people standing under a tree dressed as hedgehogs, doing the 'Hokey Cokey' – would I have paid attention to them before?

They are roaring drunk and it appears to be a sponsored 'Hokey Cokey' in aid of a hedgehog sanctuary called Mrs Tiggy Winkle's Orphanage. They are soaked to the skin, and all their quills have gone floppy, but they don't seem to have noticed.

I'm fairly sure this sort of thing never happens in Sydney.

A woman in a pillbox hat and fur coat teeters up the street to Soho in high heels like some 1950s film star. Will there be any mad, exotic creatures like her on the other side of the world?

I fold up my silly tartan umbrella and let the rain fall on my face so people won't see me cry. It's pathetic, but the tears are hard to stop now that I've worked myself up. *Dear England*. Where else in the world will I find giant pissed hedgehogs doing the 'Hokey Cokey'?

Goodbye London. Goodbye to people flapping their smelly pizza slices in my face on Shaftesbury Avenue. Goodbye to all the simply marvellous plays in simply marvellous theatres that Nash and I can never afford to see. Goodbye to Gap and Coca-Cola. Goodbye Eros. I've never arranged a romantic assignation beneath his bow and arrow and now I never will.

I look for my purse in my pocket, but it's gone. Bloody pickpockets. I could kick myself for being so stupid.

After kneeling down on the pavement to rifle through my bag, I find my make-up, keys, antique tampon collection and overdue library notices, but no purse. Well, I hope they enjoy it. They picked the wrong woman if they were looking for platinum credit cards.

There are no police anywhere. There never are. The only thing I can do is ring Nash, except my phone is still out of credit and there's no money in my pocket to recharge it. Then I realize the battery's died anyway. Great.

I don't even have enough money for a phone box. Not even a lousy 20p.

Walking home to Swiss Cottage is not impossible – Nash and I have both done it before so I know I won't die – it's just that it was summer then, and now the winter wind is physically painful.

The tartan wellies and umbrella are useless, and it's the kind of wind that gives you weepy eyes and sore ears.

I have to see Trafalgar Square one last time though. I just have to.

Suddenly, a couple in black tie step out of a taxi on their way to some event. She is wearing a tiara and silver shoes and he is wearing a black cape and bow tie. They look like characters from a fairy story, but I know that if I did a fairy-story thing and asked them for money, they would just ignore me, or possibly even use me as puddle coverage.

Then I see her. Nice Heidi.

I look away, but then something makes me look back and I see that she is waving, so I go over to her. Sometimes it's best to ask questions first and think about it later.

'Heidi!' I launch myself at her. 'My purse has been stolen. Could I borrow some money for a phone call? I'm sorry. I just need to call Nash.'

'You dropped your purse outside the lift,' she says, and pulls it out of her handbag. I'm torn between huge relief and embarrassment because it's such a pathetic purse. A silly tartan plastic thing that matches my wellies and umbrella.

'I called you but your phone wasn't answering,' she says. 'Then I called Nash and he said you'd gone to Trafalgar Square.'

What if she's looked inside my purse and seen that the only things I own are two pounds and an Oyster card? And what if she saw the Glastonbury condom that Nash bought last year? It looks like some ancient relic from an architectural dig, lying there covered in fluff, at the bottom of my purse.

'You look like a drowned rat. Do you want a drink?' she asks.

'Oh no. That's all right.'

'Come on. You're moving to Oz! Let me buy you a drink.'

'Actually – yes please.'

'I've got some time to kill before the theatre. I'm way too early. I got the time wrong,' Heidi says.

Heidi has kind eyes, and I'm sure she's telling me the whitest of all white lies, but why argue? I am freezing cold and running out of tissues to blow my nose. I can think of nothing better than sitting in a warm, dry pub with a glass of wine and a packet of peanuts.

We find a place just off Covent Garden with a table near the window and sit down while the water trickles down my legs and into my wellies. I bought them, the purse and the matching brolly at Glastonbury. It was supposed to be a romantic holiday for Nash and I, but we argued so much that weekend that we ended up sleeping on opposite sides of our two-man tent so our bodies bulged out at the sides.

'Let me tell you a secret,' Heidi nudges me once she's bought us both a bottle – not two glasses, a bottle – of wine. It's from Margaret River, she says, which is the best wine region in Australia.

'What secret?' I ask.

'You were fast-tracked. We had a note from someone in head office in Canberra. You must have good connections.'

'I thought it was because of Nash's job.'

'Nah,' she says, gulping her wine down, 'you might not have got in so easily without help.'

'Is that because of my application? Being a woman with a key in my back?'

'Sort of.'

'I knew it.'

Heidi finishes her wine, pours herself another and tops up my glass.

'Your cousin Robyn is probably the reason you got through,' she says. 'She manages one of our hotels. Did you know that? All the public servants stay at her place at Bondi Beach. Anyway, I bet she's got connections. But who cares? You're in.'

I decide to own up about the fight with Nash.

'I thought there was something going on,' Heidi says.

'I wanted champagne to celebrate and he didn't. Thank God you picked up my purse though.' I thank her. 'I've just been to church actually. St Martin-in-the-Fields. Maybe it's an act of God.'

Heidi nods sympathetically, even though I must sound like some dribbling madwoman.

We talk about the pelicans in Australia, which unlike the cruel London pelicans do not attempt to swallow pigeons whole, and we keep drinking the wine, in a new-best-friends kind of way. Heidi misses feeding the pelicans in Byron Bay where her aunt lives, and she also misses the sound of cicadas, whatever they are, and the smell of gum trees, and the fact that you can ring the local doctor and see him the same day. Not like farking London, she says, where you can wait two farking weeks for someone from the NHS.

Heidi talks and talks. I have never heard such homesickness pouring out of someone.

Most of all, she hates English Post Offices. In fact, when she talks about them she grabs her hair and pulls at it, as if she's going quite mad.

'The queues go out the *door*!' she squeals. 'There's a class system for the *stamps*!'

I change the subject back to Byron Bay before she pulls her hair out.

'What's it like for jobs there?' I ask.

'Not bad. What sort of jobs?'

'Not public service jobs. I'm useless at those kinds of things. Well, you saw my application form.'

'Oh well,' Heidi says in her kind way.

'I can do basic jobs, though. Cleaning, waitressing, cooking. I've run market stalls. I can walk dogs, that kind of thing. I really want to be a fashion designer, of course, but—'

Heidi nods kindly. 'I remember. What sort of clothes do you want to design?' she asks.

'I want to recycle old fabric, like the stuff you find in charity shops, but I also want to use vintage clothes. That's why the label will be called Vintage Alice. And I'm going to use real women to make the clothes – not kids in India – and they're going to be paid real money.'

'Wow!' Heidi says. 'Will the clothes be for real women too?'

'Oh yes. The sizes are going to go up in ones, not twos.'

'So could I be a size thirteen?' she asks. 'Because I'm not a size twelve in half the shops, but I'm never a size fourteen either.'

'Absolutely. You'll be a Vintage Alice size thirteen.'

'I want you to make me something now!' Heidi shrieks.

'Well I could, except—'

'You're going to need a job to get the business started. Hey. Do you like dogs?' Heidi asks.

'Most of them.'

'My Auntie Danielle has a boarding kennel in Byron. She's always looking for staff. You get your accommodation thrown in and you just have to walk the dogs and feed them.'

'Great.'

'Here,' she gives me a name and phone number on a piece of paper. 'Her name's Danielle Coles. We're both called Coles. The boarding kennel is called Barks of Byron Bay.' Heidi pulls a face. 'I know. She thought of it, not me.'

'Thanks. Really. This is great.'

'It's a long way from Sydney, though.'

I picture a place that's two hours away on a train somewhere and tell her I can cope.

'It's a full day on the train,' she says. 'It's like going to Europe.'

'Ah.'

'If Nash is working in North Sydney you might have to live apart for a while while you earn some cash. There's no way you can commute every day. Then again, you might need a break from him if you're having domestics all the time.'

Heidi's voice goes up at the end, just like the people on *Neighbours*.

'Thanks, Heidi.'

She glances at my silly tartan purse. 'Here. Buy yourself some champagne and take it home to your boyfriend,' she says, putting a pile of notes in my hand.

'I can't.'

'Yeah you can.' Heidi smiles and leaves quickly through the side door. I can tell she was making it up about going to the theatre. And look, she's just walked out of the pub in her lovely pencil skirt and lacy tights without a single man looking up. The men in London can be so thick sometimes.

I do not use Nice Heidi's money to buy champagne. Instead, I save it for the next great cash emergency in my life and spend the last of my coins on the ladies' loo at Victoria Station, where I know there are big, strong, reliable hand driers, unlike the broken ones in the pub. I don't care if it takes me twice as long to get home, I just have to stop feeling so soggy.

Once I'm at Victoria Station I get maximum value for money in the loo by shoving my entire head and body under the hand drier for twenty minutes, flipping my hand backwards and forwards to keep the machine on, then using every last paper towel to dry off my legs. Then I dry my wellies, my umbrella and my handbag.

In the unlikely event that I get any money ever again, I will send Heidi Coles the biggest magnum of champagne known to womankind. I wonder if they are all like her in Australia. I hope so. I feel as if an angel has just flapped her wings at me.

I find a phone booth and call Nash, who doesn't pick up, so my call goes straight through to my tired old answering-machine message from last year. It was about then that we began talking about moving to Sydney.

I look at my useless tartan boots. I should never buy footwear at music festivals. I had a good T-shirt stand there, though – it was the only reason Nash and I got tickets. Women loved my T-shirts because I'd decorated them with cut-out laminated pictures of all the bands.

They were like fan-club T-shirts from the eighties, but with lovely flattering necklines and long sleeves you could push up. I sold the lot and bought my wellies, purse and brolly with the profits. Then I gave the rest to the bank, before they could send debt-collectors to the hostel to repossess everything I owned.

I feel Heidi's money in my pocket. Now the bank debt has become a Nash debt and a mum debt. I added it all up last weekend to see how long it would take me to waitress my way to solvency once I got to Sydney. I should be in the clear in eighteen months if the only protein I eat is in the form of eggs and stop crazy luxuries like coin-operated public loos.

I think about my cousin Robyn and our fast-tracked application. The only photo I have of her in my bag shows her wearing a scuba diving mask, a snorkel and flippers while waving a dead eel. I have other more sensible photographs, but this is the version of her I most expect to see when we finally meet. In the meantime, it seems Nash and I both owe my cousin a huge favour. I just hope she didn't have to sleep with some horrible dribbling ambassador type at her hotel to get us to the front of the list.

Chapter Two

My mother's name is Penelope Templeton. My dad called her Penny. Nash calls her Lady Penelope because she has a blonde bob, like the *Thunderbirds* puppet, and because she drives a Jaguar. He thinks she's posh.

There is no point in telling Nash that the real Lady Penelope had a Rolls-Royce, or that my mother only has a Jaguar because Dad used to own a car business. Nash made up his mind about my mum the first time he met her, and that's it.

I am on the train to Hove to spend the weekend with her when Nash rings.

'Alice? Can you ask Lady Penelope if she has any old suitcases we could take to Australia?'

'Yes, I will ask my *mother* if she has any old suitcases we could take to Australia.'

'Once you've done all the shock-horror Australia news bit, of course. I've just been testing out this suitcase and the lock's broken.'

'Whatever. And I'll also apologize for the fact that you're spending the whole weekend at home working on your school Christmas concert, although this is obviously twaddle because the kids already know the carols. You're just going to drink beer and read Bob Dylan books.'

'Bollocks, Alice. I'm going now.'

'Yeah, bollocks to you as well. And Australia is not shock-horror news. It's our future Nash, try to be a bit more interested in it.'

My mobile phone seems to have a sensor which reacts to the amount of heat generated by my conversations with Nash. The more irritated we both become, the hotter my phone gets, until it feels as if it's going to scorch the side of my head. At the moment I feel as if someone has been ironing my ear.

I turn the phone off and look at my free G'day Australia pack again. I'm going to leave it with Mum, in the vague hope that she starts to understand what we're doing and why we're doing it. At the very least she might begin to get a better sense of where we're going. Geography has never been her strong point.

The last two weeks have been impossible. I have picked up the phone to tell her, then put it down every single time. Nash hasn't done anything about his parents either, and we still haven't been brave enough to tell any of our friends. There was a vague plan to have a spontaneous gathering on fireworks night at Primrose Hill, but in the end we just stayed home and watched TV.

We are breaking up with England, and breaking up is hard to do. Every time I try to find the words to tell people, I just can't. And every time we decide to organize a farewell party, it never happens.

The last time I discussed Australia with my mother was months ago, after we posted our application to Australia House. She became thoroughly confused by the idea that we could be going to a place called New South Wales and kept mixing it up with Wales – because Wales was our other idea, last year, before we settled on Sydney.

I have drawn big gold circles all over the giant map of Australia with my favourite Christmas card pen to help my mother get her bearings. There's a giant circle for New South Wales, a smaller one for Sydney and a gold blob for Bondi Beach. I've also added a gold arrow in the ocean, pointing to the location of the real Wales, just in case. To avoid further confusion, I have illustrated the arrow pointing to Wales with big wooden spoons and pictures of women in pointy black stovepipe hats.

Just looking at the map of Australia makes me feel overwhelmed. It's so big you could fit England, Scotland, Ireland *and* Wales into it about fifty times. How am I ever going to find my way around that?

My relationship with Nash has always been full of vague plans and mad ideas. The Wales scheme was one (although we were going to travel round the country by motorbike first). A possible move to Canada was another. My mother has been told about all these ideas over the last two years, then forced to forget them just as quickly. I suppose she thought the Australia plan was another non-starter. This time, though, I'm going to have to show her the letter, and Robyn's keys, and pour her the largest brandy of her life.

It hasn't been easy getting Robyn to keep quiet about our visas. When I rang her in Sydney she squealed – as much from her success at moving us up the list as anything else. I had to pass the phone over to Nash just to calm her down.

When they finished talking – or she had finished talking and he had finished holding the phone away from his ear – he said, 'Your cousin seduced someone from the Department of Immigration and Citizenship at a party at her hotel. So Heidi was right. If they find out about it they'll probably deport us.'

Nash has given me a bag of barley sugar for the train journey, and I catch myself mindlessly crunching one sweet after another, feeling more and more nervous about seeing my mother.

When we arrive she's wearing what Nash calls her Princess Anne headscarf. Mum has always worn it, and I never notice it, except when I am worrying about what Nash thinks of her. Occasionally, I tell myself that I am going to make jokes about his parents' chunky matching cardigans. They live in Cambridge and own an art gallery, and their cardigans always have such big toggles I have to fight off a secret urge to yank them.

The car, which my mother always refers to as *the* car, smells of her cigarettes, and there are library books all over the back seat, as usual. She reads the same Georgette Heyers over and over again, to the point where she can detect her own fag ash in the binding.

'How's Nash?'

'He says hello. He's doing the Christmas concert all weekend.'

'They work him so hard, don't they.'

'How are you?'

'Actually, I've just finished that wall hanging for you. For Christmas.'

Oh God. The embroidered wall hanging with pictures of labradors savaging ducks. How am I going to fit that in my luggage?

'And I thought I'd give you my old watch as well. I've decided to get another one in the sales.'

We both look at my watch-free wrist and I immediately feel guilty about the watch she bought me five birthdays ago. I sold it last year so I could buy Nash a Christmas present.

'Are you excited about Australia?' my mother lights a cigarette and winds down the window.

'What?'

'Nash rang just now and said you were going in a few weeks. Or have I gone off half-cocked and got it wrong?'

'No. Oh my God. Nash *told you*?'

'Just then, when I was waiting for you in the car park.'

My mother takes a huge drag on her cigarette and throws it out the window. Then she lights another one. Oh God. She's driving too fast. I think she may be having some kind of attack. She's going to kill us.

'He was actually ringing because he's lost his reading

specs and he thought you might have moved them somewhere. He tried calling you on the train but you kept going through tunnels. Anyway, do you have them?'

'No I bloody don't! I can't believe that Nash told you about Australia before I did!'

'It's really fine, darling, please don't worry about it. He was confused, that's all. He thought you were already off the train and that you'd already told me. I just mentioned that he might like a nice big jar of Sussex honey for Christmas and he said it might be too hard to get through Australian customs. So then the cat was out of the bag. Where are you off to again? Is it something Wales?'

'New South Wales. We're going to Sydney. To Robyn's flat at Bondi Beach at first, and then we'll look for a place of our own. God, Mum, I'm so sorry. I meant to tell you myself. It's all happened incredibly quickly. That's why I came up to see you.'

I feel the angelic Heidi's money in my pocket; the sole reason I can afford to be here today. I cannot possibly borrow any more money from Nash.

'Absolutely no problem at all,' my mother waves me away, lighting another cigarette as we screech round another killer corner.

I am trying to break up with mum – and with England – as sensitively and carefully as I know how, and now look. Her hands appear to be shaking as she grips the wheel of the Jaguar, and her cigarette ash drops all over the gearstick. Thank you, Nash, you complete wanker.

'Sorry, Alice, I'm really going to have to pull over.'

We lurch into a disabled parking space near the supermarket, and then Mum remembers this is immoral, so we lurch out again, until we finally end up parked under a tree near the station again, back where we started.

My mother is the only woman I know who can cry and smoke at the same time. She did it at Dad's funeral and she's doing it now. I hold her hand, and I realize she is wearing the same red leather gloves she has owned all my life. It's all I need to make me cry as well, and soon we are both sobbing like idiots.

'So you're definitely off then?' she asks, after she has taken off the gloves and blown her nose.

'Yes.'

'You two never got on with London, did you? I can understand Nash disliking it because he's from Cambridge and they've never liked the competition, but you were born there! You know, you could always have moved back here. It's so different near the sea. And I'm sure Nash could have found a good school near Brighton.'

'I thought we'd sort of talked about this. Staying in England isn't really going to work.'

'So you've had enough of this country. Well, many people have.'

'That's not the only reason we're going. It's complicated.'

Mum dabs at her nose. 'I'll have to come out and visit you over there,' she says, trying not to cry again. 'If you can bear an old fuddy-duddy like me following you halfway across the world.'

'Mum. Stop it. We'll come back and visit you here as well. We're not . . . dead.'

Oh God. Bad choice of word. I bet she's going to get even more upset now, because of dad, and sure enough she does.

'I know you'll visit. That's fine. Honestly, I'll stop blubbing in a minute. But Alice, are you absolutely sure about this? It's just that I've always thought Australia is one of those places where you might come a cropper.'

'I've talked it through with Nash a million times. And Robyn's been so amazing too.'

'Oh, Robyn's been helping you! Well that's nice to know. Her father was always a very kind sort of person. Mad as a hatter, of course, but never mind. Did Robyn tell you anything about him? I haven't heard from that lot for years. In fact, the other day, I realized I don't even know where to send the Christmas cards.'

'All I know is that Roland's in San Francisco, and they're all fine, I think. Robyn's managing this hotel at Bondi Beach I told you about. Roland's retired and living by himself, Joel's in India working for a charity and Aunt Helena's in Jamaica with her new boyfriend—'

'Hippy Helena,' my mother interrupts me. 'That family really did spread itself far and wide, didn't it? They were so adventurous. Roland was always much more bohemian than your father. I remember on the day they all left England, the whole family was wearing these enormous clogs.'

I laugh and blow my nose. 'I remember. I'm glad Robyn stayed in Australia, though. If she hadn't, I'm not sure it would have been that easy for us to move there.'

'Oh well,' my mother sighs. 'As long as you're sure about it all.'

'Yes,' I hear myself saying, although I know later on tonight, when I'm lying in my old bedroom, with the pink curtains and the view of the English Channel, I may well have Aussie wobbles. That's what Nash has been calling it all week – the big Aussie wobble.

After we've gone through all the hankies she possesses, my mother and I drive home through thick traffic jams and heavy fog.

'Apparently there's no traffic in Australia at all,' mum says. 'What a relief for you. It's hell here. Especially now that everybody does their Christmas shopping in November. And of course they all descend on Brighton and try to park their cars in Hove. All those cars looming out of the fog. Brrr! It's like a horror film, darling. It gives me the heebie jeebies.'

She's already cheering up. My father used to call her the trooper, and I've forgotten how quickly she can bounce back. I am worried about the number of cigarettes she is smoking, though. When she coughs, it goes on for five minutes. My mother is the sort of person you wouldn't want to let into a live television audience.

Mum starts on her newspaper crossword as soon as we get home, and after a few more polite questions about

Robyn's flat at Bondi Beach and Nash's new school in North Sydney, there is no more talk about Australia for the rest of the night. Instead, Mum and I watch a programme about stoats.

'When alarmed,' the commentator tells us, 'stoats release a powerful, musky smell from their anal glands.'

'How awful for them,' my mother murmurs.

Oh no. I'm crying now. I can't believe I'm feeling emotional about stoats, of all things, but I am. Even before the final credits roll, with their moody shots of stoats and their anal glands frolicking across the green English hills, the tears are pouring down my face.

Everything seems so richly British these days that almost anything sets me off. The chunky Kit Kats I saw on sale at the station this morning immediately made me feel homesick. So did the spotty teenage Goths who got on the train at Hayward's Heath. Every time I notice something else about England, I start missing it before I've even got to the airport.

Suddenly Nash texts me.

SORRY ABOUT TELLING LADY P.

I switch my phone off. I am so angry with him that I'm not totally sure what to do about it.

The programme about stoats is replaced by a real-life crime show, which mum immediately switches off.

'Absolute cobblers,' she comments.

'I might get an early night actually,' I tell her.

'Yes, of course. See you in the morning.'

'See you in the morning,' I parrot back.

Everyone hopes my mother will get a new partner, but we can't count on it. She looks so lonely sitting in front of the fire with all her solo possessions around her. One brandy glass. One Georgette Heyer book. One packet of Silk Cut. One embroidery kit. One packet of cards with horses on the front. Maybe I could find her an Australian man and send him over. There must be someone for her over there in Delicate Nobby.

I go up to my room and find my copy of *Should I Stay or Should I Go?* OK. One more time. Are my memories of the really, really good bits with Nash still enough to make me feel wonderful? Yes. There is no substitute for the memory of a long bike ride into the country on an autumn day, followed by an afternoon of passion on a tartan blanket.

The next question in the book is rather shocking: Has Nash ever hit me? What? Apparently, I need to think about the amount of violence there has been in the relationship.

The answer, of course, is none. Unless you count me threatening to hurl my sewing machine at him when we were having an argument about Bob Dylan.

I move on to another question, propping up my head with one hand, while outside the window the wind howls across the channel.

'Are you already spending time or money on a subtle escape route from your relationship?'

What?

I really shouldn't have had that second brandy while watching the stoat programme. Reading this book is like taking an exam. And yet, and yet . . . I want to pass this question. I want to know things will be all right.

Whoops. I'm not going to pass.

I certainly have planned an escape route, because three days ago I secretly applied for a job at Barks of Byron Bay Boarding Kennels with Heidi's aunt, Danielle Coles. It includes board, because there's a self-contained flat. Nash could visit on weekends, but that's all. If I'm going to work there, we'll have to live apart.

And . . . Nash hates dogs. He really, really hates dogs, because he was bitten in the face by a Rottweiler when he was a child, and still has a scar beneath his ear, which he's permanently embarrassed about. Hence the slightly too long but sexy curly hair. If he wasn't such a brilliant music teacher, his school would have made him cut it years ago.

Perhaps if I get the job at Barks, I'll never see Nash at all. Unless I get the train to Sydney, of course, and that might not always be possible.

I'm crying again. Oh God. They never tell you about this at Australia House. You might be among the lucky few to make it into the Lucky Country, but every day during your last weeks in England, you'll weep a canyon of tears.

Danielle Coles is bound to prefer one of the oodles of Australian trainee vets who must apply over me. Nevertheless, the letter has gone, and without even admitting it to myself, I have already put hundreds of miles between me and Nash.

When I was at the University of Huddersfield, failing

my arts degree, I walked a fox terrier called Goggles. He had patches over both eyes and was owned by an old lady who used to leave a few pound coins in an envelope for me in Goggles' dog basket.

His speciality was going into a trance. One minute Goggles would appear to be perfectly normal, trotting along on the common, the next he would plonk down on the grass with a strange, glazed expression on his face.

One day I poked Goggles with my finger and he fell over sideways, dead. I had to carry him back home to the old lady in a plastic bag – and that was the end of my dog-walking career at Huddersfield University, although I won't tell Danielle Coles any of this.

My only other canine-handling experience consists of feeding and walking our old Labrador, Charlie, who used to wander into my bedroom all the time and shred my school shoes. He was also known as Yeller, Feller and Smeller and sometimes Yeller Smeller Feller. I should have got him to put his paw print on a reference for me while I had the chance.

I can hear Mum snoring next door now, and it makes me think about Dad again. While he was still in hospital, he told me he would look after me, because life was too short to be worried about money. And now look.

He tried to do his best, but the money he left Mum and I in his will only just covered his medical bills and taxes. This house is all Mum has now, because even after we sold the business there were still debts. She had to use up a lot of her own savings to pay them all off.

I sometimes think about my school fees and wish I could have talked my parents out of it, so they could have saved their money for my mother's old age. But no. I cost them a fortune and now she's paying the price. She even dyes her own hair these days, after a lifetime of going to the same hairdresser in Hove. I saw the bottles in the bathroom. Mum shouldn't have to do that.

Dad once said that marriage wasn't about sums, and that I should never try to do any. That was probably true for him and Mum, but when I think about Nash these days, I just remember all the money I owe him.

Nash and Mum took over where the bank left off. He lent me £10,000 to get rid of the bank (and the nasty letters from their debt collection agencies) and she lent me another £10,000 just to live while I was at college.

The relationship between Nash and I was never supposed to be run along such venal lines, but on reflection, who on earth were we kidding? Every couple we know in London, married or unmarried, thinks about money all the time.

The bank let me back eventually, of course. And that's where my other debt is, the scary £2,000 overdraft that won't go away – the last trace of my student loan.

Oh, and then there's my credit card.

Thank God Robyn helped to fast-track our application. I'm sure the Australians have no idea what a dribbling pauper they're letting in.

The rain pours down while I make plans. If I get a part-time job at Barks of Byron Bay, I could get a second job as a waitress, too, so then I'd have two lots of money coming in. Maybe I would even get tips from both jobs, so I could post some money back to Mum every month and put the rest aside for Nash in a jam jar. If I found two smaller jam jars, that would take care of the bank and the credit card.

My father would put his head in his hands if he could see me now. For my entire life my finances have revolved around jars. So much for all those talks about comparative interest rates.

There is a corner shop near us, run by an Indian family whose son has installed a second-hand PC in the corner. It's connected to the world's slowest modem, so they don't charge much. Just lately, I sit on it for two hours a day, looking for jobs in Australia, and using a currency exchange website to turn pounds into dollars and dollars into pounds, just to see if I'll be a richer waitress over there. I won't be, but I'll be able to live on fruit.

According to Australian Google, denim's $6 a metre, so I could make some really groovy denim culottes and sell them, all for the price of a single-journey tube fare.

Oh God, I've got to stop designing denim culottes in my head. It's 4 a.m. now. How did that happen?

There's a knock at the door. Mum can't sleep either.

'Alice, do you want a hot drink?'

'Cocoa.' It's out of my mouth before I can even think about it. Being in my old bedroom has sent me straight back to childhood. I don't think I've had cocoa for years.

'I was woken up by my own revolting snoring,' she

says and goes off to the kitchen. 'Your father always said I sounded like something with flared nostrils that you might expect to see staggering around at the Grand National.'

When she comes back, she says she wants to talk to me about Dad's will, and sits on the wobbly wooden chair next to my bed, with a shoebox full of his old notebooks.

My father wrote everything in block letters, and it jolts me to see his handwriting again.

'I have a funny feeling you're lying here worrying about money,' she says.

'Sort of.'

'Nash did vaguely say you were both worried about money when he rang.'

Bloody Nash.

'I wish he hadn't.'

'Alice, is everything all right between you? You had a face like a boot in the car today.'

'It's all right. We're going to Australia. We're going to have a fresh start.'

'Anyway,' my mother pats the shoebox full of notebooks. 'What I meant to say was, there *is* money. Your father had it tucked away in a different account, and before he died he told me that it was just for us. A sort of emergency fund. He forbade me to touch it for any other reason. Not even to pay bills. And I woke up just now and suddenly thought, Stone the crows! This is a sort of emergency.'

'No it's not, Mum. I don't need it. You hang onto it.'

'Well, I was rather hoping we could sort something out. It's quite a lot of money, Alice. Almost fifty thousand pounds.'

'Really? Is it?' I must not look excited, I must not look excited.

'Tell me why you're really moving to Australia.'

'Because I want to design clothes. Because we'll have money again, and then I can pay everyone back. Because Nash can get a motorbike. Because we can move into a proper flat. Maybe we can even get a little house with a garden. The weather's better over there, Mum. No more tube. No more rubbish. No more zillions of people. No more CCTV cameras everywhere . . .' I pause for breath. 'No more pigeons.'

'But pigeons are very brave. Pigeons won the war for us. They were attacked by German hawks, you know, and Nazi marksmen, and they still flew straight and true with messages tied to their legs.'

'Mum! It's four o'clock in the morning. Why are we talking about pigeons' legs?' I yell.

'Why are you really moving to Australia?'

'Oh God. If you must know, to stay together. If Nash and I don't do something drastic I'm worried we'll break up.'

'I see. Look, Alice. I may be using a sledgehammer to crack a nut here, but what would you say if I asked you not to go?'

'But we've been accepted. And they're waiting for Nash to start his job.'

'This is your father's vital emergency money,' my

mother pats the shoebox. 'And I think he'd see this as a vital emergency. You're leaving England. Quite possibly for the wrong reasons. Sometimes it's better to travel hopefully than to arrive.'

'What does that mean?'

'It might be a different kettle of fish once you land in Sydney, Alice.'

'Maybe.'

If you and Nash would like somewhere nicer to live, that's fine. I quite understand. He should never have let you take that job at the hostel in the first place. And if you'd like to set up in the fashion business, that's fine too. It will be a feather in your cap. But you don't have to leave good old England to do it.'

'I think Dad meant that money should be put aside for you, if you were ever ill.'

'Not necessarily, darling. Anyway, if I am ill, what use will it be if you're in Australia? Before you say Jack Robinson, I could be in the deep-freeze in Hove with my feet sticking out of a sheet.'

Perhaps my mother is like Lady Penelope sometimes. Although it's my strings that are being pulled here, not hers.

'I can't think about this now, Mum. It's too late.'

'OK, darling. Just remember, there's money here if it's required. You don't have to take such drastic measures to help things with Nash, Alice. And I'm really, truly sure that your father would see this as an emergency. Heavens to Murgatroyd, Alice, you *know* it is.'

Eventually she goes back to bed, and the awkward

question about my debt to her – why did I ever let her lend me the money for college? – is left hanging in the air.

Counting the wallpaper roses in this room has been a reliable cure for insomnia since I was small. Perhaps it's worth trying now. I had forgotten how pink my childhood bedroom is – the lamp still turns everything rosy.

I stick my leg up in the air, examine my toes and decide I want a pedicure. My life is all charity shops, canned soup, baked beans and cheap shampoo. I am fed up with feeling guilty about the money I owe mum and sick of worrying about the money I owe Nash.

Dad's money would fix everything and it's the most tempting offer in the world. But I can't do it. I can't stay in this country. My dreams about the future in Australia are too far gone.

I listen to my mother coughing next door. If she keeps smoking a packet of fags every two days she'll probably have a stroke. Then they'll ring me in the middle of the night in Australia and tell me she's dying and calling my name.

After that, there will be a desperate rush for the airport in Sydney, followed by a lecture from her, on her deathbed, at the other end in England. It's now 5.30 a.m., according to my old plastic clock. Great. Once I'm in Australia and she's on the other side of the world, will I ever actually sleep again?

Chapter Three

Some time ago, Suzanne, my oldest friend and un-official relationship counsellor, suggested that Nash and I find a new hobby to share.

Suzanne and I spent a whole night coming up with unlikely options: joining fox-hunt saboteur groups; learning to cook Italian food; exploring the little-known world of Tai Chi . . .

In the end, though, Nash beat us to it with the coupley hobby thing. Because his mate Richard fancied Suzanne, he roped us all into the same pub-quiz team at The Bell and Dragon.

Richard is the drummer in Nash's band, The Believers. Thus, it would have been extremely convenient for everyone if Suzanne had fancied him too. She didn't, though. She made it as far as Richard's bedroom one night, then saw he had a metal clothes rack in his bedroom and pulled back. Suzanne is very wary of men in their thirties who still have tubular metal clothes racks.

Our quiz team is called The Believers, like the boys'

band. Their singer, Lisa, is also in the team, along with Michael, a teacher at Nash's school.

Tonight there are some Australian questions, which provides both Nash and I with the perfect excuse to tell everyone about Sydney. Our departure date is looming.

Nash finally told his parents after I told Mum. That means it's only a matter of time before the news starts trickling back from Hove and Cambridge, all the way to London.

Nash says his parents told him they were happy we were going. 'They said they nearly emigrated, back in the eighties. It's just that the art scene wasn't really happening in Australia then.'

I love the way his parents think they are in any kind of art scene. They run a gallery and gift shop in a little street in Cambridge with woven wall hangings and teapots with lids in the shape of root vegetables.

I think I'm allowed to have mixed feelings about his parents. In my darkest financial hour, I asked them to put some of my T-shirts in the shop, and they refused.

I haven't told Nash that mum tried to talk me out of leaving. And I haven't told him about the £50,000 emergency money either. The less I think about that, the better.

'So are we actually going to see your mum and dad before we go?' I ask Nash while we sit with The Believers, ticking off questions on the sheet.

'There's a big lunch on New Year's Day at the gallery if you're interested. They said to ask Lady P as well.'

'My mother is not called Lady Penelope, and you know she can't come to Cambridge. The trains are useless and she doesn't like driving in this weather.'

'OK,' Nash shrugs.

It says a great deal about our relationship that the other Believers – Suzanne, Lisa, Richard and Michael – have reached the point where they no longer notice our gentle bickering. I suppose it's become a pub soundtrack to them, like the pinging on the fruit machines.

The Bell and Dragon is packed tonight because the jackpot prize has gone up again. While our team wrestles with the Australian questions, I wrestle with our vague Australia-announcement plan, made up on the spot this evening as Nash and I were having baked beans on toast again for dinner.

The idea is that everyone on our quiz team will be told tonight, which should take care of most of the people we know, since Lisa, Suzanne, Michael and Richard can be counted on to spread the news far and wide.

As well as singing in The Believers, Lisa is Head of Music at Romney College in Windsor, where she seems to spend her days playing the harp on the lawns to the girls and floating around wearing a straw sun hat in the school swimming pool. Suzanne and I both know this because she sometimes brings in photographs of herself to show us. It happened so often last summer that Suzanne thought Lisa might be trying to get a job as a model on her magazine.

Michael is married to another teacher at Nash's school, who comes along and joins the team sometimes, but I'm sure he's secretly in love with Lisa. Especially since the photographs.

Apart from playing the harp and bobbing around in the swimming pool, Lisa is also a friend of Nash's ex-wife Sarah. When they both turned up at The Bell and Dragon last year, looking all floaty and sensitive together, it was one of the most terrifying nights of my life.

They had been on a sponsored charity swim for their various schools, so I couldn't protest. But when Nash, Sarah and Lisa all failed to come home at the designated time, I was very glad I had Suzanne to look after me.

Sarah has since floated off again – she teaches in Cornwall – so only Lisa remains to remind me that Nash ever had a past.

Lisa laughs in a tinkling, feminine way, not like my awful honking and Suzanne's raucous snorting. She also has hair she can sit on. It's the kind of hair that makes you think about Lady Godiva, and I can see why that would get Michael going. He's practically salivating all over the table tonight because Lisa's nipples are pointing at him through her shirt.

I look around the table and realize that Suzanne, Lisa, Richard and Michael *have* noticed our bickering after all. I squeeze Nash's hand under the table, and after a moment he squeezes mine back. We can't afford to argue tonight. After all, we're saying goodbye to The Believers for ever.

After the quiz has finished, the plan is that I will organize a big drinks night in a few days' time in the back bar. Anyone who doesn't hear about it on the grapevine will be telephoned, once I find the jam jar full of 20p pieces that I hid last summer so I can recharge my mobile phone.

My God. It's like a military operation just getting to Heathrow. And Nash and I haven't even started packing yet.

Question Four. Which Aussie won the 2005 Nobel Prize for Medicine? Easy, according to Richard – a bloke called Barry who discovered a bacteria called Helicobacter pylori. *Now, while we're on the subject of Antipodean people called Barry, did we mention we were emigrating to Australia?*

I sneak a look at Lisa. She is wearing a see-through floaty blouse in the middle of winter.

'Yass,' she's saying to Richard. 'Yass, you're absolutely right about that bacteria.'

Lisa is dating a barrister, but nobody has ever actually seen him. He's always working, apparently.

I'm not jealous of wafty Lisa, though. She's just an irritant, a reminder of Nash's clever, sensitive, ethereal ex-wife as much as anything, and soon she'll be a dot on the landscape, just like all the tiny houses you leave behind the moment you take off from Heathrow.

In a way, Lisa was a fair swap for Sarah. I've allowed Nash to have her because it's so much better than putting up with the woman he used to be married to. Sarah and Nash exchange Christmas and birthday cards, but that's it. I must have read them a hundred times, looking for scary signs of intimacy, but she always just signs them, 'Best Wishes, Sarah'. Nash seldom talks about her. And I'm not allowed to ask.

I look out of the window and watch the smokers struggling to light their cigarettes in the wind. Part of me is longing for that holidayish, Bondi Beach feeling of escape. You can run away from your life all you like by trying not to think about it, but there's no substitute for a great big 747 and a lot of tiny dots below.

We tackle a question about the most common pub name in Great Britain. Is it a) The Green Man, b) The Dog and Duck c) The Queen's Head or d) The Dog's Bollocks?

Nash is always saying that he'll miss English pubs the most when we leave. I don't think I will. The basic elements will be the same in Australia, won't they? Sticky tables, smelly carpet, a ladies' loo with a silhouette of someone from the 1950s holding a powder puff. The last time I checked on the internet, the pubs over there looked the same as pubs anywhere else.

It's the other things I'll miss: Morris dancers, dead old kings called Svein Forkbeard and Harald Harefoot, and sundials . . .

The sundial on the Hove seafront reads 'Non Redibis'. *Thou shall not come again.* My mother and I tried very hard not to look at each other when we noticed it, walking along the beach on my last night.

I'm sure she still thinks I'll change my mind at the last minute. Just thinking about her disappointment when we don't makes me feel teary.

It's Lisa's round, so she goes to the bar with Nash

in attendance. He has always been her wine waiter on these quiz nights.

'How was Twad today?' I ask Suzanne. She hates her job and her nickname for the magazine she works on is Meaningless Twaddle, usually abbreviated to Twad.

'Nightmare. We're doing "How to be Pregnant and Stylish". Well, the model was definitely pregnant, but none of the clothes fitted. We're trying again tomorrow.'

Suzanne sticks her leg out from under the table. 'Remember these trousers you made me?'

She's wearing a pair of purple velvet flares I made her years ago. They still look great, though it took me ages to get the waistband right.

'Everyone at Twad wanted to know where I got them.' She nudges me. 'We've got this stylist from New York here at the moment – Vera Van Der Meer – she *loved* them.'

Our team presses on. There is a question about Britain's most loathed dish. Do we think it is a) tripe, b) deep-fried Mars Bar, c) jellied eels or d) fruit and vegetables. The last one gets a huge laugh.

Where the hell are Lisa and Nash? They seem to have spontaneously combusted by the bar.

'Hey,' Suzanne whispers in my ear, 'are you still skint?'

'Sadly, yes,' I whisper back.

'I have a cunning plan,' Suzanne replies. 'I'll tell you later, once we've finished this round.'

Nash and Lisa finally reappear – I suppose she went

outside for a cigarette – and Lisa immediately tries to answer an extremely long question about the Scottish National Party, which is exactly the kind of boring thing she knows about.

Then I notice something. Lisa has been crying.

Richard and Michael pretend to be fascinated by their answer sheet, but no, Lisa has definitely been crying, and over-smoking too, because I can smell her from the other side of the table.

I expect Nash and Lisa have said their last goodbyes. Yes, she's definitely been howling. Suzanne gives me a gigantic kick under the table with her platform shoe.

I look carefully at Richard and Michael. There is nothing on their face to suggest they know anything about us leaving for Australia yet. Their main concern seems to be choosing between b) deep-fried Mars Bar and c) jellied eels.

Lisa says nothing for the rest of the round, even though there are lots of questions about Plaid Cymru and Sinn Fein –the kinds of things she can be counted on to know about. Meanwhile, Richard and Michael argue about the Mars Bar question.

It's my turn to get the drinks. That means I'll have to borrow some money from Suzanne, because I only have coins left in my purse and someone might go mad – Lisa? – and order something that isn't house wine.

I put my hand in Suzanne's pocket under the table, which I hope is a heavy enough hint. It isn't, though, because Suzanne is transfixed by Lisa, who openly sobs while Nash looks for a tissue.

'It's not that far.' Nash leans over and comforts Lisa. 'It's not the moon, Lisa. We'll be back. You should come over and visit us one day.'

'What's not that far?' Suzanne asks loudly.

Lisa is now snuffling into a tissue. It seems Nash has just given her the kind of news which has broken at least one big dream and possibly more. She apologizes and runs out of the pub.

'What's going on?' Suzanne tries again.

'We're moving to Australia,' I hear myself saying because Nash doesn't seem to be able to speak. 'I think Lisa might be a bit upset. Nash's got a job teaching music in a school in North Sydney and I'm going with him. Sorry, we've been waiting for the right moment to tell you. We're leaving in January.'

'I'll just see if Lisa's feeling OK,' Nash says and follows her.

'Drink!' Suzanne commands and steers me to the bar.

'Sorry, sorry, sorry,' I tell her. 'I meant to tell you before, but it's all been so mad. We didn't expect our visas to arrive this quickly.'

Suzanne turns her back on me and produces a twenty-pound note, which she flaps at the barman. Not surprisingly, he finishes what he is doing and races straight over.

'Two treble lemon vodka, lime and tonics,' she instructs him, then turns to me. 'I know I told you to get out of London to save your relationship, but I didn't mean scarpering to the bloody Antipodes.'

'Mum doesn't want me to go.'

'I'm not surprised. *I* don't want you to go.'

'I'm sorry.'

'Don't be so silly.' Suzanne gives me a shove. She has huge silver rings on her fingers at the moment, like gangsters' knuckledusters. 'Look, I don't want you to go anywhere, but Australia's going to be the making of you, Alice. It's the best thing you've ever done. Nash is going to be a changed man.'

Whatever I was expecting from Suzanne, it wasn't this. I suddenly feel a wave of gratitude. I had forgotten how brilliantly encouraging she can be. It's like standing in sunshine.

She hugs me long and hard and tries not to cry. Then she takes both our drinks and leads me back to the table, singing 'Waltzing Matilda' in a tuneless voice and getting it wrong.

'Once a jolly jam bloke, camped by a bongy thing, under the shade of a kangaroo beast . . .'

When we sit down, Richard pokes me with one of his drumsticks.

'So why are you going?'

Bugger. I knew it would be like this. We're about to get the third degree from everyone we know.

'Had enough of us, have you?' Michael adds.

I look down at the carpet and see that Lisa has left a plastic bag of shopping behind containing things like mineral water and proper moisturiser. I can't remember the last time I bought anything so civilized. Everything we eat comes from the market. Everything I wear comes from a little charity shop in Finsbury Park that helps donkeys. Nobody goes to that one and it always has black tights, even if you do have to sniff them before you buy them. It often smells as if the donkeys have been walking around in them.

Why are we going to Australia? It's so hard to list all the reasons that I can't answer Richard and Michael at all. Instead, I try to pretend I'm really interested in the next quiz question.

True or false? No whales or sturgeons washed up on British shores may be disposed of without the consent of the monarch. Richard and Michael say it's false, but I think it's true. It's like the swans. The Queen owns all of them as well. Meanwhile the rest of us are wearing tights that smell of donkeys and panicking about our tax.

'I'm going to Australia because I'm fed up,' I tell Richard at last, feeling the vodka hit my brain. 'I'm not sure about Nash. You'll have to ask him when he's finished cheering up Lisa.'

'Steady, Alice,' Suzanne puts a hand on my shoulder, but the vodka has just hit some angry part of my brain that was switched off before.

I leave The Believers to it, go to the loo, slam the door, throw the lid down and sit on it until I've calmed down again.

Then I hear the familiar sound of Suzanne's platform shoes clumping across the tiles.

'We need a frock for our pregnant model tomorrow,' Suzanne yells through the door. 'Vera Van Der Meer just rang me. There's a flap on. The model's measurements were all wrong. She's about ten times as big as she was two weeks ago. Do you think you can do one?'

'I'm not sure.'

'Vera loved your purple trousers. Anyway, I told her you ran a very cool indie label and made bespoke clothes for real women.'

'Oh my God.'

'Stop thinking about Nash and Lisa! Think about this instead.' Suzanne thumps the door. 'Now, I want you to bring your sewing machine and scissors over in the back of a taxi tomorrow at 9 a.m. and make a frock. I'll get the fabric. Don't argue, because I know tomorrow's your day off.'

Two pieces of paper are suddenly shoved under the door. A taxi charge voucher and the scrawled address of some place in Soho.

I take some deep breaths, calm down and decide to emerge. No wonder the Russians have always been so militant. It must be the vodka. I felt so angry just now about Nash and Lisa, I could have bitten a chunk out of my own glass.

'There,' Suzanne slaps me on the shoulder as I emerge. 'Come and help us out tomorrow. It's a photographer's studio. Big loft place. The model will be there from 9 a.m. and I'm picking her up, so I'll be there too. If we can both fit in the cab. Apparently she's *enormous*.'

'Can you get me some stretch jersey?'

'Oh, I've got something better than that. From the stall.'

As well as working on Twad, Suzanne runs a vintage clothing and fabric stall on Saturdays at Camden Market. A lot of the material I've used for my designs has come from there.

'Now, Alice, I've got some very nice dark green stretchy wool. Very light, but also *very* warm. This factory closed down in Milan and I got the lot. However, I've *also* got this beautiful old tweed coat from Biba I think you could do something with. I want this model to look fantastic, Alice.'

There. Suzanne has had the instant sunshine effect on me again. What is it about her that she can suddenly make everything seem all right?'

We return to our table. Perhaps Nash will be back by now.

He isn't, but Lisa is.

'He's just gone to the cashpoint,' Lisa sniffs and fiddles with her hair.

Richard and Michael plough on, trying to answer a question about James Bond. They are clearly miffed about the Australia news, but I'm not going to say any more. That's Nash's job.

Eventually, he comes back. Richard and Michael go into a huddle with Suzanne over the James Bond question, while I look sideways at Nash and Lisa and find myself thinking the worst.

It's hard not to. I try to see Nash as Lisa might have seen him all this time: cool, sexy, distant, a bit funny, undeniably fit (from the school football coaching), curly haired, multilingual, pale, interesting, a musical genius (obviously) and, above all, a woman whisperer.

She went to Nash and Sarah's wedding. There are photographs of her looking wistful, waiting to catch the bridal bouquet. She probably secretly fancied Nash the whole time. Lisa is the kind of utterly wet female you can imagine nursing a hidden crush on someone for about five hundred years.

Suzanne once told me that you can either sort relationship problems out right away, or you can pretend you're Winston Churchill and plot the right time and place for a strategic attack. In the early days of my relationship with Nash, I used to try and fix things immediately. These days I tend to wait, so that I blow up the bridges later.

The Lisa thing can be put off until I'm good and ready. I'm sure – quite sure now – that they must have been up to something behind my back. In the meantime, I'll sit on the explosives.

'I've just been telling Lisa the news,' Nash speaks at last, 'Alice and I are moving to Australia.'

'We heard,' says Michael, looking as if he's just ingested a deep-fried Mars Bar and jellied eel simultaneously.

'Fantastic bloody news.' Suzanne pumps his hand and then mine. 'I'm going to miss you like hell, but it's the best thing you've ever done. You'll love it. Trust me. You'll never, ever regret it.'

'Have you actually *been* to Australia?' Richard asks pointedly.

'No,' Suzanne pouts.

The quiz goes on. I hear none of the questions because

all I can think about is Barks of Byron Bay. Danielle Coles wrote to say there may be a vacancy for me if I'm prepared to look after the kennels on a trial basis. I was so excited when I read her email at the Indian corner shop that I even paid for a printout, so I could hold it in my hand. Barks of Byron Bay isn't much, but it's some-thing. And I desperately need *some* kind of something, even if it's my secret.

When it was very bad with Nash – around the time that I gave up fashion college – I became very good at living in the future. The more I daydreamed with Nash about where we might live, or who we might become, or what we might have in life, the more it seemed to help us.

That was when the idea of living in Wales or Canada started to appeal to us. Australia seemed too remote then, but as things got worse, we both found we needed a really big dream.

Robyn was the key. Up until then, she had never been anything more than mad Uncle Roland's daughter. Along with her brother Joel, Robyn was like a mythical creature to me, living in a far-off, upside-down place.

Robyn and I are about the same age, though, so were pen pals for a while, when we were both at school. I still have the letters. She used sunflower writing paper and I used a purple notepad with a teddy in the corner. Our handwriting was identical because we both used to write big, round letters on the edge of a ruler.

My last photograph of Joel shows him at the age of seventeen or eighteen, riding a horse in his bare feet.

He's a few years older than Robyn and I. The two polite letters I sent were returned by the post office. I wonder what he looks like now?

Joel went to India years ago to work for a Tibetan charity, and since then he's sent Mum and I the occasional postcard, but that's all. He doesn't do email, according to his sister.

I suppose Joel's family – the other Templetons – had big dreams, too, like Nash and I. They left England in the eighties to go travelling, but then a few years later, Roland and Helena divorced. Helena stayed in Sydney with my cousins and Roland ran away to America. Eventually only Robyn remained. She told me she loved Australia too much to ever leave.

None of these other Templetons have ever felt as if they belong to me, but as Australia comes closer – and even Jamaica, India and San Francisco – I am beginning to feel as if I have acquired a new family, even if they are scattered all over the place.

The quiz seems to be over. Whoops. How did that happen? I usually manage one or two questions, but the vodka has made me drift off.

Richard and Michael are talking animatedly about the Australian Nobel Prize winner. Nash is in his world, they are in theirs and I am in mine. Meanwhile, Lisa is staring out of the window, still gently weeping, and Suzanne is flirting with a man at the next table.

What a disastrous night. It's definitely time to go home.

Nash and I have the same idea at the same time, and

get up together, ready to say our farewells, but Richard looks as if he couldn't care less and Michael looks furious.

'Quickly, before you go,' Suzanne kisses me on the cheek and presses three £50 notes into my hand, 'that's for the frock tomorrow. In case you need to get any cotton or anything.'

'Wow! Thanks.'

Never mind cotton reels. That's enough baked beans for the next three weeks. What on earth would I do without Suzanne?

'Come on,' Nash says, sensing another long conversation starting up. 'See you later Suzanne.'

Once we're outside, I tell him the good news about the job.

'I'm making a dress, for the magazine – for Suzanne. The model is pregnant and the clothes don't fit, so I'm going to make something on the spot.'

'That's great, Alice, really great, but we need to have a talk.'

Suddenly Nash hails us a taxi. I am amazed. He never does that.

We sit in the back of the taxi while I watch him searching for the right words to use for his talk, and all the time I keep thinking about Bondi Beach. Whatever he's about to tell me, I have a horrible feeling I'm never going to see it now.

I think about the way Lisa ran off tonight, and the way she cried at the table.

'I borrowed a library book about the war,' I tell Nash

to fill the silence as we lurch round the corner to Swiss Cottage.

'But we're not having a war,' Nash says, as if he's talking to an idiot. 'It's just a credit crunch.'

'No, but it's a book about growing your own food. It's about gardening and cooking in the war. I can plant spinach, then bake home-made spinach pie. In Australia. When we get our own garden.'

Nash stares out of the window at a red traffic light. It seems impossible for him to articulate whatever he needs to tell me.

The journey finishes in silence, then finally we are home.

'So what are you thinking about, Alice?' Nash asks as I unlock the front door of the hostel.

'Funny, I was going to ask you the same question,' I reply as we trudge upstairs.

He vanishes into the bathroom as soon as we go inside, then suddenly Suzanne calls me. She's just made a mad decision to go away for a few weeks over Christmas and New Year. Is there any way I could look after her stall?

'I'll pay you up front. I can pay you tomorrow.'

'Suzanne, you have no idea how amazing that would be.'

'I thought you might want some dollar dosh before you go.'

I want to tell her about what has just happened – or not happened – between Nash and I, but I can't. If I start talking I might not stop. And besides, he can hear every word. That's one of the most horrible things about our rooms, the walls are so thin that every grunt, every groan and every backpacker moan is audible.

'So anyway,' I say, once I've finished the call with Suzanne and climbed into bed with Nash.

'Anyway what?'

'About Lisa. She just seemed so upset. I mean, nobody else was crying when we told them we were going.'

'She's a bit sensitive.' Nash waves me away. Then, 'Tired,' he adds. 'We do need a talk, Alice, but I've got to go to sleep.'

With that, he pulls up the eiderdowns I made at college, making more theatrical yawns, with one arm stretched up in the air and his fist over his mouth, while I am left to worry about Lisa.

I try to think about tomorrow's job for Suzanne instead. And the stall.

Sometimes I can only find comfort in thinking about fabric, and tonight is one of those nights. I fall asleep with gingham and denim filling my head.

Chapter Four

I find out all about Lisa at breakfast the next day.

Nash and I always eat downstairs in the dining room at 7 a.m., before the backpacking hordes are allowed in at 7.30 for their bread rolls and packets of jam. Because we are staff – or at least I am – Nash and I are allowed to use the microwave in the back kitchen. Honestly, there is nothing the owners of the Swiss Cottage International Travellers' Hostel won't do for us.

Over a bowl of porridge, Nash tells me that Lisa has just lost her job as Head of Music at Romney College.

'Is that all the news?' I ask him before I can think about it. 'I thought you were going to tell me you'd been having an affair.'

Nash shovels his porridge away.

'Thanks very much, Alice. She's terrified,' he says. 'It's the first time she's ever lost a job. And she's not sure she can get another one, either. Apparently the headmaster has been a bit of a problem. She's worried about her reference. She only got the bad news just before she came out last night for the quiz.'

'I would have stayed at home if I was her.'

'I think she wanted to tell me herself.'

'And then you told her you were leaving the country. That must have really finished her off.'

'Why are you using that tone of voice?'

'What tone of voice? I'm eating porridge. How can I have a tone of voice? Listen. When you told her we were moving to Australia she bawled her eyes out.'

'I'm not interested in starting an argument.' Nash shrugs. Then he takes his leather jacket off the back of the chair, picks up his school briefcase and walks out.

Our two rooms – the glorified studio we were promised when I took the cleaning job – are freezing because the owners ration our heating. Thus my sole source of warmth is a nag champa incense stick, two tracksuits and two pairs of socks.

If I didn't have Saturdays off, when I go to the library and stand in front of the heaters, I'd probably be dead from hypothermia by now.

The rooms have to be cleaned between check-out time, 10 a.m., and check-in time, 2 p.m. I wear a Walkman that I bought from the donkeys' charity shop and play old compilation tapes that one of the Pauls made for me back in the nineties. I had a portable CD player once, but one of the backpackers pinched it. Once we are in Australia I will never be able to listen to old Manic Street Preachers songs again without thinking of the smell of rubber gloves.

I try not to panic about the job for Suzanne. I've never

made a pregnancy dress in my life. I'm just going to have to take everything I know about the female form and adapt it. Thank God I had all that practise creating between sizes at fashion college, like the size 13 Heidi was so excited about.

I lie on the bed with one of Nash's old sheepskin coats over me and think about the day ahead. Because he rushed off, I've completely forgotten to wash up our breakfast things downstairs. Because I work as a cleaner here, Nash seems to assume that his mess is my responsibility, too, so I end up washing our dirty plates, cleaning his shirts in the sink and hanging up all the coats and jumpers he leaves piled on the bed.

Someone is gargling and spitting next door. I ram my fingers into my ears. I suppose they'll leave me a lovely woven mat of pubic hair in the plughole as well.

I stare up at the ceiling. I know it so well. There is a rusty brown stain in the shape of the letter B in the right-hand corner above our shelves. There is also a chipped plaster posy of flowers around the light bulb, which lost its lampshade months ago when Nash threw a book at it. There have been so many episodes like that in the history of our relationship that I can't even remember what he was angry about.

Has he ever hit me, Dr Ray Stein? No he has not. But he's chipped an awful lot of Victorian ceiling plaster-work at the Swiss Cottage International Travellers' Hostel.

I should really be getting my sewing kit together for Suzanne, but instead I find myself returning to *Should*

I Stay or Should I Go? It's now two weeks overdue from the Swiss Cottage Library, but it's also my sole source of guidance at the moment.

New question. If all my friends and family staged an intervention and told me it was fine to leave Nash, would I?

My God. The relief would be incredible. Yes, yes, yes!

I wonder if I got that question right or wrong?

And I wonder what my mother would say if I told her about Lisa? She was one of the reasons Nash and I spent the whole of Glastonbury arguing with each other. She was there too last summer, not with her mysterious barrister boyfriend, of course, but with a group of friends.

Nash and Lisa spent their time lying side-by-side in an underground dugout on the Green Fields. The dugout was supposed to be a copy of an original Ancient Briton camp, and it had seats made of earth and a little stove at the end. Their hands were just – only just – touching in the mud when I found them.

They were listening to a man playing the piano above them on a wooden platform and smiling. They looked as if they were stoned, but I don't think they were. They were just happy.

That was what hurt me the most: the intense happiness and the smiling. And then there was the fact that Nash was prepared to do such a woo-woo thing with Lisa when he point-blank refused to go and see the fireworks with me. I was dying to see the fireworks.

They were inside willow-tree sculptures on the hill and everyone was talking about them. Not Nash, though. He thought they were bollocks.

The Believers did some busking (because they couldn't get a proper gig) and they drew a small crowd. Nash and Lisa were in their element.

Here's my deep, dark secret. I don't really like The Believers. They make the kind of music that you can't dance or sing along to. Instead, you're supposed to sit on the floor of the pub with your legs crossed and *listen*.

Nash loves people who listen. That's why he likes teaching. It's a captive audience. If the boys don't devote their sole attention to his brilliance, then he marks them down. He's got them exactly where he wants them.

Lisa's attraction for him is based on the same thing. She's a listener. She hardly ever talks. Instead, she just wafts around and receives. The only time she ever says anything is when she opens her mouth to sing, and even then it's other people's words.

The one word that Nash uses the most in our relationship is 'Listen'.

'Listen, Alice . . . can you just listen? Listen to me! Are you listening?'

I know very well that's why he likes Lisa. The woman doesn't speak.

Ooh, I desperately need a good bitching session with Suzanne. She is the only person who knows me so well she won't be horrified at the way I am about to character assassinate Lisa and Nash.

If nothing else, that will get me to the photo shoot

on time. I look at my cab voucher and the £150 from last night. The temptation to go straight to the nearest beauty salon and treat myself to a pedicure is extreme, but I resist.

I lay out my clothes. It's been such a long time since I dressed for a proper job that I've almost forgotten how to do it. I have to impress the people from Twad, though. Last night, Suzanne told me we would be working with a veritable circus of glamour; not only Vera Van Der Meer, but a hair and make-up artist, a photographer, a photographer's assistant, and even a work-experience girl to be our minion.

Maybe all the thermal underwear I dyed last winter might work – if it's layered under a mad denim skirt I made at college. There's also a boxy tartan jacket from the charity shop, which I customized.

The biker boots from one of Nash's motorbike shops and an amazing crocheted cap from Suzanne's stall should finish it off. At least the cap will cover up my one-quid hair.

I apply my make-up in the taxi, resting one foot on my sewing-machine case, while the other foot holds down a cardboard box full of trims, scissors, thread and glue. That's one secret they never tell you at fashion college: when all else fails, you can just wing it with a big tube of adhesive.

Suzanne is fizzing with panic and caffeine when I arrive at the Soho studio. It's a loft on Lexington Street with a high glass ceiling and polished wooden floorboards. There's a bunk bed in one corner – I suppose that's where the photographer sleeps – and a tiny kitchen. You probably don't need a big kitchen when you're working with Twad models. The last one Suzanne introduced me to told me she was an American size zero, whatever that is. She lived on sushi and water. Suzanne said she looked like a ping-pong bat with earrings.

'Come over here.' Suzanne spirits me away as soon as I arrive and we sit on the bottom bunk of the photographer's bed, surrounded by bags of camera film and piles of magazines. 'Now. Alice. Stop thinking about Lisa and Nash.'

'How did you know I was?'

'You've got bags under your eyes. Did Nash tell you they'd had it off, then?'

'He says they didn't. She was only crying last night because she'd just been sacked. She just wanted Nash's shoulder to cry on.'

'Pesky old Lisa!' Suzanne rubs my shoulders and I smell her scent. She always wears the most fantastic perfume, thanks to all the free bottles that arrive at Twad.

'I'm a bit wobbly,' I confess.

'Right then, Miss Alice. You know who's really wobbly this morning? Natasha. She's the model who's having a baby. The very *naughty* model who fibbed about how big she was going to be. I'll introduce you to everyone in a minute.'

I glance over at the beautiful, red-haired woman sitting patiently in a chair, while the hair and make-up artist squeezes her eyelashes in a painful-looking metal curler. She is, indeed, enormous. Maybe she's having twins.

'Looks like she's having twins.' Suzanne reads my mind. 'Anyway. Here's your dosh for the market stall. I'll be back before you go off to Australia, anyway. Is that all right?'

She presses a fat envelope bulging with £20 notes into my hand, then guides me over to the corner of the studio where all the people from Twad can be found. They're all freelance, but Suzanne says she works with them all the time, and thus she calls them her meaningless twaddlings. Nobody seems to mind.

Vera Van Der Meer is extremely loud, as if she spends her whole life trying to CALL CABS in New York over the top of the traffic. I instantly want to take her plum-coloured coat-dress off her back and examine the stitching. It's a brilliant piece of work, right down to the tiny little padded shoulders.

The work-experience girl is better dressed, better spoken and far more confident than me. Suzanne tells me she is fifteen years old.

'Honestly, London teenagers! They're the next bloody master race,' she hisses.

I start cutting the beautiful stretchy green fabric. 'I'm going to channel Body Map from that old copy of *The Face* we were looking at the other day,' I tell Suzanne. 'Is that all right? Do you know what I mean?'

'Absolutely,' Suzanne says, holding up the beautiful old Biba coat to the light. 'What are you going to do with this then?'

'Cut straight up the seams and take off the buttons. They're going sideways across the skirt.'

'Vera brought a stack of stuff just in case,' Suzanne reassures me, 'so don't panic. Then again, what she found was basically rubbish, so I don't think there'll be a problem.'

Natasha glances over at us. She is beginning to look beautiful and other-worldly, like some wild red-haired woodland creature. Her dark red hair has been crimped into cascades of waves, and her skin has been powdered pink and white, like some expensive peach. Everyone is staring at her – and smoking around her while she fans the cigarette smoke away.

Vera puffs her cheeks out when she exhales, like a hamster. And she has tufty, pale orange hair and slightly buck teeth, which makes her look even more pet-shoppy.

I talk to Suzanne and Vera about my idea.

'Hi.' Vera puts her cigarette on the windowsill and pumps my hand. 'You're Vintage Alice? I love the sound of what you're doing.'

I try not to blush. If only she knew I can't even afford zips.

'So what *are* you doing?' Vera adds.

'Well . . . Because Natalie has such a beautiful long neck and sculpted collarbone, I'm going to shape the neckline of her top around that. Then I'm going to sew together a kind of second skin – a long, tubular dress which fits over the top, and skims the floor. The Biba coat will become an angular, boxy jacket and then the buttons will draw the eye up to Natasha's tummy. The whole point of this photograph is to show off her pregnancy, not to hide it.'

'She's channelling Body Map,' Suzanne tells Vera, who immediately shuts her eyes as if she is having a religious experience and makes mad little humming noises of approval.

Close up, Vera's coat dress is even more wonderful. It's all I can do not to stick my hand down the back of her neck and pull out the label.

'Break everybody!' the photographer's assistant yells over the sound of the deep dub reggae that's pouring out of the speakers.

It seems Natasha is feeling nauseous from all the smoke and must go up onto the roof immediately.

'Right then,' Suzanne stands with her hands on her hips, looking taller than everybody in her huge platform shoes. 'Cigarettes out *permanently*. Natasha, time out on the roof – don't fall off for God's sake – and we'll see everyone else back here in half an hour.'

Suddenly, the place empties and we are left alone.

'Can I watch my Bondi Beach DVD in here?' I ask Suzanne, eyeing the photographer's TV. 'It'll help me calm down and I can cut while I watch.'

Robyn has sent me a home-made DVD about Bondi Beach. There's a note taped to the cover, with her customary four kisses, explaining that although she is very bad at using the camera and her hand wobbles a lot, she has tried to film all the important things in

Bondi, so Nash and I will get a better idea about our new home before we land.

Suzanne puts the DVD on while I start cutting up the Biba coat. Robyn has certainly got a bad case of shaky hand – unlike me, fortunately – but she has also managed to type perfect opening titles in Helvetica bold. She seems like the kind of woman who would bother with opening titles.

I am excited. I know it's ridiculous because I'm so far away, but look! There's a sign saying Bondi Beach. And look! That must be Robyn's flat.

'Noice,' says Suzanne, in a bad Australian accent.

Robyn walks around the bathroom first, showing us the bath, the loo and . . . the spa. *The spa.* After that she shows us the balcony, where she has all her barbecues in the summer. I know this because she's sent me photographs of them. Her barbecues involve dozens of ridiculously attractive Australians wearing almost no clothes, standing around eating very little and wearing baseball caps. All their teeth are white, just like Robyn's.

The flat is amazing. It's not a flat at all, it's more like a house, high up in the sky. Then, when Robyn turns the camera towards the window, I can suddenly see what looks like the biggest beach in the world.

Robyn must have squashed her hand over the microphone for most of the filming, because her running commentary makes her sound like someone squeaking from the murky depths of a sock.

'Icebergs,' Robyn mumbles, and the camera wobbles

over some amazing restaurant on top of a cliff, then down to a brilliantly blue swimming pool. There seem to be just three people using it. Only three! They also appear to be quite old and a bit saggy and wrinkly. Whoops, unbeautiful Australians. The camera moves away quickly.

'Surfers,' Robyn comments as she films some tiny human dots in the distance, pinned against a series of enormous waves.

'Drongo waiter.' She laughs as the action cuts to a man's large hairy hand stabbing her with a fork while she tries to eat a huge breakfast.

'Stop it, Jason,' she says while there's a fight with the lens cap.

When the picture is restored, Suzanne and I stop the DVD and spend a long time counting all the things on Robyn's plate at the Bondi Beach café. Scrambled eggs, bacon, tomatoes, parsley, chives, bagel, avocado. Avocado for breakfast?

Robyn must be showing off, I think. Mornings in Australia cannot possibly be this decadent. Then I see that the café is packed. The clock says it's 8 a.m. How can everyone be eating breakfast outside at 8 a.m. with their work clothes on and having meetings?

The camera sweeps over the menu. Everything is nine dollars – about the same price as going one stop on the tube in London.

'That's my cousin Robyn,' I say mindlessly when the Twad people eventually drift back into the studio and sit down next to us on milk crates. 'That's Sydney.' I pause the DVD again. 'That's my new home.'

The hair and make-up artist gives us Natasha for half an hour, so I can pin her into the jacket and what will become the elongated tube dress.

The work-experience girl asks if she can rewind Robyn's DVD, and soon everyone is watching my cousin's hand-held version of Australia, engaged in a game of one-upmanship as they all claim to have been to Sydney's most glamorous bars and clubs.

'I went to Cate's hairdresser when I was there,' the photographer's assistant boasts. I suppose she means Cate Blanchett.

'Did you get up to Byron Bay?' the photographer fires back, looking impossibly smug.

'I went horseback riding with Sass & Bide,' Vera trumps them, puffing out her hamster cheeks.

Suddenly I realize I'm not going to some funny upside-down country after all. I appear to be moving to one of the hippest destinations in magazine land. If I told any of them I had just secretly applied to be a dog-carer at Barks of Byron Bay, though, they'd probably make a mass exodus.

The DVD finishes and the work-experience girl puts more deep, dub reggae on and starts dancing around in her ballet shoes.

Natasha is beginning to look like a cross between a heavily pregnant Celtic seductress and some endless, beautiful tree, which is the way I pictured her.

'No sketch?' Vera Van Der Meer asks.

'Alice doesn't need to sketch,' Suzanne explains, 'she just goes by feel. You should see the clothes she's made for *me*.'

I check Natasha's face in the mirror to see if she's feeling tired from her pregnancy, but she looks dreamily content, and so she should. Her face is immaculate and her hair is wild, red and impossibly romantic.

'Wow,' the work-experience girl says, when she returns from a coffee errand. 'She looks fantastic.'

What I have done with Suzanne's coat is not what Barbara Hulanicki would ever have envisaged during her time at Biba, but I am happy with the way it balances Natasha's proportions.

Suzanne and I have woven the light, deliciously stretchy green wool as gently as we can around Natasha's bump, and then cut the skirt so that it's comfortable enough for her to move in freely, even though it looks tight and sexy down to the ankle.

'Clever,' Vera approves as she pinches the fabric. Soon it will be time for a final hair and make-up touch-up, and then the photographer can begin the shoot.

'I think we'll go back up on the roof actually,' he muses, and tells his assistant to drag out some plastic trees from an old *Vogue* shoot. The work-experience girl is then dispatched to buy boxes of mushrooms at Berwick Street Market by Vera, who says she is 'feeling the Welsh woodlands'. Plus, I suppose, the photographer can microwave them for breakfast tomorrow morning.

The day flashes past and I am so caught up in my

work – and the excitement of the shoot – that I forget I need to go the loo at least twice.

'You'll keel over standing there like that with your legs crossed,' the photographer tells me. But I'm not listening. Vera Van Der Meer wants me to give her a call when I get to Sydney.

Her business card is the palest off-white, very thick, very expensive and engraved in hot-pink copperplate. If Vera isn't careful I may drool on it and leave little saliva marks all over her VV logo.

'If you can make a pregnant woman look hot, you can make anyone look hot,' Vera says, going outside for another cigarette.

'See?' Suzanne squeaks at me later, in the privacy of the loo. 'It's happening, Alice! Australia is already happening to you, before you've even got there. Vera is *huge.*'

The fashion industry is a funny business. If you're *physically* huge or massive they can't cope with you, but if you're *described* as huge or massive, you know you've got it made.

After this there's a loud buzz at the door, and five minutes later a courier comes up with an enormous bunch of flowers.

Nash never did write long notes, and this one says simply, 'Sorry.' Followed by, 'Good luck today.' But at the moment, that's enough for me. I'm filled with love and forgiveness. Is this the start of our Bondi-Beach born-again baptism?

Chapter Five

It always takes ages for Twad to get a fashion story to print, Suzanne says. Therefore I should stop rushing to every newsagent I see and getting disappointed when I'm not in it.

The following Saturday morning – the night after our farewell drinks for everyone at the pub – I wake up in Nash's arms. I hadn't realized we'd been sleeping together like that all night, but it's a nice surprise, like suddenly remembering it's Christmas.

'Nothing like hangover sex,' Nash says as he gets down to business.

I lie in bed for as long as I'm allowed to after that, then Nash says he's going to pick up some overdue marking from school and I begin to get ready for work.

There was no sign of Lisa last night. She had the flu, according to Nash and Richard, so she stayed at home with her boyfriend.

It was a relief, really, after Suzanne and I had spent so much time talking about her behind her back. Suzanne was in a class of her own last night, forcing the DJ to put Adam and the Ants on the turntable, then doing her own version of 'Ant Music' on her back, wriggling her legs in the air. Shortly after that, she sprayed herself with imaginary insecticide and flopped on the carpet.

Suzanne has set aside today to show me round Camden Market, so I can meet the other stallholders and she can teach me the basics of managing her stall. I've done it before, but she has more stock now, and new rules since she realized that all her best vintage pieces were being snapped up by dealers.

I meet her outside Camden tube station and admire her leather bomber jacket. She's paired it with red jeans, stripy socks and strappy sandals. She's also dissolving a Vitamin B tablet on her tongue, which has gone bright orange.

'That was a good night,' she says. Then she remembers something. 'All my emails yesterday were about you. The photos of Natasha are brilliant, apparently. The art director loves it, the agency loves it and your new best friend Vera reckons you should launch your own label for pregnant women.'

'Really?' I try not to sound too excited.

'Yeeeee!' Suzanne squeals and links her arm in mine. Honestly, there's no point in trying to be cool around Suzanne, because she's the least cool woman in London. 'Gave myself carpet burns from being an ant last night,' she says dolefully, examining her arm.

We race towards the market in the cold, passing puddles, drunks, chuggers, pigeons and the occasional pool of sick.

'Lovely,' Suzanne jokes. 'I can't understand why you want to leave London behind, darling. You must be mad.'

She unlocks her stall, which is more like a shop, at the back of Camden Market. She uses five keys and it takes fifteen minutes. As she does this, I remember reading that there are some parts of Australia that are so safe you can leave your back door and your car unlocked.

Nash and I were talking about it this morning, after we realized we'd both woken up from vaguely Australian dreams. Imagine what it would be like to live in a country where you could leave your front door unlocked.

If there's one thing I won't miss about London it's all the bloody keys we have to carry around. There are times when I feel like some seventeenth-century jailer.

Suzanne introduces me to various stallholders. There is Gary One, who sells Bob Marley T-shirts with giant cannabis leaf patterns on the sleeves, and Gary Two, who sells vintage cigarette lighters, and a woman called Beryl who seems too disorganized to do anything except throw brown paper bags around.

I have always loved Suzanne's stall. It's like a cross between a gigantic rabbit hutch and the most glamorous jumble sale in the world. She buys and sells all sorts of clothes, from vintage Dior to 1990s trainers. The only rule is, she has to find it interesting. Apart from that, anything goes.

Her stall is mentioned in all the London guidebooks, and loads of stylists shop here, looking for accessories for television programmes or special event clothes for their clients.

'Fake Pucci,' I say, spotting a scarf.

'Is it?'

'Bad print job.' I examine it more closely. 'They've snipped the label out as well, to make you think it was a sample. It's a copy.'

'Hmm. I'm not so good on my Pucci. What about this bag?' Suzanne waves a filthy patchwork handbag at me. 'I've got a funny feeling about it, but I don't know why.'

'Could you bear to rip off the patchwork to see what's underneath?'

'You do it.'

'OK.'

I rip – and keep on ripping.

'Amazing,' Suzanne says when I show her the beautiful late 1960s green leather bag underneath. It has a zippered secret compartment on the bottom, and a tiny vanity mirror on a chain sewn on the inside.

'Those posh Hermès copies were so unfashionable by the seventies that hippies used to stitch patchwork all over them. And bits of carpet. Any old stuff. But what you really want is the bag underneath. You hardly ever see those false-bottomed bags around now.'

'Alice, you are bloody amazing. I mean that. You're really staggeringly amazing,' Suzanne says.

We keep sorting through piles of bags, smelly silk scarves and trunks of ancient tweed coats. There are fox furs with beady glass eyes, beautiful old paisley dressing gowns and red leather vanity cases which still have old theatre tickets in them. It feels like time travelling. I'd forgotten how much fun her stall was.

And apparently I'm bloody amazing. There. Someone has actually told me I'm bloody amazing for a change.

The wind picks up, so Suzanne offers me an enormous tweed coat from her collection and puts one on herself. Then she finds us two big cashmere scarves and two flat caps. We put them on over our clothes, and point at each other. After that, Suzanne makes me put on a pair of gloves, knitted in the shape of pink pigs. I'm now wearing so many heavy layers I'm worried my fold-up chair will tip over.

I eye up the beautiful red Dior coat she's been trying to sell for ever. It's far too expensive for most people, even though it's worth every penny. It nips in at the waist, and the lining is so beautiful it's the kind of coat you want to hang on the back of your chair, every chance you get. It fits me perfectly. I will never be able to afford it in a million years.

'So, how is it with Nash now?' she asks.

'All right. Good, actually.'

'Thought so. A relationship is like a shark, Alice. It has to keep moving to survive. You just needed to give the shark a bit of a shove.'

'Maybe.'

I tell her about my application to work at Barks of Byron Bay.

'No!'

'Oh yes. I wrote to Danielle Coles, the woman who

94

owns it, and she asked me to ring her. Anyway, once I got the time zones right, I did. She said I could start any time after we got there. On a trial basis, anyway.'

'Nash hates dogs!'

'Byron Bay is also about a nine hour drive from where Nash is working. He won't like that either. Or maybe he will. I don't know. Maybe we need a bit of space. I haven't told him.'

Suzanne introduces me to the stallholder on her left. His name is Alan and it turns out he sells second-hand self-help books. I look at his stall. He only has about . . . ooh, twenty-eight copies of *Should I Stay or Should I Go?*

'It's a very good book,' Suzanne says, shrugging her gigantic tweed shoulders. 'Then again, you have to wonder if all those people are getting rid of it because it didn't actually help, or if they're chucking it because their relationships became so fantastic that no further advice was required.'

'Why did you buy it?' I ask her.

'I had to decide whether to get rid of Sam or not. And now look at me. I'm off to New York to stay with him. Didn't tell you that, did I? I had a last-minute change of plan. Vera offered me her apartment, so I poked Sam on Facebook, and the next thing I know he was poking me back.'

Suzanne smirks and tries not to look too pleased.

'Lucky you, going to New York.'

'Even luckier you, going to Sydney,' she replies. 'Apparently they've got it all sorted in Australia, so you can just drive up the coast from Melbourne to Brisbane, going from one market to another. People actually live like that. They do the whole boho caravan thing.'

'Sounds amazing.'

'Could be good for you,' she nudges me. 'Personally, I think you should have a go at vintage. You're bloody good at it. Or your own label, sweetheart.'

I make a horse-snorting noise because she's embarrassing me, but she has also rumbled me. That's part of my Australia dream that I haven't dared tell her. A hand-sewn label with Vintage Alice embroidered in old-fashioned, cherry-red writing.

It's not long before Suzanne starts fizzing about her trip to America again – at least until the first customer arrives.

As the day goes on, I realize I'm getting the hang of it again. Part of the trick is judging what people are wearing. Serious customers have serious vintage clothes already, even if it's just a pair of brogues or Terry de Havilland boots. They're not interested in markdowns and they certainly don't want you to tell them about the labels, because they know it all already.

Casual customers are different. One peek under the trestle table and you'll know they're wearing trainers, jeans and probably have no idea at all.

'For them,' announces Suzanne, 'the five-pound suitcase of scarves. Just tell them they make a fantastic substitute for a belt and everyone's doing it.'

When I finally peel off my borrowed vintage clothes

at the end of the day and go home, I see that Nash has gone out – he's left a note saying he's with Richard – so I run a hot bath.

At last I have hand cream. And a jar of bath salts. They were the two treats I allowed myself from Suzanne's money. I really should have set some aside for Alka-Seltzer though. My hangover is still dreadful.

I am sitting in a hot bath with a packet of frozen peas on my head when the phone rings. It's Robyn. She wants to wish me Merry Christmas before she leaves for Bali. I won't see her again until she comes back in February, so she wants to double-check that I have all the keys to her flat and that I understand the spa instructions.

'What are you up to?' she asks.

'I'm having a bath. I've got a terrible hangover. We had our leaving party last night. Nash has a hangover too.'

'Gross.'

'I'm trying this technique where you draw the pain away from your head by putting ice on your skull while sitting in hot water. We don't have any ice, though, so I'm using frozen peas.'

Robyn laughs at me. 'So how was the party?'

'It wasn't a proper party. We just saw some friends at the pub for drinks. It wasn't as bad as I thought it was going to be. Some people are happy we're leaving and some people aren't.'

'Really?'

'Some of Nash's friends definitely feel rejected. I

97

think my friends understand, though. Everyone wants to move to Sydney, don't they?'

'Hey, I got some news,' Robyn remembers why she's calling. 'Joel's coming back from India. He actually used a phone to call me. He's in Kashmir at the moment, but he'll be back soon. He's got a cheap round-the-world ticket, so he's going to see a few places before he gets back.'

'Does he know I'm coming?'

'Yes. He's really excited.'

'I don't even know if I'd recognize him.'

'He's got a beard now.'

'Beards can be sort of funky, though, can't they?'

'Trust me,' Robyn says, 'if my brother has a beard it will not be funky.'

'What sort of beard will it be then?'

'Spiritual,' she says. 'Rilly serious.'

A mental image of my cousin looking like a bit like Uncle Roland, but with a beard and an 'Om' symbol on his T-shirt, drifts into my mind.

Then Nash comes home and bangs on the bathroom door to find out how long I'll be.

'I'm *frozen*!' he complains, 'and seriously hung-over.'

I finish the call, thanking Robyn again for her amazing Bondi Beach breakfast DVD.

When I finally wrap myself in a towel and stagger out with the packet of peas, Nash shoots in like a speeding bullet, looking pale and ill and heading straight for the loo.

All I can think about for the rest of the night is that I almost have a job again. Or even two jobs.

'My designs have featured in several magazines,' I tell the bathroom mirror. 'When I arrive in Sydney I will probably be working with one of America's best-known stylists, Vera Van Der Meer. In the meantime, I'm placing vintage fashion with some of London's keenest collectors.'

It's funny how, when you say things like that in the mirror, it automatically makes your mouth go all round and pouty. God, I'm full of rubbish sometimes.

The following week goes quickly. Nash and I have a million things to do. Lisa wants him to drop off copies of all their old band recordings to her flat, because she's still too ill to move and she wants one final chance to say goodbye.

Another group of people who also missed the party call us to try and organize a last-minute drink. Then there's all the hassle of packing up and leaving the hostel.

Nash also has extra work at school, and I've got my mother on the phone every single day. She wants me to come to Hove, but I can't. She's desperate to get to London, but the trains are booked solid and she's too frightened to drive the car up.

When she says they're booked solid, I suppose she means every *first-class* train seat. She won't travel any other way, despite the fact that I've spent the last ten years trying to convince her.

The hostel people still haven't found anyone to

replace me as their live-in cleaner, but in the meantime, worried-looking couples who don't speak English very well keep turning up, wanting to see our two rooms. I don't have the heart to tell them how awful they are. Maybe they're chasing a London dream in the same way as I'm chasing a Sydney dream.

Suddenly, before I realize it, Friday swings around – with an excitable parting phone call from Suzanne, at Heathrow Airport, who promises she'll keep up with me on Facebook, shortly before remembering I don't own a computer.

The next day I wake up in Nash's arms again and breathe a huge sigh of relief. Gently, very gently, we seem to be thawing. It's still freezing in our room, but it feels as if we're turning a corner.

After that I realize it's Saturday and I have to go to work. The shock is terrible.

When I arrive at Camden Market, there are already small groups of people beginning to queue outside the main entrance. The tourist traffic at Camden is unbelievable. A license to print money, as they say.

Years ago, Suzanne found a little row of Union Jack bunting at an auction, and it's become her trademark. The first thing I do is pin it up from one end of the stall to the other. Next to go up are her fairy lights, which I'm always terrified will electrocute me (or a customer) as they are connected to an overloaded power point, which is hooked up to a generator that seems to be sitting on top of a puddle.

Suzanne has her own way of laying out the stall, and

I am under strict instructions to copy it. Cheap paste brooches at the front to draw people in, but nothing too valuable in case shoplifters are around. Show-stopping clothes high up at the back. Cardigans sorted by colour. Handbags strung up on a washing line – no rubbish, designer labels only.

As soon as the big main entrance is unlocked, people come rushing in. I sell three paste brooches in the first ten minutes – all Christmas presents, because the customers want them wrapped in tissue paper and tied with a ribbon.

My own Christmas presents this year are under the stall. I've made shortbread, iced either with everybody's names, their star signs or their favourite football teams. I thought that when business slowed down I could start wrapping them up to keep me busy.

I'm using some of my precious stall money to buy Nash a second-hand Bob Dylan book that I know he doesn't have. I saw it on one of the stalls the other day. So that's it. Shortbread and Bob Dylan means Christmas is now officially sorted.

I am determined that all the money Suzanne has given me will be spent on my debts. There are four jam jars under the bed for that very reason, stuffed with notes and covered up with a blanket.

If I am very, very careful over the next few weeks, I will soon be able to put a big cheque inside the cover of Nash's book, and another one in Mum's shortbread tin. Then I can sort out my overdraft and my credit card. The feeling of relief is incredible.

A tall woman with tufty orange hair and a black Beatles cap starts sorting through a box of cheap nylon scarves on the ground. Oh my God. It's Vera Van Der Meer.

'Hello, stranger,' she honks in her ridiculously loud voice, giving me a bucky beaver smile.

She says Suzanne just Facebooked her and told her to visit the stall before she flew back to New York because of the Vuitton.

I instantly know what she means and find the small Louis Vuitton trunk she's talking about. It's one of the objects Suzanne padlocks to the leg of her trestle table.

'Done,' she nods, inspecting it and, strangely enough, sniffing the interior. Then she asks me if I'm on Facebook and I go bright red, because if Vera Van Der Meer knew that I use the computer at the Indian corner shop, she would never speak to me again.

'I'll tell you something wonderful you can do with these,' she says, rifling through Suzanne's cheap scarf collection. 'Use them as Christmas wrapping. Look, I'll show you.'

Vera picks up a silver cigarette case from the table and turns the scarf into a kind of origami box, then she puts the case inside it.

'That's amazing.'

'You just need to use a few pins here and there, but it looks fabulous. So I'll have a few of these, thank you, Alice.'

'Oi!' the self-help book man calls my name from across the market. 'Do you want a cup of tea?'

'Yes please!' I shout back.

Vera asks me to take down a crocodile suitcase from the back wall so she can have a closer look.

'Good price,' she inspects the tag. 'Bit of water damage. It might have gone on the *Titanic*, though. So we can forgive a few drips, can't we?'

Various women come and go, inspecting a row of 1950s jackets – most of them separated from suits – then tutting and moving on.

'Sometimes I worry Suzanne's charging too much,' I confide in her.

'Right price, wrong size,' she informs me, and pulls a boxy velvet evening jacket off the rack. 'Women were smaller then. The food was crapola as it was after the war. Every single lady who's just come past this stall is at least two sizes bigger, maybe three.'

'I often think that. The clothes are lovely, but they're all so small.'

'I look forward to seeing your summer collection,' Vera raises an eyebrow at me.

Yes. Right. My summer collection.

'Anyway,' Vera says, 'May your yak butter never go rancid, as they say in Tibet. Happy Christmas. Twenty quid for these four all right?'

I notice she loves saying the word quid, as all Americans do.

I attempt to wrap the scarves, but they're already in her Vuitton trunk – now unpadlocked – before I can find the tissue paper.

'I'm such an eco-warrior, darling, I never take

wrapping these days. Think about those jackets, all right? You know the Achilles heel of most designers? They're lazy. So . . . do the work. Measure the women. Make the clothes. Oy!'

Vera waves and departs, but not before she picks up *Should I Stay or Should I Go?* from the self-help book stand. I wonder what her love life is like? Probably not great with that hamster hair and constant chain-smoking.

Customers who were too frightened to shop when Vera was waving her silk scarves around now return. Soon, all Suzanne's paste brooches are gone, so I'm forced to put out what she calls Plan B – a lot of badges showing New Romantic groups from the 1980s.

More women wander past, ignore the badges, feel the jackets, pull them out sideways, then tut and look cross. I'm trying to sort out why when I have a truly angry customer whose problem is probably Christmas – and life – but in any case, she wants to take it out on me. I feel sorry for her really. She's about my age, shortish, roundish and fed up.

'Do you have anything at all here that's a large?' she challenges me, and I can tell she hates using the word 'large' to describe herself.

'It's vintage, so I'm sorry, but they didn't actually size things that way.'

In reply, she picks up one of the 1980s badges, puts it down again, then storms off.

There's a shirtwaister dress in crisp dark-grey cotton that would look great on her if it was cut bigger. She had the kind of pale skin and dark hair that can look great against dark grey. I kick myself for not talking to her properly. I could have had a client there.

Then again, how am I going to afford the material to make clothes, never mind the time?

We'll be in Australia in a few weeks, and after that it will be difficult enough just finding a place to live. Robyn's flat won't last for ever.

I pick up the New Romantic badges. There's Adam and the Ants. I'm surprised Suzanne hasn't saved that one for herself after the other night.

The wind picks up, and suddenly all the customers vanish. I start daydreaming about Australia again, and imagine Nash and I, kissing waist-deep in the blue, blue water on Bondi Beach.

When all the brooch people have gone away, I practise my Australian accent out of the corner of my mouth as quietly as I can, like a gangster.

'Gerday.'

Nope. I can't do it.

'Heer ya gawn?'

Nope. I definitely can't do it. But imagine if I could.

I'm definitely, positively, not going to get excited about Vera's business card. Or becoming a fashion designer for pregnant women. Or becoming a designer for women – full stop.

No, I'm just going to sit here on Suzanne's fold-up chair and extend the Bondi Beach daydream, that's all.

Imagine if I moved to Australia and had my own

shop. And my own website. And hot-pink, engraved business cards. I would never have to work as a cleaner, or buy my tights from a charity shop, for the rest of my life. It's a mad idea, but now that both Suzanne and Vera have put it in my head, it won't leave me.

Now all the cheap stuff at the front of the stall has gone, I notice that people are more reluctant to stop. I suppose everyone's looking for a bargain. The women who are crouching on the ground, rifling through Suzanne's bargain hatbox, are just like me. All skint, all hoping to find something second-hand, cool and fabulous for their friends, who will be mortified if they resort to bath bombs this Christmas.

I keep wrapping my shortbread under the trestle table until lunchtime, when there's another rush. I eat the broken bits of shortbread I've put aside, and a salad sandwich, and say no to another cup of tea from the self-help-books man – every piece of spare change counts at the moment.

Eventually, it's time to go home. The day has been a blur, which is the way it should be. Not too much sitting around and just enough panic. I've made much more money than Suzanne anticipated, and I text her to let her know.

I cannot wait to go back to the flat and tell Nash about Vera.

When I arrive home, though, Nash stops me from talking before I can even open my mouth.

'Bailiffs came round,' he says.

'What?'

'Two blokes from a debt collection agency in Wolverhampton. They've sent you six letters apparently.'

'I've got the money,' I say, feeling panicked.

'I paid them. They've gone.'

Suddenly I feel trembly, as if I need a big cup of tea with sugar.

'Sit down,' Nash pats the sofa and moves a cushion aside.

'I'm so sorry,' I tell him. 'Why did they come? Was it the credit card or the overdraft? Seriously, I've been saving up my money in jam jars, Nash. Look!' I scramble under the bed, and pull them out, spilling coins and notes all over the floor.

Nash laughs at me, and then the laugh turns into a smile.

'Sit *down*, for God's sake,' he repeats.

I sit. He is smiling. Grinning, even. Why is he grinning like that?

'I have news,' he says.

'Really?'

'Good news.' He hugs me. It must be good news. He only usually hugs me like that if we're making up after an argument.

'I've been offered the best job in England,' he whispers, cuddling into me.

'Say that again?'

'The best job in England is mine. Romney College want me to take Lisa's job as Head of Music.'

I wriggle free and sit down at the end of the sofa, where I can talk to him properly.

'But we're going to Australia.'

'Ah, but do we really need to go to Australia?'

'What?'

'Why do we need to go to Australia now, Alice? I went to see them this morning and the head offered me almost one and a half times what I'm earning now, and that's before private tutoring. Do you know what these people pay you for hourly flute and clarinet tutoring on the weekends?'

'It's always money with us, isn't it?' I look at my sad little jam jars under the bed.

'What do you mean?'

'I thought we were going to Australia.'

I want to cry.

'And there's a job for you at Romney as well.'

'Is there?'

'I told them you could cook. You know it's a boarding school – a huge, posh boarding school – well, they need someone in the kitchen.'

'School dinner lady. Yeah. Fantastic, Nash.'

'We've been offered a self-contained flat in the grounds. Incredibly low rent. Half of what we're paying now. You saw the college that time. It's huge. Gym, pool, tennis court, drama theatre, music studio . . . You can use the library.'

'Do you really think my life revolves around bloody libraries? I only go there because they're free, Nash, and because there are heaters.'

'Can you stop being so uptight about this?'

'But this is a fait accompli. And you didn't tell me you

were going to see anyone about a job interview. What about our plane tickets? We paid for them ages ago. That's why I've got this thing from the bailiffs. It was on my credit card.'

'It's nothing, Alice. We'll get some of the ticket price back anyway, and I'll make up the rest in the first month of tutoring. This is serious money. Much more than I was going to be paid in Australia.'

'What about Robyn?'

'She won't mind. She can come and stay with us in England sometime. You should see the flat, Alice, it's extraordinary.'

'And what does Lisa think?'

'She'll be fine.'

'She doesn't know?'

'I'm going to clear it up with her later,' Nash waves the subject away, as if Lisa suddenly doesn't matter.

'Nash. Did you ring them up first?'

'Yup.'

'You rang up the college behind Lisa's back, after they'd sacked her? While she had the flu?'

'Come on, Alice. Be fair. It's just common sense. It's the way these jobs go anyway. The head remembered me from that charity swimathon last year. We got on well then, so I assumed we'd get on well now. And we did. He was grateful he didn't have to advertise the position. Instant offer.'

'And what if I don't want to be a school dinner lady? Was this what you wanted to tell me about in the taxi the other night? Your cunning plan? How long after

109

Lisa told you she'd been sacked did you work all this out?'

When Lisa thought Nash was visiting her in the flat to say goodbye, he was probably just checking it all out, to see how many rooms there were. Yuck.

I walk out of the room, up the corridor, past the communal hatstand at the front door of the hostel, where I grab everything I own that will keep me warm, and slam the front door so hard as I leave that the broken brass bell at the top pings.

Oh Dr Ray Stein, author of *Should I Stay or Should I Go?*, where are you when I need you? If my family and friends staged an intervention and said it was all right to walk out on Nash right now, would I pack my bags and go?

What about if Buddha said it was all right? If the sky opened up in Swiss Cottage in the next ten seconds and thousands of pink lotus blossoms dropped on my head as some kind of cosmic blessing, would I finally feel that I was justified in leaving?

I need to be somewhere else immediately, so I can think about everything. I have no idea where, but I think I need a park, a bench and a big sheltering tree.

The usual spot is on the pavement outside the Swiss Cottage laundrette. It's also freezing cold and dark. The pigeons – our English war heroes – are eating cigarette butts as usual and there are tracksuit hoods up everywhere you look. I don't want to walk around here.

Trafalgar Square? Maybe. It was strangely comforting to be there the other night.

I turn on my heel and catch the train to Charing Cross, along with all the other Swiss Cottage escapees, who are on their way to parties, nightclubs and films. It's Saturday night – I'd completely forgotten.

Most of the Saturday nights Nash and I spent together in the beginning involved The Believers and, occasionally, a band I liked. These days, because of his passion for *serious* guitar, as he calls it, Nash will only go and watch other musicians if they're a) not English and b) much older than him. Someone more cynical than me would say he doesn't like competition. I'm sure he's secretly threatened by other men. That's why he's so aloof all the time. And . . . all right, I know I'm inventing excuses to leave him now, but part of me no longer cares.

The tube is packed with couples holding hands. I wish they wouldn't. I can remember the last time Nash held my hand. It was on my birthday and he only did it because I asked him.

The train stops at Leicester Square, and I get off and walk. I now have a hole in both my tartan wellies. I may have to spend more of my vast fortune from the markets to buy replacements, before . . . Before what? Before I go to Australia? Or before we move to Romney College? Or before I am forced to move to Hove and live with my mother?

Nash has often been right about my life. He was right about fashion college – it turned out to be a dead loss. He has also been right about things like booking dentists six months ahead and talking to the bank about weekly repayments. He was right about the Swiss Cottage International Travellers' Hostel, too. If we'd moved out of there when I wanted to, last year, and rented a flat, we'd be utterly broke by now. Still. He's not right about this. Or is he? Round and round my stomach goes, like the coin-operated washing machines at the laundrette that turn everything grey while you watch.

I walk to Trafalgar Square as quickly as I can and jam my hat down on my head to stop my ears from stinging with cold.

If Nash becomes Head of Music at the college and I become a school dinner lady and we live in their flat and hang around their swimming pool and use their lovely tennis courts, will everything be all right then?

I can see the lights and the lions in the distance, and the front doors of St Martin-in-the-Fields, although it's closed for the evening. Nobody wants to go to church on a Saturday night, except mad people like me. Teenagers are texting each other, and screaming children are running in circles around Nelson's Column.

I'm not surprised that Nash has been snapped up. Even I know that he's a kind of superstar in the world of London music teachers. Plus, he can speak three languages and teach the girls how to play football. What more could they possibly want? He even owns his own trombone. It's in storage at his parents' place.

What will his parents say if I walk out on him now? What will my mother say?

I look around and realize how much I love this part

of London. I just love, love, love it. If I go to Australia, though, I will lose, lose, lose it.

I feel panicky and weird, so I try to make a list in my head and get things straight.

If Nash takes the job, and I go with him, then I will have some of the things we would also gain by moving to Sydney. I will have a swimming pool and far more money. I will probably be able to afford a pedicure. And a manicure. It's amazing how my immediate life plans at the moment seem to revolve around my stupid nails.

Nash will be much happier if he takes Lisa's job, so our relationship will probably become happier too. Maybe we'll even get married one day. We could even have a baby, and maybe the baby will be a girl and she can go to the college and end up being a musical genius, like her father.

I suppose I could be a school dinner lady for a while, at least until I've paid Nash back. Then maybe I could look at other options. Suzanne thinks I can do anything. Perhaps I should give her the benefit of the doubt. Maybe I can make jackets for her stall.

It's raining now, and I didn't bring the tartan umbrella. There's only one thing for it, I'm going to have to stand underneath a lion.

Suddenly the phone rings in my pocket. It's Nash.

'Look, I know you're probably feeling anti-me at the moment, and anti-everything.'

'Yes.'

'Where are you?'

113

'Doesn't matter.'

'Think about it though, Alice. And think about this – if I take the job at the college and end up making that kind of money, I can become the kind of man who doesn't have to *lend* his girlfriend anything.'

'What?'

'If I'm earning that sort of money, Alice, then you can forget about debts and all that kind of stuff. We can just walk away from all that and forget about it.'

'Is this a bribe?'

'*Listen* for once. If I take this job, we can have *holidays* in Australia. We don't have to move there. We don't have to leave your friends and Lady Penelope and everything here. Alice, on this kind of salary package, we can save up so much money that we can afford to go to Bondi Beach every bloody Christmas!'

'All right then, I'll think about it.' I snap my phone shut and pull back under the lion's enormous stone ears as the rain comes down.

I want to stay here as long as I possibly can, so he will be asleep when I go home, and I can quietly make a bed on the couch. I don't want to have to lie next to Nash tonight.

Chapter Six

Nash and I usually spend Christmas Day with my mother and Boxing Day with his parents, or the other way around. This year, though, he has decided to go to Cambridge and leave the rest up to me. According to his email to me this week – with the very sensible subject header 'PLANS' – this time the Christmas and January break is very much up to me. He will be in Cambridge with his parents and that's that. I can either join them or not. It takes me about five seconds to decide *not*.

Between Christmas and New Year I go into a short-bread frenzy, baking and eating about eight tins of the biscuits I made for other people. Apart from that, after I queue at the post office for half an hour to send the shortbread – nice Heidi was right to tear her hair out that day that she banged on and on about British post offices – I do nothing and see nobody.

I spend Christmas in bed with my woolly hat on, both bars blazing on the electric fire I've nicked from the breakfast room, reading *Should I Stay or Should I Go?*

– now two weeks overdue from the library – while picking shortbread crumbs out of the sheets.

I listen to the shipping forecast, because it's the only thing on the radio that isn't Christmassy.

There are warnings of gales in Rockall, Hebrides, Bailey, Faeroes and South-east Iceland, and a low Denmark Strait. Plus there's a low Trafalgar 1011 and a low Irish Sea losing its identity . . .

That was me a few nights ago. A low at Trafalgar losing my identity.

Occasionally I check the answering machine to see if there are any real emergencies, but it's mainly people wondering where I am and saying 'Merry Christmas and good luck in Australia', as well as a few wrong numbers, so on most days I am free to stay in bed.

Suzanne emailed from New York to say she was having a fabulous time with Sam and that she was sorry her stupid Twad editor had held the pregnant fashion story over. She was sure, though – absolutely sure – they would run it soon.

I emailed back from the corner shop, using a smiley face that was wholly unrepresentative of my mood.

As for the season of goodwill, I rang my mother on Christmas Day and that was it. I told her I had a cold and couldn't talk. Half true. Depression is not a word we've ever used in our family.

It is now well and truly past New Year, and I am about to take another tin of shortbread back to bed with me when the phone rings. It sounds like someone pretending to be a dog, so I hang up. Bloody kids.

A few minutes later the phone rings again to more demented barking.

'Bugger off.' I put the phone down and decide to put on a second woolly hat because the top of my head is going numb with cold.

If they ring again, I decide, I'm going to bark back.

Ten minutes later, they do, so I begin yapping like our old Labrador Charlie, as loudly as I know how, before slamming the phone down.

Five minutes later there's another call. No barking this time, though, just a worried Australian woman, wondering if she's got the right number.

'Alice?'

'Yes?'

'It's Danielle Coles. I have to apologize to you.'

'Oh God. The *dogs*! No, I'm sorry. I thought you were kids having a joke. Or I thought your *dogs* were kids having a joke.'

'No, no. I had you on speakerphone while I was washing Mr Chang.'

'Who's he?'

'This ratty little Pekinese who's got himself covered in sheep poo – Get back in the bath, Mr Chang!'

More barking. It seems I have been receiving prank phone calls from a dog.

'I just needed to find out when you're coming over, Alice. Heidi said she thought it was quite soon.'

'Yes.'

Just keep saying yes to everything, then you can crawl back to bed.

'I'm in a bit of a spot up here and I was wondering if we could try you out at the kennels sooner rather than later.'

'Yes?'

'My usual guy's got to go up north, his dad's crook.'

'Yes.'

'Mr Chang, you are not to go near King Tut or I will smack your bottom!'

Suddenly I feel exhausted.

'Danielle, do you just want to send me an email about all this? I have to use an internet café at the moment, but I pick them up every few days.'

The strain of trying to hear someone phoning from the other side of the world, shouting over what sounds like the combined racket of 101 Dalmatians is just too much.

'Yeah, sure, Alice. I must apologize again for these naughty little boys. I'll send you an email!' she yells, shortly before a gurgling sound that may or may not be Mr Chang drowning in his own bath.

I put the phone down and go back to bed.

I must take Dr Ray's advice. I must be positive about my life. I must see my options from every angle. I must take time to ground, balance and restore my centre. I must not go into a trance, like Goggles the fox terrier, every time I attempt to work out my future career path, love life – and all the rest of it.

I am not going to Australia, of course. I can keep on trying to have debates with myself about it, but it just doesn't make sense.

Some dreams deserve to go down the drain, and perhaps this is one of them. It's like my dream of becoming a fashion designer. It's madness.

Nash is right as usual and Romney College is the only sensible future we have. I did the sums after he emailed me a copy of their offer. If he takes this job, and all the private tutoring as well, we will be well and truly in the clear. My new salary as a dinner lady – if I back it up with a bit of tailoring – means I will be debt free eventually.

I try to get excited about the prospect. Cooking school dinners, plus not paying any rent, plus lots of saving in jam jars equals freedom.

Well . . . a certain kind of freedom. I'll never be able to go out again. My social life will consist of listening to Nash playing the guitar and ducking when the posh Romney College children throw quoits at my head.

I try to concentrate on Mum and what it will mean to her if I stay. For a start, if I pay her back, she can stop dyeing her own hair. I was terrified by the idea of being so far away from her, and now look, if anything happens to her, I'm just a train trip away. A mere motorbike ride away.

The last polite communication I had with Nash included the news that he has seen the motorbike he wants to buy, once he has his new salary.

The phone rings again and I listen to the answering machine click on. It's Lisa. Just when I thought I'd heard the last of her.

'I've got to talk to you, Alice. Are you there? I can't get you on your mobile. It's urgent.'

I pick up the phone.

'Hello, Lisa.'

'Phew!' She gives a floaty little pant.

'Nash's in Cambridge with his parents. Have you tried his mobile?'

'I know where he is. I need to speak to you. I need to apologize to you actually.'

'Really?'

'Yass.'

That strange, polite little voice. *Yass.* This conversation is probably the longest one we've ever had.

'Why do you need to apologize to me?'

'I've sort of been lying for Nash.'

'What?'

'I've been covering up for Nash. He's not really over Sarah, you see.'

Oh my God.

'Anyway. I just needed to ring and let you know. Now that we're all saying goodbye to you. It wasn't an affair they were having or anything like that, Alice, so please don't worry. But last year, when we all did that sponsored swimathon, Nash slept with Sarah.'

'Are you saying Nash had sex with Sarah?'

'I caught them, in the big jacuzzi next to the pool. It was dark and everyone had gone home, so I suppose they thought it would be fine . . .'

Her tinkling, frail little voice trails off. Suzanne

always said she sounds like the top notes of a posh school recorder.

I hang up on her, then I go back to bed and shake out all the shortbread crumbs until the horrible hostel carpet is covered in them.

I suppose Lisa's just found out that Nash has got her old job. I had no idea she was so vindictive. I always had her down as some kind of wafty, straw-hatted twit.

I wondered why they were all so late coming home on the night of the swimathon. Suzanne told me I was being stupid, but I knew something was up, even then.

I have never been in a jacuzzi with Nash in my life. I've never even had a bath with him.

The jealousy is awful and instant. *Sarah*. How much of an idiot have I been all this time to believe that she'd just disappeared? Ex-wives don't just vanish.

I leave Nash a message on his mobile and tell him to come home because I need to talk to him, then I off-load my shock into all the housework I can find.

There are three vacant rooms in the hostel tonight, and I blast each of them in turn, taking down nylon curtains and shaking them out of windows, scrubbing ancient stains on the mattresses, and rubbing at the cigarette burns on all the sad little Formica-topped tables.

If I am going to leave this hostel – one way or another – then I'm going to leave it clean. It's what I did when I heard Dad was dying. I vacuumed my parent's house from top to bottom, then washed and ironed every piece of linen they owned. I polished the silver, and even got the hair out of my dad's old hairbrush. I went mad.

I go back to our rooms and sweep the lino in the bathroom, then get down on my hands and knees and scrub it like a proper maid with a bucket of hot, soapy water. If I scrub hard enough, maybe I can wash away Lisa too. I never want to hear that faint, wobbly, smug little voice again as long as I live.

Some stupid line from one of Nash's songs comes into my head – *'What is to become of me?'* – or maybe it's from that compilation cassette tape one of my ex-boyfriends made me. Anyway, it's from a song. And now I can't get it out of my head.

I keep on cleaning the bathroom. I used to do this as a job and I hated it. How strange that it should be so comforting now.

Nash rings back and tells me he is at King's Cross and will be home soon.

'See you then,' I tell him as chirpily as I can – I sound like a deranged chipmunk.

What is to become of me? I can't think about that now. I should think about the state of the hostel instead. I had no idea it had become so filthy over the autumn and winter, but at the moment, at least in our two rooms, it's never looked so good.

I curl up on the sofa and flick through every page of *Should I Stay or Should I Go?* at breakneck speed, using a red pen to write notes in the margins.

Do Nash and I have anything in common, other than a long-forgotten, vaguely expressed desire to have kids? Not any more. I suppose we both used to have *him* in common, back in the days when I was content to sit at

122

his feet while he strummed his guitar. But I know better now.

Does Nash stop me from pursuing my dreams? Yes.

Does Nash make me feel like I don't matter or don't exist? Yes, yes, yes, yes yes. My God, that's it!

I close the book and feel myself gently pass out on the sofa. I don't even care what the rest of the questions are. I just want to sleep.

When I wake up, Nash is pulling the book out from under me.

'Alice?'

'Hello.'

'What's this?' he inspects the jacket. 'Oh yes. *Should I Stay or Should I Go?* Good old Dr Ray. So, have you worked it out yet?'

'Go.'

'What?'

'Go, go, go. Lisa rang up and told me you'd had sex with Sarah on the day you all did the sponsored swim. You shagged her.'

Big silence. Huge silence. Nash wasn't expecting that.

'Wow!' He sits down on the floor and crosses his legs, looking exactly like one of the boys in his music class.

'But it's not really about that, because I sort of vaguely knew something like that had happened, and the thing is, I didn't really care.'

'What do you mean?'

'I mean I didn't feel jealous. I don't feel jealous now. I just feel . . . let down. Sad. Fed up, I suppose.'

'Right.'

'Because Lisa's so lame, and so is Sarah – your bloody ex-*wife*, for God's sake Nash! – and because you went behind Lisa's back and wangled your way into her old job. She's so pathetic, that's why she's done this to us now.'

Nash looks down at his feet.

'If I ever had any doubts about how self-centred you actually are, you prick, I don't have any now. You've done everyone over, haven't you?'

Nash shakes his head slowly from side to side, smiling to himself, as if he is in possession of some precious hidden information I'm not privy to and I am really a very, very stupid woman.

'So was it just the once with your ex-wife or has it been all year?' I shout at him.

'Anything in your book, then?' Nash jerks his thumb at it. 'Because if I was to go now – and I have been thinking about it, very seriously – it would be because your sense of commitment to me is so pathetic that you actually base your decisions about our relationship on a self-help book you found at the donkeys' charity shop in Finsbury Park.'

'Don't make this out to be my fault. And I didn't find it at the donkeys' charity shop in Finsbury Park, it's from the library.'

'Whatever. You've been reading it for the last two months in front of me, and you expect me to believe you're committed to this relationship?'

'Don't talk to me about commitment. You've just changed your mind about Australia.'

'We've already talked about that.'

'No we haven't. Not properly. The book's great, Nash. Really, really great. I love Dr Ray, I think he's completely on the money. There's this question that goes, "Does your partner make you feel as if you don't matter or don't exist?"'

'Alice. Come on.'

'But it's such a great question! And it was so amazing to read it. I felt as if it was my problem in someone else's book, Nash. And all this time I've never been able to put it into words, and there it was in black and white.'

Nash stands up, sighs as if he has given up and stares at the ceiling.

'How much of your life have I bankrolled?' he asks.

'Here we go.'

'You're saying *cra-zee thangs*,' Nash says in a bad American accent, and taps the cover of the book. Then he pulls a crazy face, which I guess is meant to be me or Dr Ray Stein.

'You're just shit, Nash. I'm going.'

'To Lady Penelope. I don't know why you ever left home in the first place. You can't look after yourself.'

'You won't know where I am wherever I go.'

He turns away and stares out of the window, and when he turns back I see he has tears in his eyes.

'Nash. For God's sake.'

He stands there for ages, like a statue, until I see him relaxing again into his old familiar cool.

'Alice. We should both calm down and think about this. I'm sorry about Sarah. For what it's worth, we were stoned in that jacuzzi, me and Sarah. And . . . I am genuinely sorry that I succumbed. For all kinds of reasons. I am also unbelievably sorry you had to find out like that.'

'Don't. How bloody *dare* you have done that behind my back? Did you tell Michael and Richard as well? Has everyone else except me known about this all year?'

'Nobody knows, Alice. I promise. It was a mad thing to do. And Lisa should never have told you. I'm sorry.'

I start picking up my things from the room – cushions and books, blankets and rugs – and throwing them on the sofa in a pile. As I do, I realize I'm scaring myself as much as him. I know other couples do this all the time, this angry moving-out thing, and then they change their minds and kiss and make up and everything's OK again. We're not like that, though. This is not a dress rehearsal. And I know we're both terrified.

Nash watches me in silence as I take big, deep breaths and gather together all my stuff: sunglasses and old magazines from when I had money, albums, socks and soap. I know at a glance what is mine and what is his because I did a big inventory in my head last year.

Incidentally, that's another of Dr Ray's tests. *Have you seriously ever thought about leaving, to the point where you calculate what belongs to you, and what belongs to your partner?*

I own a chest of drawers, some hatboxes, an old drawing of my grandmother's, a dressing table and numerous other objects I can live without for the moment. I'll find a way to get them later. I'm very grateful to them, these material objects, for making these hostel rooms feel like a home. But at the moment the last thing I can imagine is asking Nash to help me lug them downstairs.

In the meantime, I silently thank my mother for her old spare suitcases. I use two of hers and two of mine, packing everything in as tightly as I can. Thank God for Suzanne's expert training in packing and sorting – thanks to her I know how to roll towels so they won't take up too much room, and how to get eight pairs of socks inside a pair of shoes.

Eventually Nash gets up and leaves, clicking the door softly behind him. I suppose he's gone to ring up Lisa, so he can shout at her. Or is he ringing Sarah to warn her, just in case I find her number and phone her?

I have no idea where Nash has gone. I just know I have to pack up my stuff as quickly as possible, before he comes back.

I go into the bathroom and pick up Ducky, an oversized rubber duck that Nash won for me at the Hampstead funfair when we first got together.

I put him down again, then I pick him up. Should I pack Ducky in my luggage or not? Oh my God. I put him down. An inanimate object is doing my head in.

Shock is an interesting thing. I feel exactly the same as I did when my mother told me about Dad. I feel as if I've just left my body in the same way that Elvis once left the building. The only bit of my physical self which currently appears to be in this room is my heart, which is banging away non-stop, and my sweat, which is pouring off me.

I now have four bulging suitcases on wheels. If I tie them in pairs with scarves I should be able to drag two on each side, at least until I can find a taxi to take me to Victoria Station. Then Mum can pick me up in Hove and we can take two bags each.

Suzanne's money has just become my running-away money. At the moment I don't give a stuff about my debts. As I empty the jam jars into an old handbag, I bless Suzanne all the way from Swiss Cottage to New York City. Then I drag my suitcases out of the room, look at the stinking hostel hallway for the last time, and slam the front door so hard that the old brass bell falls off.

It's only when I'm in the back of the taxi on the way to the station that I realize Joel Templeton has texted me. He's just arrived back from Moscow on his long trip back to Australia, and he wonders if I'm free to meet up. He has a few more nights in England before he finishes the rest of his journey.

It's one of the longest text messages I have ever seen. It is the kind of message you imagine someone would write if they hadn't actually seen a mobile phone before. He says he's going back to Australia the long way round, and the wrong way round, because it makes the journey more interesting.

'How wonderful' my mother says, when I show her his message, much, much later when we are drowning ourselves in brandy in Hove. 'Wrong way round and long way round. That's exactly the kind of thing I'd like to have engraved on my tombstone.'

I tell her about Nash and I cry. It's a relief. I held back the tears all the way to Victoria Station in the taxi, then all the way here on the train.

'I'm not going to Australia any more,' I tell her as I unpack my things.

'Not to worry, darling.'

'I've got some of the money I owe you, too.'

'Are you talking about all those old jam jars?' She looks at my collection. 'Alice. For goodness sake. There is no need to worry about money ever again. I don't want it back, not for all the tea in China. Do you hear me?'

'The bailiffs came round to the hostel. Nash paid them off.'

'I'm sure he did, and let that be an albatross around his neck.' She coughs, lighting a cigarette. 'Now, shall we talk about something else?'

She leads me to an enormous leather trunk in the hall – the kind that boys used to take away to boarding school – and flips open the lid.

'Look, Alice. All your Aunt Helena's clothes. Well, all the things she left behind when they went travelling anyway. Joel's organized it. When I told him you'd been working on Suzanne's stall at the market, he said I had to collect them and give them to you. They've been in storage all this time at your Auntie Bat's.'

Auntie Bat has been called that for years, because both Roland and my father, her brothers, maintained she had bats in her belfry.

'Bat has had the trunk in the attic for over twenty years – Joel rang Helena in Jamaica to check – anyway, she said you could have the lot. She's never going to come back for them now. She said they were all her best clothes, and her mother's and grandmother's too.'

Oh my God. Hippy Helena's wardrobe. I've seen those photographs of her from the seventies. She had *everything.*

Despite myself, I get down on my hands and knees and rifle through the trunk like a madwoman. There are monogrammed silk dressing gowns and tweed suits with velvet collars. There are tapestry slippers, pink satin dancing shoes and velvet capes.

And then there's the fabric. Yards and yards of the stuff, both pre-war and 1950s. This must be her mother's stuff, and her grandmother's. Some of it is still in Harrods carrier bags, with the old royal warrants in both corners.

'There are a few Mary Quants in there I noticed,' Mum says as she puffs away on her cigarette. 'And Ossie Clarks. Helena wasn't frightened of a mini, or a maxi.'

The trunk has three layers, each separated by a wooden shelf. I take down the first shelf, and see a sleeveless Mary Quant summer dress with the original daisy label sewn next to the zip – I kiss it.

'Who knew that fashion could inspire so much passion?' my mother muses. 'One thing that might bother you, though, is the little stoat fur collar at the bottom.'

She leans down, finds what looks like a recently deceased weasel and pulls it out.

'Do you remember that television programme?' She shudders. 'Stoats must be the most charmless creatures in the country, with their horrible glands. Chuck it out, Alice, as soon as you can.'

'I can't possibly take all this stuff,' I say, putting the stoat to one side, and pulling out a pristine Yves St Laurent tuxedo jacket. 'It's worth a fortune. Helena should have it, or Robyn.'

'Oh no,' my mother shakes her head, then shakes her cigarette as well. 'Joel said his mother was quite insistent. Nobody else in the family has ever wanted it, and she said it must go to you. I'm only sorry I've been so dopey I didn't think of it before. But then, Auntie Bat never mentioned it. Too interested in her pipe.'

I'd forgotten Auntie smoked a clay pipe. No wonder both my father and my uncle used to avoid her.

Later – much later when I've tried on the Mary Quant dress, which doesn't fit, and the beautiful Yves St Laurent tuxedo, which does – I tell Mum the whole horrible story about Sarah and Nash at the swimming pool.

'Aha!' she cries. 'The floozy in the jacuzzi! Well, the sooner you put that behind you, Alice, the better. Just think about how your fingers go all wrinkly when you've been in the bath too long. That's probably exactly what it was like for them. It can't have been much fun for her having to look down at *that* bobbing around in the water . . .'

Chapter Seven

Nash wants to put me on a regular repayment system, which he calculates should leave me free of debt by the end of this year. This, of course, depends on me working almost constantly, but he is fairly sure I can find a job as a cleaner again.

'Happy New Year to you as well,' my mother says when she reads his email, over my shoulder.

We are in Brighton for the day, and every shop, café and business is crammed with people after the Christmas break, including the tiny internet and photocopying place we're in.

'I suppose Nash is putting all this in writing so he has some kind of record about the money. How sad.'

'It's not that, Mum. He just doesn't want to talk to me, and I don't want to talk to him.'

Nash and I have exchanged more emails since I left than we ever did when we were together. This morning we seem to be typing them at the same time, so they cross in mid-air. I suppose he's using the computer at school.

At the moment we are competing with each other to see who can create the most mature, sensible and practical subject header. 'Immediate Priorities' (Nash) is followed by 'Finances' (me) and then 'Options' (Nash) is followed by 'Important Issues' (me).

Nash writes that he feels the harmony in our relationship has been damaged by my financial dependency on him and that this constant looming debt has upset the balance of our partnership. He says he thinks we need some time out from each other, but he also thinks it's time I paid him back in some structured way. He adds that overall he thinks we've had a good time together.

'A good time?' my mother asks. 'He makes it sounds as if you've been playing tiddlywinks.'

'Listen to this,' I tell her. 'He says my decision not to come to Romney College with him put his position there in jeopardy, as his application had been accepted on the basis that I would be joining him in the flat. The school prefers couples to rent the subsidized properties in the grounds.'

'Hang on, I want to read that myself. Let me find my glasses,' my mother says as she peers over my shoulder.

This is her first encounter with a computer in years, since Dad made her go on a Microsoft Word silver surfers' weekend with him in Dorset.

Dad took to computers immediately, of course, but Mum spent the whole time smoking in the garden and listening to the racing results on her transistor radio.

Now that Mum has seen the internet for the first

time, though, she is begging me to help her sign up for 'the Google'.

She calls everything connected with the internet – email, websites, spam, blogs etc. – 'the Google'.

'What else does Nash say on the Google, Alice?'

'I'm paraphrasing, obviously, but it seems that, luckily, Nash is so brilliant and charismatic that the Head at Romney is prepared to overlook the fact that I have been such a hopelessly feckless and unreliable cow – and that we're not married of course – so Nash is still being offered the flat and the job, on the condition that he signs up for two years. Oh yeah, and he hopes we can work out our issues.'

'Why don't you Google him back,' my mother says, 'and tell him you'll pay him back his loan, with interest, when you marry a rich man.'

'Mum, I'm never going to marry a rich man. I don't know where you get this rich man thing from. They don't exist. Maybe in your day, but not now.'

'He's quite mad to talk to you about money like this,' she whispers while people tap on their keyboards all around us. 'Especially after everything he's done. What about his ex-wife. What about her chap? Does she have a chap? Imagine what *he's* going to say about all this business in the jacuzzi!'

'Mum!' I hiss.

'OK, darling.' She notices a man who is obviously listening to our conversation. 'Sorry.'

We pick up our bags and leave. My mother wants to go to Brighton Pavilion because she says it's good for the soul. I haven't been there since I was a teenager, but she thinks it will take our minds off everything.

'So funny how everyone wears these American hats now,' she says as we pass one couple after another wearing baseball caps. 'I always think they make everyone look like geese from the side.'

We take a shortcut to the Pavilion, across the park, and I gaze up at the row of domes and minarets above the trees.

I wonder if George IV built the Pavilion because he thought it would make his love life better? It was never very happy. Perhaps he thought the solution to his marital problems lay in grand future plans, just as Nash and I did.

The last thing Nash and I feel like doing at the moment is sorting out the Australia mess. We've agreed to sort it tomorrow, instead. He'll call the airline and I'm going to call Australia House. Then that's it. Everything's cancelled. Over.

My mother and I pick up our free leaflets and wander through the corridors of the entrance hall to the Pavilion. It is completely silent in here, because everyone around us is far too overwhelmed by all the velvet, dragons and carved palm trees to talk. I expect even Prince George was intimidated. It's not just a palace, it's like walking into heaven.

It's hard not to ooh and aah at the hand-painted wallpaper and beautiful bamboo stairs. There's a rumour that Hitler wanted the Royal Pavilion as his seaside home after the war, which is why the Nazis never bombed it.

I find myself worrying about all the cleaning they had to do. And, of course, the cleaning some poor people still must do now. In contrast, my mother says that every time she comes to the Pavilion it makes her want to redecorate.

'I do need new curtains,' my mother says, eyeing the vast drapes in the banqueting room.

'I love it. But imagine the work.'

'Don't think about the work. It's too beautiful for that. I thought you'd like this place more now you're older. I don't think we've been here for years, have we? And when you're here you can't think about anything else, can you?'

I try to succumb. After months of baked beans on toast, wellies with holes, pouring rain and one-pound shampoo, perhaps a dose of the Royal Pavilion is exactly what I need.

It doesn't take long to give in – the palace was built for seduction after all, and it is surprisingly easy to be seduced by it. After an hour I find myself wanting to bounce up and down on Queen Victoria's lush four-poster bed.

'I've invited Joel for supper,' my mother says. 'Did I tell you?'

'You did, last night.'

'Oh, sorry. Senior moment.'

'He's coming down here to see Brighton, remember? Then going back to London to catch his next flight.'

'Could you repeat to me what he wrote on your phone message again?' my mother asks as we make our way to the music room. 'I liked it so much.'

'He said he's going back to Australia the long way round, and also the wrong way round, because it makes the journey more interesting.'

'That's it.'

'Apparently he's grown a beard. Robyn says he's a bit serious.'

'Uncle Roland was like that, too,' my mother says as we sit in the music room and gaze at the gold dragons on the ceiling. 'I think it's sad that they moved away when Joel and Robyn were so young. He was a lovely boy. Your father was very disappointed when they all left.'

'Did they just want to travel, or was it something else?'

'Oh, Mrs Thatcher,' my mother shrugs. 'Roland had a vendetta against her. He used to throw jaffa cakes at her when she was on television.'

'Shall I go and buy some wine for supper?' I ask.

'Oh no. Don't waste your money on wine.'

'It's fine. Please stop thinking about Nash's email, Mum.'

'Your father always said relationships were not about money, and I believe he was right,' she says, 'but now that you have to paddle your own canoe again, Alice, I do think you ought to stop other people taking the mickey. If you hadn't scrubbed all those floors at the hostel, Nash would have been homeless. You lived there purely because it was close to his school. It was his choice, not yours.'

She goes to the loo and I think about the money I owe Nash, and whether there's any way round it.

Our relationship – or what's left of it – has become about additions and subtractions. Giving and taking away. Dividing and bean-counting.

It's not just about pounds and pence, either. It's about time and energy, hopes and dreams.

If Nash wants me to pay him back every week for a year, I will, but I want him to know that it's because I choose to, not because he's demanded it.

'I need to get a job in Brighton,' I tell my mother when she comes back.

'Perhaps you could do his job,' she whispers, looking at a security guard – my mother is a terrible whisperer – as we make our way to the café upstairs.

Halfway up the stairs, she trips and nearly falls over. 'Crivens!'

She inspects her foot and sees the sole of her shoe has just come away. It's the same pair of Gucci loafers she's been wearing for the last twenty years. Mum used to replace her shoes when I was young. Now she doesn't.

'Ruddy things,' she complains and rubs her ankle.

I wonder what would have happened if I hadn't been there to catch her. Maybe it's best that I'm staying here with her.

We sit down in the café overlooking the gardens, and the waitress talks us through the specials. I'm having incredible flashbacks about this place now – the egg and watercress sandwiches, the pots of Darjeeling, the prints of fat old George IV on the walls – I don't think it's changed since I was a teenager.

'What do you think you'll do, Alice?'

My mother's question is so casual and easy that it takes me by surprise and I find myself telling her the truth.

'I want to make clothes with Helena's fabric.'

'Oh good!'

'I know it's ridiculous.'

'No, it's not ridiculous at all.' She waves her red gloves at the portrait of George IV. 'He loved clothes. He would have been a good customer. Do you know, after he died they found he owed his tailors nearly two million pounds?'

'He did have a big bottom. That takes a lot of tailoring,' I tell her.

'Well, if you need to work on your clothes, you know you can stay here as long as you like,' my mother reminds me.

'I know. Thank you. I thought I'd move into a shared house, though, on the other side of London for a change. I might go south or east. I've had enough of north London. Once I've saved up enough money, anyway.'

I'm trying not to think about that bit.

Our tea arrives, along with – yes, I'm still eating it – shortbread. I know one day I won't be able to look at a piece of shortbread because it will remind me of this depressing, scary Christmas, but for the moment I'm making the most of it.

'Not as nice as your shortbread, darling,' my mother whispers after she has taken a bite. 'Thank you for putting my star sign on it by the way. Although I'm never quite sure if I'm Leo the Lion or . . . what's the other one? Is it the python?'

I laugh at her.

Mum changes the subject back to clothes.

'I don't often go to the shops now,' she explains, 'but when I do I notice that people seem to be making skirts out of tights.'

'Cheap nylon. Manufacturers love it because they can churn it out in three sizes and it stretches, so the skirts can always be small, medium or large.'

'It's funny,' Mum says, 'we used to make our tailors fit the clothes around us. Now it seems to be the other way around: we have to make ourselves fit into the garments they provide. Do you know, I tried on a tweed skirt in the sales last year and it said, "Made in Turkey"?'

'Made in Turkey by fifteen-year-old girls on fifty pence an hour probably.'

I look out of the window at the wind shaking the trees. I wonder what the weather's like at Bondi Beach today?

I suppose I'll have to ring up Robyn at some point and tell her we're not coming. It's not a conversation I'm particularly looking forward to.

My mother pours me a cup of tea.

'I'm going to have to call Robyn and tell her the bad news,' I say.

'Oh, it's such a shame. We'll talk to Joel about all that

tonight when he arrives,' my mother says, discreetly hitting the shortbread with the teaspoon to see how hard it is.

We finish our tea, and my mother returns home for 'The Archers' – she never misses it – while I go for a walk along the seafront.

Watching Brighton on a windy day is like seeing a film run backwards. Seagulls fly in the wrong direction. Umbrellas blow inside out and drag their owners back along the streets. Even the waves on the beach seem to travel in the wrong direction.

I feel as if everything else in my life has gone backwards, too. I'm coming back from Australia before I've even caught the train to Heathrow. Nash has gone back on all his promises to me, and suddenly I've gone from loving him to feeling repulsed by him. He's turned from giving to taking – even grasping. I didn't show my mother the last paragraph in his email this morning, but he wants to buy everything I left behind for half the price I paid for it, which he suggests can come off my debt.

I told him I'd rather he gave it to the donkey charity shop in Finsbury Park, since that's where half of it came from anyway.

I have been replaying the last horrible conversation I had with Nash in my head ever since I got on the train to Hove. I wonder if he's called Lisa yet? Or Sarah?

Lisa in particular must know what it feels like to be non-existent now.

She thought she loomed large in Nash's world, but

she had reckoned without his ability to wave a magic wand and make the women in his life invisible. Lisa is now inhabiting the same thin air as me; we're nowhere girls – utterly irrelevant to the main action, which is always about Nash.

I think about his mother for a minute and the way Nash never mentions her. Maybe he's just got a problem with women. I'm sure that's what Suzanne will say when I finally steel myself to tell her the news.

Part of me longs to call her now, just for the bliss of being able to moan – finally – about all the awful things Nash did and that I've had to put up with and cover up for so long.

Then again, another part of me just wants to lie in bed and eat more shortbread. And have some space, of course.

I don't care if it's a silly American word and people make quotation marks with their fingers whenever they say it. Space is good. Space is oxygen, blue skies, air, stars, clouds, freedom, room and all the other things I've lacked since I moved to Swiss Cottage.

Brighton has lots of space, especially here on the edge of the sea with the sky above you. You can gulp it in, wave your arms around in it and even throw your hat into it.

Apart from the occasional old man with binoculars and a raincoat, or the odd waddling teenager pushing a pram, I am the only person on the pier. The sensation of being here without Nash – or having to worry about Nash – is incredible.

142

It's so lovely to be here without his voice in my ear, drawling, cynical and smug. Instead, all I can hear are the seagulls crying for chips.

I suppose I'm technically single now. A state that feels both terrible and wonderful. I haven't really talked about this bit with Nash, but I am sure, dear Dr Ray Stein, that if my friends and family staged an intervention now and told me it was OK to sleep with other people, I would simply go right ahead.

The last time I had sex with Nash, just before Lisa's phone call, it was so try-hard that I wished I hadn't bothered. All I remember is, my old teddy was watching from on top of the chest of drawers, and even he looked comatose with boredom.

Would anyone have me now, this afternoon, with my woolly hat, my four suitcases and my charity shop tights? I haven't looked in a mirror properly for months – mainly because Nash has ignored me for so long, I've convinced myself there's nothing worth looking at.

Poor me. I should get one of those invisible violins out, make a sad face and play Brahms's 'Tragic Overture'.

Instead, I play an old game with myself, from the days before I met Nash. I count ten men in the street and see if I could sleep with any of them. If you find one, it cheers you up and you think it's worth putting on make-up again.

On the Brighton seafront this afternoon, my man count goes like this:

Man with long woolly jumper, crocs, socks, yoga leggings and no underpants – no.

Man with Liverpool tracksuit top and fat girlfriend panting behind him in the distance – no.

Respectable fifty-something bloke whose hair is blowing sideways – no.

Bearded construction worker with sexually aroused pigeon following him– no.

Man with interesting glasses and suede shoes – yes, if not gay.

Man looking at his own reflection in a window – absolutely not.

Possible gay man with shaved head and tiny dog with bondage-style black halter – nope.

Vaguely all right bloke with shaved head, denim jacket and iPod – yes, depending on content of iPod.

Tall bloke in jeans with scruffy dark hair, sideburns, old tennis shoes and amazingly sexy, sincere, serious expression – yes, yes, yes!

Potential flasher in raincoat with possible wee stains. Looks like Peter Cook and Dudley Moore circa 1966 – no.

I cannot quite believe Number Nine. Surely he must have a ring on his finger, but he doesn't.

Gay? Possibly. But I shall claim him as heterosexual because I have counted enough members of the other team for one day, and statistically I feel I should be on the winning side.

Whoops. Number Nine has seen me staring at his hand. Oh bloody hell, he's definitely seen me staring at his hand, not to mention the rest of him, and now he's coming over to tell me to go away.

I watch and wait as he walks towards me. Suzanne would love those old tennis shoes he's wearing.

'Hi,' Number Nine says with a funny, shy smile. He looks almost as embarrassed as I am.

'Oh, hello.'

'I'm Joel. You must be Alice. I spotted your tartan umbrella. And the boots. I got into Hove early, so your mum told me to come here and look for you.'

Oh my God. I thought Joel Templeton had a beard. I thought he was supposed to be spiritual. Most of all, I thought he was supposed to still be in bloody London. The horror!

The shame is awful, but I feel so disappointed by the sudden disappearance of the extremely promising Number Nine from my life that I can barely concentrate on what my cousin is saying.

'Your heart is breaking.'

What? What did he say?

'Your heart is breaking. My mother had to leave my father, too, once. I know all about it. Do you want to go for a walk?'

'A walk?' I feel like a stunned mullet.

'A cup of tea then.'

'Oh yes.'

Joel grins. 'I knew the cup-of-tea thing would work!' He looks sideways at me. 'I remember that from when we lived in England. It doesn't matter what happens, if you put the kettle on, everything will be OK.'

We walk up Ship Street and wander into The Lanes, then suddenly I spot a newsagent.

'Can we just go in here for a minute?'

I know Suzanne has banned me from endlessly checking for my story in Twad, but I can't help myself.

While Joel stands over a pile of *Guardians* and tries to read them upside down, I flick through the latest issue of Twad from back to front.

It's there! My God. Natasha looks fantastic. Like a beautiful, pregnant green tree. The old tweed Biba coat has become a sharp, chic, angular jacket, just as I imagined. I had no idea it would look this good in the photographs.

'Joel!' I squeak and jab him in the ribs. 'It's me. This is me, this is mine!'

I realize I'm not making any sense, but then Joel quickly flips the magazine sideways and reads the credits in the margin.

'Dress and jacket by Vintage Alice. Alice Templeton,' he reads and shows me. It is the first time I have ever seen my name in print. It looks so serious. So grown-up. So . . . not like me.

Joel makes me buy extra copies for Robyn, Helena and Mum and kisses me on the cheek. 'Congratulations, Alice.'

The kiss on the cheek stays there in my mind for the next hour, like a forgotten chocolate bar in your coat pocket that you keep coming back to.

We walk through The Lanes, and it takes all the willpower I have not to keep checking my story in the magazine. It's not my story, of course, it's everybody's. But the clothes are mine and that's all that matters.

'I think your phone's making a noise.' Joel nudges me once we're inside a café having a cup of tea.

I check it, dreading a text from Nash, but it's a message from someone at the magazine, who wants to know what she should do about all the phone calls and emails they've been receiving from pregnant women wanting to know where they can buy my clothes.

'Look!' I show Joel, who smiles in his nice, warm, crinkly way. He looks nothing like any of us and not remotely like a Templeton.

'Fantastic. You're in business.'

'I'm scared.'

'No you're not. Come on, Alice.'

'But how am I going to do it?'

'Move to Australia.' He grins at me. 'Small fish, big pond. That's what Robyn said on the phone last night. She said if you want to make it in fashion, forget London, you should start in Sydney. You know there's a fantastic view from Robyn's spare bedroom. It could be your sewing room.'

I blink at him. It's all too much suddenly. Him, Australia, the pregnant women calling the magazine.

'I'll be in Sydney soon,' Joel reassures me. 'I'll help you.'

Chapter Eight

I am moving to Australia next week. I've been for many walks with Joel in that time, and things that made no sense at all before suddenly add up.

Our favourite walk has become an epic two-hour journey along the seafront to Rottingdean, and across the South Downs. There are sweeping views of the English Channel from the Downs, and somehow it's been helping me think clearly for a change.

Joel and I have been rained on and confronted by stray sheep while we walk, but I've become like Goggles the fox terrier and I can't get enough of my walks.

Along the way, Joel and I have talked about men, women, commitment, marriage, love, hearts and space. I've never heard a man talk about hearts as much as my cousin Joel, but once he started me off I found myself doing it too. After all this time it's a relief.

Joel is a bit mad, like my Uncle Roland, but he has also sat on a hill with me, high above the English Channel, until the stuck wheels in my brain started going round again.

At last I know what I'm doing, and what I'm doing is gambling.

'It sounds like the way you've been living anyway,' Joel says. 'You've taken a punt on all those jobs. Even on living with Nash.'

'Yes.'

'So if you've been having small bets, why not switch to big bets for a change? What scares you more? Giving up and going back to the old life, or risking the lot?'

'I don't even have to think about that. Giving up.'

'So there you are.' Joel smiles. 'You're better than me. I was with the same woman for five years and I couldn't take any kind of gamble.'

'You broke up?'

'She left me. She said I was incapable of making a commitment and she was right. Just like my mum.'

In all the talks that Joel and I have had about life and love, it is his mother who comes up most.

My parents never told me this, but Helena was already pregnant when she married Uncle Roland, with someone else's child. The child grew up to be Joel, but even now nobody knows who Joel's father is.

Which means Joel's not my cousin. And yet he's *still* my cousin, which is the most confusing feeling in the world.

'So what now?' I prompt Joel, as I catch up to him.

'It's been a long time since I've been with anyone.' Joel looks thoughtful. 'I'm still open to it, but that's all.'

Joel taught English to Tibetan refugees in India who had left their homes and families behind. He says he knows a lot about sitting with people who are in trouble. Right now, I want to sit with him on this hill for ever.

He has a low, quiet voice, and a steady, patient way of listening. It's such a novelty to be listened to and looked at properly. Two years with Nash has taught me to gabble everything quickly so I won't bore him or be interrupted. There is none of that with Joel.

I feel as if I have known him for years, even though he left England when I was a kid. I feel ridiculously at home with him.

The plan I have hatched with Joel is this: I am going to ring up Heidi and go to London first thing tomorrow to ask her about moving to Australia without Nash. I am also going to text Robyn in Bali to let her know what is going on. Then, if everything goes according to plan, I will get on the plane and go to Robyn's flat and stay in Bondi Beach until she gets back. After that I will catch the train to Byron Bay and start work at Barks with Danielle Coles. And then, I'll have enough money to start Vintage Alice and make tweed jackets for pregnant women.

Joel runs me through the plan again and again until it seems manageable, then he makes me breathe.

'You're forgetting to breathe, Alice.'

'Sorry.'

He makes me do a yoga pose called The Child up there on the hill. He says it immediately makes you feel safer, no matter what's going on. The Tibetans do The Child pose all the time. You curl up in a ball like a hedgehog, with only your back showing. Joel does it first and I follow. If Nash could see me now he would walk away. I feel ridiculous at first, but after ten minutes, I have to admit it's working.

'Good?' Joel asks.

'All right. Actually, better than all right. Although I won't do it in sheep droppings next time.'

We talk about what might happen if I get to Australia and realize I hate it. I know I can always come back to England and live with my mother, but Joel doesn't think I will hate Australia. He thinks I will fall in love with it, because now that there's a big space in my heart, there's room for something new to get in. I have honestly never heard any man in England talk like this.

'You should go up to Bellingen and pitch a tent on my property,' Joel encourages me. 'There's already a caravan there.' Before he left for India he bought five acres of land on the Bellinger River, which is between Sydney and Brisbane. He says the river is beautiful. You can swim in it and drink it.

After our walk we go to some tea rooms in Brighton and eat cinnamon toast, and look at all Joel's old photos.

My cousin is a funny combination of rules and no rules. He makes me feel free because he makes me feel that everything is possible and nothing is off limits. I have also received several free lectures on the evils of meat, however.

'Joel's just like Roland,' my mother said after he told her off for hoarding plastic bags. 'They may not be blood relatives, but he's certainly inherited Roland's change-the-world thingy.'

Joel pushes photographs of places like Bega and Merimbula, Bunbury and Mole Creek across the table to show me how different Australia can be. Nash would put on a silly voice to pronounce all these place names, of course.

Before he went to India to work for Tibet Aid, Joel spent a year in a camper van, driving himself all round Australia. There are numerous shots of him looking Number Nine-ish, in shorts and little else, but as he is my cousin, I have naturally moved beyond all that.

Suzanne told me about a dating website called Single Sydney and I can't wait to try it now that Joel's laptop is on Mum's dining room table.

I try to stop thinking about men and concentrate on drinking my tea.

'If you get the time to do the big Australian odyssey, you have to go,' Joel says. 'I should have done it years ago. Maybe I'll do it when I get back. But I really just want to get back to Bellingen now. Grow some strawberries. Get a cow again.'

'A cow! They're my favourite things. What do you think of England?' I ask him.

'Well, I was born here,' he laughs at me. 'I really like it. Why?'

'Australians seem not to like it. They come here to work, but once they arrive in London they just moan about it.'

'That's because they haven't tried the cinnamon

toast in Brighton,' Joel says. 'What do you think of England?'

'It's a bit like my boyfriend. I tried and tried to make it work, but it was no good.'

'Are you over it?'

'Nash? I think so.'

'Are you over England, I meant.'

'Oh yes. That bit's easy. I went backwards and forwards and now I've gone back to the start. Back to the way I felt before when I really *knew* I was ready to go.'

My mother rings. She has finished listening to *The Archers* and is worried that we have got lost.

'It's fine,' I tell her. 'Joel and I went for a walk along the South Downs. We're just having a cup of tea.'

'Isn't he nice?' she says, not waiting for an answer. 'He told me the first thing he did when he landed at Heathrow was shave his beard off in the loo. He reminds me of you, Alice, doing a thing like that, although I couldn't say why.'

'We'll be home in time for supper,' I tell her. 'We walked for miles. We're having something to eat now but I'm sure we'll be hungry by then.'

Joel and I work our way through the cinnamon toast and he admires the low plastered ceilings in the tea rooms. 'They're like the ceilings you see in Beatrix Potter drawings,' he says, showing me his notebook, which is full of pencil drawings of Indian birds and rough sketches of Hindu goddesses.

The back of the notebook has become his address book, because he says that since he's been travelling, he's run out of space. He shows me his parents' addresses in America and Jamaica, so I can write them down, and as he flicks through the book I realize there are hundreds of names in there. Joel seems to be friends with the whole world, and his friends seem to move around, like him. Their addresses are repeatedly scratched out as their phone numbers change from Australia to India to New Zealand to Thailand and back again.

He shakes out his bag to find photographs of his parents, so he can show my mother later.

'Your mother's cut her hair,' I comment.

'Oh, it's really short now. It used to be down to her waist.'

'Your dad still looks so much like my dad.'

'That's his old house in San Francisco. He's moved into this great apartment now.'

After he shows me the photographs, out come more tennis shoes, seagull feathers, little velvet pouch bags and a plastic bag full of tiny orange seeds.

'What's that?' I ask.

'Invisibility seeds. The Tibetans use them to become invisible when they escape from China across the border. They've been blessed in a special ceremony. You carry them with you and the guards don't see you. They were given to me before I left. I thought they might come in useful.'

I realize how relieved I am that Nash is not here now. There are some conversations that can never happen in his presence, and this is one of them.

'Do you mean you actually become invisible?'

'Well it's an interesting thing,' Joel says. 'Think about the people in here now, in this tea room. How many of them can you actually say you've seen and noticed?'

'About one,' I tell him, realizing it is a curly-haired child in the corner who looks a bit like Nash.

'Technically speaking, then, everybody else in here is invisible to you. That's what the seeds do. The Chinese guards see the Tibetans, but they don't. It's a very strange phenomenon, unique to their culture.'

'Why would *you* need to become invisible?' I ask him.

'Well,' Joel gives me an embarrassed half smile, 'I like being alone.'

We try to ring Robyn, because Joel has promised me he will be there for moral support when I tell her about all my mad new plans. When we ring her hotel in Bali, though, she's out.

'Probably clubbing,' Joel says.

He makes a quick sketch of the ceilings in the tea rooms, and then we walk back to my mother's house. I wonder what Nash is doing in Swiss Cottage. Maybe he's at the pub with The Believers – and Lisa.

I'm trying not to think about Sarah.

'Stop thinking,' Joel says, tapping the side of my head.

'All I ever do is imagine what could be going wrong.'

'Imagine what might go right for you, Alice. Come on. You're at the beginning of the biggest trip of your life. Don't weigh yourself down by packing all your old head baggage.'

My cousin has a strange accent, half Australian, half something else. He also has a funny, rhythmic way of speaking. When he talks to me, though, he looks straight at me, as if he's trying to read me, as if I were a book.

'It's funny that you've got invisibility seeds,' I say as we begin the long walk up the hill, past a row of doctors' surgeries to my mother's house.

'Why is that?'

'I want the opposite of them. Visibility seeds. I suppose the Tibetans don't really need those.'

'They have something that performs a similar function. Why, do you feel invisible?'

'It was only when I read the book I was telling you about – *Should I Stay or Should I Go?* – I found this question about *mattering*, about being seen, being important. And I realized Nash didn't see me at all, except in relation to him. It was like this bell going off in my head.'

'Yep.'

'So now I want to be visible again, that's all.'

'You don't need any seeds,' Joel says. 'Here—'

He snaps a photograph of me on his mad old-fashioned seventies Polaroid camera, which he picked up from a stall in Mumbai, along with a shoebox full of old film.

'Instant gratification,' I tell him, watching the developing photograph slide out of the bottom of the camera. 'I used to love these.'

'So did my dad. I always promised myself I'd have one of my own when I grew up. The white border is the great thing,' Joel says. 'And these Polaroids have a way of capturing light that you don't see in other cameras.'

I watch and wait while I sit on someone's wall and get my breath back – the hill is impossible – and finally the photograph dries.

'There,' Joel hands it to me. 'You're a very long way from invisible.'

He has made me look wonderful. My hair is golden-white and my face looks pure and demure. It's a lovely photograph. It must be over a year since anyone took a photograph of me. He puts it in his pocket.

'Nearly there,' Joel swings his bag over his back and strides off again. He is much fitter than me and my legs are beginning to ache from the three-hour walk.

We get home to find my mother has also been looking for old Templeton family photographs and is surrounded by mountains of them all over the sitting-room floor.

'I'm looking for pictures of you and Robyn when you were children,' she tells Joel, getting up to kiss him on the cheek. 'You probably haven't seen them before. They're all Polaroids. Roland and Helena used to post them to us.'

'Fantastic. I'd love to see them. I keep my photos in scrapbooks,' Joel says, 'along with other stuff – like letters, tickets and pressed flowers.'

Joel shows her the large notebook in his bag, and the

torn-off maps and scraps of Indian sari fabric he has glued in, along with some handwritten diary entries.

'I do like a scrapbook. Oh, Alice,' my mother adds, 'would you mind helping me with supper?'

I follow her into the kitchen and she closes the door.

'Do you think Joel may be gay?' she asks, looking worried.

I laugh at her. 'Because of the scrapbook? Mum! He had a girlfriend for years.'

'Oh, thank goodness.'

'I've sorted things out, by the way.'

'How?' my mother looks as if she's going to burst. 'How did you sort things out?'

'I'm going to Australia. I'm moving. I'm leaving when I was supposed to leave, next week.'

There, it's out.

'Oh dear. I have lip wobble,' Mum says, trying to keep her mouth in place with one finger.

'Don't.'

She sits down on the kitchen chair and allows herself a few seconds of crying time before she sniffs and wipes her eyes on an oven glove.

'I'm glad you're going to Sydney after all,' she says, jutting out her jaw. 'Joel is absolutely right. Now, let me tell you what I've done about Nash.'

'What?'

'I've paid him off,' Mum says quickly. 'I used your father's emergency money to pay him off, and now you need never hear from him again. Unless you want to, of course.'

'Mum!'

'It's all done, and the rest of Dad's money has gone into one of those accounts where they forbid you to touch it. So that's that.'

'*Mum!*'

'And you are not to waste any more time putting money in jam jars for me. It's forgotten.'

She turns her back, bends down and checks the roast duck in the oven.

There is no point in arguing with her. When my mother's mind is made up, it's impossible to persuade her otherwise. She's wrong about the jam jars, though. For every week that I work at Barks of Byron Bay, I'll put half the money aside for her.

'I hope Joel likes his meat well done,' she says, prodding the duck with a skewer.

'He's vegetarian, remember?'

'Oh my giddy aunt!' She nearly drops the duck, while I scoop the roast potatoes out, and put them in a bowl with some salad leaves.

I find Joel sitting cross-legged on the floor in the sitting room, while he sorts my parents' old photographs into something resembling chronological order.

The photographs begin with my grandmother in the 1930s, as a child, and go right up to my first Christmas with Nash.

I made our Christmas cake that day. It was chocolate and I made the snow out of real coconut.

I cannot even remember what I was thinking or feeling in that photograph. I look nauseatingly smug, though, to have Nash by my side. I also look as if I'm waiting for my future self to tap me on the shoulder and tell me everything I could not possibly have known then.

'I'm daydreaming in that one,' I tell Joel. 'I'm not even there.'

'Look at this.' Joel points to an old photograph of himself dressed up as a goth. 'That was my birthday party in Sydney. I thought I was Nick Cave and all the members of The Cure at the same time.'

'The black lipstick's good.'

'Here's one from America a couple of years later,' Joel shows me. 'See the difference? Before deep-fried doughnuts and after deep-fried doughnuts.'

'You have a lovely mullet, too. Is that Robyn standing behind you?'

'Oh yeah. She had a pink fringe then.'

'Your parents let you try everything.'

'Yeah.' Joel raises his eyebrows.

I wonder if that's one of the reasons Joel has so many rules. Not only does he refuse to eat meat, he also boycotts television news, credit cards and deodorant. I have seen what he uses for deodorant, it's a crystal rock.

Despite this, he always smells fantastic. He chews on Indian cardamom seeds, which he keeps in a little bag in his pocket, and uses some kind of soap which makes him smell of lemons.

My mother brings in supper, and then she and I spend the rest of the night looking for photographs of all the other Templetons to show Joel. We discover an ancient picture of Roland and Hippy Helena at their barefoot wedding in a park in London, then one of Robyn as a baby.

Joel asks if he can get some copies before he flies to Bangkok – his last stop before Sydney – then says his jet lag is beginning to kick in, so we let him go to bed.

Later on, when my mother has gone to bed, I look at an Australian dating website.

What are Australian men really like? I've heard so many differing opinions that it's hard to know what to believe.

I log onto the site, which promises that over a million single people are waiting to meet me. Hurrah! Then I look at the first four men in the top row and change my mind.

One calls himself Mr Paradox. In actual fact his name should be Mr Dickhead.

One has a full and varied life, except he doesn't.

One says his mother-in-law put a curse on him.

One has gum-diseasey teeth.

Oh God. I knew if I left Nash it would be like this. It's like hurtling back to the late 1990s all over again. Single life on the internet. Bad photos. Dreadful fake names. Boring hobbies.

Interesting things happen when you go down an age bracket, though. Australian men in their twenties are a completely different proposition.

There is a Piscean who likes Robert De Niro and parachuting and is inarguably gorgeous. There is a

177cm tall surfboard maker who has no baggage and likes crap jokes and red wine. There is also another 177cm tall person – a 25-year-old art teacher who loves giving massages (yes! yes!).

The photographs all seem to be taken on the brightest of sunny days, and in two of them I can see spectacular beaches in the background. When I go to bed, I catch myself humming.

The next morning, Joel turns on his laptop and finds my dating site still bookmarked in the margins. I go pink and pretend I was looking for Suzanne.

'Oh, she'll love Australian men.' He grins.

I farewell my mother for the second-last time. The next time I see her – hopefully – I will be at Heathrow with my luggage, passport and Australian visa.

'Bye, darling.' She kisses me on the cheek, then she puts a bar of chocolate in each of Joel's coat pockets and makes him promise to write when he gets to Bangkok.

'I'm going to get on the Google,' she warns him. 'So you'll be hearing from me.'

On the way to Brighton Station, Joel gives me one final pep talk about Australia. Even though we are both going in the same direction, we will be on different trains – me on the fast train to Victoria, and him on another to Bedford, where he's going to see some old friends from India.

'What you're about to do would scare a lot of other people,' Joel tells me, 'but you're going to have the trip of your life. Just go into Australia House, look like you mean it and get every single thing you need to do this journey.'

'Every single thing I need,' I echo.

'I'm going to see you in Sydney,' he promises me, kissing me on the cheek. 'I may be off air for a while, but I'll still be out there.'

'Thank you. Thank you so much, Joel. You have no idea.'

'Don't change your mind or I'll blardy murda ya,' he says, suddenly sounding Australian.

On the train from Brighton to Victoria I feel as if I've already gone for ever. I have detached from England, even as it disappears behind me through the train windows.

My handbag is full of scribbled notes and sketches from my cousin, and the names of people he wants me to find once I reach Australia.

Many of the names are male, and I can't help but wonder if somewhere on this roll call of Joel's most trusted and long-established friends there might be someone who is right for me.

It was nice seeing Mr Pisces and Mr 177cm on the website last night – it's given me hope – but still. Once I've begun my new single life in Sydney I'm going to need all the help I can get.

I check my texts. Heidi Coles is expecting to see me for lunch, at the same café near the Strand where Nash and I met all those weeks ago. She says she's going to tell me more about Barks of Byron Bay, because Danielle gave her a debriefing session over the weekend. After that, she says we can whip through all my last questions about the big move.

I feel guilty because I haven't told her that Nash and I have broken up, but I'm also counting on her being Nice Heidi and coming to my rescue one last time.

At 1 p.m. we meet outside the café, and I put an envelope containing a cheque in her hand, and give her the largest bottle of champagne I was able to find at the train station.

'Nash and I didn't actually celebrate in the end,' I tell her as we find a table, 'but thanks.'

'Oh. Wow! Thank *you*. You didn't celebrate?'

'We split up. I'm going to Australia by myself.'

'Faark!' she stops, with a cup of coffee halfway to her nose.

'I left him. He slept with his ex-wife. And he wanted to stay here anyway. He got a job in London at the last minute and changed his mind. Anyway, it was always bad with us; you know what we were like.'

'You poor gerl!'

'It's OK. I'm OK. But I need to ask you, can I still go? I've read the small print on the paperwork, and so has Mum and my cousin Joel, but I need to check.'

'Oooh,' Heidi says. 'Hard one.'

'Please don't say that.'

'Hard one, but I think you'll be OK. You were fast-tracked anyway, right?'

'Yes.'

'OK. What you need now is a fax from Danielle saying she's going to be your guarantor as your employer.

I'll talk to her. You're going to have to be permanent full-time, though. Full wage. All that stuff. Shit. You must be flying soon. When are you going?'

'Friday.'

'What does Nash say?'

'He doesn't know. And I don't care. He can't stop me, can he?'

'Not unless he physically throws himself under the wheels of the plane. No, Alice. They're not interested in him any more. They're only going to be interested in you.'

'Am I enough, though?'

Heidi gives me her customary kind look and I immediately panic, because I know she's seen my file at Australia House and I am not enough – not by a long shot.

I have made pottery, sold candles, cleaned houses, cooked toasted sandwiches, walked dogs, made soap, played a nun in an advert, sold vintage clothing, and even been a woman with a key in my back, but I am still not enough for Australia, not even with my jacket in Suzanne's magazine and Vera Van Der Meer's business card in my purse.

'Shall I tell you something about Australia?' Heidi says, when she sees my face. 'Everything is upside down there. Nothing is the same as it is anywhere else. So just when you think you can predict what's going to happen in Australia, or what Australians are going to do about anything, you can't. Think of the impossible, and in Australia it's possible.'

'So you're saying that even though it makes sense that they'd turn me down, they might not?'

'Exactly. Life is the other way round over there. Like a platypus. It's a furry thing with a pouch that lays eggs and swims. What's all that about? What I'm saying is, nothing will be what you expect, so expect the worst and you'll probably get the best.'

'Really?'

'Rilly.'

Heidi joins the queue at the counter for sandwiches and coffee, but I don't follow her because I'm feeling too sick with nerves to eat.

While I wait for her, I try to recapture the way I felt when I was sitting on the hill with Joel, looking over the South Downs towards the sea and talking about how everything was possible, and everything was meant to be, and everything would work.

I flick through an old newspaper that's covered in food stains. I see that we are expecting floods again and David Beckham's foot has not yet healed.

I remember Joel's photographs of those beautiful places in Australia – Merimbula, and Mole Creek, Kakadu and Alice Springs. All that space. All that light, all that freedom.

If I find out they won't have me in Australia, I'll go to Wales, or Canada. But I know one thing, I am never again cramming myself into a train full of sardine-humans in London the way I did this morning, so I can go to a café where the only vacant table is one covered in other people's used tissues.

The queue isn't moving. Instead it has come to a stop because there is a flap on behind the counter. The baristas are confused about something, and . . . I'm fed up with that too. Everyone in this country seems to be confused about almost everything, all the time, like the post office at Christmas.

No wonder I get headaches living here. Every question that needs answering in my life has to go through to a call centre. Nobody ever has a name, nobody ever knows anything and nobody takes responsibility. Everyone and everything is on hold. Including the banks.

My God. I really do have to get out. I can't stay in this relationship with England any longer – she doesn't deserve to have me hanging around, moaning about her.

Heidi pulls a 'What can you do?' face at me from the queue as some of the people behind her start tutting theatrically and walking out. Suddenly I feel guilty. This is her lunch hour. She must be starving, and I have made her come here to meet me at in the worst café in the world.

My phone rings. It's an unlisted number. Lisa? I hope not. I'm not sure I could cope with her now. But I don't know anybody with an unlisted number.

I take the call with a deep breath, but it's not Lisa, it's Robyn. She is ringing me from Bali, in the middle of the night, because she cannot sleep. She says she only just got the message I left at her hotel because she's been on a surfing trip.

'I'm really sorry, Robyn,' I tell her, watching Heidi stand on one foot and then the other in the queue.

'What?'

'Nash and I have broken up. I want to come over there, but I'm not sure I can. I'm with Heidi Coles now – the woman from Australia House. We're trying to sort it all out.'

'Put her on,' Robyn snaps. She sounds like a sergeant major in the Australian army.

I take the phone over to the queue, bumping into the people storming out. Whatever flap is taking place behind the counter has now assumed epic proportions, as one barista appears to be sitting on the floor with her head between her knees. Perhaps she's just been put on hold by a call centre in India and is trying to suffocate herself.

'Crazy,' Heidi tuts. 'Hey, who's on your phone?'

'My cousin Robyn.'

A rapid conversation follows between them, spoken entirely in Australian.

'Yeah,' Heidi says. 'He's one thermos short of a picnic. Definitely. What? Bugger that. Well, why doesn't she get her arse into gear and just do it? Yeah, well *he's* as mad as a cut snake. Rilly? That's rooted. Yeah, todarly rooted.'

The whole queue is now listening, trying to decode this strange new language, spoken at great speed, but Heidi doesn't notice. Instead, she just talks faster, standing on one foot and then the other.

It's quite a different accent, and a different vocabulary, to the one she uses with English people.

'Yeah, well, Robyn,' she says. '*If* she bungs it on then

it should be OK. Yeah. Well it's a one-horse town, for sure. Yeah. Yeah. Up to my eyeballs. All right then. Not this little black duck. Well. No worries. OK then. See ya later.'

Finally, she ends the call and smiles at me.

'I don't think you realized your cousin was a lesbian.'

The queue reels.

'What?'

'Robyn is a lesbian, and so is the woman who happens to be the Director of Australian Immigration. And she's seriously got the hots for your cousin, so we both reckon—'

'Yes?'

'You're totally fine.'

'Really?'

'Rilly. It's just going to take one phone call. The only thing is, when you start the job at Byron Bay, my Auntie Danielle's got this bugger of a dog called Mr Chang. He's a Pekinese. Permanent weekend resident. Watch out for him. He comes with his own incontinence cushion.'

I smile at her. Then the smile turns into a laugh.

'I told you Australia wasn't like anywhere else,' Heidi says. 'Now, are we going to get a proper lunch or what?'

Chapter Nine

Whenever my mother is forced to take the car to London, she gets so nervous about the drive up the M23 that she has to take herbal tranquillizers from the health food shop.

Her parting gesture at Heathrow Airport was to take two, put them in a plastic bag and hide them in my coat pocket. That was about eight hours ago. My coat is now rolled into a sausage shape, behind my head, and I am wide awake on Flight KA338 to Sydney, having been comatose – in a lovely, natural, herbal way of course – for most of the trip.

The first thing I'm going to do in Sydney is ring Mum to find out what was in the pills. They must have contained some kind of general anaesthetic because I have no memory of take-off beyond a recorded announcement – first in Korean, then in English – about storing my hand luggage underneath the seat in front of me and being careful when storing my bags in the overhead locker. The flight attendant pronounced this as overhead rocker, which Nash would have laughed at – I've really got to stop thinking about Nash.

I am starving. When was dinner? Where did the trolley go? The Korean woman in the window seat is asleep, with her head pressed against the window. There's a spare seat between us, which I suppose should have been Nash's, and it is piled high with her magazines – all in Korean, so there is no point in asking if I can borrow them – moisturizer and bottled water.

I summon up the courage to press the button with a cartoon figure of a triangular woman on the front of it, and amazingly enough, a non-triangular flight attendant appears three-quarters of an hour later.

Everyone else in the cabin is asleep. Most of them seem to be Korean. We are stopping at Seoul to refuel, then flying straight through to Sydney. The total journey time is twenty-five hours – the longest I've ever spent sitting in one seat.

I suppose my four suitcases are down there somewhere in the hold. The excess baggage charge was enormous at Heathrow Airport. It was London's last big cash extraction before I was able to say goodbye.

My mother was so zonked on herbal tranquillizers at the airport that she seemed to move like the real Lady Penelope – Nash would have been pleased. When she waved goodbye, her arm jerked up and down as if it was on strings, and her little legs seemed to jerk around in their beige trousers, as if controlled by hidden wires.

I hope she's all right now. I have to stop worrying about her. I suppose she just drove back to Hove and went straight to bed.

I look at the empty seat and wonder if Nash has found out about my girl's own adventure yet. I'm sure Mum will have emailed him for the sheer thrill of shocking him. When we were waiting for my flight, Mum forced me to go to an internet kiosk and sign her up for Hotmail – email address pennytempleton1945 – so she could enter the wonderful world of what she still insists is called the Google.

I gave her Nash's email address as well as my own, so who knows, maybe he's been fully informed of my great escape by my mother on her first foray into cyber-space.

The herbal tranquillizers have had a powerful effect on my central nervous system. I feel incredibly calm and detached about the events of the last two weeks, although I still have a cluster headache on the left side of my skull.

Of course, that may be Suzanne's fault. Her parting gift to me was a bottle of vodka, which we consumed without the necessary twenty-five glasses of water and four vitamin B tablets to negate the alcohol content.

The flight attendant brings me some aspirin, something that sounds like Bing Bang Yap and some extremely salty soup. I wolf it down and try not to be annoyed about the man in front, who has pushed his seat all the way back to my knees.

If my mother has not been able to tell Nash about my trip by email, he will probably find out for himself soon enough when he telephones Australia House. I love the fact that he never even contemplated the possibility that I would use my ticket. If he has found out, I expect he will already be predicting with Richard and Michael the date of my imminent return. I can just see him now, being smug about me: 'Alice will be back by Easter.' 'My ex will probably be back when she runs out of money.' 'Alice doesn't know anyone over there. She won't like it.'

Lisa has left The Believers quiz team, of course. I found out yesterday when I rang Richard to offer him my old chest of drawers. Richard asked me how I felt about it and I had to say I had no idea.

That's when he told me Sarah was joining.

'What?'

'Because we're two down, after you and Lisa, Nash thought we should maybe get Sarah on board.'

'Of course he did.'

I try to forget about Sarah and get out my *G'day Australia* book instead.

There's a scary back section with a list of dangerous spiders and snakes and a full inventory of sharks and jellyfish.

Nash always said the spiders would put me off Australia, and although I hate to admit it, he is right.

The back section of the *G'day Australia* book is called 'Everything you wanted to know about biting, stinging things but were too paralysed with fear to ask.' At least that's what Nash thought it should be called. The official title is, of course, 'Everything Australian that can sneak up behind you and cause agonizing death when you're on a picnic.'

The sneakiest creature of all seems to be a bluebottle. Not so much a character in my father's old *Goon Show* tapes, but a slimy jellyfish which is in fact, blue, and likes to travel in packs. It can be found all along the east coast of Australia. So pretty much where I'm going then. I think I'll stick to the swimming pool at Bondi Beach, the one with the three old people in it. At least they're unlikely to have detachable blue tentacles.

I have a close look at the pointy-headed red-bellied black snake. It is the Morticia Addams of the snake world. After that, I look at the King Brown. If it bites you, you'll die. It can be aggressive, the chart says, and has been known to give chase.

Bloody hell. *Where* does it give chase? Up the escalators at Sydney Airport?

The book has a full-colour wall chart with all these disgusting creatures on it. God knows why you'd want to stick that on the wall.

The chart says that the dangerous red-backed spider hides underneath loo seats and has killed about a dozen people. I suppose once you've been bitten on the bottom you're too embarrassed to call for help, so death is inevitable. The chart says the funnel-web spider also likes bathrooms, but particularly bedrooms, and has achieved the same evil spider serial-killer tally. It also says that one of the symptoms of being bitten is 'visible signs of anxiety'. Funny that. Surely if you were bitten you'd just kick back on the sofa with a large martini and listen to *The Best of Olivia Newton-John*?

I wish Suzanne was here so I could show her the chart.

The woman next to me is snoring, but it's a comforting sound, a bit like those dolphin noises people sometimes play to send themselves to sleep.

Apparently the Australian taipan snake's venom is so deadly that unless you're near a hospital, you may as well give up. It also turns out that everything Nash told me about snake bites is wrong. You don't wee on your skin to wash off the poison. No, you just use your shirt as a tourniquet, then crawl off, screaming in agony with a snake hanging off your leg and your best Top Shop shirt ruined.

I think about Joel, who has been everywhere in Australia, and is still perfectly healthy. He got away with it, and so will I.

There is no option available to me now except mad optimism. If I allow my basic anxiety about Nash, Sarah, Mum, money, Barks of Byron Bay, Mr Chang the incontinent Pekinese, Robyn and high-powered lesbians in the Department of Australian Immigration to be channelled into a sudden panic about snakes, I will not sleep for the rest of the flight.

The flight attendant brings me a cut-up orange and an after-dinner mint humbug. Because the man in front of me has been mean enough to push his seat right back, I do the same unkind thing to the woman behind me. Her mouth is open and she has a free eye-mask on, though, so I doubt she'll notice.

I check the time, and then I check my heart – the

heart which Joel spoke to me so much about – to see how it's faring. On a scale of one to ten, how much do I miss Nash at the moment and how jealous do I feel of Sarah, now that she has replaced me on our quiz team?

I think about it, long and hard. I probably miss Nash two out of ten and am jealous of Sarah one out of ten. Good. That may change at some point, but at least I can go back to sleep now.

I put on my free eye mask – the one that makes everyone who wears it look like the Lone Korean Ranger – and pass out.

When I wake up again we are at Seoul Airport and the cluster headache is back, with added heart palpitations. There are forms to fill in, and complicated instructions in heavily accented Korean English to listen to. Everything the flight attendant says sounds like Bing Bing Yap. Or are we talking about the menu again?

It seems we are to disembark through something then get back on again at the other end of something, but I have no idea what that something is.

I have to tell them what my job is, on the form. I only wish I knew. Fashion designer? Key woman? Potter? Candle-maker? International youth hostel cleaning supervisor?

In the end, I put boarding kennel attendant, which is what Heidi told me to say.

It's nice to be somewhere that's not Swiss Cottage, although Seoul Airport is a herbal tranquilliser-induced blur. There seem to be lots of noodles, lots of bright lights, and lots of very short women in the loo, as both the sink and the mirror have been pitched at toytown height.

I can only see the bottom half of my face, which is pale, English, scared and spotty, and some of the Bing Bang Yap, which has landed on my T-shirt in hard brown lumps.

I change the last of my English pounds into Australian dollars and hand over a tenner, wondering how long it will take before I actually forget what it looks like. I don't think I'll miss it. What's orange, brown and disappears as soon as you leave the house?

The man behind the counter makes me fill in yet another Korean-English form and gives me two Australian notes – two! – which also have the Queen's head on one side – my mother would be pleased – but fail to feel truly like money because they're blue.

I now have twenty dollars for my ten pounds, and some gold coins. It's like the miracle of the loaves and fishes. I already know what I can buy with that in Australia. I have memorized the prices on their supermarket websites by heart.

One tin of Milo, the strange national cocoa.

One pair of Razzamatazz black tights (no more donkey charity shop for me!)

One copy of *Australian Women's Weekly*, which comes out monthly.

One steak.

You see? I could only get the steak and the tights if this was England. I already feel better. Or I would if I wasn't stuffed full of Bing Bang Yap and my mother's herbal drugs.

I sleepwalk back onto the plane with everyone else, apart from the smokers, who are puffing away in a small glass room halfway down the corridor.

When we are back on the plane for the final leg to Sydney, I start doing my jam-jar sums again. Each time I do them, I slash more off my spending budget, to the point where I appear to be living on free muesli bar samples from the supermarket.

Nevertheless, if I start work at Barks at the end of this month, and stick with the dogs until Christmas – or similar – say, acting in a bad Australian soap opera or making toasted sandwiches in rubber gloves, I will be fine.

I miss Mum already, of course, but if I start crying now I'll never stop. I must remember Joel's final pep talk. I am about to do something that would scare a lot of other people. I have to summon up all the energy I have and use it.

I miss him already, too. It's ridiculous. I've only known him properly for a couple of weeks. One of the things I liked most about Joel was the way he took my World War Two library book seriously. The one with instructions about creating your own kitchen garden and making spinach pie.

'I had some spinach growing on my land in Bellingen,' he said. 'I think it's a great idea.'

Joel used to own a house cow as well, although he didn't actually have a house on his property, he had a two-man tent, so she was more of a Campsite Cow. She was a Friesian called Sunny who gave eight gallons of milk a day – enough for him to make cheese, yoghurt and butter.

Joel said that the neighbours' children used to ride Sunny around the property in exchange for mooing duties.

House cows like you to moo at them apparently. They also like to have their heads rubbed and their backs scratched. I'm sure they would like it if you bought them a foot spa as well. At one point Joel was making thousands of dollars by buying calves from the sale yards, rearing them for six weeks on Sunny's milk, then selling them on. It's this that turned him into a vegetarian, though, and eventually he made sure the only cows he traded in were for milking, not eating.

I'm so tired now, I couldn't possibly do any more provisional budgeting in my head. But imagine if Joel would eventually let me camp on his property in Bellingen and keep a house cow. I think I'd be quite good at mooing duties. It can't be too different to arguing with Nash.

Joel has already offered to buy me a cow as a late Christmas present. And, I know it's ridiculous, but I can't help getting excited about it. Perhaps all I'll need in the end is a cow, a wartime recipe book and a garden full of spinach. That would be worth any amount of mooing.

I close my eyes. I can't wear my Korean Lone Ranger eye mask again; it makes my eyelids sweat.

Then suddenly it seems we are in Sydney. What? Yes, we are definitely in Sydney, and the Korean flight attendant who was so nice to me earlier is poking me with her sharpest middle fingernail.

'We are here,' she says.

I look around me. All the blinds in the plane are up, and there are blankets, old newspapers, abandoned eye masks, empty water bottles and the abandoned detritus of fed up, bored passengers over every seat. There are Korean chocolate wrappers on the floor and old ear plugs scattered over the aisles everywhere you look. Who'd be a flight attendant?

Before I have a chance to thank her, she scoots up to the other end of the plane, then for the next hour and a half I am officially a jet-lag zombie woman.

Because I'm moving to Australia on a work permit, I have to answer more questions than anybody else in the arrivals hall. Have I been in a rural area with Foot and Mouth recently? No. Unless you count the Swiss Cottage laundrette. What are my reasons for coming to Australia? Oh my God. I can't answer that. It was hard enough when Richard and Michael were asking me about it in the pub.

I try to work out what is wrong with the world and realize that everyone is speaking Australian.

'I'm working flat out,' my taxi driver says when I finally clear customs, haul my suitcases off the conveyor belt and fall into the back of his cab. God, it's so bright outside. The sun seems to have been turned up since London.

'Why are you working flat out?' I ask, trying to be polite.

'Ah, it's always like this from Australia Day to Labour Day. Where are you from?'

'England.'

'Where in England?'

'Swiss Cottage.'

'Never heard of it. Is it somewhere near Switzerland?'

He turns the radio up so that we can both listen to a talk show that consists of people ringing up and saying, 'I don't want to make a nuisance of myself,' then proceeding to do just that.

They seem to be speaking a foreign language on the radio. Everyone is deeply concerned about the Shark's groin injury and what it will do to the Broncos next season. There is an ad for Carlton Draught, pronounced Caaaaaarldon Draaaaaught, as if someone is about to be sick. There is a lot of talk about something called Acker Dacker, until I realize it is AC/DC and people are voting for their favourite song.

I see the sun still hasn't been turned down. Joel said the light was dazzling in Sydney, but I had no idea. The buildings seem newer and cleaner, or perhaps they're just painted in paler colours, so the sunshine bounces off the walls and back onto the pavements, which have tiny glittery bits in them, like tinsel.

My taxi driver is deeply flatulent, as Nash would say. He must have been eating cabbage for breakfast. He turns the radio up again, because another caller who doesn't want to make a nuisance of herself is talking about lesbian single mothers.

I immediately think of Robyn and am glad she's lying on a beach in Bali at the moment and not in the back of the taxi with me. I wonder if she wants to be a lesbian single mother?

'Yeah, well, if they want to get up the duff that's no business of mine, but half the time they're drunk as a skunk when they make these decisions,' the caller says.

'Good on ya, mate,' the announcer says.

The taxi crawls through traffic and I watch the red numbers on the meter go up and up. So much for my two ten-dollar notes.

'How much will it cost to get to Bondi?' I ask my driver.

'About three lobsters in this traffic.'

'Thank you.'

I have no idea what he's talking about. I suppose a lobster is a note. Either that or he wants me to pay him in luxury seafood.

I stare out of the windows and recognize bits and pieces of Australian life from the television and the internet. There is a giant poster for Milo. Good. I must be in the right country.

The trees look familiar. They're definitely the kinds of trees you see on television. Flaky, patchy and brown, with dusty green leaves. I look up, like the idiot I am, in the hope of seeing a koala. I hope the taxi driver didn't see me do that.

Is this a country I can stay in? Will this really be my

new home, for ever and ever? It's like trying to decide about men.

Within two hours of meeting Nash, I knew I wanted to be with him. But look where that got me. Maybe I should take a bit longer than that this time to decide about the rest of my life.

'How long are ya here for?' my driver asks.

'Not sure yet. I've got a job in Byron Bay.'

'Beautiful up there,' he says. 'Who ya gonna support in the cricket?'

'England. Australia. England.'

Oh God, I don't even like cricket.

'Better support Pakistan then,' he says, and makes himself laugh so much that another cabbagey emission drifts into the back seat.

At last, we reach Robyn's flat. She lives in Flat 6, 10 Cooper Street, North Bondi. I'm disappointed to see that we don't pass Bondi Beach on the way, but I trust it's out there somewhere, with its packs of surfers, and its avocado-and-scrambled-egg breakfasts.

I give the driver his lobsters and get a handful of change back. I already feel poor again.

The flat is on the third floor of the same modern white building I remember from Robyn's DVD. The carpet is new. There are pot plants outside most of the doors. It doesn't smell of wee. This is definitely not Swiss Cottage.

I have had Robyn's keys clenched in my hand since I got in the taxi. When I push open the door, I'm dazzled by light all over again. Just when you think your eyes have got used to it there's another blinding flash. No wonder everyone here wears sunglasses all the time. The old people wear wrap-around sunglasses so they all look like villains in a science-fiction film.

The flat is completely white. There are white floorboards, white rugs, white bookshelves, white vases with white plastic flowers and even a gigantic white leather sofa. I don't remember it being quite this pristine in Robyn's DVD, but I suppose she's tidied all the stuff away. Or maybe she doesn't have any stuff. I know Joel doesn't.

What do I do first? Drink? Eat? Go to the loo? Put the spa on? Make phone calls? Watch Australian television? Fall in a heap on my bed and go into a prolonged withdrawal from herbal tranquillizers?

I trip over a pile of huge green plastic rubbish bags on the floor and find a note stapled to them.

'Please help yourself to these and give the rest to St Vincent de Paul,' Robyn has written.

Who is St Vincent de Paul? I picture a friend of hers – Italian, bearded, pious – who must have a secret interest in women's clothing, since that's what's inside the bags. Oh no, hang on, there's an address and a phone number. It appears to be a charity shop on Oxford Street in Paddington. That's two familiar names from London already – another thing that used to amuse Nash about the big Australian wall map. When Australians aren't labelling everything twice, it appears they're pinching English place names.

I rummage through the bags. It's like Christmas all over again, although this is a lot better than the one I had in Swiss Cottage. Robyn is throwing out a travel hairdryer, an unopened electric toothbrush and a half-full bottle of expensive shampoo. No Arabic instructions for her. She's also chucking a pedometer, a shopping basket with a tiny hole in it, a tennis racket with Sydney Gay and Lesbian Mardi Gras stickers all over it and a black crêpe Jigsaw skirt. I try it against me for size. No chance.

I suddenly realize that if I stand any longer, I'll fall over, so I sit down on Robyn's white floorboards and empty each bag out in turn. There must be hundreds of pounds – dollars – of stuff in there. How much I am allowed to take, exactly, before I deprive the mysterious St Vincent de Paul?

Robyn is throwing out a fake crocodile-skin mobile phone cover. Suddenly I want it more than anything else in the world. I find my phone in my bag to see if it will fit.

It's been switched off since London. When I turn it on I pick up a text from Suzanne, and hit the call button shortly before realizing it's midnight in London.

'Alice!' she croaks. 'I'm in bed!'

'Guess where I am.'

'Swiss Cottage? Oh no. You're in bloody Australia. Did you? Are you?'

'I'm here. By myself. I just landed.'

'Eeeee!' she squeals.

'I can't talk much. Sorry, my credit's a bit low. The main thing is, I've just let myself into Robyn's flat in

185

Bondi and she's left me this kind of treasure trove of her old stuff. There's a note saying I can keep what I want, as long as I give the rest to charity.'

'Good stuff?' She snaps awake.

'Really good.'

'Ooooh. Alice, I know you're probably jet-lagged up to the eyeballs and very little is making sense, but listen to me very, very carefully.'

'OK.'

'First of all, you *are* a charity at the moment, so don't feel guilty. *Have the lot.* Secondly, I want you to go out tomorrow, buy some rolls of film, go back to Robyn's place and iron every piece of clothing in the bags. Then I want you to pin it all up, piece by piece, on a perfectly ironed large white sheet, and photograph everything individually. Then, darling, I want you to start an eBay account.'

'I can't do that.'

'Yes you can. You can start an eBay account and learn how to do it, and then you can make pregnancy frocks, and have an eBay shop and start your own label, and then – hip, hip, hurray – as God is your witness, you'll never be hungry again!'

Chapter Ten

The time has come to find my way around.

I have inherited a poor grasp of geography from Mum, though, so despite all Robyn's carefully hand-drawn maps, I have no idea where I am in relation to Bondi Beach, the nearest supermarket, a phone box, a bus stop or anywhere else.

The heat in my head, combined with the intense heat of a late Australian summer, seems to have melted whichever brain cells are responsible for navigation. I spin round in the middle of Bondi like a Dalek in a tizzy, getting hotter and hotter.

If I had any money I'd get Australian GPS put on my phone. Instead, I am still looking for an internet café at the end of the week, when I have to give up and lie down exhausted on a bench for a rest.

When I get up again, I see the internet café staring me in the face.

There is a spare computer inside, so I sit down next to two schoolboys playing a computer game where flesh-eating mutants appear to be at war with American GIs.

I thought Australian kids just rode bikes and made friends with kangaroos.

I check my email. Welcome to me, I have 142 new messages. Most of them seem to be from friends who are in shock because they've just heard about my girl's own adventure.

The message from Nash's father is probably the best one to check first, to help me canvass general opinion. He is the person most likely to be offended by my decision to leave his son and run away to Australia, so if I can read his email, I can read anybody's.

He says he is sorry to hear our news, sorry he didn't get a chance to see me at Christmas and sorry that he and Nash's mother did not get the opportunity to give me my present this year – a unique ceramic teapot from the gallery, with a lid like a pumpkin.

I can't even be bothered to write back and tell him about Sarah, Lisa and all the rest of it. Part of me wants to set the record straight in the interests of truth and justice, but the other part just thinks, Go away, Mr Nash, with your cardigan and your big toggle buttons.

There is a picture of the teapot from Nash's parents attached to the email. If I look very carefully I can see the marked-down sale sticker creeping over the base. Thank you very much. I hope you liked my crappy shortbread, too.

I open an email from the person most likely to approve of my sudden departure from Nash and England. It comes from Rosie, an old university friend from Huddersfield who came all the way to our leaving drinks in London. She's always been a free spirit.

Whoops. She is sorry, too. Sorry that I have just fled the country by myself without calling her first. Sorry that I have forgotten some of my oldest friends. Didn't I know she was there for me?

Delete.

On balance, though, most of my friends are in favour and completely understand why I have run away. Almost everyone seems to have heard about Nash's affair with Sarah – and his new job.

There are messages from Heidi and Danielle Coles, checking that I have landed safely and letting me know that everything is in place at Barks, ready for me to begin.

Danielle's email comes inside a special Barks of Byron Bay design box, like a little note. There's a dachshund wearing a crown in one corner and a golden retriever with an orbed sceptre in the other.

My mother has written me her first ever email, which has the following in the subject header: 'Anthony Andrews, Pears Soap, Dad's Bicycle, Overdue Library Books, Nanny and Mango Chutney.'

I read the email over the noise of flesh-eating mutants attacking American soldiers:

Dear Alice,
I see that you must begin every email with a subject. This is rather difficult, as there is so much to tell you in this letter, and there are

so many subjects. Nevertheless, I have done my best.

Anthony Andrews is meant to be holidaying in Australia at the moment. Have you seen him? I saw a photograph of him this week in the *Radio Times*. He has hardly changed since he was in *Brideshead Revisited*.

There is a special offer on Pears Soap at the moment, so I bought twelve for the price of eight. Would you like me to post you some?

I tried to ride Dad's old bicycle the other day to the chemist to buy the soap. Unfortunately I fell off because I was wearing Dad's old Barbour and the cord caught in my spokes.

Nash rang to say you've left some overdue library books in the flat, but he's been unable to reach you by telephone to discuss the fine. Would you mind calling him? (I'm so sorry to have to pass this on, Alice, I do realize he is a complete wanker.)

My God. I had no idea that word was even in my mother's vocabulary, but there it is, in black and white. She continues:

My Nanny had a marvellous recipe for mango chutney which I will send you in my next email. Now that you are in Australia I am sure you can buy mangoes very cheaply.

All my love, Mummy xx

I move on to Nash's emails, even though I'm thinking about Joel as I read them.

He is annoyed that he cannot get me on the phone and wishes I would switch it on again. Is it because I have run out of credit as usual?

Oh, shut up.

He is sorry about Sarah (again) and wants me to know that if it hadn't been for the breakdown in our relationship, he would not have been tempted. It meant nothing to her and it means nothing to him.

He says he will post me all the stuff I left behind if I send him the money to pay the shipping company.

Finally, he wants me to know how much he still cares about me, and that when things go wrong in Australia I only have to call.

When things go wrong? He clearly wants me to be eaten alive by a shark, feet first, just so I can call him and he can be smug down the phone from Romney College, while my lower limbs are being severed from my torso to the der-der der-der *Jaws* soundtrack.

There is nothing about the fact that Lisa is no longer in The Believers (the team or the band) and nothing about Sarah replacing her on quiz nights either. Well, *quelle* bloody *suprise*, as Suzanne always says.

After that, it's time to sell Robyn's stuff on eBay.

I feel guilty, embarrassed and ashamed, but I am also desperate. Perhaps there's no point in even pretending any more. I'm at her mercy. If I don't get some dollars on my credit card soon I'm going to be in serious trouble, and this time there's no Nash to bail me out.

I am too scared to open an Australian bank account yet – just the thought of the forms is enough to put me off. Sydney isn't as cheap as I expected, either. I was completely mad getting a taxi from the airport, though I didn't have much choice because of my luggage – it cost me half my weekly food budget.

I log on and try to register as a seller. It takes four attempts because I can't understand the wavy words at the end.

Tharways?

Pernifor?

Weebur?

Isbun?

When I finally master this, the computer makes a sad little 'beee' sound, trailing off at the end, and crashes.

I sit back in my seat and breathe out, then suddenly there is another sad little 'beeee' sound, and the screen goes black. 'Bloody computer.' I kick the grey plastic box under the desk.

'Speak nicely to it. Don't kick it like that.' The voice is English – you cannot hear the letter 't' at all.

I turn around and see a tall, tanned man wearing a Ben Sherman shirt and cut-off denim shorts. He is ridiculously good-looking in an untrustworthy kind of way.

'Sorry. I've just had enough,' I tell him.

'They'll kick you out of here if you kick the computer,' the man says. 'What's the problem?'

'I can't do the eBay code thing.'

'I can sell it for you.'

'Can you?' Oh no. A cockney cyber-spiv. I've come halfway around the world and run into a character from a Guy Ritchie film.

'I take twenty per cent and sit here doing it all so you don't have to.' The man holds out his hand for me to shake it and tells me his name is Matty.

'Alice,' I tell him, wishing it wasn't such a drivelly posh name.

'Are you interested then?' he asks.

I look at the wavy passwords. There's no contest really. It has to be Matty.

'It's just stuff from my cousin's flat, really. Before I move to Byron Bay.'

'Nice. I love it up in Byron. I live just round the corner. Drop in any time. It's a party house. Very friendly. What did you do in London then?'

'A bit of everything.'

I really shouldn't be talking like this to a complete stranger, but Matty is the first human being I've had a proper conversation with since I landed.

'There's nothing wrong with a bit of everything,' he says, putting his trainer on the side of my chair so I can admire the inside of his tanned, lightly fuzzed thigh. 'I do Bondi Markets as well.'

'Oh, I heard they're really good. My friend Suzanne told me about them. I used to look after her stall in Camden.'

'Ever meet a bloke looking after a second-hand book stall there? Down the back of the market?'

'Yes!'

'That's Alan. He used to live in my manor,' Matty says. 'Why don't you come round now for a cup of tea? You'll like Jade. She's my girlfriend.'

Oh. So I won't be having an ill-advised fling with an eBay trader, then.

'We've got an open relationship,' Matty continues. 'Anyway. Maybe you can take over the stall when she goes to Perth. We'll 'ave a talk about it.'

Aha, so Jade is going to Perth and Matty wants to let me know they have an open relationship. Very well then. Matty has quite a kissable mouth, actually, if you can overlook the number of drugs he's crammed down his gullet. Oh, stop it, Alice. I just haven't had sex in a while, that's all.

I glance at Matty's business card. It hasn't been printed on a machine at a supermarket as I'd feared. It looks serious, glossy and expensive. Matthew Riddup – Web Commerce. I'm surprised he hasn't engraved the word 'Diamond Geezer' in copperplate below his name.

'Thanks,' I say and follow him out. I'll be really annoyed if I accompany Matty back to his flat and discover that he and Jade are the Bondi Beach equivalent of Fred and Rosemary West.

Matty recognizes at least three people on the way back to his flat.

''Allo Charlotte, all right?' he says to a girl in a sarong.

'John! Wot you up to then?' He gives a bald man a thumbs-up.

'Phil! Over ere!' He waves across the street.

He reminds me of an old boyfriend of Suzanne's who was a roadie for some Britpop band who have since disappeared. She now refers to him as Ageing Lad. Matty is too young for that, but he is certainly keeping laddism alive in this distant corner of the world. I sense that for Matty there will always be some far corner of a foreign field that is for ever *Loaded*.

We get into the lift in his building and I am overwhelmed by Matty's aftershave, or is it cologne *and* deodorant? I can just imagine what his bathroom looks like.

He presses the button marked Penthouse and tries not to look smug. I don't think I've ever been in a penthouse before. I steel myself for potted palms, polar bear rugs and sofas shaped like lips.

Their flat is like Robyn's – a white, light-filled shell – although it's about five times the size. There are ashtrays everywhere, along with bits of clothing, odd trainers, empty CD cases and old pizza boxes. And – hey I was right! – old copies of *Loaded*.

Matty tells me they are looking after it for a friend of theirs who has gone travelling. I guess that things like this happen to him all the time.

Jade appears and offers to put the kettle on. She is a stunning six-foot black supermodel. I wish Matty had given me some kind of warning. If they are having an open relationship, he's certainly doing all right out of it.

'Alice is from Camden.' Matty introduces me, and I don't bother to correct him.

'I used to work on the markets there,' I tell Jade. 'I looked after my friend's stall. Just vintage clothing, that kind of stuff.'

'Up the back?' Jade enquires, crossing her legs.

'Yes. Her name's Suzanne. The stall had Union Jacks all over it.'

'I love that place!' Jade shrieks, and waggles her foot at me in its giant platform sandal. 'These are Terry de Havilland,' she says proudly. 'I got them last trip.'

'They're amazing.'

'So what you up to in Bondi then?' Jade asks, switching the kettle on.

'I said she should help you out on the stall when you go away,' Matty cuts in.

'That would be nice,' Jade agrees. 'I want to go to Perth. Oh, baby, I am so dying to go to Perth! I want to see some dolphins.'

Matty brings out a bowl of jelly babies while we're waiting for the kettle to boil and gives me an intense look. He appears to be waiting for some kind of reaction.

Are they special jelly babies? Do they have Matty and Jade's cocaine stash sprinkled on them? Then I realize they're proper Basset's jelly babies. Rare exotica in Australia.

'Fantastic. It's so nice to see these again,' I tell him, and he passes the bowl to Jade, satisfied.

'You been down to Bronte yet?' Jade asks me with a mouth full of jelly babies. I thought supermodels weren't supposed to eat that kind of thing.

'No. Should I go?'

'Get yourself down there' – Matty takes over, pointing through the window – 'and follow that path along the clifftop. There are signs everywhere. See that swimming pool underneath Icebergs?'

'Icebergs has the most fantastic bar,' Jade interrupts him.

'Yeah, well, just get yourself as far as the cliff path and go from there.'

Oh no. More incomprehensible Australian directions. I've been following this kind of well-meant navigational advice for a week. You have to pretend you understand when people are trying to help you, though, or they get offended.

'Thanks, Matty. I might try Bronte this afternoon—'

'Watch out for the yucky lizard sculptures, though,' Jade interrupts.

'Yeah, watch out for them,' Matty adds. 'Jade thought they were real. Nearly fell off the cliff. Keep walking and you'll get to a beach called Tamarama. Don't go swimming there, though, cos you'll drown. Keep going and you'll end up at Bronte.'

'Tell her about the blue jellyfish, Matty.'

'Yeah. If you see people running about screaming with red marks on their legs and little blue tentacles on the sand, get straight outta the water.'

'OK,' I promise. I decide I'm never, ever going to walk to Bronte.

I finish my tea and Matty and Jade invite me to watch

EastEnders with them. Jade's sister sends them DVDs from London every week.

'I'd absolutely love to, but I think I should go back and sort out this stuff for eBay.'

'Oh yeah,' Matty remembers. 'Well, when you've got it sorted, give us a call and I'll come and get it. We take the photos, do the auction, post it out, the lot.'

'Wow. Thanks.'

I wonder which English backpacker minion he employs to do all that for him?

They walk me to the lift and I am asphyxiated by Matty's aftershave all over again. I wonder if Jade dresses like this every day – tiny denim shorts, platform shoes, transparent pink shirt – and what the locals think of her. They probably love her. Maybe they think she's Naomi Campbell, especially when she puts on her enormous sunglasses.

Once I'm outside again I decide the time has come to draw my own map of my new home town. I can't understand Robyn's tiny drawings, and her Sydney street directory is mental torture.

I have already worked out the only things I need to find in Bondi, and they are the bank, the supermarket, the phone box, the internet café, the sea, the funny little street with all the great shops I can't afford and the bus stop.

It takes me all afternoon, but finally I manage it. You've just got to stop mixing it up with Brighton or Blackpool, that's all.

Will there ever come a day when I know where

everything is? Australia is so vast it seems impossible. Bondi is sprawling, Sydney is vast. No wonder my taxi driver had to look up Robyn's street in his directory. In London, they know where everything is.

I go back to the flat and sort through the pile of rubbish bags again. I have already taken a discreet glance at the clothes my cousin actually possesses, so I am not surprised that she can afford to throw out so much stuff. Robyn has a wardrobe like a boutique. You walk in one door and out another. She has an entire cupboard just for shoes.

Her bathroom is like a small section of the cosmetics department at Selfridge's. Her book case would make the librarian at Swiss Cottage weep.

I have no doubt at all that my cousin is well off. It's quite different from English well off, though. Everything about this flat is new, while everything about rich English homes is very, very old.

I need a swim. It's hot enough now, and anyway, I'm Australian these days. It's what they do.

The Bondi Baths are built on a cliff jutting out over the sea. It's not like any public pool I've ever seen. There is no smell of chlorine, no posters about disgusting verrucas and no cackling fat boys with tight nylon trunks and bottom cleavage belly-flopping into the shallow end. Best of all, there is nobody in the pool at all, just one man with the body of a Greek god, slogging up and down in the far lane.

I am so used to having to jostle for space in London that it's hard to believe I can have a lane all to myself, or even make a leisurely decision to swim under the ropes and choose another one.

I get changed, try to ignore how white my body is and get in the water. It's clean and cool, and within minutes it starts to feel warm. The sky is blue, and the sea is too. I have space above me and space all around me. Lovely, lovely *space*, a million miles from my horrible relationship with Nash. I have absolutely no idea what I'm doing here yet, or even who I am any more, but why would I want to be anywhere else?

With every lap, the fines on my overdue library books in Swiss Cottage – oh you wicked woman, Miss A. Templeton – seem further and further away.

When I'm doing backstroke, I look up and see glamorous people in sunglasses standing above me at the bar having cocktails. This never happens at the Tooting Bec Lido.

I suppose Matty and Jade come down here all the time and do laps. Or maybe it's just Matty by himself. I allow myself a small, forbidden fantasy that he might come along for a swim one day – when I have developed a suntan and bought a stunning pink bikini – and invite me upstairs for a Piña Colada.

Then I get real, get changed and go to the Bondi Beach post office to send my mother a cheque.

Chapter Eleven

I am cleaning Robyn's flat ready for her arrival when the key turns in the door and she bounces in.

'Alice!' she squeals, and as she rushes towards me, I realize she's not wearing a bra. She's like one of those posters for an Australian gym come to life, all muscles, bounce, white teeth and perfect skin.

Robyn has short, jet-black spiky hair, enormous diamond studs in her ears, a pristine white tank top – what my mother would call 'your father's vest' – and black tracksuit pants. Her socks are white, her trainers are white, her watch is white.

She makes me feel so . . . Swiss Cottage International Travellers' Hostel.

I am trying not to think about the lesbian thing, but it's not working – mainly because the first thing she does is unpack her suitcase in front of me, and throw out something that looks like an egg with a long cord and a battery charger. God, is that a vibrator or a piece of kitchen equipment?

'I've got a present for you here somewhere,' she says,

bobbing down on the floor and squatting like a frog. 'Where the blardy hell is it?'

Eventually she pulls a small box out of the zipper compartment at the front. Please let it not be an egg with a battery.

'Balinese pearls,' she explains before I can open the box.

'Robyn, thank you. You really shouldn't have.' I put them on immediately, to please her. I suppose she thinks because I'm English I like my jewellery to be the same as Princess Anne's.

Once Robyn has finished unpacking, we sit down and open her duty-free vodka, drinking it with the mint and fresh limes she picked up at the supermarket on the way. My cousin is impressively well organized. I would never have thought of doing that in a million years. I suppose that's what happens when you manage a hotel. You organize everything so that it comes with ice cubes and a swizzle stick.

'Welcome home, Robyn. How was your holiday?'

'Oh, man.' She pushes her hair behind her ears. 'It was fantastic. I just chilled. I did yoga on the beach every day and just hung out. You have to go to Bali, Alice.'

'Well, places like that are so close now that I'm living in Sydney, aren't they?' I say, sounding like my mother.

'So what's the story with Nash?' she assumes a cross-legged yoga position on the sofa.

Aha. The story with Nash. It's something that's best

explained methodically, but instead it all comes out in a mad rush.

'The thing is, he always thought he was better than me. Anyway, basically he had sex in a jacuzzi with his ex-wife Sarah. And this other woman – Lisa, who was on our pub quiz team, lied about it for him. Then he went behind her back and got her old job, so she rang me up and confessed. I really did love him at the beginning, but that was before I realized how awful he is. I got this book out from the library called *Should I Stay or Should I Go?* and in the end, I just thought, Go . . . The only trouble is, when I found out about Nash and his ex-wife, it felt like he'd left *me* first.'

'Wow!' Robyn sympathizes, sitting back on her heels. 'What a total prick.'

It's intensely gratifying to hear someone insult Nash like this, and I savour the moment, until my cousin comes over and starts mini-massaging my shoulders. I try not to leap away because that would be hurtful and insulting, but still, it's a relief when she has to go to the door to let a delivery man in.

'Looky, looky here!' she says, accepting a huge bouquet. Then she checks the note and pulls a face. 'Huh. Just corporate wank as usual: "From all at Phaeton Financial Management Solutions, in appreciation of your efforts at our annual Christmas party."'

She goes off to find some old family photos – more polaroids I haven't seen before. There are three of Joel as a teenager and I have to stop myself lunging at them.

'That's a nice photo of your dad there,' Robyn says.

'He didn't really get on with Roland, did he? My dad was such a hippy back then. Yours was pretty straight, I reckon.'

'I suppose so.'

'So how was Joel when you saw him?'

I go pink. She notices and then I go even pinker and cannot stop. She pours us both another vodka.

'So you saw Joel then?' she tries again, watching for more blushing.

'Yes.' I fight the urge to talk about him. 'Joel came up and stayed with Mum for a while.'

'He really likes you.'

'Oh.'

'No, Alice, he's rilly got a crush on you. I can tell. But I don't think he wants to make a move on you, because he's worried that you'll think it's weird.'

'Well, it is a bit weird.'

'Not rilly. Put some more vodka in that. It's hot today, isn't it? Yeah, I think Joel's holding back because he thinks that *you* think it's all wrong. Even though you're not related at all.'

I hug the secret knowledge that Joel likes me while Robyn sloshes more vodka into my glass. She's just like her brother. Strangely honest and straight to the point, as if all communication has to take place as simply and quickly as possible because it's just too damn hot. Maybe it's an Australian thing. In this climate, you don't want to faff around like everyone seems to in England.

Just look at the way Joel told me about Helena and his faintly embarrassing status as a bastard in the Templeton family. With anyone else – Nash for example – the whole paternity thing would have taken days, even weeks, to uncover. It would have involved complicated tactical manoeuvres, awkward silences, changes of subject and all the other things that usually happen in English life when anything personal is up for discussion. It took Nash five months to tell his parents about me.

Australian television, I have already noticed, is wonderfully unsubtle. There was an ad last night for some kind of herbal pessary for men that consisted of a woman shouting, 'CAN'T GET IT UP? GET THIS UP YER!'

'Oh look, Alice. There's a party on soon,' Robyn says, checking the text messages on her phone. 'There'll be lots of Pommies there. It's their Australian Citizenship celebration. Do you want to go?'

'I'd love to.'

'Hey, how about that chick from the Department of Immigration? She was keen. I had to beat her off with a stick.'

'Do you mean the woman you had to talk to?'

'I had to do more than talk to her.' Robyn smirks. 'But it's cool. She's fallen in love with someone else anyway. Do you know about Dykes on Bikes?'

'No. Sorry.'

'Well anyway. She's in love with one of the dykes. Hey, what are you doing tomorrow morning?'

Robyn's energy is relentless. It is pours out of her like sweat. I feel tired just looking at her.

'I've got to work at Bondi Markets tomorrow morning,' I explain. 'I said I'd help someone out with her stall. She's trying me out, really.'

'Who is she?'

'Her name's Jade.'

'Really gorgeous? English? Black?'

'Yes.'

'See, everyone knows everyone around here.' Robyn jerks a thumb out of the window. 'It's the Bondi mafia or, if you're a lesbian, the Bondi muffia.' She laughs at her own joke.

Wow! So Matty and Jade are having an open relationship and Jade is a lesbian. Or bisexual? I have a sudden mad thought that Jade might actually be a man who's had a sex change – she does have enormous feet – and I'm about to dismiss it when Robyn puts me straight.

'Jade used to be called John in London,' she explains. 'She's a trannie. She came out here to have the operation done because it's cheaper. Everyone's in love with her in my spinning class. She's got a boyfriend, but they're pretty free.'

'Matty.'

'Oh, you met him, did you? Did he try to sell you anything?'

I suddenly remember about the eBay sale and go pink again. I have sworn Matty to secrecy, but if Robyn ever finds out what I've done, I'll never be able to look her in the eye again.

I try to change the subject but she's having none of it.

'Matty's the Sheikh of eBay.' She laughs. 'That's what they call him at the gym. I should have got him to sell all my stuff.' She winks at me.

'Well actually—'

'I saw you beat me to it, though.' She elbows me in the ribs. 'Someone emailed me and said, "How come your tennis racquet's on auction? Good call to ask Matty, though. He rakes it in.'

'Sorry, Robyn.'

'Don't be sorry!' she shrieks at me, looking genuinely shocked. 'I don't care! Hey, you should join our gym. It's called Bondi Hot Bods. Jade and Matty *live* there. It's rilly social. By the way, do you want another voddie? Shall we go out tonight? Do you want to come salsa dancing?'

Robyn and I are about the same age, but she makes me feel very, very old. When I decline, she salsas around the sitting room anyway, clicking her fingers and throwing her head back as if she's in a video.

Right now I just want to lie on my bed and take in what she's just said about Joel. I want to gaze out of the window at the stars above Bondi Beach and daydream.

It's a very, very long time since I've felt like this. I think I'm in love. In lust. Infatuation. Insane, because I have only recently become single and besides, he is my cousin. Maybe I'm just inebriated.

'I'll leave you to it then,' Robyn says once she's changed into the tightest no-bra black dress she can find, and a sparkling pair of gold flip-flops. 'If you want me, I'm on my mobile. Hey!'

I look up.

'It's so great to see you again.' She blows me a kiss from the door. 'I'm *so* glad you're coming to live here.'

The next morning, I am at Jade's stall at Bondi Markets at 7 a.m., as instructed. Jade, however, is nowhere to be seen. Maybe she went to the same nightclub as Robyn.

I sit on the fold-up chair behind the table bearing her name, and a reserved label, and wonder how long I'm going to have to wait.

A man selling goldfish in empty fruit-juice bottles sets up on my left-hand side, and I watch the fish swimming around for a while. I have a terrible headache from Robyn's vodka, and slugging water from the kettle throughout the night had no effect. If I don't find something to drink soon I may become so desperate I'll have to decant a live fish.

There was no sign of Robyn at the flat this morning, so I expect she got lucky. I imagine she probably has dozens of admirers, quite apart from the woman from the Department of Immigration who is now with a dyke on a bike. She told me she is on the Sydney Gay and Lesbian Mardi Gras committee, so I'm sure she has plenty of takers.

While I am enjoying the sun, a psychic sets up her table on my right, using a garden table, umbrella and a padded Victorian balloon-backed chair. She doesn't shave under her arms but she does use a lot of aromatherapy oil; the smell of peppermint and eucalyptus wafting my way is amazing. She's wearing a leotard under her skirt and boots that lace up at the front. A fringed shawl goes over the garden table and a hand-painted sign goes up: 'Blossom Promise's Psychic Readings'.

I think about it. I have never had a psychic reading in my life, but I really want one.

Blossom Promise looks my way and smiles. 'You're better off without him,' she says.

'Sorry?'

'Your man. Better off without him.'

Well, that was a lucky guess. That could have been any man from any point in my history.

'The new one's better,' she continues.

'Really?' I leap on this information.

'Kissing cousins,' she smirks.

Oh. My. God.

'You've got two saints looking after you,' she goes on.

'Which saints?'

Blossom Promise shakes out her fringed shawl and settles herself in the Victorian chair. 'You got Saint Vincent and Saint Martin, sweetie.'

I check to see if the goldfish man is listening to this impromptu psychic reading, but he's too busy on his mobile phone. What does she mean, I have two saints looking after me? I don't even go to church.

'You got St Vincent de Paul and St Martin-in-the-Fields,' she says. Then she closes her eyes and sinks into meditation.

This goes on for some time. I watch, hoping for another prediction – preferably about Joel – but nothing happens.

'Mim, mim, mim,' Blossom chants to herself. 'Mim, mim, mim.'

An official in a bright green vest comes over and moves her on.

'You're in the wrong possie,' he says. 'You're supposed to be at the car-park end.'

'No I'm not,' she confronts him unspiritually.

'This is goods. You're services.' He shoos her along and I catch a flash of hairy armpit as she scoops up all her things.

'You need that book!' Blossom Promise shouts at me, as he shepherds her out with the balloon-backed chair, the umbrella and the fold-up garden table. 'Buy that book!'

Goldfish man smiles at me and twirls his finger on the side of his head. I expect he thinks that Blossom is – what was Heidi's memorable phrase at the café that day? – one Thermos short of a picnic.

I make up my mind to find her later. I want to know about Joel. And after that I need to interrogate Robyn further for some hard, factual, non-psychic information. Why does she think her brother has a crush on me? Was it something he said? Something he wrote in an email? I have to know.

Blossom Promise is just too weird. Perhaps I *was* being looked after by someone up there in heaven on the night I went to St Martin-in-the-Fields, and Heidi found my purse. And without Robyn's rubbish bags for the St Vincent de Paul shop, what on earth would I have done for money? I think about the possibility that my father might be my guardian angel, then dismiss it. He played snooker, drank whiskey and voted Conservative. If there was one thing he couldn't stand, it was people talking about ghosts. He is the last person I would actually expect to become one.

"Allo, Alice!' Jade appears, talking through a cigarette as she hauls a trestle table and two fold-up chairs past the goldfish stall. I try not to look at her breasts or her man-hands. The fingernails might be long and pink, but the fingers are like sausages.

Jade is half an hour late but doesn't mention it. Instead, she's fizzing with good news about her Australian citizenship test. She and Matty passed with flying colours and will be lining up to receive their certificates before what she promises will be the biggest party in Sydney.

'My cousin Robyn told me there was a party on. She goes to your gym. Robyn Templeton.'

'Yeah, we know her. Everyone knows everyone, darling. I'm just gonna get the rest of the stuff from the taxi, all right?' Jade teeters off in her platform sandals, shorts and – a new addition – an ancient oversized Madonna T-shirt.

I recognize it immediately from Robyn's garbage bags and make a mental note to tell her not to wear it in her presence. Matty was supposed to have sold that.

For some reason, Blossom Promise's verdict on Nash has made me feel comforted. It's the same feeling I had when I was reading *Should I Stay or Should I Go?* when Dr Stein asked if I would feel relieved if my family and

211

friends staged an intervention and told me it was all right to leave. I suppose Blossom Promise was a kind of intervention in a way. Anyway, I feel . . . better.

Jade comes back with two enormous suitcases on wheels. 'I got more stuff at home if we run out,' she says. 'And Matty's on the way.'

While we wait for the market to warm up, she explains the Matty–Jade business model to me. It seems to consist of selling the possessions of every departing English person in Sydney at 20 per cent commission on eBay and flogging the rest at a slightly lower commission at the markets. The rest of their stock they find at auction – Australians are frightened of auctions, according to Jade. They're too laid-back to bid.

Jade specializes in old fifties and sixties swimming costumes. She also snaps up Hawaiian shirts when she finds them, and natty little beach accessories – striped duffle bags, ancient towels with fringing on the ends, enormous Mexican sun hats and beach wraps with boomerangs all over them.

It's a fantastic stall, but she hasn't got enough stock.

I could use Aunt Helena's fabric and make all kinds of things to sell here. Wrap skirts and sundresses, maybe, with headscarves and bags. The skirts and dresses would be easy enough to run up using my in-between-sizes idea. I could do them for pregnant women, too. Maybe I could photocopy the story in Twad and pin it up at the front of the stall.

My Dad was so right about me. He used to say I was

a born capitalist without capital. Still, a woman can dream. Even in the middle of a credit crunch.

'By the way.' Jade clicks her sausage fingers at me. 'Matty did well with all your gear. He's gonna come over later and give you the dosh. That was lucky for you that your cousin was having a throw-out, wasn't it?'

She's embarrassing me now by making me feel poor. 'Do you know that psychic Blossom Promise?' I change the subject.

'Never heard of her. Here, tell me if you could get these questions right, all right?' She crosses her long legs and reads from her Australian citizenship test.

'What is Australia's floral emblem?'

'I don't know. Gladioli. Something to do with Dame Edna Everage.'

'Wattle.'

'What is mateship?'

'No idea.'

'What percentage of Australian migrants are born in the UK?'

'I know that one. About twenty per cent.'

'Yeah, too bloody many.' She laughs. 'Which creature can be found on West Australia's flag?'

'Kangaroo. Koala. Platypus. Dame Edna Everage. Pass.'

'The black swan,' Jade says, tutting at me. 'Can you sing the Australian national anthem?'

'No. Something about girt. Our home is girt by sea.'

'What role did Private John Simpson Kirkpatrick play in Australian affairs?'

'No idea. Actually, hang on. I do know.'

'Come on, time's ticking away.' Jade taps her wrist.

'It was in the First World War. Simpson was a medical officer. He used to put the wounded men on the back of his donkey and take them back to the camp. Simpson and the donkey were both killed at Gallipoli. It was so sad.'

'Ah, bless,' Jade pulls a face. 'You're absolutely right there. I'm impressed. 'Ow did you know that one?'

'I used to go to a donkey charity shop in Finsbury Park. There was a poster on the wall of the changing room. I must have read it a hundred times.'

Matty turns up with more wheelie suitcases, wearing a baseball cap with a lightning bolt on the front.

'Gewd morning,' he greets us as if this is the first time he's seen Jade in twenty-four hours. Maybe it is.

'I've just been telling Alice about the citizenship test,' Jade says.

'Piece of piss,' is Matty's verdict. 'You going to do it, Alice?'

'I might,' I say. 'Actually, maybe I should.'

'Ooh, you've made her go all serious.' Jade nudges him. 'Hey. Did you bring Alice's money, darlin?'

'All good, all tax-free,' Matty says, and I try not to look too desperate as he counts out one hundred dollar bill after another, putting them carefully in my hand.

'Well I probably will declare the tax,' I tell him, but Matty and Jade are already in a world of their own, rolling cigarettes and reading this morning's screed of text messages from London.

'I think I'll go and get a coffee,' I offer. 'Anyone want one?'

'Yerr, ta,' they say in unison.

The coffee is hard to find. What did the man in the green vest say about services? Were they near the car park or away from the car park? And where is the bloody car park anyway?

I check the money Matty has given me and put it straight back in my purse. Then I stuff my purse down the front of my bra just to be certain. I can't have St Martin-in-the-Fields looking after me all the time.

I can certainly look after St Vincent de Paul, though. I am determined to give him his cut from Matty's pile of cash. It's one thing to be skint, it's quite another to be cheap, and I want to be able to look Robyn in the eye when I next see her.

She explained the rubbish bags to me last night. She said she cleared out her apartment in preparation for her detox in Bali, so she could bring in good chi for the new year, realign her meridians and get the energy pumping in her love corner.

Sometimes I have absolutely no idea what my cousin is talking about.

I see a second-hand book stall and go over. I wonder which book Blossom Promise wanted me to buy? What in the name of merry jingo, as my dad used to say, was she blithering about? Then I see the book she means immediately: my old friend *Should I Stay or Should I*

215

Go? by Dr Ray Stein. I suppose Nash will give it back to the library eventually, if he doesn't burn it first. I flick through the book, remembering every word. I don't need it any more, though. I shouldn't have stayed, Dr Stein, and I didn't.

There is a cheap pile of books underneath it marked 'AUSTRALIANA – HALF PRICE'. I pick it up and untie the string. One of the books is about the First World War. I look in the index and there is Simpson's donkey. There's a photograph of Simpson in the centre pages and I immediately want to buy it. Maybe Blossom was talking about this instead. It could be good for my citizenship test.

I will take my citizenship test eventually, for exactly the same reasons Matty and Jade are taking theirs. I want an Australian passport. I want to make it easier to get a proper job here. Maybe one day, if a miracle occurs, I'd even like my future son or daughter to have an Australian passport. I can't think of a better country I'd like my descendants to belong to, if I ever find a man to have descendants with, of course.

I want to belong to this country, too. I don't want to feel like an interloper. I already feel I owe Australia that much, even though I've only been here a few weeks.

I look at the other books. The story of Phar Lap, the greatest racehorse Australia has ever seen – so great, it seems, that they stuffed him – and a very smelly book called *Selected Poems of Henry Lawson*. I'm not surprised it's whiffy; it was published in 1918. Someone has also scribbled all over the front of it.

A nosey woman in big sunglasses is hovering, looking over my shoulder.

'Do you want that lot, love?' the stallholder asks me.

'Yes, please,' I hand the money over and get a filthy look from Big Sunglasses as the stallholder puts the books into an old plastic bag.

I collect three cups of coffee in a cardboard tray and go back to the stall. Jade and Matty are snogging, ignoring their customers while they investigate each other's recently whitened teeth.

I suppose if you didn't know that Jade used to be John, you'd find Matty's insatiable lust understandable. Then again, maybe her man-hands turn him on.

'Been shopping?' Jade enquires when Matty finally gets up and lets me sit down.

'Just some Aussie books. I thought if I had to do the citizenship thing, they'd come in useful.'

'Yes dear,' Jade interrupts me as she spots a customer hovering. 'Can I help you?'

It's Big Sunglasses, but she's not interested in Jade's old clothes, she's interested in my books.

'My husband would love those for his birthday,' she confronts me. 'In fact, he had his eye on them before. I was about to pick them up. Would you take a hundred dollars for them?'

I'm just about to be all middle-class English about it and say, 'Oh God, sorry, of course you can, I do apologize,' when Matty cuts in.

'Come on, love, if it's his birthday you can afford

to be generous, can't you,' he says, watching her like a hawk.

'I spent loads and *loads* on Matty's birthday,' Jade says sweetly, backing him up.

Big Sunglasses waits, watching for my reaction, then storms off – as much as any woman can in Birkenstocks.

'Give us a look at the books then,' Matty sighs, inspecting each page with his fingertips.

'You wait,' Jade promises me. 'He'll sort it for you.'

'It's the Henry Lawson,' Matty says, thumbing the book of poetry. 'Not because I know anything about Henry Lawson – although I prolly should, having just sat the bloody Australia exam – but that's his name there in the front.'

Jade and I look carefully and see the letters, written in spidery copperplate in ink that dried a long time ago.

'It's a signed first edition,' Matty says, 'and that woman knew it.'

'If she was offering you a hundred dollars, girlfriend, it's probably worth ten times that,' Jade says, fanning herself.

'Guard it with your bloody life, Alice,' Matty waggles his finger at me. 'And put it in the safe at home, orright?'

And then, just as St Vincent de Paul and St Martin-in-the-Fields join hands and set off joyful fireworks and exploding dollar signs above my head, my world comes to a mini-end because there, coming towards us, is Joel. And he's holding hands with a pretty dark-skinned, dark-haired woman in a sarong who can't stop gazing at him.

I duck my head, but it's too late, and anyway, Robyn has probably sent him to look for me.

'Hey, Alice!' He kisses me on the cheek, and I introduce him to Matty and Jade.

'You're back,' I say stupidly.

'Came back a bit early. This is Rebecca.'

Well, thanks very much, Blossom bloody Promise.

Chapter Twelve

The Henry Lawson poetry book is worth one hundred times what I paid for it, so Blossom Promise was right about that bit.

Matty photographs, prices and auctions it for me on eBay and we watch the bids increase by the hour, until time runs out and Jade punches the air with her man-hands and yells, 'Yessss!'

I do the sums on the back of an envelope, converting dollars into pounds, and realize I can afford to send Mum another cheque, *and* pay for Nash to send my things from London. More importantly, I can now afford to have Aunt Helena's trunk sent over. And maybe, just maybe, I can afford a pedicure too. After all this time, the feeling of freedom is incredible.

I am desperate for my things now, even Ducky the rubber duck. I feel as if half of me is stuck in London. When Matty has paid the money into my account, the first thing I do is write to Nash.

An email comes straight back – he's bought himself a laptop now and seems to be on it first thing in the morning and last thing at night – with the very businesslike subject header: 'SHIPMENT TO AUSTRALIA'. All our emails are like this at the moment, keeping it sensible and civilized. It's still a competition to see who can be more grown-up about breaking up.

Nash has typed a list of everything I left behind and it's not exactly an auction catalogue at Sotheby's.

Bangles, dental floss, face flannel, loofah, packet
of felt-tip pens, melted pink candle, petition
against scrapping of Routemaster London bus
– damn, I forgot to give that back to Suzanne –
Swiss Cottage library card, rubber duck, four pairs
of black knickers . . .

I am surprised at how much I've left behind. The Duran Duran key ring I was given for my sixth birthday, for a start. Oh, and the inflatable dolphin lilo, which Nash and I took to Cornwall on our first summer holiday. Maybe I could float around Bondi on it.

I appear to own a lot of relationship self-help books from charity shops, too. Funny that. I tell Nash to chuck those. Apart from that, I want everything, mainly because I only have four suitcases and a sewing machine to my name and I feel as if I have nothing.

I notice that anything Nash and I bought together is not on the list. Mysteriously, Nash seems to have interpreted these shared purchases as his property. If I argue about that, though, I'll never see my packing crates.

'Thanks for making the list and offering to pack everything up,' I write, gritting my teeth. 'Hopefully you'll have more room in your new flat once my stuff is out of the way.'

The last time I was this polite with Nash was the first time we met. I wanted him so much, my restraint was incredible. He was polite, too. When the relationship really took off, though, he used to take my bra off at the front door. The memory of it now makes me feel surprisingly wobbly. Why is it that your brain knows when a relationship is over, but your heart always lags behind?

I try to persuade myself that Nash was just a habit, like smoking. That was hard to kick, too; even when I was long past the cravings, I used to walk into a room and look for an ashtray.

I read Nash's email again. He is quite happy to organize the packing and delivery of my stuff, as he thinks it's only practical that I have my things around me in Australia, for the time that I'm there.

'For the time that I'm there.' So, he still thinks I'm coming back. Does that also mean he hopes I might be coming back to him at some point?

Well he can stuff that. I might be marshmallow on the inside, but I'm hard as nails on the outside. I'm a human Wagon Wheel now, baby, and there's no going back.

I have braved the walk from Bondi Beach to Bronte and I love it. The lizard sculptures didn't scare me at all and I didn't see a single blue jellyfish, instead, I dived into the water at Bronte like a madwoman and stayed in the sea for an hour.

Australia has see-through water. You can see sand and shells at the bottom, instead of murk and crisp packets. I want to stay here for ever.

I like my new country. I like the way everyone sounds the same. Nobody is posh, nobody has a *background* clunking along behind them. There is no class system for stamps. You can make your dream come true here. Everything I thought was impossible in London suddenly seems possible here. Everybody says yes almost all the time. Even if they think you're bonkers, they still say yes.

I saw a kookaburra the other day and it cackled with laughter, just as the guidebooks said it would. It had a punk Mohawk and a big beak and it seemed properly Australian.

Matty and Jade have been teaching me about property in Sydney. You save up for a deposit on a cheap unit – not a flat, a unit – in an up-and-coming area, then you rent it out and use the money to rent somewhere even cheaper for yourself – preferably miles out of town because nobody wants to live there.

'Distance don't matter, though,' Matty advised me a few nights ago when we were looking at a map on the internet. 'They've got the cheapest trains in the world here. The Aussies don't like them; they live in their cars. We're used to it, us Brits. We can do it – we're used to the pain. Use it to your advantage, Alice. Save up and get yerself a deposit on something in Woop Woop.'

Woop Woop, Matty explains, is local parlance for the middle of nowhere, but Woop Woop is also the only place to live if you are broke like me and want to buy your own home.

It's a shock to realize I might own a flat one day, or even a house. It's always seemed like some mad dream, but Matty and Jade are talking about it as if it's a perfectly normal thing for me to consider.

Later on, I discover that Matty is right about the train trips anyway. Australians don't like them, or at least Danielle Coles doesn't like them. When I ring to tell her I will be arriving at Byron Bay station, she sounds deeply shocked.

'You're not bringing your car up?'

'I don't drive actually.'

'You're not flying to Ballina?'

'I thought I'd take the scenic route on the train. See a bit of the country.'

'But it's nine hours, Alice!'

'Oh well. Hang on, I need to put some more money in the slot.'

'Are you in a *phone box*?' More shock.

I am fairly certain Danielle Coles is a rich woman. I have Googled her and have found her to be the happy owner of not one, but three dog-related businesses in New South Wales. Along with Barks of Byron Bay, she also owns Pampered Pooches of Parramatta and Diva Doggie Day Care in Double Bay.

I've asked Nash to send my packing crates to Robyn's address because I don't want them to arrive at Barks of Byron Bay, where Danielle will have to watch me unpacking tatty old underwear and a face flannel and suffer yet more shock.

In the meantime, I need to go shopping for some dog-friendly work clothes. Perhaps it's time I paid a visit to my good friend St Vincent de Paul in Paddington, so I can do a few Vintage Alice conversions. I am secretly going because I want an outfit that will impress Joel, of course. We're having dinner tonight.

I know he has a lovely new girlfriend with long, dark plaits and I also know that she is a much better human being than me, because she works for Joel's charity and helps Tibetan refugees. (Robyn, as always, has been a goldmine of instant information.)

Nevertheless, I live in hope. I *have* to hope. As Joel himself said on the hills above the English Channel that day, it's the only proper response to life. Even if it's hope of the pointless, deranged variety.

I get the bus to St Vincent de Paul's in Paddington and try not to look in the other shops, which aren't second-hand and have eye-watering prices. Instead, I buy two chicken satay sticks and revel in the luxury of eating takeaway food for a change.

When I go into St Vincent de Paul's life begins to feel even more luxurious. The first rack I look at has the kinds of clothes Suzanne and Jade would snap up for their stalls: nearly new English labels, all recently shed by well-dressed expats on their way back home.

As well as my pedicure budget – yes! – I am letting myself keep a small amount of spending money from my amazing Henry Lawson book miracle. Once I have tried everything on, though, I realize I have more than enough to buy two pairs of jeans, three skirts, a bundle of tops and even a coat for next winter. Australia's like a fruit machine at the moment. Every time you do another pound-to-dollar conversion in your head, you find more gold coins in the tray.

Joel would really like one of the tops. It's white cheesecloth with drawstrings and it looks a bit Indian. If I bleach the red-wine stain out of the sleeve, it could even pass for new.

I realize I've also lost weight. Result! All that swimming and tramping around Bondi Beach and Bronte has given me back the kind of shape I had when I was a silver-painted key woman. Now all I need do is stop looking so English and white.

I try not to obsess too much about Joel as I pay for the clothes, but dinner with him is just a few hours away, and I cannot wait. Then suddenly he walks past the window. What?

I rush out in time to see him disappear into a jewellery shop. It's definitely Joel. Scruffy dark hair, tennis shoes, beaten-up old shoulder bag . . .

Maybe I should just sneak off. I have no foundation on and I am carrying three big plastic bags full of clothes, like the kind of hopelessly superficial capitalist shopaholic he would cross the road to avoid.

I edge towards the window of the jewellery shop so he can't see me but I can see him. God, he's gorgeous.

Then Joel looks up, sees me, smiles and waves.

'Hey, Alice!' he emerges from the shop and beckons to me. 'Come and tell me what you think of this.'

I go in, trying to breathe normally. The woman behind the counter looks me up and down, then looks away as if she wishes she hadn't bothered.

'I really like this bracelet,' Joel shows me a bangle decorated with unmatched stones. 'On the other hand, I also like this necklace.' He shows me a huge piece of amber on a long silver chain. 'What do you think?'

'Nice,' I say mechanically.

'It's for Rebecca,' Joel explains. 'It's her birthday on Saturday. She's back in Sydney for a while.'

'The necklace,' I say, at the same moment as the shop assistant says, 'The bracelet.'

'Both, then,' Joel jokes while I try to keep the smile on my face. I cannot keep it there for ever, though, or I'll develop paralysis of the jaw. I go and look at the rings in the front window instead.

How long is Rebecca back in Sydney? What does he mean, she's back for a while? Why buy her a necklace *and* a bracelet? Oh God. Joel must be really in love with her.

'Thanks for that.' Joel squeezes my arm once he's made his purchase and we're outside again. 'What are you doing up here?'

'Just getting some work clothes for my new job at Barks. Once I've moved out, you and Rebecca can have my room,' I test him. 'Or are you both staying somewhere else?'

'Alice. Are you OK?'

'Fine. Just a bit tired.'

'That makes two of us. Do you want a cup of tea? Maybe we could just do that instead of the dinner thing, if you're really tired.'

'Sure.'

We walk in silence to the café in the park at the end of the road, then suddenly he stops and makes me look at him properly.

'What's wrong?'

'Dunno.'

We walk into the park, through some vast stone gates and past two strange sphinx statues. It's like Victorian England, transplanted halfway across the world.

'This is a good place to sit,' Joel suggests, showing me a bench overlooking a pretty nineteenth-century bridge.

'I suppose the English were so homesick once they got here they tried to recreate London in Sydney,' I tell him.

'Is that the problem?' he asks. 'Are you feeling homesick?'

'Dunno.'

He laughs. 'Could the problem possibly be that I bought a bracelet and necklace for Rebecca?'

I give in. 'Maybe.'

'She's in Sydney for a week, for her birthday, then she's going back to New York,' Joel tells me. 'She runs the marketing department for us in Manhattan. I'm her

holiday fling – that's what she said on the weekend –
and that was perfectly fine by me.'

I note the tense and try not to feel too excited. *Was*
perfectly fine.

'Alice,' Joel squeezes my hand, 'you are going to Byron
Bay tomorrow and I'm probably not going to see you for
a while. We're also cousins, which I'm sure you're aware
of. Not genetically linked, but nevertheless cousins. You
only just broke up with someone. I've been by myself
for a long time. My last relationship went nowhere
because she said I couldn't commit. I'm not . . . *good* at
this stuff.'

'Yes. All right.'

'Of course there's something there between us, but
I don't know what it is yet and I'm not even sure we
should act on it. Does that make sense?'

I look at his steady, serious eyes and feel his hand in
mine. I fight the urge to kiss him.

Then he sees the chicken satay sticks, poking out of
the paper bag in my pocket and gives me a lecture about
battery-hen farming.

'Sorry,' I apologize. 'I was absolutely starving.'

'Come and stay with me in Bellingen,' he nudges me.
'Once you've seen real chickens laying real eggs you
won't want to eat the ones stuck in cages.'

'Can I really come and stay? I'm dying to see it.'

'Any time.' Joel smiles. 'Just leave your plastic bag
collection at home, OK?'

'Oh God, Joel. I'm such a sinner, aren't I. Any more
lectures?'

'I've booked a vegetarian place for dinner. Is that all right with you?'

The next day I catch the train to Byron Bay, and after a farewell breakfast with Robyn, Joel sees me off at the station, taking one photo of me after another on his ancient 1970s Polaroid camera.

We are at Central Station, which is like a grand old London station, complete with old-fashioned clocks and marble walls. There's something incredibly romantic about trains – I can't believe Australians are so reluctant to use them. Maybe it's just Matty talking rubbish, though as my train is heaving with passengers, all equipped with pillows, chocolate, magazines and bottles of water. I look at the timetables and realize the train to Queensland takes all night to get there – and that's only one state away. Imagine trying to go to Perth. I'm sure the train must be full of skeletons holding coffee cups, by the time it arrives at the other end.

Joel kisses my cheek on the platform and shakes my hand for good luck through the window. Once the train sets off and I am by myself, I know I will think about that perfunctory kiss for hours.

Soon, Joel will be able to move back to his block of land at Bellingen, too, and then I can come and stay. Even though he says we'll be roughing it.

I wave goodbye through the window until I finally lose sight of him, then I worry that all the other single women on the platform will leap on him as soon as

I have disappeared – or that the beautiful and good Rebecca will change her mind about New York and stay in Australia after all.

The train finally leaves Sydney and its houses far behind, then crawls on between roads cut out of mountains and past tiny islands I didn't even know existed. I fall asleep somewhere between the legendary Woy Woy and somewhere with a place name that sounds like a man falling down a fight of stairs – Tumble-along? Thud Wallop?

The woman in socks beside me, who has been doing sudoku since we left Central Station disappears half-way through the journey, leaving me with a spare seat to lean sideways on. I'm so tired – I was up all night, talking to Joel for hours after we left the restaurant.

I wake up to an announcement about our immi-nent arrival at Byron Bay. I have seat-creases on my arms and sleep in my eyes, and all the make-up in the world isn't going to make me look presentable, even though I'm wearing a new work outfit from St Vincent de Paul.

There is an old-fashioned rule about double denim – Suzanne would kill me if she could see me now – but the faded jacket and skirt I found somehow look right together, with the addition of a stripy T-shirt from Jade's stall. Right now I feel ready for anything, even Barks of Byron Bay.

I stagger off the train just as the sun is setting and see a tanned forty- to fifty-something woman – a new breed I have noticed in Australia – with flaming red hair and three dogs on a lead. One of them is a worried-looking Pekinese wearing gingham rompers, the other two are excitable Labradors.

'Hello, Alice!' Danielle Coles pumps my hand. 'Let me take your luggage! I can't believe you wanted to take the train, you crazy girl!'

In common with many forty to fifty-something Aussie women I have seen, Danielle is wearing her gym gear at eight o'clock in the evening, although her hair is beautifully blow-dried. She has a bottom like two boiled eggs in a handkerchief. It's a Pilates bottom – according to Danielle, anyway.

'These are some of the little people you'll be looking after.' Danielle introduces the dogs as we wheel my mother's old suitcases to her car.

Dad would have been impressed. It is an enormous silver BMW with 'BARKS OF BYRON BAY' painted on each side together with the company logo, featuring dogs in crowns waving sceptred orbs around.

'Now, Alice. A bit of info for you. We've spoken about Mr Chang – he gets carsick, so we'll have him in the front by himself in case he does a little chuck on the way. And these two gorgeous boys are called Zoltan and Tikyo.'

Zoltan and what? It hadn't occurred to me that I would have to memorize the names of all the dogs at Barks of Byron Bay. What if I forget? They sound as if they've been named after alien fighter missiles.

'What I'm going to do with you, Alice, is drop your bags with the dogs back at the kennel, then take you straight out to dinner. I thought you might like to meet up with some friends of mine.'

'Lovely.'

Danielle insists I call her Dani as we bundle into the big silver BMW.

'Put the iPod on shuffle, darl,' she instructs me, and I try my best. Soon we are listening to random Sting, followed by random Enya and then more random Sting. By now, Nash would be sticking his fingers down his throat and pulling faces.

When we finally arrive at Barks I try to take in as much as I can, even though it's dark. It's vast, like a health farm, and appears to be bordered by live electric fences and monitored by a Colditz-style CCTV system.

Dani – as I must now call her – takes the two Labradors in first, while I am left to talk to Mr Chang in the front seat. He has indeed been carsick down the front of his gingham rompers. I suppose the rompers have a nappy built into them. I wonder where his famous incontinence cushion is? Poor thing. I pat him on the head and he tries to lick my hand off. I'm sure nobody ever shows him any affection.

Should I be doing something? I'm not sure. Perhaps I still have guest status at the moment and am not obliged to carry out any dog-wrangling duties. Then again, Mr Chang looks desperate for a wee.

Before I can make my move, though, Dani is back, wearing a pair of rubber gloves with frills on the ends.

'He can pee like a brewer's horse,' she advises me before lifting him out of the front seat and taking off his rompers. I wonder if Mr Chang has a selection of pants to choose from. I certainly hope so. Otherwise I expect I'll be hand washing the gingham rompers once we return from dinner.

'There are about fifty dogs here on the weekend,' Dani explains once she has lugged my cases into the house, and we drive off again towards the centre of Byron Bay. 'We have our regulars, too. I call it my little dog therapy clinic. Mr Chang is a permanent resident from Friday to Sunday because his parents have a weekender up here. They're going to be at dinner by the way. Robert and Georgie. Robert's got a few vineyards along the North Coast.'

Poor Mr Chang. He must be like one of the forgotten, adopted children of Hollywood celebrities, who leave their offspring with nannies while they jetset around the world. No wonder he pees everywhere, so would I.

Dani is a terrible driver, mainly because she talks into what she calls her Blueteeth while she is supposed to be keeping her eyes on the road. Blueteeth appears to be some kind of magic invisible telephone. She can hear the person who has rung her up, but I cannot. I can hear her replies, though, which, along with the robotic monotone of her GPS tracking device, makes for a very odd atmosphere in the car.

'Yiss, he's been having a bad trot lately,' Dani says as we narrowly avoid crashing into a lamp post. 'So I basically said "Up your nose with a rubber hose darling, I could care less."'

'Turn right at the roundabout' the GPS instructs.

Dani has a lot of stickers on her back window. 'Magic Happens', 'I Heart My Dalmatian', 'I Heart My Corgi', 'No McDonalds for Byron Bay'.

'Yiss, if his brains were dynamite they wouldn't blow his hat off,' Dani goes on with her Blueteeth conversation and I realize she must be talking about my predecessor at Barks. Suddenly I find myself wondering how many kennel assistants Dani has employed before – and what happens to them. Maybe she rolls on them with her Pilates ball.

We go into the restaurant after an amazingly bad piece of parking by Dani, and there is a copious amount of what Nash would call mwah-mwah kissing among her friends.

The group of smiling, kissing people around the table is a silver blur. Platinum rings, metal chairs, gleaming candlesticks, shiny hoop earrings and metallic handbags. All the silver contrasts with the tans, which are deep and golden, and the whole thing is reflected in an enormous mirror standing on its side against the back wall.

I am introduced to everyone and instantly forget their names, except for Georgie, wife of Robert, because she is sitting next to me.

The restaurant is BYO so we are drinking wine from Robert's vineyard. Because he is slightly drunk and not listening to me properly – and because the music is so loud you can't hear anyway – he makes the mistake of thinking I'm a businessperson too.

We order our first course and Robert starts talking. And talking. He talks across Georgie and Dani, and then across me, occasionally sending tiny bits of spit flying across the table.

'See the way Danielle parked her truck out there?' he asks me without waiting for an answer. 'She's a shocking driver. Women shouldn't drive at night. Man's got the right-brain spatial ability. He's got the hunting vision.'

I try to think of a reply.

'But a woman can see better in the dark than a man,' I tell him at last. 'That's been proven.'

Now Robert doesn't know what to say.

'Do you hunt?' he asks.

'No. It's been banned in England, actually.' Much to my mother's disappointment, of course, but I'm not about to tell Robert that.

Robert immediately loses interest and moves on to the man sitting on the other side of his wife, who is the first man I have ever seen with cosmetic surgery. He looks most peculiar, like a fifty-year-old fifteen-year-old.

'So you're working for Dani,' Georgie says, leaving her wine untouched.

'I think I'm looking after Mr Chang. He's yours, isn't he?'

'He's Robert's dog,' she says. 'Actually, he belonged to Robert's son Ryan, but then he got his tennis scholarship.'

Georgie sounds as if she doesn't know whether to be smug or annoyed about this.

'Dani said you were over from London,' she continues. 'That's exciting. Byron Bay's so bewdyful. I'm doing a big detox spa next week. You must go.'

'Sounds great.'

'Are you here in Byron on your own?'

'Yes.'

Suddenly Georgie has nothing left to say to me, and I have nothing left to say to her. She is the detoxed wife of a successful vineyard owner with a son on a tennis scholarship, and I am a sad old single, toxed-up Pommie dog-minder in second-hand clothes – a distinctly unbewdyful creature, wearing double denim in the middle of bewdyful Byron Bay.

I miss Joel so much. As soon as I find a phone box to call my own, I'm going to phone him, but Dani is watching me like a hawk and there is no escape.

Robyn told me all about Byron Bay. She said it's where the sea-changers go. Sea-changers are people who sell their homes in the city and move to the coast so they can live in enormous houses and live the Australian dream, with all the swimming pools, yoga classes, ocean views, silver handbags, four-wheel-drives, flat-screen televisions, expensive restaurants and designer dogs this entails.

Poor old incontinent Mr Chang. He must be the only part of Georgie and Robert's dream that didn't go according to plan. I suppose that ultimately they'll have him killed.

Chapter Thirteen

The following day I discover that Georgie and Robert do, in fact, want to have Mr Chang put down.

'If you could just run him to the vet later on for his . . .' Dani pulls a face, because she's too delicate to say the words, 'lethal injection.'

I don't know what to say. I'm not even sure I can do it. But this is my first Australian job, and this is the first task I have been asked to perform.

As I listen to Dani making calls in her office, I realize that although she hearts Dalmatians and hearts corgis, she doesn't actually seem to have a heart. Nor does she actually own any dogs.

Danielle and Heidi Coles share a common Australian vocabulary – little black ducks, mad cut snakes, various rooted situations – but that's the only thing they have in common. Heidi is nice and Dani is not.

Before I can even begin to face the full horror of ferrying Mr Chang to the vet, there is an embarrassing money discussion.

'I've taken some admin costs out of your first week's

pay,' Dani says when I'm trying to sort out all the sacks of dog biscuits in the kitchen. 'All that business with immigration cost us quite a bit, Alice, just so you know.'

I take my cue, because she is looking at me as if she wants me to be grateful.

'Thanks so much for that, Dani. I really appreciate it.'

'It was a pleasure to be able to help yew,' Dani turns her Pilates-perfect bottom towards me and strides out.

I am in the Barks kitchen – vast, stainless-steel, indisputably doggy – when it occurs to me that I may not stay here beyond the first month. The list of instructions is overwhelming and the smell of canine crap is overpowering. And I'm not taking poor Chang to the vet to be put down. I have decided that already. Georgie, Robert and Dani can give that task to someone else.

Dani has lists everywhere, laminated and decorated with dog stickers.

Under the heading 'KLEPTOMANIACS', she has written a list of lawless animals who must be watched night and day in case they make off with anything on the premises. Dani is particularly concerned about a spaniel called Johnny who has been known to take other dogs' squeaky toys, and a mixed-breed named Whispering who digs up other animals' bones.

It doesn't stop there. When I add up the items on Dani's computer printout there are forty-seven things I must do – or not do – as part of my duties at Barks:

Stereo tuned to bass notes only, no high-pitched music, and especially not violin. Dogs howl at Nigel Kennedy, Dexy's Midnight Runners, 'The Devil Went Down To Georgia' etc., etc.

The following dogs have been known to break into delivery vans if doors are left open: Hickory, Sophocles, Meatball, Twinkle, Zack, Punkboy, Rabbit and Travis.

Bruce (Boston Terrier) pulls down washing.

The following dogs jump up: Kisser, Cisco, Otis, Mr Whippy, Winchester, Teddy, Mooch, Nike, Psycho, Woody, Hollyoaks, Zed, Tubs and Mr Chang. (Aha, the unfortunate Mr Chang.)

Buddy, a Maltese Terrier, makes physical attacks on any human seen watching television, particularly *Oprah*, and must be squirted with water.

The following dogs are whiners: Lady, Calvin, Monsieur Henri, Robertson, Scoop, Tricky and Leroy.

The following dogs attack lawnmowers, motorbikes, skateboards and cars: Cinnamon, Frosty, Monty, Mavis, Mr O, Rambo, Jet Boy, Bunny, Cooper and Farfalle.

The following dog regularly goes into a trance: Nipper (Oh please let Nipper not fall over dead like Goggles when I poke him, so I have to carry him home in a plastic shopping bag.)

The following dogs have criminal records: Pegasus, Willow and Jock.

The following dogs are leg-riders: Outrageous, Lily, Chunky, Jelly and Whistler.

Ollie (Kelpie-Staffie Cross) is a licker and must not be allowed near anyone with bare arms.

It goes on for several pages. No wonder Dani Coles has been through so many staff.

I found out all about it, of course, when I inspected my carer's quarters. Everyone who has ever stayed there has written their name on a bare piece of concrete, underneath a loose tile in the fireplace.

Because the staff have to clean the fireplace – another task on the laminated list – Dani doesn't go near it. If she did, she would see that the loose tile covers up an unofficial visitors' book containing a variety of one-star reviews.

Will I end up hating Barks as much as the other staff who lived and worked here? I'm not sure. But I now understand why Dani was so quick to take me on as a full-time employee, sight unseen, from the other side of the world.

At the end of the day the subject of Chang comes up again.

'Sometimes yew just have to be cruel to be kind,' Dani says.

'But he's not in pain. He's just incontinent, isn't he? Lots of dogs are like that. And he gets a bit carsick.'

'I think his owners are the best judge of that.'

'I thought this was a boarding kennel. I thought I would be walking the dogs, feeding them, playing with them and bathing them. I didn't expect to be doing this.'

'There's a little saying we have in Australia. Love it or shove it.'

'It's exactly the same in England,' I add.

In the end I obey orders and take Chang to the vet, but only because I want to hear what he has to say about his health. The vet turns out to be a she, not a he, though, and she is on my side. She says she cannot possibly proceed with the lethal injection.

'This is a Barks' dog, I suppose. Apart from anything else, you're not authorized to do this. There's no signed letter here from the owner, or from anyone else.'

'Dani seemed to think it would be simple. She said Phil would look after it.'

'All the Barks animals are usually seen by my colleague, Phil Hodain. He's on leave and I'm the relieving vet – I usually work at Ballina. I don't know what kind of arrangement Phil has with Dani, but I'm sure he wouldn't proceed on this basis. Was this an impulsive decision by the owners, do you know?'

'Sorry. I haven't been told anything.'

'Well, you'll have to take Chang back. But I would advise against this procedure altogether: he's not in any pain or extreme discomfort, and the incontinence can be controlled with medication. It's no big deal.'

Poor Chang. He looks terrified, shivery and cold in the corner of the surgery in his ridiculous rompers – tartan today – and matching collar.

When I take him back to Barks, Dani is furious and says she has better things to do, because she is training for a triathlon and she's going to sack me if I don't clean up my act.

'Alice. I don't have time for this.'

'Can I take him then?'

'Take who? The *dog*?' she looks at Chang, and then at me, as if we are both completely mad.

'I'm happy to take him. Georgie and Robert won't care, will they?'

'Do what you like with him, but you're not keeping him here.'

'I might have to leave, then. Sorry.'

'You're quitting?'

'I'm sure you were about to sack me anyway, weren't you? It's probably going to save us both a lot of time and trouble in the long run.'

'It's been a frigging *nightmare* to get you over here, Alice. Are you crazy?'

'I'm sorry.'

Before Dani can shout at me, I jog-walk back to my poky little dog carer's flat with Chang as fast as I can and pack up my suitcases on wheels – and my poor old sewing machine – at record speed. I know there's no point in talking to Dani about money. Instead, I stand on the side of the highway and hail a taxi, then head for the nearest phone box. Please let Joel be there.

It's wonderful to hear his voice when he finally answers.

'It's Alice. I'm having a problem.' I try to sound businesslike and fail.

'Where are you?'

'In Byron Bay with this Pekinese dog, Chang. I've run away from Barks. We've run away. They were going to put him down. I don't know what to do. I've got a dog,

243

a sewing machine, all my suitcases and I'm in a phone box.'

Joel doesn't miss a beat.

'Come to Bellingen and stay with me. The caravans are already there. There are no locks, just go in. There should be towels and stuff.'

'Joel, I can't even walk down two consecutive streets in Australia without getting lost. How am I going to get to Bellingen?'

'Get a taxi to the station, then jump on the train to Urunga. You'll have to hide the dog, though.'

'Argh!'

'Alice, don't sound so worried. People do it all the time. I'll try to get my neighbour to pick you up at the other end. Have you still got the map of my property that I drew for you?'

'Yes. Oh, Joel, it was so awful at that place. It was like Colditz for poodles.'

'It's over now. I'll be there as soon as I can. OK?'

'I don't want to drag you away from Sydney.'

'And I don't want you to be by yourself at the moment. How's Mr Chang feeling?'

'We can't call him that any more. It's just Chang. He already seems a bit happier.'

'He'll love Bello. It's dog heaven.'

Bello. Anything with three or more syllables in Australia is automatically shortened. Even two syllables is too long sometimes. I suppose at some point I will be turned into Al.

I flag down a taxi. My ticket to Urunga uses up

a precious fifty-dollar note, so far untouched, but I would give anything to put some space between me and Barks of Byron Bay. Not to mention Dani's boiled-egg bottom.

Because I am climbing on board with so much junk – old suitcases, a sewing machine and various plastic bags – Chang, who's hidden in a cardboard box, goes undetected.

Once I'm on board, I traipse through carriage after carriage, dragging my stuff behind me until I find two unoccupied seats within range of the loo doorway. Every time I open the flaps of Chang's cardboard box to give him some air, he wisely declines. I wish I could. Instead, I try to avoid the smell and fall asleep.

After a long journey when I veer between dreaming and waking, we finally hear the driver announce that we are approaching Urunga. I immediately turn to the window and see two pelicans flying overhead. Please let that be a good omen.

'G'day,' a bearded man walks up to me in the car park, and offers his hand. He says his name is the Wizard Formerly Known as Wayne, and that he's Joel's neighbour. He says Joel has told him all about me and the situation – whatever that is – and if there's anything he can do, I only have to ask.

I look at him properly to see if I've heard the wizard thing right. He doesn't look particularly magical. His beard is short and clipped. He has no pointy hat. No purple cape with stars. No shoes that curl up at the end, although he does have tanned, bare feet and a toe ring.

'I'm Alice,' I introduce myself.

'Call me Wiz,' the Wizard Formerly Known as Wayne offers. Then he takes my bags while I let poor Chang out of his box and we make our way to his VW camper van.

Wiz drives with a can of beer on the dashboard and walks like John Wayne after a week in the saddle, and when he sits in the front seat, his legs are so far apart his knee keeps bumping into mine. What the hell has he got in his underpants? A jar of magical pickled onions?

'Got the dog on the train, did ya?' he nods at little Chang, who's cowering at my feet.

'They didn't check. Maybe they were just being nice. Chang's been very good, though. He didn't pee anywhere and he wasn't sick. That's a bit of an achievement for him.'

That is the extent of my conversation with the Wizard Formerly Known as Wayne for the rest of the journey. I try, but in the end I give up because he would clearly rather keep his eyes on the road and concentrate on the art of truck-dodging.

As trucks scream past, I check my phone. There's no reception.

'Depends where you are,' Wiz informs me.

I try to take the countryside in.

I'm slowly getting used to the Australian landscape. So far, I have only seen it framed in car and train windows, but there are some things that are becoming familiar – the enormously fat, healthy cows, for a start, and the brilliant green grass. In this part of the country, at least, there is no drought and it looks positively lush.

I see a river through the trees and assume this must be the Bellinger, which Joel loves so much and where you can famously drink the water you swim in. Suddenly I long for a swim – and a drink, come to that. I had wanted to explore the beach at Byron Bay, but I suppose I'll have to do that another time. Another year. Another decade.

We pass a swimming pool and a golf club, and then we are in Bellingen itself. It's just as Joel described it: one street, one pub, one supermarket, one chemist, one newsagent, one garage, one library, one war memorial.

There are Christmas lights up everywhere, even though Christmas is long gone, so the whole street appears to be celebrating something.

'Well, it's not London,' says the Wizard Formerly Known as Wayne, offering me a bag of nuts.

We drive for miles, leaving the war memorial far behind. I'm too afraid to ask Wiz how far away Joel's property is, in case he loses concentration and runs into a truck. His whole approach to driving seems to be based on avoiding them.

Trucks in Australia don't carry orange juice or chocolate, as they do in England; invariably they have huge logs on board, or herds of cattle.

'You're probably wondering about me,' Wiz says,

although I'm not. 'I used to be known as Wayne O'Halloran. Then I got in with some bad mojo people and they took my power away. I had to change my name for business reasons.'

'Did you get the idea from Prince?' I ask him.

'Yeah,' he gives me a sly look and turns on his cassette player, whereupon I'm blasted with the very best of Prince, specifically 'Little Red Corvette' – 'Whoo! Whoo!' hoots Wiz – and assailed with much finger-clicking and foot-stamping.

Eventually we move from a sealed road on to a bumpy dirt lane, then we rattle our way down a winding track at the bottom of a long mountain range.

I recognize the hand-painted, numbered sign outside Joel's property from his hand-drawn map and try not to get too excited.

'You're Joel's cousin,' Wiz announces rather than asks.

'Yes, but we're not related.'

'Yeah. You'll like it here,' Wiz says. 'Do you do much astral travelling?'

'Not really.'

'That's a shame. You can go a bloody long way from here.' He points upwards.

Wiz parks the van, hands me Chang in his box and drags my cases, bags and sewing machine over to the two caravans, which are parked side by side in a clearing beneath a canopy of trees.

'Thanks so much, Wiz. You must come round for dinner.'

My neighbour looks at the caravans, looks at me and smiles – at last. I suppose it's the most ridiculous thing he's heard all week.

'Tell Joel some goat's runnin' around,' he grunts before driving off.

I see the goat as soon as I let Chang out for a run and take off the dreaded rompers. The animal is white, like the billy goat in the English children's fairy story. He even eats grass sideways, the rest of his furry face remaining immobile while his jaw shunts back and forth.

Chang is thrilled and gives little barks of excitement; it's probably the first goat he's ever seen, or maybe he thinks it's some kind of gigantic poodle.

The caravans are lit by fluorescent strips, and when I look in the mirror it's like looking at some kind of dead vampire woman. I find a packet of tea-light candles in a drawer, and light them instead, turning the larger caravan into a shadowy cave.

I open and shut every drawer in turn. All I can find are ancient saucepans, bits of old picnic-set cutlery, smelly newspapers and the occasional mousetrap. Then I check my phone reception – nothing.

I sit down on the mattress and read the paper. Here is the news from Bellingen last year:

The Bellingen Potato Festival this year will feature an Iron Man competition where each contestant must spring 40 metres carrying a 20kg bag of potatoes, drink a raw egg, eat a cold meat pie and blow up a balloon until it pops. Prize: 20kg bag of potatoes.

The annual Bellingen Chainsaw Races this year will be replaced by Bovine Bingo, due to lack of interest.

There is also some news about something called the Urunga Swingers, but it turns out to be a ladies' golf club, rather than some Australian married couples' sex club.

I give up on the newspaper and look in the second caravan. It's even emptier, but the sheets and pillowcases seem cleaner and there is even a proper bath-sized towel, so I settle in there and put a blanket under the van for Chang.

London never seemed further away than it does now. I can't wait for the stars to come out. Joel said you can see everything from his property, including the Southern Cross.

I wonder what Wiz's house is like, and imagine some purple-painted shed, with silver-foil wallpaper and lots of incense. My God. I hope Wiz doesn't astral travel to my caravan tonight. The way he was grinding his thighs together when he was singing along to Prince was just awful.

I try to think of something else – preferably Joel – and fall asleep, but when I wake again, I've missed the stars altogether. Instead, it is almost seven o'clock in the morning and there is a goat trying to get into the caravan and what sounds like a rooster trying to coach him.

Suddenly I realize that Chang is on the end of the bed. Oh no.

I lift him off and look for the wet patch, lifting up each blanket in turn, and finally the sheets. Everything is dry and clean.

'Chang, did you sleep on my bed and not pee? Did you? Did you manage to stay here all night and behave yourself?'

He snorts and skips out of the van as if I'm a complete tosser, and immediately chases the rooster away from the van.

I step outside into the sunlight, still wearing my clothes from the night before. It's already warm, and it looks as if it will be boiling hot by lunchtime. Joel said there was a creek on the property that I could use as a temporary water supply until he buys a rainwater tank.

I try not to think about the King Brown snakes or the Red Bellied Black snakes on my wall chart from Australia House as I go looking for the creek. Instead, I concentrate on the nice-cup-of-tea aspect. I have left a lot of my old life behind in England, but one thing I cannot get rid of is my addiction to builders' tea.

Slowly but surely, things on Joel's property begin to make sense. I find the creek at the bottom of a steep slope, then I find four tin buckets in the storage cavity underneath the caravan beds and return to fill them up. The water is incredible. Clear, cool and up to my knees. No pollution, no murk, no old crisp packets or tyres.

I make a cup of tea, then I take Chang back down to

the water, while I strip down to my bra and pants and sit in the creek as if it's a bath, hoping that Wiz's bearded head won't suddenly appear over the top of a tree.

I am quite alone, though, and I spend the whole morning exploring the deeper parts of the creek, watching more punk-rock kookaburras cackling at me through the trees.

I am starving, but there is no food in either caravan. I suppose I can do a hippie-fasting thing until Joel gets here, but I'm also beginning to feel faint.

Chang leads me to a grapefruit tree, like Lassie.

'Good boy!'

He loves the attention and jumps up – the forbidden jumping up Danielle Coles loathed – then he lifts his leg on a gum tree to celebrate his cleverness.

The grapefruit are sweet and juicy, not like London supermarket grapefruit at all. There is also a patch of spinach nearby, just as Joel promised.

After that, I discover rhubarb, tomatoes, potatoes, cabbage, pumpkin and even – once I taste-test it – coriander. Despite Joel's absence the vegetables are flourishing all by themselves.

Chang leads the way and eventually we find a hen house. There are a few chickens inside, asleep, but I can't see any eggs and I don't want to disturb them. I suppose they're just like me at Huddersfield University, riddled with performance anxiety and desperate to stay in bed all day. I'm sure if there was a television inside they would be watching quiz shows and eating Pot Noodles.

I try not to feel too anxious about Joel's arrival, but

it's like every other time I've waited for anything nice to happen. The more I count the hours, the less anything happens.

In the end, I fall asleep with Chang lying on my stomach, until I'm woken up, hours later, by Joel whispering my name.

'Hey, Alice,' he says, standing in the doorway.

'It's you!' I say stupidly.

Later, much later, when we have drunk a vat of tea, and I have told him all about the horrors of Barks, he laughs at me about the chickens.

'You've been living on boiled spinach and grapefruit because you didn't want to disturb the chooks? Just lift them up. The eggs will be right underneath.'

'Oh, Joel. You know I think that all eggs come from Tesco's.'

We swim in the creek as the sun goes down, after Joel has shown me a deep waterhole further down the hill. I never thought about water in London, but I'm beginning to see how much it matters here.

We both have good intentions of christening the caravans with the bottle of wine Joel has brought up from Sydney, but in the end, we go for a long walk and never get that far.

He tells me that my preferred caravan can be my home here for as long as I like. So that's it, then; we'll be caravan neighbours. Non-kissing cousins. Any silly daydreams I had about an instant relationship vanish in a second. I should have known that Joel was far too sensible for that.

253

'So you met the Wizard Formerly Known as Wayne, then?' he asks.

'God, yes. How could you do it to me, Joel?'

'Wayne's all right. He's just done too many mushies.'

'Magic mushrooms?'

Slowly but surely I'm learning to translate the Australian language now. You just stretch out every compressed word and phrase until you have added back all the extra letters or syllables the locals have taken away.

The next day, Joel buys two ancient bicycles because he says we cannot rely on lifts for ever. He was lucky to hitch a ride yesterday, he says, but he can't count on it happening again. 'I should hope not. My God. You could end up in pieces in someone's car boot.'

The Wizard Formerly Known as Wayne kindly picks us up on the way into town, then drops us at the second-hand shop, where we find the bikes.

Mine is a proper girl's bike from the 1970s – pink, decorated with daisy stickers and equipped with a funny straw basket at the front and a big vinyl carry-case on the back. I ride around Bellingen with Joel, pinging the bell for the hell of it, then pick up my emails at an internet café.

There is nothing from Danielle or Heidi Coles. I feel bad about Heidi, though, so I write her a short email about Barks, using the magical phase 'it just didn't work out'. Suzanne taught it to me years ago, and although Nash used to curl his lip in utter contempt any time he heard me saying it, it's still the emergency life raft of the English language.

At one point in my career, though, I would really like *something* to work out. Is that too much to ask?

All my good intentions about Vintage Alice seem to have been defeated by Barks, money, time, life, the universe and everything.

Danielle's silence in my email inbox is deafening. I suppose she will never speak to me again. She and her horrible friends have to be grateful for one thing, though – I saved them a vet's bill by kidnapping Chang.

My mother writes three emails containing the same information, reworded each time, because my silence over the last few days has convinced her that her Googles are not getting through.

She is excited about a new online dating site she has discovered called Greydates UK, for widows and widowers of a certain age, and wonders if I agree with her that it's time to make new friends again. Oh my God. Greydates UK? And what does she mean, *friends*?

I can't even think about it now, but I tell her she is free to Greydate as much as she likes – if she feels ready. It's been three years since Dad died.

She says she has accidentally sent Aunt Helena's trunk to Barks of Byron Bay. I can only hope Dani sends it on. Oh God. What if she chucks the lot, in a fit of revenge? Or worse still, makes natty little dog coats out of the Mary Quant dress?

While Joel picks up provisions at the supermarket, I trawl through the rest of the news from London.

My friends want to talk to me about everything I'm

missing on the television, but all I want to do is tell them all about Joel. Instead, I sit on my hands. How can I possibly explain any of it to anyone? I don't even understand it myself. And underneath everything lurks the thought that although it feels right, right, right, it's wrong, wrong, wrong.

Even if I went to a phone box now, rang Suzanne and got her out of bed to talk about it, I still couldn't find the right words.

Nash has sent me two emails. One is headed 'COMMUNICATION TO AUSTRALIA' and insists that I make more effort to stay in touch. We may have broken up, he says, but that is no reason not to remain friends. Yeah right. I write back and tell him I'm staying in a caravan on a country property with no water, a generator, no phone line and no proper loo, thus COMMUNICATION TO AUSTRALIA is a bit limited. That should shut him up. I do not tell him about Barks.

Just the thought of entering into discussions with Nash about that makes me feel overwhelmed. All I really want to do is get back to the grapefruit tree, the chickens, and the creek.

What did Joel say last night? 'Welcome to the real world.' I think I'm beginning to understand what he means.

Nash's second impossibly polite email is about the packing crate he has just dispensed, and like Mum he's also sent it to Barks of Byron Bay.

My God. I hope Danielle Coles doesn't open it – if

she sees my donkey charity shop tights collection she'll never recover.

I don't think the internet is a very good idea at the moment. Every time I check my messages from England my head feels like it's going to explode. Even Suzanne's emails are too much – full of Camden Market news and local celebrity gossip. It all seems too far away.

While I wait for Joel to finish at the supermarket, I wonder how long I should wait before ringing Dani about my shipments from England. Maybe I should tell her I know Sting or something. That might help.

Chapter Fourteen

Now that I have a new life in Australia, with a new dog and a new caravan, it feels like New Year's Eve. Thus, I make a new resolution: I am going to pay Joel back for everything, even if it kills me.

We are having a beer in Bellingen one evening when I push two $100 notes over the table.

'What's this?' he asks.

'The bicycle you gave me. Our food. The loo rolls yesterday. This beer. Everything you've spent on me so far.'

'I'm not keeping a tally. Are you?'

'Sorry.'

'Don't be sorry. I get it. But if I was broke and you had some cash lying around, wouldn't you want to send it my way?'

'Yes.'

'Well then. No tally. You'll be helping me out soon enough if you get going with your clothes. You know, the Vintage Alice thing.'

Joel gives me one of his funny, friendly, crinkly

258

smiles, and I try to smile back, although I feel like a complete fraud. There are dozens of pregnant women in England at the moment just waiting for me to make them frocks, but at this rate they will have given birth by the time I've organized myself.

We cycle home, unsteadily, in the heat – it is the kind of day when the roads seem to shimmer and wobble – then I help Joel pull weeds out of a patch of land south of the caravans, which he thinks would make a good home for a worm farm.

We wear thick rubber gloves as we work, and I try not to sneeze as pollen flies everywhere. The previous owners have left an old concrete slab behind, and a rusty car trailer without tyres.

'Poor old flying fox,' Joel notes a black, leathery corpse lying on the ground. 'Must have hit something on the way home.'

Chang inspects it and makes little whining noises. I think it may be the first bat either of us have ever seen. Australia continually presents me with live versions of things I've only ever experienced on television.

'So tell me about the worm farm again?' I ask.

'Everything organic goes into the tank,' Joel explains as we sit down on the concrete slab. 'Paper, cardboard, sewage, the lot. The worms process it, to put it nicely, then it all goes back onto the fruit trees and veggies, as a kind of super juice.'

'You make it sound so lovely.'

'Are you OK with that?'

'Oh yes,' I swallow hard. 'I can be an Australian worm farmer.'

He picks up an old stone tool, which is lying on top of an old car battery near the slab.

'Someone else found this before me,' he says. 'I'd forgotten I left it here. It's Aboriginal.'

'Wow.'

'The other Australia,' Joel says as he helps me up.

'So they were here, on this land?'

'Yeah, before they were driven out. Who knows when that got left here. It might have been hundreds of years ago.'

He points at the sun, which is shining over the top of the mountains, and says he wants to build a house here using solar power.

'I'm so hopeless,' I say, feeling very Swiss Cottage all of a sudden. 'I don't know anything.'

'Neither do I! I'm going to teach myself, while I'm here. But imagine this place in a couple of years' time. Everything on your plate could be grown here. You could cook using the sun for your electricity. Drink rain water from the tank. Gather honey from your own beehive . . .'

'The goat's here,' I tell him, pointing as it stumbles towards us, bleating.

'You can give him a name if you like. He's not mine by the way. He might have belonged to the squatters.'

'What squatters?'

'I've been hearing about them in town. Apparently a bus just rolled up one day when I was in India, containing half a commune, kids, goats, chooks, the lot.'

I think of Nash in London, who hates squatters so much that he's been known to pelt gravel at their boarded-up windows, and compare him with Joel, who is completely untroubled by it all.

'They probably left the chooks and the goat behind as payment.' He shrugs. 'That's often the way it works around here. Anyway, the animals seem to have found a way to get by.'

Later on, when Joel thinks I'm not looking, I sneak a glance at him swimming in his boxer shorts in the deepest part of the creek. The fact that he is so unconcerned by my presence bothers me. When I was falling in love with Nash, at the beginning – and he was falling in love with me – we were so twitchy and self-conscious around each other we could barely get through a night at a café without jumping every time our legs touched under the table.

Joel just doesn't seem to care. Meanwhile, I am beginning to care more and more about his close proximity to me. Does he really think we can stay like this for months, just being neighbourly cousins, or cousinly neighbours, living side by side in a couple of caravans?

He's seen me in my bra and pants in the middle of the night, wandering off into the bush for a pee. Nothing happened. I've seen him washing himself over a plastic bowl, naked all the way down to his rolled-up pyjama bottoms. Still nothing.

Maybe it's Rebecca with the plaits. Maybe he likes her more than he's letting on. In any case, I am beginning to feel as if nothing will ever happen between us.

The next day – the hottest morning yet – I cycle to the Bellingen library and borrow a book about goats. I also give ours a name – Henry, after Henry Lawson. He is not the donkey I want – who will be named Simpson – but he's a start.

There is a lot to learn. Henry has lice, to begin with, which is why he's scratching all the time, and unless I'm careful the lice may hop onto Chang, and then presumably me. The solution is a large teaspoon of sulphur every day for as long as Henry can stand it.

He also needs a doe, if I am ever going to make goats'-milk yoghurt, but I have to make sure she doesn't have big knees. Big knees, apparently, are a huge problem in the goat world. I must tell Suzanne in my next email. It's exactly the same in the world of fashion. One big knee and you're out of the collection. Two big knees and you'll never work again.

I talk to Joel about Henry the goat and his lice.

'Maybe we should try sheep instead,' I suggest.

'Except they get crutch run, blowfly strike and pulpy kidney,' he advises me.

Bugger, or as they say in Bellingen, buggery. If I have to deal with a sheep's disgusting pulpy kidney after a hard morning's work throwing buckets of sewage at worms, I think I may have to throw in the towel, or as they also say around here, 'chark it all in'.

Joel cheers me up by bringing home some mint,

parsley and basil plants from Wiz, which he has ex-changed for a box of fresh eggs. He is dripping with sweat in the heat.

'Wiz says he can help us with a beehive as well,' he tells me, 'but we'll have to change our clothes if we do.'

'Why?'

'Bees hate black.'

'You're joking. Almost everything I own is black.'

'They don't like beards either. Wiz had big problems with his bees; they used to attack his chin.'

We have peanut spinach loaf for dinner, made with Joel's spinach, and something he calls apple ambrosia, which I have never heard of, but think I may become addicted to.

I suppose I'm becoming an accidental vegetarian. It used to happen sometimes in London when Nash and I were particularly broke, but now it feels like something I could live with for the rest of my life.

I don't even mind Joel's lectures now. In fact, I'm almost beginning to understand the point of them. All those farting cows and global warming, how could it possibly hurt to eat asparagus instead?

Oh my God. Suzanne was absolutely right in her last email. Thanks to Joel, I am turning into a fully-fledged, card-carrying Aussie hippie chick.

The days roll by, as the heat builds – the weather is abnormal for late summer, according to the locals – and we make plans for the autumn instead, to make ourselves feel cooler.

Joel and I say polite goodnights to each other from our caravan doorways, then wake each other the next morning with billy tea made from water boiled in a billycan on the campfire, with proper unpasteurized cow's milk that has blobs of yellow cream on top. We could just plug a kettle in, of course, but Joel prefers it this way.

He's a romantic. I've already worked it out. And yet, for all our late-night stargazing and convivial beer-drinking at The Federal Hotel, we seldom seem to get any closer.

I long to talk to Suzanne about it, but she is so busy these days that even when I can get through on the phone, all I get is her voicemail. She seems very, very far away, even though Twad is on sale in the Bellingen newsagency. It comes on a ship, the newsagent tells me, which is why it's always three months out of date.

I am dutifully pulling out more weeds near the concrete slab one morning on another intensely hot day when the postman delivers a kind of instant Christmas: Aunt Helena's trunk – sent on from Barks of Byron Bay – and all the boxes from Nash.

I kiss the trunk, which has been squashed inside a wooden crate. Thank God for Nice Heidi: she must have talked Nasty Dani into sending it on, because her aunt still refuses to reply to my emails.

Joel helps me carry the crates into my caravan, and I rip off the tape with a bread knife. Suddenly, all that remains of my old life in England is decanted onto my bed.

'You look like you're going to enjoy this,' Joel says, smiling. 'I'll leave you to it.'

I prop myself up against the caravan wall with pillows and sort through the bits and pieces of my recent past. Nash hasn't left a note. It's still strange to see his handwriting on the boxes, though, after all this time.

I pick my way through my grandmother's button collection, which he has wrapped up in one of my old pink towels. I wonder if I could make jewellery from them and sell them at the Bellingen Market? The market is my new discovery of the week, along with a chicken food recipe that's supposed to prevent fowl pox.

Amongst my possessions, there is an old black beret that saw me through several hard winters in London, though if I wear it here our black-hating bees may boycott me.

I try out a half-full tube of concealer and lipstick that I made Nash send, squinting at myself in the sunlight in a tiny hand mirror that arrived cracked on one side. Not only is my face divided into two halves, I look like a goth panda. The red lipstick is too hard in the bright sunshine and the concealer is far too white. Without even trying, I have picked up a tan in Bellingen, just from riding around on my bike.

My old A–Z of London is in the second box, scribbled with arrows, pointing to long-forgotten locations for job interviews, from Kentish Town to Putney.

There are other scribbles on the dog-eared pages, reminding me about parties I have been to in the days when it was still possible to have a good time with Nash.

Oh look. He's sent me *The Best of Motown*. Now there's something I thought Nash would never let me have. He was always such a dictator about music. I can't believe he has passed up this opportunity to edit my collection at last, but no, he has carefully packed it into the box, along with everything else.

All those petty annoyances with Nash seem so far away now, and so long ago. I wonder how The Believers are faring with Sarah on board? The news must either be very good or very bad, because Nash is saying nothing about anything.

I unpack old soap-making equipment; four fat, dusty paintbrushes left over from my pottery days; a hand-knitted stripy scarf with glittery wool. These were all the ideas I had before Vintage Alice. Suddenly I'm not sure if I should feel comforted by my old possessions or depressed by them.

I find a family tree I half-started and gave up on. How funny. There's Joel's name next to Robyn's, growing out of the left-hand fork in one of the trees. And now here I am, living on the same branch.

Suddenly he bounds into the caravan.

'Hey, guess what I've just found?' I wave the family tree at him.

'Get up on the bed.'

'What?'

'Just hop up on the bed, Alice, quickly, and look straight at the wall. Don't look down.'

I step up onto the caravan bed, and despite his instructions, immediately look at the ground, following his eyeline. And then I see it. A long, skinny black snake slithering from the doorway towards the old caravan kitchen cupboards.

'Argh!'

'Shhh. It's fine, Alice, the snake won't hurt you. I just need you to stay up there on the bed, that's all. And *don't look.*'

I turn my head and face the wall. Please, please, Saint Martin-in-the-Fields and Saint Vincent de Paul, make the black snake go away. I'm not sure I can remain standing on this wobbly mattress for much longer.

Joel pounds the floor in his boots, and I try not to whimper in case he has just stamped on the snake's head. What happens if you do that? Does the head explode?

'There you go. I've got him. No worries,' Joel mutters, reassuring himself as much as me, then I finally feel brave enough to turn my head and see him holding up a hessian sack at arm's length.

'Take it away!' I yelp.

'One Red-Bellied Black snake to go,' Joel jokes, taking a huge jump off the bottom caravan step, swinging the sack as he goes. 'Stay here, Alice. I'll be back.'

My legs feel as if something is crawling all over them – probably of a reptilian nature – and I am momentarily paralysed. I'm not sure if I should run out of the caravan or stay where I am. What if the snake has a wife? What if there's another one in here right now? Or a whole family of them, slithering around under this bed, looking for my legs?

Joel wouldn't have left me if it wasn't safe. I have to trust him. But maybe I should close the caravan door to be safe. I get up, cringing, trying to avoid the few feet of lino where the snake was slithering a few minutes ago. Then I slam the door, whimper and get back on the bed.

I must concentrate on something else. Aunt Helena's trunk. Yes. I must forget all about snakes and find the Mary Quant and Ossie Clark dresses, and all the magnificent old shoes and fabrics.

There is something stuck on the side of the trunk: a polite note from Dani on Barks of Byron Bay writing paper, decorated with the usual royal dogs wearing crowns and carrying orbed sceptres. Perhaps she's forgiven me after all. Maybe I won't wake up tomorrow morning to find myself issued with a deportation notice from the Department of Australian Immigration.

I try not to worry about the fact that Joel seems to have disappeared. What if he's been bitten? Where's my *G'day Australia* handbook? I have already forgotten what you're meant to do about a snake bite. Do you pee on it, or not pee on it?

Suddenly, the handle of the caravan door turns and Joel bolts in, panting.

'Smoke!' he yells. 'That's why the snakes are all out. We have to get out of here.'

'What?'

'Fire coming.' He takes my hand and pulls me out

of the van. 'There's smoke all the way down near Wiz's place, but it's on the other side, too. That means the fire's already jumped the road.'

A fire *coming*? I am about to correct him when I remember where I'm living. It must be a bush fire.

'See that cloud?' Joel squeezes my hand and makes me look east. 'It's bush fire smoke. It's a long way off, but I'm worried about the wind changing.'

I suddenly remember the snake and ask him about it.

'I let him go. He's a long way off. Don't worry. But we need to get out of here.'

'Will all the snakes be trying to escape now?' I suddenly feel terrified.

'They won't hurt you if you don't hurt them,' Joel tries to reassure me, but I've heard that one before, and all I can think about is a whole army of them slithering down the hill.

Joel says Chang has detected a bush fire, too, because he's shivering and will not leave our side.

Then I blink – there is something in my eye.

'Ash.' Joel looks worried as he holds out a finger to catch more of it – tiny black specks blow around in the air. 'It's coming from everywhere. Alice, get one case from the small van. I'll sort out another case in the big van. We're going to have to bike it, so don't overload yourself. I'll take Chang if you can get him in a rucksack. We'll have to leave Henry and the chickens. I think they'll be OK – but we have to get out.'

'What about all my stuff from England?'

'Leave it.'

'Oh God, Joel. Helena's trunk, my sewing machine. It's everything I have!' I feel like crying.

'We have to go, Alice. Leave the sewing machine, I'll get you another one. Get your passport, papers, photos, some clothes. I'm giving you three minutes.'

'What?' Suddenly I feel like killing him.

'Two minutes now,' he says, racing ahead of me to his van.

We run, panting in the heat, with Chang following us.

For the second time in a few months I find myself trying desperately to grab as much as I can of everything that's precious to me. It's just like that horrible day with Nash. I cram my passport into a plastic bag and stuff in everything else I can see, all the while conscious of Joel yelling at me from his caravan.

There. One minute and I've done everything I can. Maybe the bush fire won't get us. Maybe the Mary Quant dress will be OK. Perhaps Joel's just overreacting.

'Come on,' he pulls me out of my van and bundles Chang into the rucksack, swinging him on his back and squashing his head down, though it just pops straight back up again.

'There's even more smoke now,' I tell Joel as a dirty grey cloud goes higher over the tops of the trees.

Suddenly we hear a honking sound and see Wiz in his camper van at the top of the road, waving frantically.

Joel is panting now in the thick dust and ash.

'Got another five minutes,' Wiz waves us back and shouts through the window.

'You sure?' Joel shouts back, but I'm already tearing off back down the hill again. All I can think about is the extra room in the back of Wiz's van. I can put Helena's trunk in there. I have to. If it all burns I'll never forgive myself.

Joel catches me up as I start running. 'Get all the blankets from your van and soak them,' he pants, and starts filling one bottle after another with water. 'Fill everything you can with water and bring it. We might be able to get some of the chooks and Henry in, I'm not sure.'

'Bugger off, Henry!' I try to shoo the goat away from the caravan door in the direction of the van, but he won't go. Instead, he stumbles towards the creek.

'He'll be fine. It's OK.' Joel gasps for air. It feels like all the oxygen is being sucked away from the land, as if an enormous fan heater is blowing dust the other way. There's no sign of our hens.

I try not to think about the little bits of black, flaky ash going into my lungs. My eyes are already starting to water.

'Now!' Wiz yells, leaning out of the van window and beckoning us over. We stumble towards him, Chang swinging in the rucksack on Joel's back, juggling bottles of water and sopping-wet blankets.

'Helena's trunk . . .' I hear myself saying.

'Can't go back. Water's more important,' Joel cuts me off.

'Wiz, we're so glad to see you—' I start to thank the Wizard Formerly Known as Wayne as he helps us into his van.

'Git in there,' he says before I can force any more of my time-wasting English politeness upon him.

The smoke cloud is enormous now, hanging high above our heads.

'Nothing tethered?' Wiz checks. I suppose he means the animals.

'No,' Joel reassures him. Then I realize we are sharing the back seat with a large dog and an ancient cat. No wonder Chang is trembling like a jelly under my arm. Then after a few minutes I realize what is in the front seat. It's a large goanna that looks like a junior extra from *Jurassic Park* and is flicking its tongue and waving its tail from side to side.

'Kiss me,' Joel whispers.

'Aaargh!' I cannot stop cringing at the awful goanna, which is staring at me with its cold reptilian eyes from Wiz's passenger seat.

'Kiss me, Alice.'

Joel pulls me towards him and I breathe in mint, lemon and patchouli, and all the other wonderful hippyish things he always smells of.

'You just want to take my mind off that . . . thing,' I whisper when we come up for air.

'But was it good?' He nudges me.

'God *yes*!' I blurt out, like some deranged, sex-starved idiot.

I give myself the giggles, and they go on and on until

Wiz gives me a fierce look in the rear-view mirror and I realize I may be having some kind of hysterical fit. But . . . he kissed me. Joel kissed me. Goanna or no goanna, it's happened.

The van lurches forward over the unsealed road.

'Look,' Joel warns me after a few minutes, and I see that the fire has raced ahead of Wiz's van, so it's now on either side of us. My heart starts banging and will not stop, and suddenly I want to go the loo more than anything else in the world. My brain wants to be brave, but my body is a coward.

Wiz looks straight ahead, hunched over the wheel as if his hands are glued to it. Suddenly, the beautiful, sunny day has turned dark. Where did all the light go?

'Wet your face.' Joel passes me and Wiz a water bottle. 'My eyes are stinging,' I croak. 'My throat's burning.'

'Keep blinking hard and try not to rub your eyes.' Joel squeezes my hand. 'Keep your eyes closed. Breathe normally – as much as you can – and take little sips. Don't talk.'

As we drive on, I realize the roaring sound I thought might be wind is actually the fire. It has raced across the road in front of us, making it impossible to pass.

'Can't go back,' Wiz says, looking in his rear-view mirror. 'She's all gone back there. I'm going to put the headlights on and then I'll drive straight through.'

'Shit,' Joel says. 'Are you sure?'

'Sure as I'll ever be,' Wiz says and punches the cassette player so Prince bursts into life. I realize what we are about to do. Our lives are completely in Wiz's hands, and we are driving through a fire listening to 'Purple Rain'.

I bury my head in Joel's T-shirt and breathe in the smell of his minty, lemony, chest. The shirt stinks of smoke but his skin is still the same, thank God.

Whatever happens now, I think, it has to be right. Everything else about the last few months has been right, so this must be, too. And . . . it feels like we're together now. We've jumped the gate, just like one of the chickens, and now we're over the fence.

I stroke Wiz's cat and dog, who are wide-eyed, panting and terrified, while Joel holds Chang. Meanwhile, the dreadful goanna huddles low on the passenger seat.

'Good on ya,' Wiz pats the goanna absent-mindedly as he grates the gearstick and crunches over another bump in the road.

The water bottle goes around the car again, and this time we sluice it over our skin, not caring. Wiz pours a handful over the top of his head and licks his lips as it runs down his face.

Flames go over the bonnet of the car and I try not to look, while Joel pushes the animals down on the floor so they can't see.

Suddenly a horse runs past us along the side of the road, away from a burning house, and I find myself praying that he won't race into the fire. Perhaps he's on fire already, but we can't stop to save him. We have to keep on driving.

Then, without any warning, the engine stalls.

'Shit,' Joel says.

'Shit,' Wiz echoes.

We sit and wait. Wiz tries again. Nothing.

'We'll get through,' Joel tells me. 'We're nearly there now, Alice. The town's not that far away. There'll be a fire break soon. Just hang on.'

Wiz tries a third time and miraculously the van springs into life. We drive forward just as a burning tree crashes behind us.

'Prince is a real master of his game, isn't he,' Wiz says to nobody in particular; the goanna sticks out his tongue in reply.

'So tell me again why you're known as the Wizard Formerly Known as Wayne,' I ask, trying desperately to take our minds off the flames outside.

'My ex-wife got nasty,' Wiz explains croakily. 'She made a voodoo doll out of scone dough and wrote Wayne on its back – and this happened . . .'

Wiz keeps one hand on the steering wheel and lifts up his T-shirt with the other. He is covered in pimples.

'Those are some spots,' Joel whistles, then Wayne pulls his T-shirt down again.

We drive on through the smoke, and I rub my eyes, over and over, trying not to think about Wiz's horrible spotty back. I bury my face in Joel's shoulder, wishing it could all be over. It all feels like some kind of mad dream.

'Look!' Joel yells and points out of the window. 'Blue sky, Alice. Just a patch, but you can see it now.'

'Yeehah!' Wayne whoops and honks his horn.

I think about the poor horse, left behind, and realize

I must have been crying steadily for the last five minutes without realizing it. My eyes are so sore I've barely registered the tears.

We keep driving until two policemen appear in the middle of the road, shaking their heads, grinning and waving us on. In reply, slowly but surely, Wiz's thumb appears, upright, over the steering wheel, and he waggles it backwards and forwards.

'You're a miracle man,' Joel slaps him on the back, but Wiz still only has eyes for the road.

'There!' I yell, as I spot a large State Emergency Services sign, propped up outside what is normally a row of cafés and a car park, but which has become a makeshift rescue centre, lined with trestle tables, bottles of water and fold-up chairs.

Wiz stops his van and we fall out, hot, dazed and shocked at the way the fire has turned his VW camper van from pale blue to dirty black.

Wiz carries his goanna in his arms, to the nearest bowl of water. Then Chang follows Wiz's cat and dog straight past the line of fold-up chairs, the rows of parked vans and cars – all charred black like ours – and into the nearest stretch of grass. In just a few weeks, the lush green fields I saw on the way in from Byron Bay have turned straw-yellow. Still, there is water over there somewhere, and the animals seem to know it.

'Let him go,' Joel puts his arm around me as I watch Chang run off. 'He knows what he's doing.'

Wiz has been recognized by the locals, despite his dirty face and singed beard, and is being given bottle after bottle of cold water, which he doesn't know whether to drink or pour over himself. I realize we are both shaking – Wiz quietly and me uncontrollably. Joel, by contrast, is perfectly still.

Fire trucks are pulling in everywhere, and people seem to be reacting in two ways: smiling and laughing too much from relief and nerves, or just staring into space like stunned mullets.

'Do you want to sit down or lie down?' a woman wearing a bright orange SES waistcoat asks – and I see that there are dozens of blow-up mattresses lining the street.

'I don't know. I saw a horse trying to get out,' I tell her. 'We had to leave our goat and chickens.'

'I know, love.'

She has kind eyes, like Heidi Coles.

Wiz sits in a fold-up chair, shaking quietly.

'They need to treat him for shock,' Joel says.

'We're treating you *all* for shock,' the SES woman puts her hand on his shoulder.

The rest of the day is a blur. I find myself panicking about Chang and Wiz's animals, who are eventually found and brought back, then kept inside an air-conditioned rescue truck.

At some point Wiz, his animals and his few possessions are rescued by relatives, who have driven in from Taree to evacuate him.

There are radios blaring everywhere, offering a series of news bulletins. There seems to be a fire update every ten minutes, and I hear a roll-call of unfamiliar place names, all of which have been caught up in the blaze.

Suddenly I feel unbelievably tired, but I also need to talk, and keep on talking.

'He saved our life,' I tell a man with red hair who says he's Wiz's nephew. 'Tell Wiz he saved our life. I'm never going to forget it.'

'We still call him Wayne in our family,' says the red-haired man.

As Joel and I watch Wiz's family drive him away, bits and pieces of conversation drift past our ears. It's the worst fire Bellingen has had for ten years. Half the houses on the Darkwood Road are expected to be gone by tomorrow. The fire was deliberately lit, or, in another version, the fire was an accident, started by tourists who left a barbecue burning behind them.

'Hey, Joel,' a dark-haired man approaches us. It's John, a friend of Joel's who has come to volunteer.

'John. We're homeless, mate. This is Alice and her dog Chang.'

'No worries. Come to our place.'

'Is it safe?' I ask John stupidly. Everything feels un-safe at the moment.

'We live on the beach,' he explains with a small smile.

John drives a huge truck. Joel and I share the wide front seat, and I put Chang on my lap after bundling our sad collection of bags, blankets and water bottles in the back.

'Chang was incontinent,' I tell John, trying to make conversation, 'but now he's not. Obviously.'

A pause, then Joel and John both start howling with laughter, and I find myself joining in until I can't stop.

I remember my grandmother telling me about the mad giggling that went on during the worst days of the war. If you've been badly scared, you'll laugh at anything.

John's house by the beach turns out to be wonderful – an old-fashioned wooden bungalow with a separate studio in the garden. We sleep there with Chang at our feet and throw all the blankets off because it's so hot. Eventually we're covered only by a sheet.

A fan chops away on the ceiling, while tiny frogs stick to the window, using the suckers on their feet to stay on the glass.

'This cousins thing is going to be weird, isn't it,' I ask Joel, snuggling into him.

'Too much explaining.'

'It's going to be *very* hard work trying to make people understand.'

'Already is,' Joel pulls me towards him.

'I've wanted this for ever and ever,' I tell him, 'but now I'm just so tired.'

'Sleep,' Joel kisses me and pulls me towards him. We both stink of smoke, and as I fall asleep I catch myself thinking that I'll always associate the smell of singed hair with a strange kind of happiness.

Joel and I both have mild burns – like painful sunburn – and as we cling together under the sheet we both have nightmares throughout the night. Mine have nothing to do with the fire, instead they're about snakes, escaping in their hundreds over the property. Joel's are all about the fire, though, and at one point he has a lucid dream that the horse we saw running along the road is trying to push us off the edge of a cliff.

I cannot believe how angry I feel the next morning. It's a generalized anger – at the fire, at the person who started it, at Australia itself.

'The bush can be a bitch,' John agrees as he pours us some orange juice. Joel and I are both so dehydrated that we can't stop drinking, and we gulp down anything from tap water to coffee, like people who have been walking through a desert.

We laugh at our eyes in John's bathroom mirror. They are so bloodshot they look exactly like the eyeballs you see in silly fake glasses in fancy-dress shops. Even Chang's little round eyes are red.

We ring Wiz's nephew, but he doesn't answer the phone.

'At the pub,' John jokes. 'Bet you. First place you're going to find Wiz, after everything he's been through.'

After that, Joel and I have the longest, coldest showers in the world. I have seldom craved water so much.

'I've got to take you back into town to fill in your registration forms,' John tells us. 'Otherwise you're going to be a missing person statistic.'

We drive back into Bellingen, listening to the news on the radio. The fires have been widespread and two people are dead, with three missing.

Joel and I look at each other, terrified. Then he starts

blaming himself for not evacuating us earlier, for not having a plan, for not reading the weather more carefully.

'Stop it,' I say and put my hand over his mouth.

The makeshift car park and emergency centre at the café, so crowded yesterday, is now reduced to a neat little camp of buses, trucks and ambulances.

Joel and I register our names and address and supply Wiz's as well, in case the police haven't heard from him.

'Alice Templeton,' I say.

'Joel Templeton,' Joel follows me.

'Ah, so you two are married?' John asks Joel when he hears. 'You kept that one quiet, mate. Congratulations.'

'Not married,' Joel looks embarrassed. 'Cousins.'

Now it's John's turn to look embarrassed.

'Not actually related by blood,' I explain. 'Don't worry.'

'It's a long story, mate,' Joel puts his hand on John's back. 'I'll tell you another time.'

'You goin' back?' a woman from the SES asks. 'They've given the all-clear now. They'll give you a lift if you want one.'

'We are going back,' Joel confirms. 'Who do we speak to?'

We're unable to let go of each other, or Chang, who's on the other end of my long stripy scarf, which is acting as a makeshift lead. Joel and I wear each other like security belts.

'Becky can drive you,' the SES woman tells us, and

after we've bid John farewell, we find Becky – another volunteer in a bright orange vest – with large bottles of water in both pockets.

'Get ready,' she warns us as we drive off in her van.

All we see for the first mile or so are dead or dying cows.

'I can't stand it!' I hide my face in Joel's shirt.

'What are they doing about the animals?' he asks Becky while I burrow into his chest.

'They're onto it. We've got WIRES, the RSPCA, the whole lot. Don't you worry about the animals. You're priority one; they're the *other* priority one.'

Trees are still on fire everywhere we look. Even worse, houses have been reduced to burning shells, with only their frames still standing. The smell of smoke is inescapable, even with the windows up.

Finally, we reach Joel's property.

'I only had a couple of caravans here,' he tells Becky before she asks. 'There wasn't much to lose.' He doesn't tell Becky it's everything he and I own in the world.

We get out of the van, leaving Chang in the back, and walk down the hill. There's nothing left of the postbox. Neither caravan has survived. Instead, there is a black mess covering about half an acre of Joel's land. It's hard to tell what used to be caravan and what used to be trees.

'You save much?' Becky asks.

'Just bits,' I reply, then I realize the enormity of what I have just said and start feeling shaky. I want to cry, but

I can't. I'm too tired. Even our bicycles have burned to nothing.

We find Henry the goat, whose feet, nose and ears are red with blood. Joel's eyes fill with tears as Becky and I lead him back to the truck for the long drive back to the Bellingen football oval, which has been set up as an emergency animal shelter.

'We should have put him in the back of the van,' I say.

'No time,' Joel says sadly.

The chickens are dead at the far side of the property. We find other animals who couldn't get out in time – possums, wombats, kookaburras and even a poor little wallaby. It's so unfair, I can't stand it.

'How did the fire start?' I ask Becky, whose eyes are as red as mine.

'Vandals,' she says, looking grim. She tells me she has been back and forth to six properties in two days, all destroyed – with dead and dying native animals everywhere she looks.

'Your friend's house is all right,' she says, and I realize she must mean Wiz. 'He left his hoses running over the roof, and he'd been soaking the grass since the sun came up. He's lost about half of it, but there's enough there to build on. Not insured, though.'

'Not insured?' I look at Joel.

'Crazy,' Becky shakes her head. 'You wouldn't believe how many people weren't. But he's the Wizard Formerly Known as Wayne, yeah? So he's obviously got . . .' she makes quotation marks, 'supernatural powers.'

We get back in the van, with Henry lying across our knees. He puts his head in Joel's lap like a human, as if he's asking for help.

And then I see it – a lone brown hen with wet tail feathers – running towards us, clucking in panic, from the direction of the creek.

'Hey ho,' Becky says. 'Some old girl's had the brains to sit it out in the water.'

Joel and I cackle like idiots.

'She's alive!' I say, pointing at the hen, who's excitedly making bock-bock-bock noises, and Joel laughs at me again, then we start cackling again. The van is almost shaking now. I suppose Becky is used to it – I expect everyone she has transported in here lately has been in hysterics.

'You're staying up at Urunga, is that right?' she asks us once we've calmed down and returned to the make-shift car park in town.

'For the moment. Then we'll probably go and stay with my sister in Sydney,' Joel tells her.

'My cousin,' I say at the same time, getting a strange look from Becky.

'Then make a fresh start, eh?' she suggests, catching my eye in the rear-view mirror.

'I'm sort of getting used to it,' I tell her as I put my hand in Joel's.

When we get out of the car, Joel, Henry and I are immediately snapped by a newspaper photographer. It's only when he stops to reload his camera that I realize I'm still holding Joel's hand.

'It's just for the appeal,' the photographer explains. 'For the fires.'

It seems a fund has already been started up for us – and everyone like us – who lost their homes.

'People round here aren't rich, but they'll give everything they can,' Joel tells me once the photographer's gone.

'We can't take money from them,' I protest.

'It's just neighbours being neighbours,' Joel shrugs. 'We'd do the same if we'd escaped and other people had got stuck. It's like that round here. People look after each other.'

Then he kisses me, and this time I don't care who sees.

Chapter Fifteen

Joel rings Robyn to let her know we are OK, then he rings his parents. His sister says we can stay as long as we like. She has been desperate to get hold of us, she says.

'She called us crazy hippies.' Joel sighs when he tells me about it. 'But she's glad we're alive.'

I call my mother as soon as I can, before she has a chance to find out about the North Coast bush fires on the internet. I needn't have worried: she's more concerned about a forthcoming bicycle ride with Greydate UK.

They're all cycling to a village where Princess Alexandra is rumoured to have friends, and because all the Greydaters are having lunch at a restaurant afterwards, mum is worried that Princess A. will swan past their table and see her tatty old shoes.

'Just wear your wellies, Mum. They're very fashionable at the moment.'

'Oh, I don't think I can do that!'

'Look. I've been staying in Bellingen with Joel. We

had a bush fire, but we're OK now. We might go and stay with Robyn at Bondi Beach for a while, though.'

'Oh dear. What sort of bush fire?'

'Joel had a couple of old caravans and we had two bicycles. Everything melted. Our chickens died. Well, all except one.'

'The chickens are *dead*?'

'Our goat is at an RSPCA shelter. They've set up a special centre for all the livestock. He couldn't get away. It was awful; he's covered in burns.'

I stand in the phone box for half an hour after this, as my mother forces me to work backwards through the story – *all* of the story.

'Cousins can marry cousins,' mum says thoughtfully after I've confessed about Joel. 'It's perfectly normal in the Middle East. Though I believe it's illegal in America. What about Australia?'

'Mum! I'm not even considering marrying Joel.'

She asks me about my job at Barks.

'This woman Danielle was going to do *what*?' she interrupts when I tell her about the day I was supposed to have Mr Chang put down.

'Dani was a bit of a fitness freak,' I explain. 'I think that came first.'

'I don't like those giddy gym bunnies.' She sighs.

'She did Pilates as well.'

'Oh, how ghastly. It sounds like a disease.'

My mother asks me what I have left after the fire. I can count it all on the fingers of both hands. Three black skirts; five T-shirts and shirts; three pairs of knickers;

one pair of flip-flops – which Joel insists I should call thongs, because I'm Australian now – one book on Yves St Laurent; my passport, immigration papers and address book; my photographs.

'It's making me cry,' I tell her. 'Can we talk about something else?'

'Oh, Alice, yes. Do you know, I have two hundred and fifty friends in my Greydate UK local forum? I only found out this morning. I had no idea. I feel as if someone has filled up my dance card without me noticing.'

I think of Mum's spatial skills, which have never been particularly good, and imagine her with hundreds of other similarly confused Greydaters, cycling in a pack up the M23 while an out-of-control truck careers off the road somewhere near Princess Alexandra's friend's village.

'Anyway, darling,' she finishes, 'if you've been in a fire, that really is an emergency, isn't it. So I'm going to put some of Dad's money into your account this evening.'

'No, it's for you.'

'He meant it for both of us.'

'Mum! First Nash and now this? There'll be nothing left!'

'Don't argue, dear. There'll still be plenty left. You can't live in three pairs of knickers.'

I feel like two people. One of them is New Australian Alice, who can manage perfectly well on her own, no matter if the problem is a worm farm, a bush fire or a snake. The other one is Old Alice, who is so relieved and excited to hear about the sudden arrival of some money that she simply gives in. In the end, I make peace between both of me. If Mum puts too much money in my account – more than I need to get by, anyway – I'll deposit it straight back.

When I go back to John's on the bus I see that someone has left an old newspaper behind and I read the jobs section. I'm not an accountant, backhoe operator, boiler maker, bus driver, butcher, cabinet maker, concreter, driver, electrician, forklift driver, glazier or panel beater, though. Are all Australian jobs designed for hearty women?

I spot two jobs Joel and I could do, if we were desperate enough: selling advertising for volunteer magazines over the phone – call Jason now! – and selling boutique wine over the phone – call Trevor now!

We have already talked about asking Robyn for jobs at her hotel, but neither of us want to do it. We feel we're imposing enough as it is.

There is a small part of me that wishes she would just offer, though, even if it means hurtling back to my days as a cleaner. I never thought I'd be grateful to have the chance to vacuum other people's mess up again, but now it seems like a lifeline.

Joel is convinced we would eventually be better off going back to his property, pitching a tent and slowly starting to build up the chickens, vegetable patch and fruit trees again, living on the very last of his savings while we try to live off the land.

The bus hurtles on towards Urunga while I worry

about all this. The cool change which the locals were talking about has now arrived and the sky is pale grey through the windows.

Perhaps I think about money all the time because Dad did, too.

My father worked like a dog – or at least a Barks dog carer – all his life. Or perhaps he was more like a hamster, going round and round on a gigantic wheel.

The second-hand Jaguars and Mercedes Dad bought had to be repaired, cleaned, insured and maintained. Expensive security systems had to be installed, to protect the cars from thieves – and any drunk who felt like chucking a brick. After that, the tax usually used to finish him off.

My memories of my father, from the time I went to university, to the year he died, revolve around paperwork, late-night accounting, frantic sessions with calculators and a constant supply of aspirin, washed down with a glass of red wine after dinner. And now look. Even his old bank is going broke.

I love the idea that Joel and I might be self-sufficient one day. I'm longing for a time when I'll never have to think about money again. It seems impossible at the moment, though, with only one chicken left and burned-out trees all around us.

I remember my post and open it. There's nothing remotely interesting, just bank statements, which Nash has redirected from London.

Amazingly, one of the letters actually manages to

spell my name right. I am usually known as Miss A. Templeton to the HSBC, but today there is an envelope from one of their rival banks. It's a credit card offer. I can transfer the debt from my old card and pay no interest for six months.

I stare out of the window at cows lying on their sides in the sun. I have only just managed to escape being a serial debtor, with any number of collection agencies threatening me, and already some finance company is trying to woo me back. There's a toll-free number to ring, and a promise that a decision can be made over the phone. The card can be mine in fourteen working days.

It's hard not to be tempted. Then an enormous bull stands near a fence at the side of the road and craps dramatically, and at length, on the grass.

'Thank you,' I mutter through the window. The universe has spoken. I've had enough of banks.

When I arrive at John's house, Joel is on the phone, making notes. After he has finished, he pours me a beer – John brews his own – and tells me we have been offered a new caravan if we want it. And a tent. And a new generator.

'Wow! Where from?'

'People I don't even know,' Joel says. 'Someone's started a donation centre in Coffs Harbour. They've just had a whole container of new sheets offered by a department store in Sydney. Look, I've written it all down. All we have to do is turn up and put our names on the waiting list.'

'Mum's going to put some money into my account from Dad's emergency fund.'

'Did you say yes?'

'Joel. I don't want to, but part of me has to.'

'OK.'

'Some bank is offering me a credit card as well. No interest for the first six months.'

'Do you want to take it?'

'No.'

'*Good*. Now come here.' Joel holds out his arms. 'Let's go for a walk on the beach and watch the storm. Look, it's on the way.'

We pick our way along some sand dunes, then crisscross through a jungle of trees and bushes to get to the beach.

In the days when I was still weighing up the wisdom of moving to Australia, several people told me I would find the people impossible to deal with. They were too taciturn, they said. Too hard to get to know. Too rough. They may as well have been describing Wiz – or even John – but Wiz is also the man who picked us up, checked that Henry wasn't tethered, waited for us to pack our belongings, then drove us through miles of flames that could have killed us all.

Meanwhile, John has turned over his home to us, and everything in it, as if it were our own. Joel says he's always been like that, even though they don't know each other particularly well.

As we walk along the beach, Joel shows me the full list of things people have offered at the donation centre in Coffs Harbour. Almost everything that we lost is on there, from hairdryers to boxes of baked beans, pillows to pots of paint.

Joel's list reveals an incredible outpouring of generosity, and I know it's coming mostly from areas outside Sydney, where there is very little money. These are the places that Matty pointed out to me on the day we were talking about buying a unit and getting onto the Australian property ladder. Nevertheless, everyone seems to be giving what they have.

I think about Wiz's burned-out house and promise myself that I will do whatever it takes to help him build another. Even if I have to sew pyjamas out of charity-shop sheets and sell them on Jade's stall, I'm going to try to make it up to him.

'Here comes the rain,' Joel promises, and we run to find shelter underneath a tree that's growing out of the marshy land that runs behind the sand dunes.

In London, rain was always irritating, boring and something to be avoided. Here, I don't mind if I get wet. Anything's better than fire.

I'm still having nightmares about our escape. This time they don't involve snakes, but they do involve flames chasing me down the road. I haven't said anything to Joel yet, but when we finally go back to Bellingen, I'm not sure I can live indefinitely in a tent or a caravan, or more importantly without a water tank.

Even if we have to build everything ourselves, I need to know I'm living somewhere I can stay and defend.

Time and again this week I've been told that we should have stayed and fought back the fire. If I'm ever going to be able to return to Joel's property, I have to know that next time we can beat nature before it beats us.

When I was a teenager, I used to ride on the South Downs with a friend called Lucy. Nearly everyone at our school went through a horse-mad phase and I was no exception, then one day my horse bolted and I came off and broke my arm.

I was told to get straight back on again by my parents, as soon as the arm healed, but it didn't work. I still don't want to get on a horse as long as I live.

I feel differently about the threat of another bush fire, though. The other night, John told me that if we'd had a proper house instead of a couple of caravans, we could have stayed on and saved what we had.

I talk to Joel about it as the rain pours down across the beach.

'I don't know how we're going to do it, but I need to live in a house if we're going to stay there permanently,' I tell him after we have watched the lightning over the horizon.

'The fires won't come again. Not for years. There's nothing left to burn. A house is going to take time, Alice. I've got some money left, but it's not enough.'

'That's it,' I make my mind up. 'I'm going to get it.'

'How?'

'I don't know, but I'm going to make the money some-how. We've got to have a house, Joel.'

The rain pours down while I mourn the loss of

my tartan wellies and umbrella. Perhaps some kind person will have donated something I can replace them with.

I look along the beach in both directions and count my blessings. Nobody in their right mind would be here on such a wet and windy day, but it is still incredible to see miles of white sand, all unoccupied.

'It's so beautiful here,' I tell Joel.

We agree that it really is an upside-down country. We've seen dolphins cresting on this beach, in water so warm you can dive straight into it. Joel has seen sharks here too, though, swimming so close to the beach that you can see them snapping at anything that moves beneath the waves. He's seen a shark bite into driftwood here before; he was out of the water in ten seconds flat.

Just when you think Australia is some kind of post-card paradise place, it bites you on the bum – as the Wizard Formerly Known as Wayne would say.

I still haven't changed my mind about it, even since the fire. I want to belong here, even if citizenship is only a piece of paper. I want my name on a certificate, beneath the emu and the kangaroo, so I can frame it on the wall of the house we're going to build.

'Will you come with me to my citizenship ceremony?' I ask Joel.

'It would be an honour and a privilege,' he says, kissing me.

'This rain's not going to stop,' Joel says, taking my hand. 'Do you want to make a run for it?'

We race towards John's house, ahead of the thunder, and go in to find a message on his answering machine, telling us he's gone fishing.

'Tibetan incense,' Joel produces a box from one of his bags. 'It's good for Lhoong. I think we should burn some.'

'I can't believe you saved that! What's Lhoong?'

'A disequilibrium of mental and emotional events,' Joel reads from the label. 'It's also said to be good for tinnitus, swelling in the abdominal region and dry tongue.'

'John's beer is pretty good for that, too.'

We settle down on the sofa together and play an old Led Zeppelin album – John still believes in vinyl and record players – while Joel lights the incense. Led Zeppelin were banned from my life when I was with Nash. They were too low down in his musical class system. It feels good to have them back.

'There was a moment when I looked at some photos of Nash back at the caravan, and I really had to think about saving them,' I tell Joel.

'Hmmm. You know you'll have to tell him about us some time.'

'We'll both have to tell everyone *everything*.'

We sit and stare at the incense for a while without talking.

'Joel. Do you mind me mentioning Nash?'

'Not at all.'

'Damn,' I pout, pretending to be annoyed.

'I wasn't going to tell you this,' Joel squeezes my hand

and smiles. 'But when we were driving through the fire, I realized I would have been happy to die with you.'

'Me too.'

'John won't be back for hours,' he leads me to the studio and throws his clothes on the chair.

'Your skin.' I touch his shoulders. 'It's still so red.'

'Not all of it.' He smiles and pulls my shirt off.

I have fantasized about sex with Joel so often, it's a shock to realize how completely unlike my daydreams it actually is. In my imagination it's always been quick – urgent and intense – but now it's finally happening, everything seems to go in slow motion. My bra comes off, little by little, and finally my pants.

'So wet down there,' Joel says, touching me softly with the tip of his finger. Then he finds a condom and unwraps it for me, as if it were a chocolate.

It's hard not to compare him to Nash. I am already amazed at how brown he is, how warm he feels, how different he smells. There are no chemicals on Joel Templeton.

Nash was a woman-whisperer, but he always made me feel as if he'd done it all a million times before. Joel makes me feel as if everything is being made up on the spot, just for me.

He strokes my hair then meets me halfway. I want him so much I don't think I can wait.

Suddenly, we hear John's truck in the driveway. He's home early.

'Later?' Joel stops and kisses me, but I have no desire to wait. I've already waited too long.

'Shhh!' I hold my hand over his mouth, but it's no good, once I have switched places and got on top, I come before he does, then I can't stop my moaning, let alone his.

'God,' Joel says at last, rolling off me. 'Oh my *God*.'

As we lie together side by side, I realize the sheet is soaked with sweat. It is, in every sense of the word, the hottest sex I have ever had in my life.

We fall asleep, and when I wake, Joel has gone. When I finally get dressed, I wander into the sitting room to find him chatting to John and drinking his home-made beer. I suppose it's the Australian way.

I go back to the beach for a moonlit walk, and try to work out what I am going to say to Nash. I don't owe him anything, but I'd like to be more honest with him than he ever was with me. Besides, there is a small, smug part of me that wants to boast about my new boyfriend, even if he is my cousin.

In true Alice Templeton fashion, though, I spend the rest of the night dithering, then all of the following morning in Bellingen, I do everything except go into an internet café.

As a distraction, I even go to the post office to see if there are any parcels for me, not that I'm expecting any. Instead, I find a postcard of Bondi Beach. It's from Matty and Jade. Their stall will be available from – oh my God – next weekend for three months. The postcard has been sitting there for days. The address is simply: Alice Templeton, Bellingen.

I ring Matty immediately, and deflect all his questions about the bush fire and Joel, making him tell me about the stall instead.

'It's paid for in advance,' he says. 'Just take that out of whatever you make on the gear. Are you going to put your own stuff on there, too?'

'I want to, once I get another sewing machine.'

'Sweet,' he says. 'I'll tell Jade.'

'I'll be on the next plane to Sydney,' I promise, then I call Robyn, who says I can have her spare room whenever I like.

I run to a phone box and call Joel, who is helping John in the garden. As always, the more I flap, the more unflappable he becomes.

'It's all right,' he reassures me. 'You go now, I'll come down later when everything's settled with the property. John says he can give you a lift to the airport if you ring up now and book a flight. John reckons you should be able to get a seat, no worries.'

The rest of the day disappears in a frantic rush as I pay for a flight, pack up everything I need, blow-dry my hair on John's old travel hairdryer and find at least one clean pair of pants – all in the space of three hours.

John drives Joel and I to the airport with Chang in the front seat.

'Good luck,' Joel kisses me at the airport door as John hovers, looking embarrassed. 'Say hi to Robyn for me.'

The flight to Sydney is just under an hour, and I have only just finished my plastic tub of water, my suspiciously mouldy-tasting sultana cake and my free magazine when our tray tables have to be folded back again as we prepare for landing. I can still taste Joel through the sultana cake. I wonder who his father really was? Maybe Helen did shag some famous actor at a seventies party, as Robyn once joked. Someone has to take responsibility for those long, long legs.

Chapter Sixteen

I'm beginning to understand Joel's love of roughing it,
but there is also no substitute for a bath that doesn't
have insects landing on it. Robyn's bath has bubbles
instead, which I decant from her *Doctor Who* dalek
bubble-bath container. It's bliss on a stick, as Robyn
says, although I have to point the dalek's exterminator
stick at the wall.

'You and Joel are in*saaane*,' she drawls, when I've
finished my bath and she's made me one of her
wonderful vodka and lime drinks. 'The eco-hippie
thing is great, but you've got to be contactable. When
the bush fire was happening, I didn't know if you were
dead or alive. There's no reception there. You and Joel
have got to get back in the real world.'

'Sorry.'

After that, she says she's going to Hotbods for her
spinning class and tells me I can check my email on her
computer.

My first message is from Heidi Coles. It seems
that Dani is selling Barks of Byron Bay and that I am

(apparently) the last farking straw that broke the farking camel's back. Heidi is writing to let me know that nobody blames me, though, least of all her. I suppose I have been forgiven, then.

After that, I move on to my mother's email. She is moving in with a man from Greydates. What?

I read the first long paragraph again to make sure I've got it right, but all the details seem to be there. The Greydates man is called William Bastable, and my mother met him playing conkers at a Greydates UK Back-to-School dressing-up party.

William worked in the music business for years, but before he retired he invested in *Saturday Night Fever*; consequently he's now a multi-millionaire with homes in France and Rye. She has enclosed a photo or, as she insists on calling it, a JPEG, as if it's a clothes peg.

William Bastable's photograph looks like a 1980s corporate ID shot, taken for the purposes of annual reports or possibly name tags at seminars. He has that telltale stunned look, like a fish that's just had its head banged on a rock. Still, he had a nice tan back then, and most of his own hair. It's obviously the photograph that lured my mother to his Greydates UK profile.

I read on.

For no apparent reason, she has enclosed a recipe for home-made lemonade at the bottom of her email, along with the news that she is sending all her old fur coats to me by sea mail, because winter is coming in Australia, and she thinks we might be able to wrap Henry the goat in them. She is worried his coat won't grow back after the fire.

I can just imagine what William Bastable will be like when we finally meet: a giant overgrown schoolboy in baggy shorts, with some horrible disco past. What would my poor father say? Mum says he is in his late seventies and 'rather attractive', as I should apparently be able to see from the corporate photo.

As always, she leaves a chain of PSs at the end of her email.

PS: I hope Dad's money is now safely in your account.

PPS: William wants to buy this house so he can sell his home in Rye and move in with me. We plan to live between Hove and Provence. Hope this is OK with you.

PPPS: I have decided to give you half the proceeds from the sale of the house. Please don't try to argue.

PPPPS: William and I thought we might hire the Bee Gees for our wedding. Could I have your candid opinion on the wisdom of this?

It takes me some time to fully comprehend my mother's email in all its enormity. I should never have let her loose on the internet in the first place. I am sure her relationship with William Bastable has been aided and abetted by constant emailing, and at her age she may be about to make a terrible mistake.

Then again, what would I know? I made a terrible mistake at an age when most women are supposed to know better, and it was done without any emailing whatsoever.

She is selling the house and giving me half – already, it sounds like the kind of good news that's too impossibly good to be true. It will never happen, though. Nothing ever does.

I contemplate the idea of having some old shorts-wearing, conker-playing reprobate as a close relative. What does she mean, can she have my opinion on the wisdom of hiring the Bee Gees for their wedding?

I cannot even begin to think about the old fur coats for Henry, or the recipe for home-made lemonade. I wish she wouldn't try to cram everything she would have discussed with me over the course of a fortnight into one paragraph.

She's only known William Bastable for a few weeks. I know almost nothing about him, apart from the fact that he looks good on paper. She's about to make life-changing decisions, based on nothing more than a night of passion – probably blotto on cheap Greydate UK punch – and a misguided sense of what love is.

In other words, my mother reminds me of myself when I first raced into living with Nash, and I would be a total hypocrite if I tried to stop her. No wonder it's making me feel so wobbly.

I wonder how much the house in Hove is worth these days. I hope Mum's going to do it all through an estate agent. In which case . . . I let myself have the forbidden fantasy. In which case, of course, I need never worry about money again, and Joel and I can build our own house. On his land. With a new hen house and new hens. And I can get a baby donkey!

If my father was here now he would have his head in his hands and be asking my mother for three aspirin and a glass of red wine. It is utterly typical of me that the only issue which is of any concern at this crucial crossroads in my financial destiny is the purchase of a baby donkey.

I mentally move my mother's offer into the too-mad-to-be-real category, which has taken up a lot of my brain space over the years, then I move on to the other emails, which are all from friends, who are mystified at the rumours they've been hearing about me and my cousin; worried that I have gone completely broke; deeply miffed that I have apparently been involved in a bush fire and not bothered to let them know.

I knew it. You can try to keep secrets in a small town like Bellingen, but sooner or later the smoke signals will cross the world and that will be the end of you.

Finally, I move onto Nash.

It seems that a photograph of Joel and I kissing after the fire ran in the *Guardian*.

What?

Snide remarks about keeping things in the family follow. It's a horrible email and I wish I hadn't opened it. I can already hear him laughing at me, even though he's thousands of miles away.

Why on earth did we let that photographer near us?

I thought it was just something for the local paper. I didn't realize Joel and I would end up as the *Guardian*'s Australian bush fires photo of the week.

I decide I have had quite enough of the computer for one day. There is something about emotional matters transmitted by unemotional electronic messages that's not good for the soul, especially when Nash is at the other end of them.

I go for a walk along the cliffs from Bondi to Bronte and think about the importance of tea in my life. All the things I have just been facing in my email inbox would normally have been the result of fairly measured developments in my life in London, accompanied by long conversations and many cups of tea.

They never tell you this when you go to your interviews at Australia House, but once you live upside down on the other side of the world, ten hours in front and two seasons out of synch, everything goes pear-shaped.

Cups of tea and conversation become a thing of the past. The normal speed of everyday events vanishes. Suddenly you get news all the time, or you appear to be the subject of it.

So many Brits in Australia, like Matty and Jade, have told me that the price of emigrating is learning to let go. Joel said it best – you have to accept that life is going to concertina around you from the other side of the world, and you won't be there to stop it from happening.

I was worried that my mother would have a stroke while I was at the other end of the planet, but instead she's fallen in love. I was worried about how I was going to tell Nash about Joel, but he's just found out for himself from a newspaper.

These are the things that should happen over cups of tea, or possibly not happen at all. They should certainly take place with my active participation.

I look at the surfers on Bondi Beach, hopping onto waves the way other people jump on buses. If I am to remain in Australia, I must get used to the not-invited feeling about life in England, and they will have to learn how to let me live my life apart from them as well.

I keep walking along the cliffs, wondering if I will ever be brave enough to swim at Tamarama, where they say the currents can sweep you away.

I suppose in time, everything will sort itself out at this end of the world. Once I have rung Nash and talked to him properly, maybe we can move on – until one day I will look at his name in my address book and realize I haven't heard from him for years.

My mother's situation may eventually take care of itself, too. There will come a time when I will no longer feel miffed if she makes a decision without me, and she will no longer feel moved to let me know about everything that's on her mind, whether it's William Bastable, Anthony Andrews, mango chutney or Princess Alexandra.

When that day comes, it will be the real break-up with England. It doesn't happen when you are waving goodbye at Heathrow Airport, or even when you are standing in Trafalgar Square, trying not to cry. It's only real when the emails slow down and the phone calls stop.

I don't regret leaving London for a minute. If I was given the choice between Swiss Cottage and Joel's creek, I'd take the creek any day, even if insects do land on you, and leeches get inside your socks.

I used to live in a place where people wouldn't give up their seats for anyone on the train. Now I'm living in a place where a neighbour is prepared to give up his life for you in a fire. It's not what I expected to happen, but I am beginning to realize that Heidi Coles was right and nothing about this country is predictable.

I cannot believe I seriously entertained the idea of moving to Wales – or Canada. Now I am here with Joel – despite everything, even the red-bellied black snakes – I feel as if I could never be anywhere else. The homesickness is still there, but it's like any other addiction. I might *think* I miss sundials, people dressed up as hedgehogs and Tunnock's teacakes, but it won't last long.

I decide to sit at Bronte with a glass of wine, and wait until the sun has well and truly set before calling Nash. I'm sure he won't mind talking to me over his breakfast cornflakes. As soon as the clock hits 6 p.m. in Sydney, I'm going down to the phone box. We have to talk. Properly. And I have to let him know that my future lies with Joel.

I watch the locals walk onto the beach, and admire the mothers in their work suits, disappearing into the changing rooms and coming out transformed, like Superwoman, in dazzling bikinis with children hanging onto both hands.

If Joel and I ever have children, I would love them to be water babies. More than anything else, though, I would love them to have two passports, so they can have the best of both our countries.

I hug this thought to myself, finish my wine, and gaze at the funny dark-blue line where the edge of the sea meets the sky. Maybe one day I can tempt Mum out here to visit, if it all works out with William the conker Conqueror.

I order more wine and watch the day slip away. It's seven o'clock now and I can't put Nash off any longer. I drain the glass, hoping it will make me feel braver, and walk to the nearest phone box, armed with a purse full of gold coins.

'Would you mind telling me exactly what is going on with your Australian cousin?' is the first thing Nash says when he picks up.

I suppose it's early in the morning so he's allowed to be bad-tempered, but his anger is frightening, even at this distance.

'His name's Joel, and he's not really my cousin. You know that.'

'I rang Robyn as soon I saw that photograph of you and Joel in the paper. All I got from her was 'Yiss, yew'll have to talk to Alice.''

'Don't be like that. Robyn just did what she thought was best. We were in a *bush fire*, Nash.'

'What the hell were you doing out there in the out-back with your bloody cousin, anyway?'

'Nash, I am standing in a phone box on Bronte Beach, looking at the most beautiful sunset. I do not need you shouting in my ear. Can you just calm down for a minute? Can you just *listen* to me?'

Listening is not Nash's way, though. It never has been. The whole point is, you listen to him. The memory of his awful self-absorption comes flooding back to me now as I listen to him barking in my ear.

It's the same old thing. He knows what's going on and I don't have a clue. He's right and I'm wrong.

I feel as if I have time-travelled back to my old life in London, even though I am staring at a beautiful red Sydney sunset over a dark-blue sea.

'Nice one, Alice. There was a solid chance that we might get back together there for a while.'

'Not with me there wasn't. You screwed your ex-wife behind my back.'

'Whatever. We didn't screw.'

'Whatever. You must be now. How *is* the quiz team going?'

I slam the phone down, feeling shaky and slightly drunk from the wine. I wonder what the photograph of Joel and I was like? I'll have to get a copy of the *Guardian*, even though it's caused all this trouble.

I have already decided I'm not going to tell Nash about my mother's impending marriage to William Bastable, or the fact that she wants to sell the house and give me half the money. I refuse to discuss anything

310

about my life with Nash ever again, unless I absolutely have to.

I walk back to the café and consider ordering another wine with my remaining coins, then I see Jade and Matty, toasting each other with champagne in the corner.

I hope they haven't seen me as I'm in no mood to talk. Instead, I slink away and look at the phone box, fantasizing about what I would say now if I called Nash again.

It is so absolutely typical of him to refuse to apologize about either Sarah or Lisa, but instead to seize upon the fact that I have begun a relationship with Joel.

Nash must be single. He must be desperate. Sarah must have given him the flick, otherwise he wouldn't be feeling this pissed off. I don't believe he is genuinely jealous of Joel; he lost that particular emotion about a year ago.

We were addicted to the most hormonally charged kind of love once, and now we are addicted to a kind of loathing. Of course, I don't hate Nash – not really – but the idea of bickering with him is so seductive it's hard to keep away. How can you resist an argument you know you're going to win?

I thought Joel might have got me over that kind of thing, but still the phone box is calling me. I must have the last word with Nash. I *absolutely* must have the last word. That's it, I'm going back.

Then . . .

'Over here, Alice!' Matty beckons me over as Jade waggles her fingers in a cool, supermodelly hello.

They are celebrating Jade's new job in London, Matty tells me. There is a new soap starting on ITV called *Australia Street* and she has been offered a one-year contract.

'It's a bloody load of rubbish,' Matty says, 'poor woman's *Neighbours*, really, but the girl's done good.'

'It's like *Home and Away*,' Jade explains, 'except there are a lot of gay characters. People are already calling it *Homo and Away*.'

'It's gonna be huge.' Matty looks smug.

'They're really nice people actually,' Jade enthuses. 'They said they were going to build the part around me. Apparently they saw loads of people, but nothing really clicked for them, so they decided to rewrite the character. She's an Olympian gymnast, or at least she was, before she became a nun.'

'It's a big co-production with English telly,' Matty explains. 'Loads of money. You should see what they're going to do with it. They're going to make her a *star*.'

'Congratulations!' I say.

'Is it all right about the stall, then?' Jade asks.

'Fine. Fantastic.'

'You OK after the fire and all that?' Matt suddenly remembers what has happened.

'We survived.'

'I never really thought about acting before,' Jade goes on, slurring her 'r's, 'but my friend said they were looking for English ladies, so I thought I'd give it a try. It was so easy. I could quite get into it, I think.'

'Just learn your lines and try not to bump into the

furniture.' Matty winks at me. 'Anyway. You were in the paper in London, Alice. Did you know?'

'I do. My ex saw it. That's how he found out about me and Joel. We're sort of together now.'

'Oh my *God*!' Jade shrieks, pouring me another glass of champagne.

'Robyn said the house burned down or something.'

'We were living in two caravans and we lost them both. That's why we had to evacuate. You should really stay, apparently, and fight the fire before it has a chance to take hold. We'll know better next time. We'll be living in a house, for a start. That's a safer bet than a caravan. Joel wants to build one.'

'When Robyn told us, we was quite surprised. It's funny about him being your cousin, isn't he,' Jade twirls her champagne glass around in the candlelight.

'Yes, but we're not blood related. His mother only married my uncle after she'd become pregnant by somebody else.'

'Naughty, naughty,' says Matty.

'Joel and I are going to stay with Robyn for a while until we get ourselves sorted out.'

The waitress brings over the pudding menu, which they pore over. I have already decided that anyone I meet from this moment onward will never be told that Joel is my cousin. It's all too hard. I'm going to change my second name to something else. Tonks? That was my mother's maiden name.

I try it out in my head while Matty and Jade choose between pavlova and banoffee pie. Alice Tonks. No, it's rubbish. It rhymes with honks and bonks for a start. Oh why couldn't my mother have a normal name?

A few days later, Matty and Jade send me a farewell text message from the airport as I'm setting up my trestle tables at Bondi Market on Saturday. Suddenly Blossom Promise walks past the stall, with her fringed shawl tablecloth, her garden table, a pack of tarot cards and an enormous lump of crystal.

'Hiya!' She waves across the path.

'You were right about buying the book!' I wave back.

'Destiny works in mysterious ways!' she yells back. 'Are you having a boy or a girl?'

'What?'

Oh no. It can't be. Joel and I have been so careful. He's the king of condoms. What on earth is she talking about?

She disappears, dragging her tablecloth along the ground behind her as she shuffles along in her boots. How can I trust a clairvoyant who is so lacking in foresight that she can't even do up her shoelaces properly?

I size up Jade's stall from the front, as if I were a buyer, not a seller. It's an old trick Suzanne taught me at Camden. Always get in front of the table before you sit down in your chair and make sure you're seeing the stock the way the punters do.

Selling Suzanne's vintage clothing at Camden was deeply satisfying. She had such an amazing eye for detail that I ended up selling exactly the kinds of things

I wanted to buy. She had handbags to drool over, the most extraordinary tulle party frocks and the most staggering pre-war velvet jackets.

Vintage clothing is different in Australia. There's less of it, for a start. Jade has tried her best, but most of her stall is padded out with nylon flares that don't pre-date 1980 and retro sun hats, bought cheaply in Chinatown and marked up for the tourists.

The only thing I think she's got right is the old swimwear and beach accessories. The sunglasses are priceless – it's an entire wardrobe of Elvis Presley eyewear, boxed up and never opened. She also seems to have unearthed a treasure trove of all-Australian bikinis, decorated with palm-tree designs, frangipanis, wattles and tiny kangaroos.

If this is going to be my life, for the rest of this year and beyond, I had better start doing something about it. Australian vintage beachwear is beyond me at the moment, but maybe I can ask Suzanne for some advice.

A tutting woman in an enormous hat and dark glasses looks through the few dresses on the rack and heaves an enormous sigh.

'Sorry, we'll have more stock later,' I promise as I search for something, anything, that might fit her in the pile of suitcases behind the stall. She has the classic body that fashion designers find hard to cater for – even though it's the body every other woman is born with.

'Hang on,' the woman says, taking off her enormous, jet-black sunglasses. 'It's Vintage Alice, right?'

'Hello, Vera,' I say, recognizing the tufty orange hair sticking out from under the hat.

'Long time no see.' She raises her eyebrows. 'Suzanne said you were in Australia now, but she's had trouble getting hold of you. So have I. You still got my card?'

'Oh yes. I'm sorry. I've been in the country.'

'In the bush, dear. That's what they call it here. Hey, when are you going to make me some frocks?'

Chapter Seventeen

William Bastable wants to know if I have a camera on my computer so we can engage in some kind of long-distance video conference call. I am too embarrassed to tell him I don't even own a computer.

He seems to think I might be on Skype as well, but . . .

'I'm like Mum,' I tell him on the phone. 'I'm a bit of a Luddite.'

'No problem!' he booms.

They are thinking about setting a wedding date near Christmas, which is why William wants to introduce himself by video conference call. The sale of my mother's house is already underway and he will be moving his things from Rye at the weekend.

I try not to get too excited about the fact that the house sale might become a reality. I already feel guilty about looking up a Hove property agency online and trying to value my family home. It's plummeted, of course.

William has one of those old smoothie voices that I

associate with the men who used to sell Dad their old Jaguars. I must try to like him more. I must try to trust him more. Just because my relationship with Nash was a financial and emotional disaster doesn't mean my mother is similarly doomed.

Sometimes bonkers, fantastic things just happen – and work. Just look at people who circumnavigate the globe in rafts made of orange-juice bottles.

I listen to William ramble on about the house. They have done everything through an estate agent, he says, to keep it simple. He wants me to know I am welcome to stay with them any time. My old bedroom will remain just as I left it. The only change he intends to make is the addition of a swimming pool and a gazebo. Clearly, William has escaped the credit crunch but—

The addition of *what*? What about Dad's old potting shed? I suppose he's going to throw ten sticks of dynamite under it.

'Isn't he lovely?' my mother says when she takes over the phone; I suppose he must be lurking in the background, eavesdropping. 'We're so excited about the swimming pool. William's very fit. He used to have a pool at the house in Rye, so we thought we'd put one in here.'

My God. What does a fit seventy-something look like? It's been a long time since I heard my mother use the 'we' word. It may take me a while to get used to it.

William takes over the phone again. I must stop being such a suspicious cow. I'm sure he is among the nicest of the Greydaters – my mother wouldn't be marrying a mad, bad old cad. Would she?

I know that he's been married before – Mum says William doesn't like talking about it. Perhaps because he kept his previous wife in the cellar and made her wear rubber scuba-diving gear. *No, Alice!*

'It's the *Saturday Night Fever* thing,' I tell Joel later, and he tries not to laugh. 'I wish he hadn't invested in it. I know it's made him a fortune, but every time I try to picture him, I just see some dodgy old disco bunny doing business deals with the Bee Gees.'

'William probably invested in a lot of things. He was in the music business for years, wasn't he?'

'I'm sure he bankrolled half the albums Nash loves to hate. I must find out.'

I'm back in Urunga on a cheap midweek flight when Joel and I have this discussion – it's a precious break with him before I return to Bondi Beach for Saturday's market.

It's our last week at John's. He has been the perfect host throughout – always willing to look the other way when I come out of the bathroom, always ready with home-made beer, always ready to drive us to Bellingen if we need to go into town . . . but nevertheless, Joel and I are looking forward to moving out and it being just us again.

'Make sure you remember to find me a woman when you're in the big city,' John says, dropping us off at the internet café one morning.

'I will!' I promise, but the only women who

immediately spring to mind are Suzanne and Vera, and that's never going to work.

I check my email and Joel wanders off for a walk along the Bellinger River.

My mother has written to say that the sale of the house is now complete and she has deposited the money in my account.

It won't have cleared, so I won't get my hopes up, but I have a look at my bank website anyway, just to make sure it's absolutely real.

The money has cleared in three days – William Bastable must know how to do those kinds of things – and I am rich. Rich, rich, rich.

I am so used to seeing the letter D next to anything in my account that it seems quite wrong to see the letter C instead.

I can go to England with Joel and watch my mother become Mrs Bastable II.

I can have a pedicure.

I can start Vintage Alice – properly.

I can buy a baby donkey.

I can afford to have a baby. Oh my God, a baby!

I can do *anything*.

I have to find Joel and tell him. I leave a pile of coins on the counter of the café – the first tip I have left since arriving in Australia – and race down to the river.

When I eventually find him, he is swimming in his boxer shorts in a deep waterhole two miles upstream. The rest of his clothes are on the bank.

'Are you coming in?' he yells.

'I'm rich!' I scream, then I jump in, fully clothed.

We wade towards each other until we are close enough to talk properly. 'William's paid Mum. Mum's paid me. It's all in my bank account. Oh my God. Come and look!'

'I don't need to look.' He grins at me.

'We can build a house! We can do everything.'

We hug each other in the water, dancing around on the mud at the bottom of the river like mad people.

Is this what it feels like to be rich? Is this how the Queen feels? Or Bill Gates? It's not so much what the money can bring, I think, as I dance around with Joel, it's what it takes away.

No more shampoo with Arab instructions on the back. No more out-of-control politician's eyebrows, because I lost my only good tweezers in the fire and can't afford to buy new ones. No more skipping lunch. No more panic in the pub when it's my turn to buy drinks.

Most of all, though, no more guilt. I am never borrowing money from anyone ever again, even if our house has to be built from hay bales.

'We should go to England,' I tell Joel. 'We can go to my mother's wedding.'

'You want to?'

'I feel so cut off from everything that's been going on. I want to see William Bastable. I want to be part of her life again. And it will be Christmas soon. I want to show you what that's like over there.'

'We could buy tickets today.' Joel grins.

'We can do anything today. It's the *day* of days.'

The first thing I do after we take a taxi – luxury! – to John's is ring Suzanne. It's midnight in London and I know she'll be up.

'Hello?' she yells over the sound of some noisy club.

'It's Alice. I'm ringing from Australia.'

'ALICE!'

'I want to buy that red Dior coat from you. Have you still got it?'

'Sure. Of course. Alice, my God, have you come into money or something?'

'Yes. Don't laugh. Mum's marrying this bloke who used to be in the music business. He's bought her house and she's given me half.'

'Ooh I say,' Suzanne puts on her best *Carry On* voice.

'We're coming to England for the wedding.'

'You and the cousin?' she shouts over the music.

'Me and Joel.'

'When? When?'

'Soon. When everything's sorted out here.'

'The sooner the better. You should hear the things I've heard about you lately. Romantically involved with a goat!' she shouts down the phone. 'Completely destitute and living like a hippy in the outback . . .'

'Don't tell me.'

'You should stay in touch a bit more often Alice. Saves us having to look at pictures of you in the papers.'

'I know, I'm sorry, I'm useless.'

'You're in love, that's what you are. Don't worry, you're allowed to go off the air. And listen, if you're into your

322

Dior coats at the moment, you need to look at the stuff I just got in Paris. I've been at the flea markets all week. I've got Dior, Yves, Chanel. I've even got someone's old Galliano.'

'Really?'

'I'm gonna take this phone outside for a minute,' Suzanne announces over the doof-doof bass and screeching, inebriated Londoners.

'So anyway. Now I've got some money—'

'Darling,' she interrupts, 'we should go into business and create a global market empire together! You can import from me and I can export to you!'

'Actually, Suzanne . . .'

She's got it the wrong way round, but the right way up. We *should* go into business together. Instead of me buying from her, though, she should be buying from me. If Jade is prepared to hand over her stall – and a few of her secret auction addresses – I can send Suzanne the kind of exotic Australian swimwear Londoners only dream about.

Suzanne has always moaned about the lack of decent summer clothes on the stall, and Jade has discovered a goldmine of exactly the kind of vintage sarongs, shorts, bikinis, sun hats and sunglasses Suzanne has been dreaming of. There may not be much of it, but what there is, Suzanne could sell at a huge profit.

I'm sure Matty could help me with the boring paperwork side of things, and Jade could help with the sourcing. She might be a soap star now, but that won't last for ever.

I don't remember much about fashion college, but I do remember the golden rule about cash flow: get your first business on the go, then start your next one.

Vintage Alice is my next plan. At long last, Vintage Alice.

I do a little dance on John's rug. It almost feels like a proper shop already.

'I'm dancing, Suzanne,' I tell her once she's agreed to my idea, and she tells me she's started dancing too. So there we are, like a couple of nongs – a fine Australian word I have learned – hopping around, thousands of miles apart.

Later on, I bombard Joel with my plans. There is no Nash to pour cold water on my dreams or moan about how much it's going to cost him. There is only Joel, massaging my shoulders on the sofa, as I throw my ideas at him.

I am doing what he talked about all those months ago in England: taking the wrong way round in my life, and the long way round. Joel is right, though, it's always more interesting.

A few days later, we pack up our cases ready for Bondi Beach and buy John the new canoe he's been lusting after. We want it to be a surprise, like Wiz's new camper van. It's the least we can do, since he's volunteered to look after the property, and the remaining animals, in our absence.

'Trust me,' Joel said, once we'd paid for the canoe and the camper van to be delivered to them from Coffs

Harbour, 'these are not the kinds of guys you want to make big gestures to. I think it's better for everyone if we're away when they arrive.'

As we say our goodbyes at Urunga Station, John holds Chang in his arms and makes him wave his paw up and down.

'Thanks, mate,' Joel says in an Aussie-blokey way.

'Any time,' John says.

'Hopefully there won't be another time,' Joel says.

'Gotta get on and build that mud brick house and get that tank up, mate,' John replies. 'Anyway,' he says, 'me and the dog will still be here when it happens.'

I call Suzanne when we are on the train, interrupting her in the middle of a late dinner at home.

'What have you cooked?' I ask.

'I'm having a can of tuna and a tomato on a tray in front of the television. I'm trying to lose weight. I'm doing the Dr Robert Fatkins diet. It's perfectly safe, he only slipped on ice, you know. Hey, I sent the Dior coat off this morning.'

'I can't wait.'

'Listen. You know Speedos?'

'Yup. Of course. Legendary Australian label. People love it, especially if it's seventies. As long as the gussets are all right, of course. My customers seem to prefer an intact gusset.'

'I thought I'd bring as much stuff as I could over to London.'

'Sure, darling. Straight through the green channel and over to me. Perfect.'

Joel and I spend our week at Bondi Beach preparing for our trip to London. William Bastable has set a wedding date with my mother, and they are hunting for a suitable venue for the ceremony and reception.

So far, Mum is voting for Chelsea because it's where Judy Garland got married, but William quite likes the idea of doing the deed inside a capsule on the London Eye.

'Jeez no, you don't want them getting married inside a vomit comet,' Robyn says. She decides to ring my mother up immediately to offer her advice on the reception.

When she finally hangs up, she mixes Joel and I two of her vodka, lime and mint drinks, then adds an extra slug of vodka to her glass at the last minute.

'What's that English word that means a bit vague?'

'Dotty,' I supply.

'And what's that other English word that means a bit mad?'

'Potty.'

'It's great to reconnect with Auntie Penny, but this wedding is sending her dotty and potty,' Robyn concludes. 'She's running around like a chook with its head cut off. She hasn't even rung round for quotes. There's some place in Kensington that wants to charge them a fortune just for the hire of their rooftop. And it's extra for the farking pink flamingos. She has no farking idea.'

Nash would love it, not that he will ever be invited. My mother has gone totally Lady Penelope after all, getting information from Claridges, The Ritz and The Dorchester. There will also be an announcement in *The Times* and the *Daily Telegraph* this weekend.

'William Bastable is a sir,' Robyn tells us. 'Did you know he was a sir?'

'Are you sure?' I ask.

'She told me to slip it into the conversation with you because she didn't want to be indelicate. Indiscreet. Impolite. Inappropriate. Whatever. Of course, as soon as she drops his name on the phone when she's talking to the hotels, the price just goes up and up . . . Maybe I should get over there right now and do the talking for her.'

Robyn says she is definitely coming to the wedding now – nothing will stop her – and there's even a chance that Roland or Helena might make it, too.

'Instant family reunion.' Joel shakes his head. 'I think this might be the first nuclear family I've ever had. It's . . .'

'A bit weird?' I interrupt.

'Really great,' he says.

'Your mother's banking on two hundred guests, including the website people – what are they called again?' Robyn asks, looking at her laptop computer.

'Greydate UK.'

'Yeah them. Anyway, she's gonna do two hundred people, allowing one bottle of Bollinger per head,' Robyn continues. 'Plus she wants asparagus rolls, chicken vol-au-vents, smoked salmon, pink fairy cakes, a four-tier wedding cake – probably with all the hairy

Bee Gees jumping out of it. I'm just warning you,' Robyn raises her eyebrows at us, 'in case you weren't *todally* prepared.'

We spend the rest of the week at Bondi, swimming and enjoying the luxury of having Robyn's flat to ourselves while she's at work.

I'm not sure what to do about the market plan with Suzanne, Matty and Jade. Dad would have told me to get a lawyer and organize contracts. Instead, I write my plan out on some Snoopy writing paper I found at the market, lick the envelopes and hope for the best. Sometimes you just have to trust people.

Then, in the middle of the night, I get a text message from my mother.

'WEDDING NIGHTMARE – URGENT PLEASE CALL.'

I check the time and ring her, suddenly terrified that William Bastable has disappeared and everything – her happiness and mine – has vanished with him.

'Mum? What is it?'

'Oh, Alice. I don't know what to do. It's all gone a bit belly-up.'

'What do you mean?'

'The wedding has to happen next week, darling, or it's not going to happen at all. Everybody's booked up for months. The good news is, though, we've got The Dorchester for both the wedding and the reception. Such a relief. So William and I were wondering, could you possibly catch the next flight over?'

328

'Is that all? My God, I thought William had buggered off.'

'Oh no. Why ever would you think that, Alice?'

Three days later, after finding someone to man the stall the following weekend, Joel and I fly to London after a long night with Robyn on the vodka and limes. I enjoy three completely new experiences in my life. One is flying with a hangover, another is the novelty of paying for somebody else's trip and the other is travelling with an airline which actually has room for my knees.

This time I complete the journey without my mother's knockout herbal tranquillizers, and Joel and I spend most of the trip greedily watching films. In the whole time we've been together, we have never been to the cinema once. Joel doesn't even own a television.

When we finally arrive at Heathrow, my mother is there with William Bastable, who is looking very formal in a navy-blue jacket with shiny buttons, even though it's only six o'clock in the morning. I am worried about calling him sir, and so is Joel, but we've decided to pretend we don't know about the title, thus avoiding the problem.

'Should I curtsy or something?' Joel jokes as we stagger through the green channel at customs, pushing all my luggage.

I have somehow managed to pack Jade's finest selection of fifties sunglasses and seventies Speedos into two suitcases and two squashy nylon bags, and still found room to wedge in our own clothes.

'Alice!' William steps forward at the arrivals lounge and shakes my hand. 'Joel!'

'Hello, darling.' As my mother welcomes me back, I notice that she is wearing an enormous sapphire ring on her finger.

Joel kisses her on the cheek and congratulates her, and she holds the ring out for him to see.

'Beautiful,' he says. William looks quietly pleased.

We all notice a horrible smell and realize that it must be time for Heathrow's morning rubbish collection – either that or they're removing a lot of illegal French cheese.

'There's a bit of a pong in here,' William says, looking around the airport suspiciously. 'I think we should get a move on, don't you?'

We find his car – something far too new and shiny for my father to have ever sold – and drive to Hove, listening to Radio Four all the way.

'I was worried he was going to play us *The Best of the Bee Gees*,' Joel whispers in my ear.

'Saucy,' William says, when my mother leans forward to fiddle with the volume knob, revealing too much bra. 'I'm going to zoom straight up the M23 and kick on home – is that all right with you in the back?'

'Fine,' Joel says, trying not to yawn. I know it's not William Bastable's company – he's far too intriguing for that – just a bad case of jet lag. Neither of us slept much on the flight. Instead, we did what we always do in Bellingen, which is talk for far too long when we should both have gone to sleep.

I decide that William is what my father would have called a good egg. I was right to be suspicious at the beginning, but there is something about the way he overtakes other cars, pokes two fingers in the air and tells the other drivers to 'eff orf' that reminds me of Dad and Roland. More than anything, he seems like family.

My mother has found her man at last. And despite her unlikely belief in rich husbands and effortlessly happy endings, she seems to have conjured up both of them. I have to hand it to her. She may be dotty and potty, but she's also been proven right.

I feel a huge wave of longing for all the ordinary, English things I am seeing and hearing as we zoom – William's favourite word – towards Sussex. There is something incredibly comforting about all the familiar London voices I am hearing on the radio, and the sunken green hedges that line the motorway. Even the crisp packets stuck in the hedgerows are strangely endearing. Ah, English litter. So familiar.

'I hope you'll get to see a little of the country while you're here.' William passes Joel a guidebook from the glovebox. 'You should go off for a few jaunts. See what you're missing in Aussie land.'

'Thanks.' Joel takes the book. 'I only had a few days here last time.'

I look over Joel's shoulder at Cornwall, marked with wavy red lines on the map. The homesickness was supposed to hit me when I was in Australia, not now, but I find myself longing to go and see the Furry Dance

331

at Helston and wander down to Land's End for a bright yellow ice cream or walk around Cambridge again, reminding myself what a cobblestone looks like.

As we make our way towards the coast, I am filled with regret for the way I left England: worrying about Nash and the future and what would happen once I left everything behind. I should have left the country dancing with hedgehogs, and instead I left worrying about debt collectors. I left England the way I left Nash: angry, confused and barely capable of putting one tartan wellie in front of the other.

Joel was right. I did have a huge empty space in my heart when I left London, and Australia filled it perfectly. Perhaps I just did it too prematurely. England is a different place when you can afford to live here, and now I can, I want to take my time. I want to pay my last respects in the appropriate manner, I suppose.

'I love this.' Joel shows me a photograph of a stone circle in the guidebook. 'The Hurlers. Do you know about them? They're prehistoric stones on Bodmin Moor. The stones used to be men, but they were turned to stone as a punishment for throwing balls around on the Sabbath.'

'I'd love to see them.'

'And look at this – Dozmary Pool, the mysterious lake next to Bolventor that is the last resting place of the sword Excalibur.'

'Good for tourists anyway,' honks William from the front seat when he overhears our conversation.

'I want to see everything there is to see.' Joel closes the

332

book. 'And I want to play cricket at Cricket St Thomas as well.'

'Oh, that's where they filmed *To the Manor Born*!' my mother says, getting thoroughly overexcited in the front seat. The only woman finer than Judy Garland, as far as she is concerned, is Penelope Keith.

Once we get home, Joel and I are installed in my old bedroom and handed two hot-water bottles and two large cups of tea.

'We're just off for a walk,' Mum says. 'Make yourselves at home, both of you. Have a look at the garden, Alice, and you'll see where the new swimming pool and gazebo are going to go. We're spending our way out of recession, darling!'

Joel and I wait until they have gone, then we fall asleep in each others' arms on top of my old pink eiderdown. The last time we were this exhausted was after the bush fire in Bellingen.

'It's one of the most incredible countries in the world,' Joel says much later when I have woken up. Mum and William are still out, apparently, having decided to see some Greydate UK friends in Lancing.

'Incredible in what way? I left it, remember.'

'It's just so hard in England,' Joel tries to explain. 'Really tough and really cold. But everyone still daydreams. In fact, I don't think they ever stop. That's what I mean. It's quite incredible. It's all Alice in Wonderland and the Queen and Vivienne Westwood.'

'I'm glad you remember everything I taught you about her.'

'Everything's like a fairy story. Or a panto. Goodies and baddies. Beautiful princesses and evil stepmothers . . .'

'But it has to be like that, because otherwise it would just be too . . .' I try to think of a word and fail.

'You tried really hard to make it work here, didn't you?' Joel asks.

'Yeah, but your history follows you around. You can never get away from your mistakes, or even the mistakes your parents – or their parents – made. You don't have any of that in Australia. It's all new. You can be what you like and do what you like.'

I think of Jade, who is about to become a TV star of sorts, and Matty, who is creating a business empire. I can't imagine either of them daring stretch their luck this far in Camden. She would have been a hairdresser and he would probably have been on the dole, selling cocaine in the pub. Jade was discovered in Sydney, not here.

'Witches in the Wookey Hole,' Joel says suddenly.

'What's that?'

'A place in Somerset called Wookey Hole. I want to go there, too. It's all limestone, and there are waterfalls below ground. The Witches of Wookey used to live there, according to the locals.'

'Hmm. I think Nash's parents went there once.'

I see Joel's face and suddenly wish I hadn't mentioned Nash. We've been able to forget about him lately, but sooner or later, I'll have to see him and talk about . . . everything.

'Now that you're back here, does it remind you of him?' Joel asks, staring out of the window at the sea.

'I suppose so. The bad bits and the good bits. Mostly the bad bits, though. I seem to have spent my relationship freezing to death. No heater, no warmth.

'But you're going to sort things out with him now, aren't you? Once and for all?'

'Oh yeah,' I agree. 'Closure is such a stupid word, but it's right in a way. It's like closing the curtains or closing the lid on the biscuit tin. Finishing things. When I bolted to Sydney before, I didn't have time to close anything. Now I can. I'm going to ring him tomorrow.'

Chapter Eighteen

A few days later I go to Romney College to see Nash. It takes half a day to get there after I've missed my train because the ticket machines aren't working. I failed to get a packet of crisps because the girl behind the counter was ignoring me and lost an hour because the bus was late on account of a late driver. By which time I am well and truly fed up with England again.

So much for *The Wind in the Willows*. So much for prehistoric stones who used to be people. It's all business as usual: complete and utter chaos. Nothing's open and everyone's got a cold – or a hangover probably. I ring the train company to see if I can get my money back and I'm put through to a call centre in Scotland. Oh that's all right then. I suppose it's an improvement on Mumbai.

Once again I bless William Bastable's money. In the old days, any failure to get my money back on a train ticket would have forced me to live on apples for the rest of the week.

The people in the queue are so patient – in Sydney they

would have started a riot by now. But this is England, there's a system, and even when it's not working, people still try to pretend it's worth going along with.

When I finally arrive at Romney College, Nash has finished teaching for the day and is wearing his old grey tracksuit, from the time when he used to coach school football.

His hair is shorter, and the curls have gone – he looks harder and older, and sexier too. I hadn't counted on being attracted to him all over again. I had forgotten about his noble Roman nose. I had forgotten about the way he can look at me, long and hard, until I have to look away first. It's partly because he needs glasses, of course, but is too vain to wear them.

'Come in,' he leads me into his flat and I remind myself that he's all wrong for me now. Quite wrong.

Nash's flat is decorated with posters I have never seen before. Two of them are reproductions of jazz album covers from the 1960s, and another two posters advertise art exhibitions I have never heard of, although I can see by the dates that they both occurred in London this spring.

Nash smells different, too. Spicier, somehow, and slightly sweeter than normal. When I use his bathroom, I see why. He's using some new matching shampoo and aftershave.

We sit down in immaculately upholstered armchairs, which I suppose must have come with the flat, and I try to fight the feeling that he is still mine. It's just an old, dumb instinct really, like automatically feeling a sense of ownership about our shared CDs which I can see on the shelf.

'Great to see you,' Nash says in a twitchy, nervous way. 'You're looking well. Very suntanned. Very Aussie.'

'The winter's so sunny over there.'

What a completely moronic thing to say. Nash immediately gets up to make us both a cup of tea, and says he's sorry about the phone call when I was in Bronte – he wasn't thinking straight.

'It's all right,' I answer. 'Neither was I.'

While he is fiddling around with teabags and asking me stupid questions like whether or not I take sugar – how could he have forgotten so quickly? – I get up and inspect his shelves. All his old Bob Dylan books from Swiss Cottage are there, along with – hang on – some books I thought were mine. He also appears to have been buying cookbooks. I suppose he had to learn how to cook some time, useless twat.

There. That's better. I almost feel back to normal.

'So what are you up to?' he asks.

'I'm working full time in Australia now. I'm sort of organizing a business between London and Sydney. And I'm starting up Vintage Alice.'

'Not skint any more then?'

'Mum gave me half the money from the sale of her house. Her fiancé bought it from her.'

There. That's knocked him for six, as my mother would say.

'Very nice.' Nash puts on a silly posh voice and I can

see that my sudden fiscal turnaround has made him nervous.

'Anyway,' I change the subject, 'how's the quiz team? How's the band? How's life?'

'I've got some news actually.'

'Really?'

'I'm leaving the college. I've sort of been asked to leave. I've been seeing a girl here. Not everyone thinks it's a good idea.'

'Do you mean a *schoolgirl*?'

'It's all perfectly OK. She's eighteen years old, an outstanding sixth-former, and she's getting ready for Oxbridge. I've been tutoring her. She's incredibly bright, extremely mature, and I'm not the first.'

'Not the first what? Teacher?'

'It doesn't matter. Anyway, someone told the Head and I've been asked to go more or less immediately. I expect I'll move to Oxford. She's bound to get in. And I've been offered a place at one of the schools there.'

'Bloody hell, Nash.'

'Don't make a big thing out of this, Alice, because it's really pretty straightforward. Some schools dig it, some schools don't. This one doesn't. She's happy and I'm happy. You're happy with your bloke, aren't you? Your cousin?'

'Will you stop calling him my cousin as if it's incestuous and terribly weird? His name's Joel. I'm not telling you again.'

'Fine.'

'Yes, it's all absolutely *fine*. So it didn't work out with Sarah, then?'

'I'm not going to talk about her, Alice.'

'What about Lisa? Any contact with her now?'

'You're being cruel,' he gives me a lopsided smile, 'and that's not like you. Has Australia made you cruel? Is it living in such harsh conditions?'

'Don't be silly.'

'So you're rich.'

I laugh, embarrassed.

'Lend me some money then?' he asks, and I suddenly realize he's serious. 'About my finances, Alice,' Nash says, twisting his hands together. God, the number of times those hands have been all over me, but I can't think about that now.

He tries again. 'About my cash situation. The girl I've been involved with, well, it's all totally cool, but it did get a bit legal for a minute, with the school and her parents, and that costs. And I'm not entirely sure about my next job.'

'You want me to lend you some money?'

A long silence. 'There's absolutely nobody else I can ask.'

I sign a cheque for exactly the same amount he once lent me – £2,000 – then I get up to leave.

'Nash. I can't believe you're seeing one of your students. She's practically half your age. It's pathetic. There, that's the last time I'll ever talk about it.'

'So are you going to marry Joel, then, and stay

in Australia for good?' Nash asks as I walk out of his flat.

I don't reply because I can't. But it's all I think about on the train back to London, as the tea trolley clanks up and down the aisle.

Chapter Nineteen

Joel often goes off by himself, but I seldom do. When he's around, I want to be with him. Today, though, I am craving solitude.

'All right?' he rubs my shoulders at breakfast. He is the emperor of impromptu massages.

'It's all the Nash stuff, I think. I just feel like a big, long walk by myself. Is that OK?'

'It's fine.'

I told him about Nash last night – and the schoolgirl and the cheque – Joel was good about it, but I need to be by myself just to take it all in.

Joel decides to go out with William Bastable to see the Bluebell Railway, which he had hoped would turn out to be a train made entirely from bluebells, but is actually just Pommie trainspotter heaven in the middle of Sussex. It turns out that William Bastable's other passion, apart from catchy 1970s chart music, is old steam engines.

Once they have gone – Mum is out shopping – I leap onto William Bastable's computer and look for Nash's schoolgirl.

He has emailed me about her, almost as if he's proud to be with her, which unfortunately I think he is. Her Facebook/Myspace title is Constancia Dover and she is stunning – part Italian apparently – and the recipient of several music scholarships. She's a regular little culture-vulture, so I suppose that's where all Nash's new posters come from, not to mention the new cookbooks.

I don't think it will last between them – not for a minute – but I suppose I wish him some kind of luck. When I tell my mother, though, I know she will fall sideways on the sofa and fan herself with a copy of the *Daily Telegraph*.

I am not going to tell her about the cheque for Nash, though. The only person I'll ever tell about that is Joel.

I drift from Facebook to a relationship self-help site. I'm not entirely sure why. Perhaps it's a knee-jerk response to being back in England, and in the immediate vicinity of Nash.

There is a quiz on the site for couples who are breaking up. It asks:

Why did you fall in love anyway?

What went wrong?

When did it go wrong?

When did you give up?

Why did you give up?

Do you think you could still make it work?

Do you hate him/her?

Do you love him/her?

If not, then why not?

I feel a sudden rush of sympathy for Sir William Bastable, who must have been down this route before, if not on an internet quiz, then in some discreet corner of Sussex with a marriage guidance counsellor. He still doesn't speak to his ex-wife and she hasn't been invited to the wedding at The Dorchester.

I am glad William and Mum found each other, in the end. I can even forgive them for dressing up in school uniform and playing conkers.

I wonder about every other couple I know, and how they will fare in the end. Matty and Jade? They'll probably be OK. As long as she keeps earning and he keeps dreaming.

I think about Suzanne, who I guess will ricochet back to Sam in New York until the day he finally commits and moves to London. Then I think about Richard from our pub quiz team, whom I hold no hope for, with anyone, ever, and Michael and his wife, who I think will be fine in the end. I worry about Danielle Coles in Byron Bay and her obvious leanings towards affairs with her friends' husbands – not to mention the local vet – then I take comfort in the fact that John – good, kind John – will probably go to the Bellingen pub at some point in the future and bump into the beer-guzzling, fish-crazy love of his life.

Love is a scratch card.

But what kind of scratch card was I gambling on when I fell in love with Nash?

I stare at the photo of his schoolgirl on Facebook again and remember the time that Nash was dancing with me at a party somewhere and refused to see out the song because it was Motown; he said he was bored with Motown. He left me standing there by myself rather than let himself down. Nobody was watching and nobody cared, but Nash still had to walk off the dance floor by himself.

I think about the day he told my mother we were moving to Australia before I'd had the chance to tell her. Then I remember the way he apologized for it, with a bloody text message.

I contemplate his schoolgirl, who will reject him as soon as she meets someone her own age in Oxford. What a waste of time. But it's so typical of Nash. It's just like Lisa and Sarah all over again. I suppose he thinks he's a romantic or something.

I have a nap and try to shake off the last of my jet lag. Maybe I can dream Nash out of my system, together with all the sadness he brings with him.

Eventually, I hear my mother coming home – she has been looking for fabric so I can make her a wedding suit – and then Joel and William return.

When Joel wakes me up, I smell him before I see him. He has brought his funny lemon soap with him, together with his mint-tea habit. It's a smell that's easy to become addicted to.

'Hello.'

'Hi.'

I tell Joel about the photo of Nash's schoolgirl on the internet, and we make bad jokes about it, then try to rationalize it, but nothing works. Some things are so awful you just have to sit and digest them, like putting up with bad food on Christmas day.

'I like William Bastable,' Joel says while we are having coffee in a café in Brighton later. 'He's a great dancer.'

'Is he? How did you find that out?'

'He showed me a film of his wedding reception, the first time round. He knows how to shimmy.'

'How can you shimmy in Hush Puppies?'

'He can. You should have seen him. And here's another thing. He wants me to call him Bill.'

'Does that mean I'm allowed to call him Bill as well?'

'Not sure.' Joel grins as I hit him with a cushion.

I am pouring muesli into my bowl the following morning – Joel is still in bed – when Suzanne rings. She wants me in Camden tomorrow, at her stall, so I can check all the prices she's putting on Jade's Australian bikinis.

'I think I'll go out walking tomorrow,' Joel says hastily before William can take advantage of my absence to show him any more steam trains.

On the way to London the next day, I read the newspapers – floods and David Beckham's feet, as usual.

Suzanne greets me at her flat in what she calls her Benny Hill couture look – long shorts, a Fairisle V-neck sweater, long woollen socks and brown lace-up boots. As always, she looks fantastic. On anyone else it would just look silly.

She shows me all the price tags she is putting on Jade's Australian bikinis and asks me what I think.

'You can't charge that, Suzanne! Flipping heck, woman. It's as much as a microwave oven.'

'It's a two-piece with matching skirt. Oh yes I can, baby.' She smiles, and glides around the floor, holding a pair of gigantic, hand-embroidered bikini bottoms up against her hips.

'You're under-charging for that Pucci dress, though,' I tell her.

'Mmm. I was rather hoping you'd say that. You do know your Pucci.'

She loads all her trunks onto the back seat of her ageing Volkswagen, and I take the rest of the stuff in the front, in plastic rubbish bags that fill every inch of available space from the floor to the bottom of my chin.

I tell her about Nash's schoolgirl and try not to feel embarrassed. Talk about humiliation by association.

'So is that it with Nash for ever, then?' she asks, turning a sharp corner into the least-full street behind Camden Market. 'Not even friends?'

'I don't know. I don't think so. He's moving to Oxford, I'm going back to Australia. Wow! Maybe that is it. Is that what happens? It just sort of comes to a complete stop?'

'London's just dire.' Suzanne changes the subject as we drive past a towering block of flats with 1980s-style lettering on the mailbox, still trying to find a parking space. 'Isn't it awful? It's so crowded here. Nobody knows what's going on. Everyone's got bags under their eyes. Everyone's on bloody drugs all the time. All they do is watch telly. Don't you just want to leave and never come back?'

'Stop it. You know I want my kids to be half-English. I want them to go on the Bluebell Railway and visit Soho at night and dance around like hedgehogs.'

'Don't they do that in Australia?' Suzanne yells, over the sound of her ancient car engine.

'Put it this way, they don't take silliness as seriously as they do here.'

'Aha!' Suzanne shouts back. 'That's it. The English seriously believe in everything that is silly, because if they didn't they'd throw themselves under a car.'

We pull up at the markets and dodge past all the waiting hordes. I can moan about the crowds in London all I like to Joel, but there is nothing like a heaving queue in the early hours of the morning to give a casual stall-holder hope.

'Here we go,' Suzanne chants under her breath. 'Here we go, here we go, here we go . . .'

The Union Jack bunting goes up along the top of her stall and I plug the extension cord into the generator, then watch the fairy lights go on.

'Boom shanka, boom shanka,' Suzanne chants to herself as she pins Jade's polka-dot bikinis up on the washing line that flanks the back of the stall.

She lays out Ray-Bans, and imitation Ray-Bans, and rows of shark's-tooth necklaces. She pins up Tiki necklaces from New Zealand and strange brooches made from abalone shells.

A man in a huge tweed jacket stops and looks through

the bikinis. He is followed by a woman in a beautiful pair of pink pants – Escada, late 1980s, I tell Suzanne – who cannot stop cooing over the Hawaiian shirts Suzanne has just hung up next to her usual selection of white dinner shirts and silk-fronted waistcoats.

'All right?' Suzanne checks as people descend upon us from all directions. We are being surrounded, like the victims of a Roman battalion in turtle formation. They are above us, to the left and right of us, behind us and sometimes below us.

'I should have increased the price of those bloody Ray-Bans,' Suzanne reflects half an hour later. We both know she's joking though. She has doubled her usual take, and she has four business cards sitting in her cashbox, all from professional stylists who cannot believe how she managed to find so many pristine 1960s swimming costumes, all with clean gussets.

'We're on a roll,' Suzanne promises me. 'We're on an egg-and-bacon roll, Alice, and quite frankly, it's going to gather no moss.'

'When do you think I should launch Vintage Alice?' I ask her.

'Australia or here?'

'Maybe everywhere. I was thinking I could get a website.'

'Launch in the European Spring,' she says automatically. 'That's what Chanel did. Be lucky.'

'That's it, then,' I promise myself, 'the European Spring.'

It's only when we take a tea break that I notice I have a text message – from Nash.

I call him back straight away, then almost wish I hadn't, because the first thing he does is cry.

'Are you OK?'

'No. Yes. I just wanted to say—'

'Yes, Nash? Are you sure you're all right?'

'I just wanted to say I'm sorry,' he finally gets the words out and hangs up.

In all the time that we were together, I never saw him cry.

Chapter Twenty

Uncle Roland is coming to England for the wedding on Saturday. Helena cannot make it, but he will be here with ding-dong bells on, he says.

'Does your dad talk like my dad used to?' I ask Joel. 'I thought he'd be a bit more San-Franciscan.'

'It's in the DNA. All Templetons of a certain age talk like that,' Joel replies. 'We both will too one day.'

The excitement of the wedding is turning my mother into an insomniac, and one night I hear her talking in her sleep from about 5.30 a.m. until 8 a.m. Her conversation with the strange people who are populating her dreams goes something like this:

'No, it's my badger.'

Then:

'You have NO idea.'

Then:

'Take the asparagus and have done with it.'

I had forgotten that she talks in her sleep. It's one of the most endearing things about her.

'Badger. Crucial to wipe it off,' she mutters to herself,

stirring slightly as I come in to see if she wants a cup of tea. William went out ages ago, probably in search of the paper; he's usually up around six.

Mum's eyelids are flickering – doing that thing that makes you look demonically possessed – so I make a quick exit and forget about the tea.

When I go downstairs, I find her wedding notebook full of scrawled ideas about what to drink, who to invite and, interestingly, who *not* to invite.

Some of the Greydaters William has pencilled in have been carefully crossed out by Mum. Anne Horton-Bills has gone, with this comment from my Mother: 'Annus Horribilis!' Someone called Nicholas Lowry has gone, too, on the grounds of his greenhouse gas emissions.

Other than that, it seems that hundreds of G-Daters, as William calls them, will be coming to The Dorchester on Saturday.

There are catalogues from Asprey and Dunhill on the table, along with their congratulations to the happy couple, and a pile of business cards from photographers.

Then there is my mother's scribbled sketch of her chosen suit – nipped in at the waist, flared out at the hips (but not too much) and pulled in at the knee with a classic pencil-skirt tapered pleat.

I am quite proud of the suit I ended up making for her on my new sewing machine, but I drew the line at the lime-green linen she asked for. In the end, we compromised on a beautiful bolt of raw silk from Suzanne's stall, dating from the fifties, which time has faded to the creamiest shade of coffee.

The hat I have no control over, though – I think it looks like a small UFO trying to return to its mother ship, but this is something I have only confided to Joel.

Joel is out too this morning, on one of his long walks along the seafront. Later on he texts me from The Mock Turtle, where he is having a cup of tea and sorting out his family.

'Is everything OK?' I ask, when I call him back.

'Bit of politics.'

'What?'

'Roland's not coming. He's had second thoughts.'

'But why?'

'Roland created some problems for the rest of the family when he broke up with my mum,' Joel says at last, and my heart instantly goes out to him.

'I'm sure he did.'

'That's why your parents didn't visit us in Australia for all those years. I think your dad was furious with him. It's possible they didn't speak, although I'm only guessing. Nobody talks about it.'

'Wow!'

'Roland came back from India one Christmas when we were kids and planted his stash of dope on Helena. He thoughtfully decided that if he was going to take some hash back to Sydney, he may as well be really clever about it and hide it in her stuff. He nailed it into this painting she had – of the Buddha, can you believe it? – and they found it. She protected him at the airport. Robyn and I saw her do it. She took the rap, and got busted.'

'Oh my God.'

'End of marriage. Enough was enough. But Roland was like that: totally selfish and completely irresponsible. And he wasn't a good dad to me because he knew I wasn't really his son.'

'Oh, Joel.'

'He rang me last night when everyone was asleep, and I blew it.'

'What did you say?'

'Just something stupid about Helena not coming, and how great it would have been for you to meet her. Anyway. That was all it took to set him off, and then we ended up arguing about everything.'

'Mum has no idea you feel like that about him or she wouldn't have invited him to the wedding.'

'Families keep secrets. When our kids are old, are you going to tell them about Nash and all the stuff that happened there? Of course you won't.'

'I'm so, so sorry, Joel.'

Later on we go for a walk along the seafront.

'Ooh, I've just remembered something that's cheered me up,' I tell Joel. 'When we go back to Bellingen, it will be snake-free, won't it? Because of the bush fire.'

He laughs at me. 'Sorry, Alice. You're never going to get round it that way.'

'Oh well. I miss Bellingen anyway.'

'I *really* miss it.' He gives me his sexy, serious look. It is the expression I fell in love with when I chose him as Number Nine not far from this spot all those months ago.

'Joel. When we went back to the property that day, when the chickens had gone and the mailbox had disappeared and our caravans had been burned to the ground, I finally understood why you went to work with Tibetans.'

'Because . . . ?'

'Because they didn't just lose their homes, they lost everything.'

'It's the same for all refugees.'

'I want them to have half the money Mum gave me. I want you to give it to Tibet Aid.'

'You could. Except, as usual' – Joel laughs at me – 'you've got no idea about money.'

'I really have absolutely no idea, do I?'

'Nope. For a currently homeless woman you really should rethink this. Half your money is *way* too much. But we should go to India and give them something. Money, time, energy – whatever.'

Joel and I have often talked about his time with the Tibetans but he has always stopped the conversation before I've wanted to. Now he cannot stop talking. It's like his journals, full of odd memories, funny stories, and brilliant sketches.

Afterwards, we walk past a large tourist coach parked outside the West Pier and hear some Australian accents.

'Wow!' Joel steps back and looks at me. 'I suddenly feel homesick.'

The two women who are talking are annoyed about something and are telling each other how rooted it is.

'It's not like any other language, is it?' I ask him.

'As good as French or Italian or Spanish.'

'Better.'

We decide to keep walking, to give my mother a chance to catch up on her sleep at home, and cross the road to the gardens behind the Pavilion.

'Can you help me with something?' I ask him.

'Sure.'

'I need to do my Australia homework. I've decided I want to apply for citizenship when we go back, or even before. I could go and see Heidi Coles in London and ask her about it.'

'OK.'

'The only thing I know about is Simpson's Donkey and it's pathetic. I bet those women back there on the coach know *everything*. I don't even know what the national flower is. I told Jade I thought it was gladioli.'

'Wattle,' Joel reminds me. 'We've got it growing on the property. Or we did.'

'Let's plant some more. I want to plant a whole new garden when we get back.'

Joel gives me a progress report on Henry the goat. John – who has been charged with the task of keeping us updated – says that Wiz thinks his fur is slowly growing back, although he has become unbelievably randy and must be kept away from all the other recovering goats when he goes for his regular RSPCA goat health check-ups.

'What about our chicken?'

'John went up there the other day and says she's still around somewhere. We'll have to get her some friends, though.'

'Do you think she could become friends with a sheep?'

'I suppose so. What have you got in mind?'

'The French make cheese out of sheep's milk. It's a real delicacy. I'd love to do that. Am I mad?'

'Not mad at all. The sheep will keep the grass down as well. And fertilize it. I know a guy who'll do the shearing, and then you can wash the wool and spin it.'

'This is such a nutty conversation to be having in the middle of Brighton,' I say, looking up and seeing the pickled-onion domes of the Pavilion in the distance.

'Not at all. In fact, I know more than you might think about sheep. Mainly because the Tibetans knew so much about yaks.'

'So could we do it? What about foot rot and fly strike and all of that?'

'Trim their hooves and you won't get rot. It can't be all that different to a pedicure.'

'Argh! A pedicure. Do you know, when I was in Swiss Cottage with Nash, I used to dream about having a pedicure. And a facial. And a massage. And now I can afford it and I haven't done the slightest thing about it.'

'That's what weddings are for, aren't they?' Joel asks. 'It's about all the fun stuff. I think you deserve some fun.'

He buys a disposable camera in a gift shop and takes some photographs of me, because he has left his clunky old Polaroid at home. After that, it's my turn to take some photographs of him. I wonder if Joel looks anything like his real father and suppose he must. Perhaps one day we will both find out.

It's one of the things about him that I leave alone. That and Tibet.

I don't mind Joel knowing all about me, from my awful days as a Woman With Key in Back to the time the bailiffs turned up at my door. Something tells me that Joel will always need a small, private space for himself, though.

I follow him around the park, snapping as I go. I have never seen anyone so determined to go left when everyone else is going right, or vice versa. If there is a short cut, Joel doesn't take it. Instead, he'll choose the least likely option and stop and smell the flowers on the way.

Life with him is definitely the wrong way round and the long way round, but I can't imagine how I ever lived without it.

'Actually,' Joel says, picking me a flower, 'will you marry me?'

'Yes,' I say instantly. Then I laugh at myself because I sound like such a hopeless Bridezilla.

'Is it too soon?'

'I said *yes.*'

This time Joel laughs. And now I'm crying. Just a bit.

'Quick, let's take a photo,' I grab the camera with one hand and him with the other, then lean my head in towards his. I'm sure it will all be hopelessly out of focus, but I suddenly want to have a record of this moment.

When we return to the house, William is on the phone to a friend, giving motorway advice. 'Penny's gone into Hove to see about that Mendelssohn CD she wanted,' he says. 'I wanted something a bit more modern, but then again it's better than having her trotting down the aisle to "Here Comes the Bride, Short, Fat and Wide."'

We go upstairs to my old bedroom and I take Joel's jeans off on the bed.

'I love you,' I say. I've never actually said it, although it's always in the back of my mind at the silliest times.

'Bugger,' Joel says, looking in his wallet. 'We've run out of condoms.'

'Later then?'

'Bill'll have some.' He zips his jeans up and swings his legs off the bed.

Before I can protest – I do not want William, sorry *Bill*, to know that we are doing it right now, in this room, above his head – Joel has disappeared.

He returns some time later with his prize, not one, but two condoms, which he says Bill keeps in an empty Maltesers packet in his briefcase.

'I told him we were engaged and he said, 'Congratulations, have two.' Joel laughs.

'Oh for God's sake,' I say, putting one back in my bag.

Then we sit and stare at each other for a while, realizing two things. Firstly, we have managed to terrify and excite each other at the same time by agreeing to marriage. And secondly, there is no way we can embark upon a celebratory shag now that Sir William Bastable has provided the contraception.

In the end, though, I just want Joel too much. Please let that never change . . .

The wedding is an absolute hoot, as my mother would say, from start to finish. It begins with her lying on the sofa at sunrise wearing a full face of Nivea cream, and ends with a drunken tour of their bridal suite at The Dorchester, where everyone agrees the bed is big enough to accommodate all of the Bee Gees at once.

Of course the Gibb brothers do not leap out of a giant cake with their guitars strapped to their chests; instead we have my mother's Mendelssohn and, later on, William is allowed to play what sounds like The Wombles' song.

I cannot stop adding up the cost of the reception in my head. It's like the bad old days in Swiss Cottage, when I used to stand in the aisles of ASDA with a pencil and paper and add up everything until it came to four pounds.

Even though those days are long gone, I can still remember everything. Own-brand cola was 20p and own-brand orange juice was 16p. Own-brand crisps were 51p and I can even remember the price of the loo roll – 38p for four.

The lavatory paper in the bridal suite at The Dorchester is so thick and soft you could make a blouse out of it. It's probably 38p a sheet.

'What are you doing?' Joel asks, when he finds me sitting on the stairs. He is covered in synthetic Day-Glo spaghetti because Sir William went mad and seized all the cans that were intended for the bridal car, spraying the lot on Joel's head instead.

'It was his way of congratulating me on becoming engaged to you,' Joel explains when I complain. 'By the way. Everyone knows now. After you disappeared, your mother seized the microphone and broke the news. Then Robyn got the microphone and made everyone give us three cheers.'

'Oh no.'

So much for our vague ideas about keeping it low key. I really wanted Mum's wedding to be out of the way before anyone began thinking about ours.

'Here,' Joel hands me a fistful of scribbled-on napkins, bits of paper and business cards. 'All these women downstairs want you to make them a suit.'

'Really?'

'They loved the silk most of all. I didn't tell them it was second-hand.'

'Vintage,' I correct him.

Chapter Twenty-one

'How's Chang?' Joel asks, taking over the phone when I ring John a few days later.

It seems our dog is alive and well and has taken to digging enormous holes on the beach. John thinks he's trying to dig to England so he can see us. Even Henry the goat is better, his momentary randiness having subsided with the arrival of another, older male goat.

Having survived bush fires, Bellingen is now enduring the threat of floods. It has rained for weeks, John says, and the river is steadily rising. He thinks we should buy a water tank while we still can and take advantage of it, so Joel takes him up on the offer.

'I suppose this is mateship,' I say when John has gone. 'It was one of the questions in the Australia citizenship test, but I didn't know what it meant. People just do things, like randomly offer to buy you a water tank.'

'It's an interesting question, the mateship thing,' Joel says. 'Everybody would have a different answer.'

'I have to find out,' I tell him. 'Heidi said I could

borrow some books from Australia House if I wanted to. She's really excited that I'm taking the test.'

We are staying in Suzanne's spare room in London in order to get away from the post-wedding madness that has engulfed my mother. They are going on honeymoon to Paxos, but so far they seem to be taking an awfully long time to leave.

Suzanne's spare room has become a vintage clothing emporium since her last trip to Paris. There are so many Chinese silk dressing gowns it's difficult to see any light at all coming in through the window.

I recognize all my swimming costumes and sarongs from Sydney lying in dry-cleaning bags.

'Our new stock,' Suzanne says proudly. 'Isn't it great?'

'Fantastic.'

'Where are you off to today, then?'

'Joel's gone back to Mum's place to catch up on some Tibet Aid work. And I'm going to Australia House to find out how I can become an Australian . . .'

'Get an extra leg, diddle, diddle.' Suzanne pretends to be Rolf Harris doing 'Jake the Peg' and fails. 'While you're there, see if you can find out about a working visa for me.'

'Really?' I try not to sound too excited.

'If I'm going to go all the way to blimmin' Australia for your wedding, I want to hang around afterwards,' she says.

When I arrive at Australia House, Heidi Coles greets me with a Euro-kiss – once on each cheek. Her accent seems to have changed as well. The twanginess has gone and been replaced by strangely rounded vowels. She says she might be marrying her new English boyfriend next year if they can book the church in his village for the summer.

'There's no point in doing it any other time,' she says, 'or we'll just get drenched. I attract rain, you know.'

I have to admit she's right. Every single time I have seen Heidi it has been pouring down – or threatening to – and today is no exception. We are standing in the library at Australia House when it starts to bucket down without warning.

'I can just give you all the right answers from the files if you want?' she whispers. 'You don't have to do the research thing. I don't mind. Hey, if you still want a job in the public service, I can give you all their old exam papers as well.'

'Thanks, but I'm running a stall at Bondi Market, and doing my fashion label thing.'

'You're joking!'

'I took over the stall from some friends of mine.'

'Fentestic. Hey, sorry about Danielle.'

'I'm sorry, too. Thanks for all that; it seems like such a long time ago now. But you got me to Australia. Really, you did.'

Heidi photocopies a book about Simpson and his donkey for me. 'Are you sure you're not going overboard with this?' she asks.

'It's just for me really. I've always liked donkeys. Joel

says we can have one, once we sort out the cows and the sheep and everything else.'

'You were living in a hostel in Swiss Cottage and now you're running a farm – you're one of our success stories,' Heidi tells me.

'It won't be a farm. We just want to be self-sufficient, that's all. Or as much as we can be anyway. You know how much organic tomatoes cost in London? We grow them just by walking to the compost heap and accidentally dropping a few seeds. Bellingen's incredible. Everything just grows as soon as you look at it.'

'It's supposed to be bewdyful up there,' Heidi says wistfully.

I buy her lunch at the nearest pub because we have both decided the café near The Strand is jinxed.

'How is your ex?' she asks as I put our drinks on the table.

'Having it off with a schoolgirl.'

'You're kidding?'

'The school have thrown him out.'

'Remember that day when you dropped your purse and I found it? I listened to everything you two said and I thought, they're never going to make it.'

'You were right.'

On impulse I tell her that Joel and I are engaged, and she squeaks at me, then shakes me by the hand.

'You look scared,' she says. 'Don't look so blardy scared.'

'Maybe I've had too many girl's own adventures lately.'

'Can't be any more frightening than moving to some place you've never even seen before.'

'I suppose not.'

'We get so many people coming here,' Heidi says, 'wanting to move to Australia. The good, the bad and the ugly. Some people want to go because they're desperate. They don't give a stuff, basically, but someone told them their pounds will be worth thousands of dollars and the weather's really good.'

'That was Nash. That was why he wanted to go.'

'Yeah, and look what happened. Even if you had got on the plane together, Alice, I guarantee he would have turned tail and come back to England. A lot of people do.'

'It hasn't been easy,' I tell her, 'but I never, ever thought I'd do that. I liked it too much from the moment I got there.'

'That's because you're one of us,' she says, and I feel ridiculously pleased, until she adds that I am mad by nature and therefore ideally suited to life in a country which is upside down, back to front and impossible for most normal people to deal with.

'You know you'll get a question on mateship in the test, don't you?' she warns me. 'They ask everyone.'

'I was talking to Joel about that. We decided it was two people we know in Bellingen. One of them probably saved our life in a bush fire. The other one took us in.'

'Those fires were *bad*,' Heidi winces. 'Shit! But they looked after you?'

'They looked after us and it was no big deal; they just

got on with it. This one man – Wiz – drove us through the fire and probably saved our lives. Australians just seem to keep on rescuing me for some reason.'

'Ha!' Heidi looks pleased.

'A bit like the phone call you and Robyn had that day, in the café, when I was worried they weren't going to let me in.'

She beams at me and shows me a photograph of her boyfriend, who is dying to come to Australia with her once they're married.

'Come and stay with us,' I offer.

'I'd rather stay with you than Auntie Danielle,' she hisses. 'Do you want to know what she's doing since she sold Barks?'

'Another dog thing?'

'No, she's started a colonic irrigation centre – for humans. It's the scariest thing I've ever heard of.'

'Please don't tell me what it's called.'

We clink glasses and she congratulates me on my forthcoming Australian citizenship – she won't be there, but because she knows they'll take me.

'Are you going to have kids, do you think?'

'Not sure. I hope so, but not yet.'

'Have them in Oz, then they can have two passports. Lucky kids. Best of both worlds.'

After I bid Heidi farewell at Australia House, I walk back down to Trafalgar Square, where I tried to say goodbye to England the last time – and failed.

I have been dying to go to the loo all day, to use the pregnancy-testing kit I bought at the chemist this morning, but the pub didn't seem the right place to use it. I've been feeling sick for days.

I know I should go home and do it properly, with Joel waiting on the phone, but when have I ever done anything properly in my life? In the end I can't wait, so I throw some money in the donation box at the National Portrait Gallery and walk in.

A large painting of Princess Diana looks down at me, and I give her a little wave underneath my coat. Wish me luck, Diana.

If I am pregnant, I'm definitely going to be one of those morning-sickness women.

I go into the loo, and wonder if I am the first person to do a pregnancy test in here. Probably not. I bet it happens all the time.

I look at the condom in my bag, which has been there since William decided to congratulate Joel and I on our engagement, by kindly supplying us with two.

As Suzanne said when she saw it, some things from the eighties deserve a comeback, and some things don't, and a rubber condom date-stamped 1989 definitely doesn't. She is amazed that neither of us felt the first one break. It was twenty years old for God's sake.

I flip the loo seat down, sit with my legs crossed, sort out all the bits and pieces in the kit and watch the little strip of paper like a hawk. I am so nervous that I read the instructions eight times to make absolutely sure I have got it right, and then . . .

It's a boy! It's a girl! It's something! It's just a bit of purple-looking paper at the moment, above the line, but I have never been more excited by anything in my life.

I bolt out of the loo, find a quiet doorway to make a phone call and ring Joel.

'Hello, Alice,' William Bastable says. 'I'm afraid he's not here. He's gone out for a walk. He said he'd be back later.'

'I'm pregnant!' I shriek at him like an idiot.

'What?'

'You had nineteen eighties' condoms! I just did the test. Tell Joel I'm pregnant. Tell Mum!'

'Oh, what marvellous news. Penny's seeing her friends in Brighton I'm afraid. But she'll be back later. I'm afraid she doesn't like mobile phones, as you know, otherwise I would have lent her mine. Goodness. Am I the first to know?'

'You are!'

'Many, many congratulations,' William says. 'I am so deeply sorry about my condoms, but perhaps in time you will come to think of me as a living saint.'

Suddenly, Blossom Promise and all her strange predictions pop into my head.

'I wish you all the luck in the world,' William continues. 'And as soon as I can get hold of Penny and Joel I will pass the good news on.'

I ring Suzanne and the call goes straight to voicemail. Damn.

After that I rush into a clothes shop near Charing Cross, where I immediately feel moved to tell the assistant I'm pregnant.

'I'm having a baby. I've just found out I'm pregnant, so I need some trousers with a really loose waistband. It's my stepfather's fault. He gave me a twenty-year-old condom from his disco days and it exploded.'

'Maternity's that way,' she points, trying to get rid of me.

Instead, I take a tip from Princess Diana and walk in the direction of what my mother always calls *the* Park, as if there is only one park in the entire world. It is, of course, Diana's old park. And my dad used to bring me here when I was little. It is the most amazing feeling to think I could take our children here one day.

I have only just seen a strip of paper turn purple in a loo, and already I'm planning an entire family. Joel would laugh at me. But why stop at one?

I feel an incredible sense of achievement as I walk along the Serpentine. Being pregnant is like hearing you've got the best job in the world, even though you think you're the least likely applicant.

It's hard to believe that the last time I was here Nash was having his weird flirtation with Lisa. It was in the summer, the week after Glastonbury finished, and there was some outdoor concert he wanted to see. I can still remember worrying about how I'd pay for the drinks, ice creams and deckchairs. I never want to live like that again. Joel was right about hanging on to most of my money: I can't put my children through that either. It's time I grew up and went to talk to an accountant for a change. No more jam jars.

Nash and I had a world-class argument when we were here and I was so miserable about Lisa. I never want to have any more of those, either. I think Joel and I can get through marriage without them. I hope so. Our kids should never have to listen to the kind of fighting that split his own parents up.

I follow Princess Diana's trail of roses along the walk that bears her name. This is such a pretty park, even when the leaves have come off the trees. How did all those English women cope, when they settled in Australia all those centuries ago and found themselves confronted by bush fires and snakes? I wonder. Our children will know it all, every last bit of it.

Oh my God, I can't wait to tell Joel. It's only when I walk back through Knightsbridge that I get jelly legs and realize I am a pregnant lady now and I really should find somewhere to sit down.

When I finally make my way back to Suzanne's flat, her answering machine has been crammed with messages from my mother, and one from Joel. But first, she cries and cries, because she has just remembered a drunken promise I made her years ago at The Bell and Dragon about being godmother to my kids.

'Did you mean it?' she sobs. 'I understand if you've changed your mind, but do you think you still want me to be?'

'Completely. You're a godmother. Whooosh!' – I wave an imaginary fairy wand over her head – 'I hereby pronounce you godmother to this baby.'

Then my mother calls.

'A grandmother and a Christmas bride!' she shrieks. 'I never thought. Here's Joel.'

We are on the phone for over three hours, which is a record even for us. Every time I mutter about going, he keeps me talking, and every time he says he really should hang up, I find another reason to keep him there.

We spend a long time talking about his real dad. Now that he is going to be a parent himself, Joel wants to find him.

'He'll be a grandfather, wherever he is. He deserves to know.'

'Would Uncle Roland have any idea?'

'No, I'm going to have to ask Mum. She won't like it, but it's time.'

Joel says he cannot believe how much has changed in his life. In India, the Tibetans were his extended family. Now he has one that includes new faces, old faces and more surprises than he ever imagined.

'Bill's gone nuts,' he says. 'He already wants to put the baby down for Eton.'

'It could be a girl, though. He might have it all wrong.'

'It certainly could be a girl.'

We talk about all the names we have both secretly reserved for future baby girls. None of them are the same. Some of his – in my opinion – would be better suited to the new hens we're going to buy. He says all my ideas are too English. I say all his names are too silly.

'I'm going to fill our room with flowers when you come back,' he says, 'and if I can't find any flowers, I'm going to drag in branches.'

'It's early days yet,' I remind him.

'What are the rules on those things?' he asks. 'Can we tell everyone?'

'When did either of us ever do what you're supposed to do? Of course we're going to tell everyone. At some stage, I might even ring up Nash.'

A few days later Matty arranges to meet me. He wants to talk about our business plan, he says, but things might be different now, because Jade has left him.

''Ere,' he says when we meet up in The Bell and Dragon, 'this is my old mobile. It's on a proper network – works all over Australia. Stop living like a hippy and you can have it. If we're going to do business, you've got to sort yourself out.'

'That's exactly what Suzanne said,' I tell him. I've asked her to join us later, once she's finished a styling job.

Matty tells me that Jade is going to be a star. 'They were sort of hinting at it, but then it got serious,' he says. 'The other girl they had in mind wasn't up to it. So they gave Jade the lead and this other woman walked out.'

'Wow!'

'Jade's going to be on the sides of buses in Australia.' Matty shrugs. 'She got a big head – you can't blame her. All these blokes were suddenly after her and I was coming second.'

He thinks about it. 'Nah, I was actually coming third. She even got one of them toy dogs for her handbag.'

'Nightmare. I used to look after those kinds of dogs once.'

'I'm well out of it.' Matty sighs and pushes his beer mat around the table. 'Was this your local?'

'We used to do the pub quiz here,' I tell him. I have made a deliberate effort to come back here today so I can exorcize the past. It's a great pub, and there's no reason why my memories of Nash and Lisa should be allowed to spoil it.

'Your mate's late,' Matty says, checking his much more impressive new phone.

'Suzanne's hopeless. Do you want another drink?'

While I am organizing Matty's pint, Suzanne walks in and introduces herself. There is some confusion as Matty stands up at the same time that she is trying to sit down, and more flapping as he tries to kiss her on the cheek while she offers him one of her business cards.

There's a buzz there, a definite buzz. I can't imagine they'll ever be attracted to each other, but then again, stranger things have happened.

'I brought me laptop,' Matty gets it out of his bag and proceeds to show us his new website. It's called downthemarket.com and is based on a real street market, like Bondi or Camden.

'Be careful, though,' Suzanne warns him, 'it might sound a little bit too downmarket. You don't want that, darling.'

'No offence taken,' Matty suddenly gets sniffy and pretends to be interested in his computer keyboard.

'So will all our clothes be on there?' I ask.

'Yep,' Matty says. 'I was thinking about it on the plane. I've had it with Aussie-land. I'm never living there again after what happened with Jade and me. But if you keep things going at the Sydney end, I can keep everything going over here. I'll just need to come over every so often to make sure everything's ticking over.'

'Lovely, lovely tax-deductible holidays to Bondi Beach,' Suzanne's eyes widen. 'Now you're talking, Matty.'

'You ever been to Australia?' he asks her.

'I'm dying to go – when Alice has her wedding.'

'Didn't tell me that bit,' Matty nudges me.

'It was a bit sudden.'

Then I kick Suzanne under the table, in case she suddenly blurts out my other news too.

'Ooh, this website is so exciting!' she breathes, kicking me straight back. 'Did you design it yourself?'

'Mate of mine did it,' Matty replies. 'You girls have got to get off the streets and get on Web Two. The Americans are all over it like a rash.'

'God. I didn't even know what Web One was,' Suzanne confides once Matty has gone to the bar for more drinks. 'He's all right, though, isn't he?'

'He's a good egg,' I confirm, thinking about my father again. For some reason, being with a bad egg like Nash seems to have helped me develop the egg-character-reading radar I have lacked all my life.

'What about his girlfriend?' she asks.

'They've broken up. The TV network wants to turn her into a star.'

'So he's coming back to London and you're staying in Oz.' Suzanne smirks. 'You're replacing each other.'

'Well, it keeps the population level.'

Matty returns with a tray of drinks and I try to see him as Suzanne sees him. There are elements of her previous boyfriend in him – the ageing Britpop lad – and I believe she might be weakening.

'This website does require an investment,' Matty says, looking at each of us in turn.

'Not a problem,' Suzanne shrugs. 'Alice, are you in?'

'I'll need to see an accountant,' I reply, worrying about jam jars, and the price of loo paper at ASDA, while Suzanne looks at me with a stunned expression on her face.

'Glory be, Alice Templeton's getting herself an accountant,' she says, fanning herself with a beer mat.

'Right enough,' Matty agrees. 'If we're going to do this properly, then you need to get sorted.'

'I'm hopeless with money and I always have been,' I tell him. 'There's no point in hiding it. The last time I was in this pub I was so desperate I was looking for change on the carpet. Honestly.'

'But now she's quids in,' Suzanne explains to Matty, 'I'm sure she can make a modest investment in—'

She immediately forgets the name of his website, and I have to remind her before she calls it downmarket. com and loses all the ground she has just won.

The conversation moves to local Camden gossip and Suzanne and Matty realize they both have the same contact in the London market mafia. As they talk, I drift off into my own world and feel a sudden shot of panic about working and looking after a baby at the same time, not to mention helping Joel look after sheep, chickens, hens and a worm farm. I think I might resign from the worm farm.

I have a vision of myself in a mud-brick house at some point in the future, working on my sewing machine while my children play with Chang and Joel builds a hen-house.

By that stage I may even have overcome my fear of spiders and snakes.

Robyn asked me to take her to London Zoo the other day and I didn't even flinch when she mentioned the Reptile House. Who knows, in ten years from now I might even be able to look a goanna in the eye – even if he is sitting in the front seat of a VW camper van.

I drift back again. The conversation has moved on to Miss Great Britain, because Matty thinks Suzanne looks a bit like last year's winner.

'That slapper!' Suzanne fakes indignation.

Suddenly I feel unbelievably tired and realize I have to leave. We all agree to meet again the following week, and I am about to put my coat on when Richard and Michael walk in. They look the other way, but I'm not going to let them get away with that.

'I think we'll go, too,' Suzanne says as she waits for

Matty to get his stuff. 'We're going to split a cab. He's on my way. Well, actually, he's not remotely on my way, but we've got a lot to talk about.'

'Bye,' I kiss her as Richard and Michael look on.

'Bye, honey. Ooh, hello Richard and Michael. And goodbye Richard and Michael!' she gives them a little wave, then teeters off in her heels.

I sit down with the remains of our legendary quiz team, The Believers. They say they haven't been here for weeks and that the team has gone to ground a bit, but they are hoping to find new members again. I wonder if that means Nash has left them for good? I suppose it's a long way from Oxford.

It's funny to think that the quiz night here was supposed to help save my relationship with Nash. In retrospect, nothing would have worked. He was always capable of infidelity, and now I've found out he's the kind of man who's capable of having a relationship with a schoolgirl as well. He always was lazy. Nash could never be bothered to reach very far for what he wanted, whether it was a new roll of loo paper or the light switch.

'Very convenient, Nash having an affair with one of his students,' I tell Richard. I'm feeling a bit merry now. Matty was far too generous with the drinks.

'I think that might be over now,' he says, raising an eyebrow at Michael.

'Nash is leaving us to go to Wales,' Richard continues. 'The Oxford thing didn't work out. He's just going to teach piano for a bit. Part-time tutoring, that kind of stuff.'

I realize I will never see my money again and try not to feel too upset. Maybe it's karma. That's what Joel would say anyway. It all goes round in the wash, like some spiritual version of the Swiss Cottage Laundrette.

I start telling Richard and Michael about Australia and Joel and the bush fire, but their eyes soon glaze over.

Their world is this pub, all the trivia they talk about and the streets outside. I am discussing something that might as well be on planet Mars. For all their quiz brilliance and pop-culture knowledge, they don't really want to look beyond North London.

Perhaps I'm turning into a foreigner. They certainly seem to be looking askance at me. I want to tell them I'm getting married, but then I remember I still haven't had the courage to tell Nash, so I shut up.

I say my goodbyes; I expect I will never see them again, unless I come back here on a Tuesday night for the pub quiz.

I go back to Suzanne's, pack my bag and go to Victoria, nearly missing my train because of the queue behind the ticket machine. I don't care any more. All the effing, blinding and harumphing that is taking place in the queue is the funniest thing in the world. My children will love it when they're old enough to see it for themselves.

There are two little kids in my carriage on the way to Hove. They have colouring-in books and are both plugged in to the same iPod – proper London children on their way to the seaside for the weekend.

Joel meets me at the station in Brighton with Mum and William. I tell them about Matty and the website idea, then they tell me that Robyn is trying to organize a farewell dinner before she flies back to Bondi and Mum and William set off on their honeymoon.

Joel holds my hand in the back seat as I jokingly stick out my stomach, as if I was several month's pregnant, and see if I can get my seat belt around it. I have already practised with cushions, of course, and realized that Suzanne's beautiful red Dior coat will never fit after all.

Later on, Joel and I go for a walk along the seafront, wrapped up in hats and scarves. I stand near the spot where I first saw him – my own Number Nine. My Australian cousin.

I tell him about Heidi and the Australian citizenship test, and how she wanted to smuggle me all the old answers.

'What you forget is that Heidi is probably descended from a long line of smugglers,' Joel points out. 'It may even be how her ancestors got to Australia.'

'So dodginess is in the blood.'

I tell him more about Matty and Suzanne, and about running into Richard and Michael at the pub.

'How was that?'

'It made my past seem very . . . *past*.'

We think about the last few years of our lives and how everything has happened at the right time.

'Even the things that went wrong helped make it right,' Joel says.

Joel says he is already seeing Jade being written up in the papers here. He agrees that it's sad that she and Matty broke up, but right that he should have come back here.

'He emigrated back,' I say.

'Wrong way round, long way round. It usually works in the end.'

THE END

I'M A BELIEVER

Jessica Adams

'An original and entertaining novel
about life after death'
The Times

Mark Buckle thinks he's an ordinary bloke. He teaches science at a
junior school in south London. He'd rather read Stephen Hawking
than his horoscope, he's highly suspicious of Uri Geller, Mystic Meg
and feng shui, and he wouldn't be seen dead at a séance. Most
importantly, he absolutely, positively doesn't believe in life after
death. Then, one terrible night, Mark's girlfriend Catherine dies in a
car accident, and even worse, starts communicating with
him in the middle of her own funeral.

While Mark forces himself to the doctor for checks on his mental
health, Catherine continues to find new ways to get her message
through. But the biggest message of all must be from Tess – the last
woman in the world Mark thinks he should be with.

'A heart-warming, funny book with a serious core'
Glamour

9780552772808

SINGLE WHITE E-MAIL

Jessica Adams

'Sexy, funny, smart, for any woman who has ever been single'
Cosmopolitan

Dumped on her 30th birthday by the man she thought she
would marry, Victoria Shepworth – known as Victoria
'Total Bloody Relationships Disaster' Shepworth
to her friends – is feeling desperate.

So desperate that she cuts her hair, contemplates becoming
a born-again lesbian and even throws herself into internet
dating. Armed with a new computer and an anonymous
nickname, she soon starts to feel human again – especially
when she starts receiving e-mails from a fantastic
Frenchman in Paris who claims to be a single
white male seeking single white e-mail.

Soon, everything else in Victoria's life begins to seem boring,
from her job in advertising, to her old friends and neighbours.
It's only when tragedy strikes that her potential Monsieur
Right is finally unmasked, though, and Victoria realizes that
her love life will never be the same again.

'*Single White E-Mail* has an innate honesty about it that
keeps you entertained to the end. At times disarmingly harsh
and decidedly candid, Adam's début into the literary
world is fresh, frenetic and fun'
Elle

9780552772785